PRAISE FOR VIVI HOLT

The writing was superb staying true to all of Vivi Holt's writings. Vivi Holt never disappoints in her writing and the amazing books that she has published. She has a gift for writing intriguing and entertaining stories.

— AMAZON REVIEWER

My first time reading Vivi Holt, I believe she will be one of my favorite authors.

— AMAZON REVIEWER

Wonderful! Vivi Holt pulls at your heart strings and then some

— KIT MORGAN, BESTSELLING AUTHOR

COTTON TREE RANCH

TRILOGY

VIVI HOLT

BLACK LAB PRESS

ABOUT THIS TRILOGY

Meet the Williams' family - Dalton, Eamon & Parker! Three brothers, one ranch in south Georgia, and not a woman in sight. That is until Hazel stumbles into their lives and turns everything upside down. Find out what happens when city girls fall for country boys in these three sweet and inspirational western romance stories from a bestselling author.

DALTON

ABOUT DALTON

Everything in Hazel's perfect life is going according to plan. Every moment is accounted for. But she's in for a surprise. When her best friend and roommate takes ill, Jenny begs Hazel to fill in for her on a trip to South Georgia. But life on a horse ranch in her Jimmy Choos isn't exactly what Hazel had in mind for her summer break.

When Dalton Sullivan takes a spill from a bronc at the last rodeo of the season, his life changes forever. Uncertain about his future, his fortunes take another turn when Grandpa Joe bequeaths him a dilapidated horse ranch in his will. Dalton's plans to refurbish the place and turn it into a working ranch again are interrupted when a beautiful woman shows up pretending to be someone she's not.

Even though Dalton knows Hazel's hiding the truth, there's something about her that makes him want to change his solitary ways. But will he be able to convince her to do the same before their time together runs out?

CHAPTER 1

*D*alton Williams scanned the crowd packed into the arena. Wide eyes peered through fence rails, button-down checked shirts and blue jeans crammed the rows of stadium seating. Eager mouths chomped on burgers, hot dogs, corn dogs, fried pickles and cotton candy and exclaimed over the spectacle below. The glare of stadium lighting illuminated the entire arena with an eerie glow.

Dalton's gaze drifted to land on the cowboy sitting astride a bronco in the bucking chute. The man adjusted his seat, locked his gloved hand around the leather strap and nodded. Stuart "Buck" Handley was the man to beat. He'd won the National Bronc Riding Championship trophy five years in a row – something no one thought could be done.

But last season Dalton had won, against all odds, throwing the whole circuit into a spin. Dalton had ridden against Buck for years and never come close to beating him. But last season had been different – he'd been at the top of his game after years of focus, prac-

5

tice and strength training. His dream of winning the championship had finally come true. Pundits were certain it was the start of a new era, one with Dalton at the helm.

But when the circuit started up again after the summer break, he'd torn a rotator cuff at the first event of the year. Now Buck Handley was back in the lead.

Dalton watched the bronc jump out of the chute, bucking and twisting, its hindquarters almost vertical above its head, ears laid back against its neck. Buck held on tight, his body flexing with the movements of the animal, one hand high in the air.

The buzz of the eight-second timer rang out and the crowd erupted into cheering and catcalls. Dalton shook his head and spat in the dirt as the announcer went wild, his voice echoing loudly through the cool night air.

"You ridin' tonight?" asked a soft feminine voice behind him.

He turned and nodded. "Yup."

Carrie Finnick stood there, her torn denim short-shorts and knotted flannel shirt leaving little to the imagination. "I'll be cheerin' for you," she said, laying a perfectly manicured hand on his forearm.

He glanced at it, then smiled. "Thanks, Carrie. I sure do appreciate it. I'll need all the support I can get."

"Oh, you're gonna win for sure – everyone knows that," she drawled, letting her fingers trail softly down his arm. His skin goose-pimpled beneath her touch.

He cleared his throat. "Well, I don't know about that. Buck just had a good ride that'll be hard to beat. But I'll sure try." He hated to be rude, but he had no interest in Carrie. She followed the circuit whenever they were in Texas and had hit on him every season. He'd taken her out to dinner once after a breakup, but hadn't felt any kind of spark. Not being the kind of man to lead a woman on, he'd left it at that. But she didn't seem to take 'no' for an answer – not where he was concerned, anyway.

The truth was, he hadn't dated anyone seriously since Jodie left him back in Chattanooga. If he was honest with himself, he hadn't given anyone a chance. But there was no time to think about that now. His ride was coming up and he had to get his mind straight. "I'd better go get ready," he said, touching the brim of his hat with his fingertips and nodding in her direction.

"I'll be lookin' out for you," she called after him.

He strolled over to the bucking chute and surveyed the animals corralled behind it, ready to go. He got to pick the one he wanted to ride and by now knew them all pretty well. The red roan was a solid performer, but tended to travel in a straight line with a standard bucking style. If he wanted to beat Buck's score, he'd need a horse with more of a twist to its stride.

His eyes landed on a gray quarter horse named Benny. At first glance, Benny looked like a mild-mannered old boy, but he knew differently. He pointed to Benny, and the cowboy with the rope nodded in acknowledgement. That done, now he just had to focus, to concentrate on what he had to do.

A group of children ran past with a bucket of popcorn, spilling kernels on the muddy ground as they went. They laughed and chattered amongst them-selves, excited that the rodeo was in town and they got to watch the cowboys, arguing about who would win and who would be thrown. Dalton remembered doing the same with his friends when he was a boy in Chattanooga. He'd loved the rodeo and never missed it if he could help it.

He'd always wanted to be one of the cowboys who got to ride the wildest broncos around, and when he started on the circuit it was all he could do to keep from pinching himself. He couldn't believe he could ride for a living and have people cheer for him, look up to him, admire him.

But lately, things had been different. Ever since Jodie called to tell him she was through waiting for him to come home and had fallen for someone else, the spark had gone out of everything. The rides, the crowds, the bright lights – none of it filled him with the same excitement any more.

Buck stepped through a gate nearby and brushed off his chaps with both hands, dust swirling around him in a soft cloud. He spotted Dalton and grinned. "How'd ya like that, huh?"

"Sure was a good ride, Buck. It'll be hard to beat."

Buck raised an eyebrow. "But you're gonna try, I bet."

Dalton chuckled. "I sure will."

Buck leaned back against the fence and crossed his ankles. "How's yer shoulder?"

Dalton lifted his arm and circled it around a few times, stretching out his shoulder with a grimace. "It's been better."

"Well, good luck to ya."

"Thanks, Buck. You staying to watch?"

"Ya bet. Wouldn't miss it." Buck's eyes glinted and he tipped his hat. "Gotta watch ya lose, boy."

Dalton laughed and strode toward the chute where Benny awaited him. He and Buck always teased each other that way. But after each event was over, they were first and foremost friends and usually ended the night playing blackjack over glasses of coke, each balancing bags of ice on the various body parts that hurt the worst.

"You ready?" asked a cowboy in a black Cowboy hat.

Dalton nodded, his eyes focused on the gray in front of him. The horse stamped a foot and pranced as far sideways as he could within the confines of the fence palings, breath expelling from distended nostrils clouding the cool fall air. He'd done this so many times before, he knew what was coming, and Dalton saw the whites of his eyes as he snorted and shook his head.

With a deep breath, Dalton climbed the rails of the chute and swung a leg over the animal's shivering back. His heart pounded and adrenaline coursed through his veins, exaggerating every sensation. Colors seemed brighter, every sound was amplified and the rough inside of the glove covering his hand as he clenched tight to the leather strap scratched at his skin.

Time stood still.

Then the gate swung open, Benny leaped forward and Dalton dug his heels into the horse's sides. Benny swung left and spun in a circle, his heels kicking high above his head. Dalton held on tight, leaning back and forth, rotating with the movements of the animal beneath him. The noise of the crowd cheering him on swelled in his consciousness.

Then the eight-second buzzer sounded. The loud-speakers declared that it was a good ride and Dalton released his breath in a huff of relief. But as he loosened his grip on the strap, Benny spooked and bucked harder than ever as he swiveled to the right, crashing against the railings of the arena fence.

Pain shot through Dalton's leg and he cried out, grabbing it as the horse galloped out from under him. He felt his head spin, and everything faded to black as he landed with a thud on the grass to the gasps of the crowd.

* * *

DALTON'S EYES flickered open and he glanced around the room. He was in a hospital bed, surrounded by four white walls. A vase of fresh-cut carnations sat on a square table beside his bed, along with his cell phone and a horse magazine. He grimaced and lifted a hand to feel his head. It throbbed, and his throat was dry. A nurse strode past the room, then a cart piled with dirty food trays squeaked by on noisy wheels in the opposite direction.

"Hello?" he croaked. He cleared his throat with a cough and tried again. "Hello?"

A nurse poked her head in with a smile. "Did ya need somethin', hon?"

"Could I get some water, please?"

She nodded and disappeared.

His thoughts wandered back to his ambulance trip to the hospital. Two paramedics arrived in the arena after he regained consciousness, a big man with a handlebar mustache and a petite blonde woman. They'd rolled him onto their stretcher and carried him to the ambulance, making chitchat the whole way while he writhed in pain. They hadn't bothered with the lights or sirens for the journey, since he was stable, and they'd given him a whistle to suck on, which had made him loopy.

He grinned and rubbed a hand over his stubble. He had a feeling he'd asked one of the paramedics out on a date. He hoped it was the woman.

His leg was stretched out in front of him, encased from hip to ankle in a hard white cast. He frowned. Six to eight weeks, he'd been told – that's how long he had to wear it. Even when it came off, the doctor had warned him he shouldn't ever ride broncs again, not unless he wanted to risk permanent damage.

The nurse bustled into the room with a jug of water in one hand and a plastic cup in the other. "Here you go, cowboy," she said with a smile. "You just let me know if you need anythin' else. There's a button right here on your bed – if you press it, I'll come as soon as I can, okay?"

He nodded. "Thanks."

She set the pitcher and cup on the table beside his bed and left.

Dalton leaned over to grab the cup and heard his phone vibrating. It bumped around in a circle on the hard surface of the table, buzzing quietly. He picked it up and ran his finger across the screen. "Hello?"

"Dalton, honey, you're awake." His mother's chipper voice echoed shrilly through the speaker.

He grimaced, laid it back on the table and sipped his water. "Yeah, I just woke up. I haven't seen a doctor this morning, but I'm assuming the surgery went fine, seeing as how I have a great big cast on my leg." He chuckled and took another sip, enjoying the feeling of the cool liquid as it traveled down his parched throat.

"That's good to hear," she replied, her voice catching.

"Are you okay, Mom?" He heard a sob. Susan Williams hardly ever shed a tear. The sound shook him. "Mom?"

"Yes, hon. Sorry … it's just that I have some bad news. I didn't really want to burden you right now, but I think you'd want to know …" She sobbed again.

His chest tightened, and he set the cup on the table and straightened, staring at the bright screen of the cell phone where it lay. "Mom, what is it?"

"It's Pa – your Grandpa Joe. I'm afraid he passed away last night in his sleep." His mother choked up and she sobbed again.

"Oh no! I'm so sorry, Mom. I know how much you loved him. He was always so good to us, especially after Dad died." Dalton frowned, and he lay back on the pillows stacked behind his head with both hands pressed to his eyes. Grandpa Joe was strong and fit, the life of any party. It was hard for him to believe the old man was gone. He listened to his mother's strained voice fill in the details of Pa's passing as a lump formed in his throat.

* * *

HAZEL HILDEBRAND PACKED her violin into its case and passed a delicately manicured hand over her hair, smoothing it into place. The performance had gone off without a hitch as usual, yet there was something bothering her. She wasn't sure why, but she felt deflated.

She'd dreamed her whole life of being in the Atlanta Symphony Orchestra, and this was her third season playing violin with them. She should have felt exhilarated, but instead she just felt flat, though she had to admit the Chastain Amphitheater was certainly one of her favorite venues to play. She glanced up to see audience members still chatting, sipping wine and eating from picnic baskets beneath the shade of umbrellas.

"Hazel, are you going away over break?" asked Frieda Brighton, flipping her long black hair over her shoulder and smiling warmly as she packed her instrument. The first-chair violinist had been with the orchestra almost a decade.

"Well, I don't have big plans, which isn't like me. Actually, I think I might go and spend some time with my parents."

"Oh? I was under the impression you didn't get along too well with your folks." Frieda arched an eyebrow and slipped her stocking feet into a pair of black pumps.

"Well, we've definitely had our differences But, Mom called me a few days ago to complain that they never see me and invited me to their summer house on Jekyll Island next week. I thought I might stay a while out there with them." Hazel took a deep breath. The thought of spending time with her parents made her stomach clench. She shook off her slippers and pushed them into her shoulder bag, then retrieved a pair of red flats and stepped into them with a sigh. "How about you? Big plans?"

"Yeah, Jerry and I are taking a cruise. We're leaving from Miami and going around the Caribbean. It's going to be fantastic – I can't wait!" She looped the strap of her purse over her shoulder.

"Don't you have that rehearsal for the ballet performance the week after next?" asked Hazel, standing to pick up her violin case.

"Yes, but the cruise is only for a week, so we'll be back in plenty of time. You're not playing?"

Hazel shook her head, her chestnut curls fanning out over her shoulders. "No, not this time – they didn't ask me. Maybe next time."

Frieda tipped her head to one side with a tight half-smile. "Yeah, next time."

"Okay … well, see you after the break, then. Have a great time on your cruise." Hazel waved goodbye to Frieda and the others who were still packing up their instruments and strode off the stage, her brow furrowed. Frieda had known full well she hadn't been asked to play for the ballet. She sniffed – one day she hoped to be first chair. She wouldn't hold it over others the way Frieda always did.

The bright sunlight of the summer day hit her full in the face when she emerged from beneath the roof of the stage. Outdoor matinees in the throes of summer weren't her idea of a good time, especially when they were all expected to wear head-to-toe black. The heat had coated her entire body in a layer of sweat. She blew out a breath and fished around in her purse for her sunglasses, putting them on with a grimace.

The drive home to the Atlanta neighborhood of Virginia-Highland wasn't far, but first she'd have to deal with the city's bumper-to-bumper traffic. She inched forward with the car's air conditioning blasting, listened to the radio and let her mind wander over the four weeks of vacation stretching out before her. She didn't do well without structure in her life. Her usual routine was to have every moment of every day accounted for, planned out, full.

She'd wake early, go for a run, shower, then have breakfast while reading the news on her phone. After breakfast, rehearsal, followed by errands in the afternoon. She'd always practice on her own after that, then sometimes had a performance at night. Other nights were planned out well in advance: social events, book club, church, gym, even shopping trips scheduled, to ensure she didn't waste any time or find herself with nothing to do. No wonder her roommate Jennifer Barsby complained she hardly ever saw her.

Jen was the one unstructured thing in Hazel's life. She was scattered, disorganized, spontaneous, loud – everything that Hazel wasn't, but she loved her like a sister. They'd attended the University of Georgia together – Hazel majoring in music, while Jen studied veterinary science. Thrown together as roommates their freshman year, they'd never lived apart since. And though she hated to admit it, Hazel liked the loud, messy energy Jen brought into her otherwise tidy life.

She pulled the car into the driveway of their small bungalow and shut off the engine with a frown. It was the middle of the day and Jen's car was in the garage. It was unlike her friend to be home at this time of day. Jen worked five days a week at a quarter-horse ranch in Walton County, just outside of Atlanta. She headed inside, the kitchen door swinging shut behind her. "Jen! Jen, are you home?" she called.

Her voice echoed through the quiet house. Jen usually cranked her favorite country tunes through a Bluetooth speaker when she was home, but the house was ominously still. Hazel leaned her violin against the wall of the study and dropped her shoulder bag in the kitchen.

A moan from Jen's room caught her attention and she ran down the hall. "Jen?"

Her friend lay on the bed on her side in a fetal position. She moaned again.

Hazel rushed to her, knelt next to the bed and laid a hand on Jen's face. It was flushed, and a trickle of sweat ran down her temple. "You're burning up," said Hazel, running her hand over her friend's damp hair. "What's going on?"

"I don't know," she whispered. "It hurts."

"We should get you to the doctor, sweetie."

She shook her head. "No, I'll be fine. I might just take some Tylenol."

Hazel frowned. "I know you don't like going to the doctor, Jen. But I'm afraid you have to this time."

"No, I… ughhhh!" She moaned and rolled back and forth, her face contorted in pain.

"Okay, come on, stand up. You can lean on my shoulder." Hazel tried to help her to her feet.

Jen fell back onto the bed with a cry. "I can't!"

Hazel stood for a moment, her hands on her hips, watching her friend. What should she do? Then Jen moaned again, and she knew she'd have to call an ambulance.

CHAPTER 2

*W*ith one hand shielding his eyes from the blazing Georgia sun, Dalton stared at the lopsided wooden sign that hung from two tall posts on either side of a broken-down gate. The sign read *Cotton Tree Ranch* in faded lettering.

With a frown, he kicked a two-by-four that lay in the middle of the road out of the way, then strode back to his blue pickup idling in the driveway. He still favored his left leg, which had been broken in two places. But it'd healed well, according to his doctor. Even though the cast had been removed weeks ago, a slight twinge every now and then reminded him of the accident.

Releasing the brake, he pressed down on the gas slowly and drove through the open gate and along the rambling dirt drive to a long, dilapidated single-level ranch house. It squatted in the middle of a green pasture, all peeling paint, broken porch rails and grease-covered windows. It looked like a lot of work and not much else. He parked and got out of the truck, careful to keep the foot of his injured leg from hitting the ground too hard.

He considered the phone call from Grandpa Joe's lawyer, Mr. Sanderson. The man had informed him he was to inherit part of Pa's estate, and his heart had pounded in anticipation. What would it be – money? Property? Debt? He'd known his grandfather was an entrepreneur, but didn't know much about the specifics of his investments. The old man didn't talk about it and Dalton never felt the need to pry. They were much more likely to discuss baseball scores, or which quarterback was expected to go first in the draft.

He turned slowly to look at the pickup, his belongings stacked in the back beside his Ducati motorcycle, then scratched his stubbled chin and scanned the property. Acres of overgrown pastures, rickety fencing and weeds greeted his eyes. A rundown barn and a set of stables stood – just barely, it seemed – fifty yards from the house. A chicken coop, long since vacated, jutted from one side of the barn.

He wandered over to take a closer look and discovered an old tractor parked beneath a shelter. The barn was well stocked with tools, saddlery and farm equipment, though much of it was mildewed or rusted. A black cat meandered out to greet him, its tail held high, eyes half closed. It appeared to be well fed, probably due to a ready supply of mice.

He continued out to the pasture and draped his arms over the top fence paling. A small herd of horses grazed in the distance. Mr. Sanderson had told him about the herd. Apparently the property had been a working ranch years earlier, but the manager his grandfather hired had bled the place dry and let it fall into ruin during Pa's final years, when he hadn't the energy to check on it.

A buzz in his pocket made him start. He pulled out his cell, checked the caller and pressed it to his ear. "Hi, Mom."

"Hello, honey. Are you there yet?"

"Yep," he sighed.

"What's it like?"

"It's a beautiful property, that's for sure. Big too. But it'll need a lot of work." He absentmindedly scuffed the dirt beneath the fence with the toe of his boot.

"Well, I know you can do it. You can do anything you put your mind to. You've always been able to do that." His mother's voice was calm, but he could hear the worry in her bright tone.

"It's only a year, right? The lawyer said I've got to stay here a year, and then I'll inherit the whole thing. Otherwise, it reverts to Nana Dixie." Silence on the other end of the line. "Mom?"

"I can't believe Pa did that. I mean, really, couldn't he just have sold the place and given you the money? Now you're all the way out in rural Georgia on your own. I worry about you."

"Don't worry about me, I'll be fine. I'm glad he didn't sell it – it's really a spectacular piece of land, and I'll bet he thought so too. He believed in me and I want to make him proud. Anyway, what else would I do with myself? I can't go back to the rodeo circuit – the doctor said another fall could mean permanent damage to my leg, and my shoulder aches all the time. If Pa hadn't left me this place, I don't know what I would have done."

She sighed loudly. "That's true, I suppose … I just

don't want you doing something you'll hate. I want you to be happy. Preferably up here in Chattanooga with me." She chuckled.

He laughed along with her. "Yeah, yeah. I know. But I really think I could be happy here. I love working the land and I've always wanted to breed horses. I think I'll turn it back into a horse ranch – stock horses, like it used to be." He hadn't given it much thought until that moment, but standing there as his eyes roved the property in the afternoon sun, the words just poured from his mouth. And as he said them, he felt their truth. Owning a stud farm had always been his dream, one he'd never thought would happen. But now … maybe this was his chance.

"You know, Nana Dixie's grandparents, Della and Clement White, moved down from Montana to Georgia when Clem's health deteriorated. I remember Mom, your Nana Dixie, saying they built a ranch in south Georgia, and when they died they left it to Pa in their will since their only son, your great-grandpa Stan, had already passed on. So when you think of it, that ranch is a family heirloom of sorts. It really would be a shame if it had to be sold, and that's probably what Nana Dixie would do with it – she certainly couldn't run it herself."

He pondered her words as he watched a bay mare nip at the hindquarters of a chestnut colt, sending it running. He smiled. "A family heirloom, huh?" He turned, rested his back against the fence and studied the ranch house. "Well, it doesn't look as if the house is original – they must have rebuilt this place in the 1970s or something. It's rundown, but it's not that old."

"I hope you don't work yourself too hard, my boy. And call me if you need anything, okay?"

He grinned. She was always taking care of him. He wanted to show her he could do this. When he invited her down for a visit, he wanted to surprise her with how well he was doing. "I won't, Mom. I'll call you soon. Love you. Bye." He hung, rested one heel on the lowest rail of the fence and breathed the fresh country air deep into his lungs.

If he was to turn this place into a horse ranch, the first thing he'd need to do was to buy a breeding stallion with good bloodlines. He'd saved a decent nest egg from his years on the rodeo circuit – he'd likely have to sink every cent into this place before things turned around. But a stallion was a necessity, one he couldn't forgo. If he found one with an impeccable pedigree, he could start letting him stand at stud for a sizable fee, bringing mares from all over the South to be covered. And while he waited for his own foals from the grazing herd to arrive next spring, he'd use his remaining funds to fix the place up.

Long shadows clung to the house and barn, throwing the grasses beyond into darkness. The sun would set soon. He'd better get inside, unpack and assess the damage before it got too dark. He pressed his Stetson more firmly onto his head and returned to the truck. He reached inside for his backpack, shoved the door closed and headed for the house.

With a few quick steps, he climbed the stairs, then stopped to pull the keys from his pocket. Mr. Sanderson had given them to him right before Dalton left for Georgia, with a warning that he should be prepared to find the place in disarray. *That was putting it mildly*, he thought with a snort.

The key ring was full, and he flicked through them, looking for the one that fit the front door. Before long he found it and tried it in the lock. When the door swung open, he glanced cautiously inside before stepping through. A musty smell hit him full in the face, and he covered his nose and mouth with one hand and winced.

He blinked a few times in the darkness of the entryway, then let his backpack slip to the ground and shut the door behind him. The first thing to do was open the drapes and windows and let some fresh air in. He hurried to do it, and the sunlight that drifted through the windows illuminated millions of dust particles floating through the air around him.

A search of the kitchen revealed a bucket and some expired cleaning supplies. He found a pair of rubber gloves, still unopened in their packet, and pulled them on, then filled the bucket with soap and water and began cleaning the place. The water was cold, since he hadn't thought to get the electricity turned on before he arrived. That was next on his to-do list – which was growing longer by the moment.

A few hours later, the kitchen was passably clean, along with the bathroom and bedroom, the three rooms he figured he'd be using most. By then it was too dark to do any more, and he'd had about all he could take after the long drive from Tennessee. He called for a pizza, grateful to be near enough to the town of Tifton that he could get delivery – and use his phone.

He slumped onto a faded brown leather couch in the living room, with a freshly washed glass filled with lukewarm water, to make some calls. After talking to the electricity company, internet service provider and cable company, he pulled up the Notes app on his phone and considered what to do with his newly acquired ranch. There was so much work to be done if he was to make it a fully functional business, but what should he prioritize? He tapped at the phone, building a list of tasks to get things started.

He'd eyeballed the small herd of brood mares grazing comfortably in the pasture. They looked to be in fine health, with shining if somewhat shaggy coats and plump sides. The more he thought about it, the more certain he was that he should continue the property's breeding tradition. He'd grown up on a horse ranch and knew the ins and outs of running a breeding program. He'd ridden stock horses since he could walk and loved the breed. They were a noble, beautiful, intelligent and highly trainable horse. It made sense.

He smiled and leaned back on the sofa, his hands linked behind his head and his thoughts spinning. Yes, that was it. Cotton Tree Ranch would become one of the premier stock farms in the country under his leadership.

The sound of a car on the drive made him jump to his feet and fish his wallet from the back pocket of his jeans. The pizza delivery boy looked to be around sixteen, his spiked hair stood on end with razor-short back and sides. He pushed spectacles up his pimpled nose and held out his hand for the cash that Dalton quickly handed over. When he closed the door, the smell of baked dough and cheese filled his nostrils. His stomach growled as he carried the pizza to the newly-cleaned kitchen table.

Through the kitchen windows he spied the stars coming out, and lit a candle he'd found in a closet. There was something so appealing about this place, something earthy, homey and real. Just the thought of what it could become set his blood racing. If he failed, it wouldn't be for lack of trying.

Satisfied with his plan, he opened the pizza box and sat down with a sigh. He pulled a slice out and watched the cheese stretch, still warm, from one end. And for the first time in months, he felt a buzz of excitement and anticipation well up from deep within.

* * *

HAZEL'S FOOTSTEPS echoed loudly in the still morning air. They pounded against the pavement as she ran, a steady rhythmic beat she couldn't help matching to the music in her earbuds.

She'd left Jen at the hospital the previous evening after an emergency appendectomy. According to the medical team, she'd be fine, and was sleeping soundly when Hazel left. She'd certainly given Hazel a scare.

She stopped and bent forward, leaning her hands on her knees and puffing. She always pushed herself harder toward the end of a run – it gave her a rush of adrenaline and a sense of satisfaction to take herself to the limit of her ability. With a deep inhale, she stood straight and squared her shoulders, stretching one arm above the other.

A man with a large white dog on a red leash stopped beside her and smiled, then focused on his FitBit, pressing buttons with a furrowed brow. The dog pushed its wet nose against her leg, then gazed up at her with its mouth agape, its long pink tongue lolling out one side of its mouth.

Her lips pursed, she stepped aside, mouthing, "sorry, I'm allergic" to the man who raised an eyebrow at her. She wasn't really allergic, but why couldn't people keep their animals under control? Now she had a sticky patch of dog slobber on her leg. Really, was it too much to ask that she not be drooled on in the park?

Her cell phone buzzed. She unclipped it from the clear holder strapped around her arm and swiped her finger across the screen. "Hello?"

"Hazel, it's Jen."

"Jen! How are you? Shouldn't you be sleeping?"

"I was sleeping. But my boss just called. He needs me to do a job for him."

Hazel frowned. "Didn't you tell him you're in hospital?"

Jen groaned. "I couldn't. He was all stressed and in a hurry – he didn't give me a chance to say anything, really. I've just started working there and you know I really need this job. I can't afford to lose another one."

With a huff, Hazel leaned forward to touch her toes, letting the tension ease from her shoulders and neck as she tipped her head from side to side. "Well, you can't go to work – you've just come out of surgery. You'll have to call him back."

"It's just that ..."

"What?" Hazel's eyes narrowed. She recognized the tone in Jen's voice, and it made her nervous.

"Well, it's a really easy job – accompanying a breeding mare down to a ranch outside of Tifton in south Georgia. There's a stallion there for her to frolic with. Really, it's nothing but riding in a truck, waiting around for her to do her business and riding back again. Easy."

Hazel's heart thumped. "Why are you telling me this? You're not suggesting I go, are you?"

"I know it's a lot to ask, and I wouldn't even think about asking if it wasn't important. But I reeeeally don't want to lose this job, and you're on vacation now, aren't you? So it would be like taking a road trip. And there's nothing for you to do, because there'll be a driver for the trailer and the rancher will take care of things at their end. You're really just ... horse-sitting."

"You can't be serious," fumed Hazel. "A road trip? To a ranch, with horses and mud and who knows what else? And how long would it take, anyway? I'm planning on going to Jekyll Island for a few days, and my mom will kill me if I back out now."

She could hear Jen's victorious smile through the phone line. "Oh, a day or two at most. You'll be back in plenty of time to visit your folks. Thank you so much, Hazel! I owe you, really. Anything you need, you just ask me."

Hazel sighed and squinted up at the fluffy clouds floating by. "Really? *Anything* I ask? How about this – don't make me spend my vacation at a stinky ranch in south Georgia."

Jen laughed. "Thanks, Hazel. I'll text you the details, but I have to go now. My doctor's just come in to give me an update. Really, you're a life saver, I mean it – you're the best friend a girl could ask for. Bye!" The phone line went dead.

Hazel stared at the screen in disbelief. What had just happened? How had she agreed to horse-sit for a big-time horse breeder? Likely the mare was valuable – what if something went wrong? She didn't know the first thing about horses. What a disaster!

She couldn't understand why Jen just didn't tell her boss the truth. There was no way he'd fire her for a burst appendix – it was completely out of her control.

But that was Jen all over – always making everything far more difficult than it had to be. And usually ending up in a big mess as a result.

She sighed again and tucked her cell phone back in its sleeve. The man with the dog had moved on and so did she, falling right back into her regular jogging rhythm as music filled her earbuds again. She supposed she could do Jen this one favor. After all, her friend had always been there for her in the past – giving her a shoulder to cry on, a sympathetic ear during the hard times, cooking a comforting dinner when she knew Hazel had a bad day. If this was what Jen needed from her in return, she figured it wasn't too much to ask.

After all, how hard could it be?

* * *

WHEN HAZEL PULLED up at Green Peach Ranch the following day and parked her convertible in the thick mud beside a set of immaculate stables, she knew immediately she was in trouble. She stepped from her car with a frown, her silver Steve Madden pumps sinking immediately into three inches of muck.

A horse trailer hitched to an impressively large red Ford truck was backed up close to the stable. A man dressed in a faded blue-and-white-checked shirt and dungarees with a tan cowboy hat, greeted her with a tug of his hat brim. "How ya doin'?"

"Fine, thank you," she replied with a grimace. Every step she took, her heels got stuck in the mud, and she had to jerk them out before she could continue.

"You Jennifer?" he asked, one hand on his hip, the

other rubbing where a beard would be if he'd let it grow.

"Actually, I'm filling in for Jennifer. I'm Hazel." She stopped in front of him and thrust out a hand.

He raised an eyebrow and shook her hand. "Okay, then. I'm Gus – pleased to meetcha. If Bill's okay with it, then I'm okay with it. You can get your stuff and get in the truck if ya like. We're 'bout ready to head on out. I'll just grab the filly and load her up."

"Great – nice to meet you," she responded with more enthusiasm than she felt.

Gus nodded in her direction, then strode into the stables.

Hazel closed her eyes and took a deep breath. All she had to do was get into the truck, ride to south Georgia and wait for some stallion to do his thing. That was it. A cinch. She opened her eyes and trudged back through the mud to her car.

Jen owed her. Big time.

CHAPTER 3

The country road stretched long and straight between cotton fields. White puffs held by green claws stretched as far as Hazel could see in every direction. Then the fields were gone, replaced by pastures – thick, green and lush.

The truck slowed and she glanced at Gus, who'd chewed the end of a toothpick for the entire drive. He'd been silent for most of the trip, occasionally humming along to a favorite country song on the radio, one arm leaning on the edge of the open window, the other hand gripped the steering wheel. She'd tried to start a conversation with him several times, but after a few grunted responses, she took the hint and let him be. Even when they'd stopped for lunch at a Waffle House by the freeway, he'd barely spoken except to the waitress.

He pulled to the side of the road slowly and care-fully, then turned the truck neatly into a driveway. The gate looked new, constructed from bright raw timber. And a new wooden sign hung above it, reading

"Cotton Tree Ranch" in clear black letters. Her gaze followed the path as it wound through green fields. The grass was cropped short on either side of the gravel drive, but only a few feet away it rose tall, swaying in the afternoon breeze.

She lifted a hand to wipe the sweat from her forehead and pushed her sunglasses back up her nose. They kept sliding down in the heat, and no matter how many times she mentioned it, Gus had refused to raise his window and turn on the air conditioning.

Now he looked across the bench seat at her, his eyebrows arched in expectation.

"What?" she shrugged.

He nodded toward the gate, and she rolled her eyes with a sigh. Of course – he was waiting for her to get out and open it for him.

She pushed open the truck door and climbed cautiously down. Her pointed heels dug into the soft red earth, and she wobbled through the gravel and mud to swing the gate open. She caught a splinter from the raw timber in her finger and shoved it into her mouth with a curse. This day just kept getting better and better.

As Gus drove through, she saw him smirk and shake his head, and felt a bolt of anger course through her veins. He was laughing at her – no doubt he had been all along. He didn't think she was up to the task. Well, she might not know what she was doing, but she was good at faking it till she made it. She'd show him she could be every bit the country girl if she put her mind to it.

As the trailer trundled past her, she saw the chestnut tail of the mare through the back of it and frowned. She'd just act confident and the horse would know she was the boss. That was how it worked – at least that's how the Dog Whisperer seemed to do it. She'd accidentally watched the TV show once while channel-flipping and had gotten caught up in the drama. Of course, she'd never actually tried any of his techniques, but it all seemed straightforward enough.

When they pulled up in front of the house, a man opened the screen door and wandered out to watch them park by the stables, his hands on his hips. She smiled and waved, and he nodded in response. He wore jeans, a green-and-white-striped button-down shirt and a tan cowboy hat, and he was in his stockinged feet. Muddy brown boots sat by the door, and she watched him pull them on as Gus parked.

Her heart jittered and her head felt light. "You've got this, Hazel," she whispered under her breath. "It's just an animal, and he's just a cowboy. You've made small talk with heads of state over cocktails and negotiated to play third-chair violin with the legendary head of the Atlanta Symphony. You can handle a cowboy and a horse."

She climbed out of the truck, stumbling on the uneven ground and almost twisting her ankle. As she rounded the front of the vehicle, she landed against the cowboy's hard chest, her arms wrapping around his shoulders and neck. Her cheeks burned, she lifted her eyes to meet his – and time stood still.

His eyebrows rose in surprise and he gently pried her free, setting her on her feet. "You okay?" he asked with a hint of a smile. His dimpled cheeks seemed to mock her.

She smoothed her flyaway curls behind her ears, smiling with a confidence she didn't feel. "Fine, thank you. I'm sorry about that – I'm afraid I didn't select the most practical shoes when I left the house this morning."

He glanced down at her feet and pursed his lips. "I guess not."

She offered her hand. "Hazel Hildebrand."

"Dalton Williams – pleasure to meet you." He shook her hand with a firm grip, then tipped back his hat. "So you're the vet?"

"Well, I'm … I'm here to keep the mare, um …"

"Contessa's Charity?"

"Yes – I'm here to keep her company."

"Good to know."

Gus rounded the back of the trailer with the mare in tow. She looked remarkably calm after the long journey, her tail swishing around her hind legs. Her head bobbed as she walked and her eyes flitted around, taking in her new surroundings with seeming curiosity. "Howdy. Ya must be Mr. Williams. I'm Gus, and this here's Contessa's Charity – just Charity fer short. She's stayin' here for a bit, I understand."

Dalton grinned and shook Gus's hand. "Pleased to meet you, Gus. Hey there, Charity." He ran a hand lovingly down the mare's forehead, tracing the long white blaze there.

"Here ya go, then. I'll just get the paperwork fer ya to sign and I'll be on my way. Miss Hazel here's gonna stay with Charity 'til the deed's done, then she'll call me and I'll come on back to collect her. Sound good?"

Hazel marveled at how loquacious Gus was all of a sudden. He'd said more to Dalton Williams in one minute than he had to her in hours.

"Sounds fine to me." Dalton took the mare's lead from Gus and watched as Gus foraged around in the truck cab for the contract.

Hazel felt very out of place. She chewed on her cheek and folded her arms.

Gus's head emerged from the truck, his eyebrows arched. "Ya want yer bag?"

She nodded and hurried around to the passenger side, dragging her wheeled luggage from the cabin. It thudded to the ground below and she pulled and tugged it across the lumpy ground. It was almost as bad a choice as the pumps, she realized – now that it was too late.

Once finished with the contract, Gus waved good-bye, backed out of the yard, turned the truck and trailer around and headed down the long drive. Hazel watched him leave, her heart pounding. She wiped the sweat from her brow again and turned toward the rundown house with its cracked paint and rotting siding, and the ancient barn and adjoining stables. Finally, she looked at Dalton, who was talking quietly to the mare. Then his eyes met Hazel's with a bemused expression.

She smiled, her heart in her throat. What had she gotten herself into?

DALTON WATCHED Hazel mince into the stable in her absurd city shoes. The building had a wide opening at one end, and its floor was coated in a thin layer of straw mixed with dirt. Stalls ran along both sides, some occupied but most empty. This time of year, he preferred to keep his stock out in the pasture.

He turned and led Contessa's Charity into a stall, then unclipped the lead from her halter. She immediately dropped her head to the pile of fresh hay he'd thrown in earlier and began munching away. He smiled – she already seemed at ease there. No thanks to her handler. He glanced over his shoulder at Hazel standing there awkwardly, her hands clasped in front of her skirt, her wide eyes gazing around the stable.

Frowning, he turned back to the mare and backed out of the stall, snapping a rope into place to keep her there. She was a good-looking animal, with a shiny coat and finely shaped head. A decent height as well. With a mare like her, his new bay stallion Rocket Peak would sire a fine foal.

"So how long do you think it will take? You know, to …"

"Have her covered?" he finished, wiggling his eyebrows.

"Um … yes." She flushed pink and chewed nervously on the side of her mouth.

"Well, I don't know. I'm going to bring Rocket Peak into the next stall in the morning so they can get acquainted. Then I'll let them out into the small field beside the house together, in the afternoon. So maybe day after tomorrow? But there's really no way of knowing." He ran his fingers over his lips and flashed her a smile.

She sighed and frowned at the ground. "Oh great," she grumbled.

He frowned. She really was something – though he wasn't sure what. "I'm sorry – do you have somewhere else to be?"

Her lips pulled into a tight line and she shook her head. "I wasn't told it would take that long. I'm supposed to visit my parents."

He shook his head. City women, always in a hurry, always with so much to do. And why on Earth would she wear high heels to a horse ranch? Not to mention designer clothing and a pound of makeup on her face. She'd sure be pretty if she weren't so made-up. "You're more than welcome to leave her here and go do what you gotta do. I'm happy to watch her and call you when the deed's done. I'm sure a woman like you's got better things to do than sit around on a horse ranch." He didn't hide the annoyance in his voice.

She shook her head. "No, I promised …" Her cheeks flamed pink. "I'm supposed to stay. So …"

His forehead creased and his eyes studied her face. What was going on? Promised – promised who? She was hiding something, or at the very least not telling him the entire story.

She shifted uncomfortably and crossed her arms. "What do you mean, a woman like me?"

"You know." He waved toward her. "Dressed up, made up, perfume, the whole nine yards."

Her eyes narrowed. "You've got me all figured out, I see."

He laughed and adjusted his hat. "Lady, I read you the moment you stepped out of the truck."

Her eyes flashed and her nostrils flared. "Well, ditto to you. I've known men like you. You just think you're *so* special that no woman could possibly resist your charms. Well, I've got news for you – you aren't God's gift to women, even with that dimpled smile of yours."

He grinned, flashing his dimple as best he could and letting his baby blues sparkle just to tease her. "Yes, ma'am," he drawled, tugging the brim of his hat. "On that note, why don't I show you to your room so you can get settled in?"

She smiled, her eyes cold, and nodded. "Thank you. That would be fine."

* * *

Safely ensconced in her room, Hazel slumped onto the bed and lay back on the covers with her hands pressed over her eyes. She couldn't believe how much of a jerk Dalton Williams was. She seethed, reliving that moment in the stables. He thought he knew all about her just by the way she dressed? Well, she'd never let him push her into a box like that. She was more than fancy clothing and flawless makeup – she was a woman of substance, and she hated that for a moment he'd made her feel like less.

She groaned and sat up to survey the room. As much as she'd like to fling his lousy housekeeping skills in his face, she had to admit the room was neat and clean. The house itself was in a sorry state, but he seemed to have scrubbed the interior until it sparkled. He'd even added a few decorative touches to the guest room to make it warm and welcoming. The pale blue comforter was complimented by a set of throw pillows. The dresser had a vintage lamp. There was even a cozy-looking afghan over one arm of the wooden rocking chair in the corner.

She stood and unzipped her Louis Vuitton suitcase, shaking her head at the mud-caked wheels. In a few minutes, she'd moved everything into the dresser, with her toiletries sitting on top of it. She changed quickly into athletic gear, pulled her hair into a ponytail, plugged her earbuds into her ears and selected an upbeat track. She needed to run a few miles to work the fury out of her system before she could face Dalton again.

She poked her head out of the doorway to peer up and down the hall. Good – the cowboy was nowhere in sight. She slunk down the hallway and out the front door, being careful to shut it quietly behind her.

The afternoon sun was setting, and the stifling heat of the day had finally begun to lift. She stood still for a moment, looking out at the yard, fields and grazing horses. It really was pretty in a rustic kind of way. She doubted she could ever live in such a place – it wasn't likely there'd be a good sushi restaurant within easy driving distance. And she couldn't imagine going without her sushi. She put her head down and set off at a run down the long drive, the music pounding in her ears.

When she returned a half-hour later, she was dripping with sweat and the sun was disappearing over the horizon. The farmhouse slid into darkness, apart from a single porch light that had likely been turned on for her benefit. She sniffed. Too little, too late, Mr. Williams. She removed her shoes, set them next to Dalton's work boots, and tiptoed back through the front door.

She could hear him banging around in the kitchen. He had music playing – country, of course – and was singing along off-key. She grinned. He really did sound adorable, even if he was hopelessly obnoxious.

By the time she'd showered and changed into denim shorts and a white T-shirt the singing had stopped. Only the faint strains of a lonesome melody floated out to greet her. She marched into the kitchen to find him sitting at the little round dining table in the breakfast nook, a plate of steaming hot food in front of him and a fork poised over the plate.

He smiled at her and set his fork down. "Evening, Hazel. I made chicken parmagiana if you want some."

She shook her head. "No, thank you – I'm going to

order in. Do you have a number for the local sushi place?"

He laughed and combed his fingers through his thick brown hair, his eyes twinkling. "Sushi? Sorry, you won't find any of that 'round here parts. The only thing delivered out here is fried chicken, pizza and Chinese food. Would you like the numbers for them?"

Her chin dropped and she sighed. "No, thanks. I suppose I'll just have to make something myself."

"Like I said, you're welcome to a plate of –"

"I can manage just fine on my own."

"Well, then," he responded. "Help yourself. If you can find something you like, have at it."

"Thank you."

She wrung her hands together, then opened the refrigerator and found a loaf of bread, some butter, a few vegetables and a carton of milk. The pantry contained more options, but since she hardly ever cooked for herself, she wasn't exactly sure what to do with them.

Finally her gaze landed on a box of instant macaroni and cheese and she pulled it from the pantry with a grimace. How many calories were there in that stuff? She decided not to look and instead grabbed the milk and butter and a saucepan. She studied the instructions on the box carefully, following line by line with her fingertip.

A chuckle behind her made her gasp. "You sure you don't need some help with that?" Dalton asked.

She spun to face him with wide eyes. She'd been concentrating so hard on the task at hand, she hadn't noticed him sneak up behind her. And she didn't like how he looked her up and down, his eyes gleaming in appreciation. "No, thank you. I'm fine."

"You look as though you've never made mac and cheese before." He crossed his arms over his thick chest and raised an eyebrow.

She frowned. "Actually, I haven't. I don't eat a lot of carbs ..."

His laughter stopped her. "Of *course* you don't. Well, don't let me interrupt – I'm gonna go and watch some TV. Just holler if you need anything." He left the pan of chicken parmagiana sitting on top of the stove, beside a pot of strained pasta and wandered out into the living room, letting the kitchen door swing closed behind him.

She wrinkled her nose at his departing back, then returned to the task at hand. While the water boiled, she peeled a carrot and bit into it with a smile of satisfaction. She was starving after the long day of travel and the run. She'd pushed herself to the limit and was pretty sure she'd beat her own personal record. Her stomach growled at the smell of Dalton's dish right in front of her. Her eyes kept roving to it, but she'd tear them free and re-focus on her own boiling pot.

Finally, the macaroni was cooked and she drained out the water with a spoon, losing some of the pasta down the drain. She dumped the flavor packet, butter and milk into the pot, stirred it for a minute or so and grimaced. It didn't look very appetizing – not like Dalton's meal. But she'd be burned alive before she'd give him the satisfaction of knowing she'd caved and eaten the food he prepared. She had to prove to him she was capable of feeding herself, at the very least.

She dished a hearty serving of mac and cheese into a bowl, sat at the table, took a deep breath and put a spoonful into her mouth. It wasn't bad. But it wasn't very good either. Her eyes flitted back over to where the chicken parmagiana sat, tantalizing her.

Oh, the heck with it. She leaped to her feet, hurried to the drawer to fetch a fresh bowl and piled pasta and chicken parm into it. It was still warm, and gooey cheese and rich tomato sauce spilled over the noodles. She smiled and closed her eyes to inhale the delicious aroma.

Hazel returned to the table and dug into the dish with gusto, the first mouthful making her groan with delight. She couldn't remember the last time she'd had pasta, and this was as delicious as any restaurant she'd been to. Her eyes drifted closed and she savored each flavor as it danced across her tongue.

When her eyes opened, she gasped to see Dalton leaning against the door jamb, his arms folded over his chest and a smirk lighting up his handsome features. Her cheeks blazed and she dropped the fork on the table. "It just ... looked so good ...," she mumbled helplessly.

He laughed and turned to leave. "You're welcome, Slick," he called over his shoulder.

CHAPTER 4

*H*azel pulled the covers up to her chin and closed her eyes, then opened them again and sniffed. Slick? He'd called her Slick. Was that short for "city slicker" or something? She'd seen the way he looked at her, as though he pitied her. And so far she'd done little to prove him wrong. So she guessed the nickname was *not* a compliment.

Her phone buzzed on the bedside table. She sat up, flicked on a lamp and picked it up, her blood still boiling over Dalton's insult. "Hello?"

Jen's voice on the line brought a smile to her face. "Hi, Hazel. How's it going?"

"Fine, thanks," she lied. "And you?"

"Fine, fine. Enough chitchat – tell me everything. Did it all go according to plan?"

Hazel laughed at the worry in her friend's voice. She'd never seen Jen so serious about any job before. She must really want to keep this one. "Everything went fine. I pulled up in front of the stables and avoided the office, just like you told me to. Gus was there already and he loaded Charity into the trailer. I didn't really have to do anything. Gus is the strong-and-silent type, emphasis on 'silent' – he barely talked the entire trip. I chattered away, of course – you know how I get when it's too quiet."

"I hope you didn't say too much."

Hazel, leaned back against the pillows she'd stacked just so. "What do you mean?"

"You know – he was expecting me, Jennifer Barsby. So even though he's never met me before, it's important to keep up the ruse."

Hazel slapped her forehead and took a deep breath. "You didn't tell me that."

"I didn't?" queried Jen, panic in her voice. "What did you tell him?"

"Nothing about you. I just introduced myself."

There was silence for a moment. "As Jen, right?"

"No, as Hazel Hildebrand."

Jen screamed, and Hazel held the phone away from her ear with a grimace. "Oh no! I'm dead. He's totally going to tell my boss and I'll be fired!"

"Maybe he won't. Maybe he won't say anything and it'll all be fine. I'm sorry, Jen. I didn't know."

Jen sighed. "It's not your fault. I should never have asked you to fill in for me. It must have been the medication they had me on – it made me crazy. I'm sorry for making you do it – you're the best friend in the world for following your ridiculous roommate's stupid plan." She took a deep breath before continuing. "So what's he like?"

"What's who like?"

"The owner of the ranch. Dalton Williams?"

Hazel growled. "Rude, obnoxious, totally full of himself and not even slightly chivalrous. I thought

42

cowboys were supposed to be chivalrous. All I can say is, I'll be glad when the job's done and I can leave this death trap."

"That bad?"

"Worse. And now he's nicknamed me 'Slick'."

Jen laughed, then stopped herself as if she'd clapped a hand over her mouth. "That's terrible," she sympathized. "I heard he's hot, though."

"What?" exclaimed Hazel, her eyes wide.

"Is he?"

Hazel grunted in annoyance.

Jen chuckled. "I knew it."

Hazel pictured Dalton's grinning face, white teeth, dimpled cheek and twinkling blue eyes. She was certain he got plenty of female attention wherever he went, but she wasn't going to succumb to the charms of an arrogant jerk like him. She had standards when it came to men, expectations of how they should behave and how they should treat her. And Dalton Williams did not live up to any of them.

* * *

DALTON SLUNG a bag of seed over his shoulder and walked over to the tractor. He'd managed to get it running with a bit of oil and some TLC just after he'd arrived at the ranch. It was old, but it ran like a charm. He emptied the bag into the seeder, then wiped the sweat from his brow with the back of his sleeve. Dang, it was hot.

A glance at the horizon told him a storm was on the way, and he wanted to get the alfalfa planted before it came. He'd decided to sow a few of the fields with crops, to bring in some extra money come harvest time and provide feed for the horses through the winter months.

He climbed into the cab and started the engine, then set off for the already-plowed field on the south end of his property. Another peek at the sky revealed dark, angry clouds churning toward the ranch. He shook his head. He'd have to be quick if he wanted to get this done before the storm arrived.

HAZEL PUSHED the porch swing with one foot, the other tucked beneath her, and laid back. She could see Rocket Peak, the stallion they'd travelled so many miles for, on the other side of the nearest fence, grazing happily. The mare, Contessa's Charity, wandered along the far fence line, her tail swishing at flies as she chewed a mouthful of grass.

With a sigh, Hazel shook her head. She'd been watching them all morning long and they seemed to want nothing to do with one another. It was all so frustrating. She'd hoped they'd be headed home the following day, but it certainly wasn't looking hopeful.

She put in her earbuds and opened the Spotify app on her phone. With a quick search, she located a recording of the London Symphony Orchestra live at the Barbican and pressed "play." She smiled and let her eyelids drift closed, as the music swelled to envelop her, shutting out everything around her.

But it wasn't working. She'd expected the rapture, the joy, she should feel listening to one of the premier orchestras in the world play the *Symphonie Fantastique*, but it just didn't come. In fact, it hadn't happened a lot lately – as if her passion for the music had dimmed.

Instead, her stomach churned with anxiety whenever she thought about work. And listening to this piece made her mind turn to her work.

She wrinkled her nose as the phone buzzed, muting the sound of the orchestral piece. A quick look revealed a text from Jen: *Have you been following the news?!!!*

Hazel frowned and opened a browser on her phone to skip to the local news site. The headline read: *Tornado warning for Tift County – take cover, secure outdoor furniture and pets.*

She yanked her earbuds out, stood and went to the porch rail to look up at the sky – nothing but a few gray clouds. She hurried to the other end of the porch and peered around the edge of the house. Angry black thunderheads filled the horizon, twisting as they headed toward the ranch house.

Her eyes widened and her hands dropped to her sides. What should she do? She was supposed to take cover, but where? What about Dalton and the horses? Come to think of it, where was Dalton? She'd seen him head off on the tractor earlier, but she hadn't paid much attention to where he'd gone. She'd simply been glad to be on her own for a while without his snide grin reminding her of how she didn't measure up to his expectations. But now she was worried.

She shoved her phone in her pocket and ran down the steps into the yard. With her hand above her brow, she stood on tiptoe and scanned the surrounding fields, finally spotting him in the distance. The tractor was moving slowly, pulling some kind of equipment in its wake. He wore his trademark hat, and looked to be facing away from the approaching storm, his attention on the ground behind him.

She shouted and waved, but he didn't see her and was too far away to hear her. The noise of the storm, the rush of wind and swish of leaves drowned out everything else, as if the storm was sucking any sound up into a vacuum. Every glance over her shoulder revealed the clouds were closing in fast. She couldn't tell if they would bring a tornado, but figured it wasn't worth the risk to wait and find out.

She frowned, took off her patent-leather flats and set off. "Dalton!" she yelled as loud as she could, waving her arms over her head as she ran toward him.

The tractor slowed to a stop as she approached, its engine idling. Dalton leaned forward. "What's up?" he shouted.

She pointed a finger toward the clouds. "Tornado warning!" she yelled back

He turned to follow her finger and pushed his hat back, surveying the sky with obvious concern. "Climb on," he replied, patting the seat beside him.

She hurried over to the tractor and pulled herself up into the cab. He grabbed her hands and yanked her up the last step, moving aside for her to sit next to him. The seat was just wide enough for both of them. He shifted the tractor into drive and set off toward the barn as fast as it would go.

They bounced and jolted over the uneven ground and Hazel held tight to the seat with both hands, knuckles white. She glanced at Dalton. His face was serious, and with one hand on the steering wheel and the other on the gear shifter, he looked strong and confident. Her heart skipped a beat.

* * *

DALTON STOOD in the doorway to the stable, hands on his hips. He'd pulled an old boom box from his bedroom closet and plugged it into an outlet to listen to the news on the radio. Gusts of wind buffeted the ranch, and the bushes and trees planted around the house and barn leaned low to the ground, branches waving as the wind whistled through them, almost drowning out the voice of the newsreader, He'd already confirmed a tornado had been sighted near Tifton.

Behind him, Hazel was pressed up against the stable wall, her eyes wide. He turned to face her. "We have to get the horses out of here."

She nodded. Thankfully, there were only a few in the stables – most were already out in the pasture. He could see them trotting together in a herd up and down the long fence line, tails and heads raised high. They'd be safer where they were if a tornado touched down. There weren't many trees or much potential debris in the pasture, and it would give the animals a chance to get out of the storm's way if it came to that.

He strode to the nearest stall, unclipped the rope and stood aside as the mare trotted out into the yard. She was soon cantering off to join the rest of the herd with a shrill whinny in their direction. Hazel did the same for a colt in the next stall, who followed the mare.

Before long the stable was empty, and the two of them stood side by side watching the herd pace the length of the pasture. "Will they be okay?" shouted Hazel, squinting into the wind.

"I hope so."

"Now what?"

"If you can get all the windows in the house open, I'll put away anything that's been left out in the yard."

She nodded again and ran for the house. He watched her go, with the long easy strides of a dedicated runner. Her chestnut curls hung loose around her head, still damp from her morning shower. He'd been right about her – she was gorgeous without the makeup and fancy clothes. Her bright green eyes sparkled, and a smattering of freckles across her nose made him want to kiss each one.

He shook his head and hurried outside to put away the tools he'd left beside the air conditioner that morning. He dreaded the idea of it dying in the middle of summer, but it wasn't looking good. He'd done what he could to fix it, but it needed an HVAC technician and he wasn't one. He could just imagine what Hazel would say about it if the air went out while she was staying at the ranch. Though likely she'd be gone in a day or two, so it wouldn't be an issue ...

The thought made his heart sink, and he frowned. He'd be glad when she was gone, so he could get back to work with no distractions. She was nothing but trouble, and trouble was one thing he didn't need more of. But for some reason, the idea of being on his own again at the ranch without Hazel there to frustrate and annoy him had begun to feel mighty lonely.

It only took a couple of minutes for them to finish their tasks, and Hazel emerged from the house with a wave. He beckoned her toward the barn and leaned into the howling wind to pull the door of the tornado shelter open. It was old, built decades ago – maybe by his forbears, Della and Clem. The thought made him smile and he pointed down into the shelter – the noise of the storm forced him to communicate with gestures alone.

She nodded and skipped down the stairs into the shelter. He took one last glance around the ranch, now shrouded in a dark grayish-green light, then followed her inside, pulling the door shut behind him.

The howl of the wind outside sounded eerie as it whistled through cracks around the shelter door. Hazel was seated at the far end of the concrete structure, her knees pulled up to her chest and her arms wrapped around her legs. With wide eyes, she stared at the wall in front of her, unmoving. No doubt she wasn't as accustomed to tornadoes as him, being from Atlanta. He'd spent time all over the South and Midwest, including Oklahoma and Kansas. He was used to taking cover like this, though it shook him up more this time knowing it was his property and his horses under threat.

He pressed his back against the cold hard wall of the structure and slid down to sit beside her. "Thanks for your help," he said, taking off his hat and setting it on the ground beside him.

"No problem."

He ran his fingers through his hair and pushed his legs out in front of him with a grimace. He laced hands beneath his injured leg and shifted it into a more comfortable position. It ached at times, especially if he overdid it – and he probably had, with all the running he'd done to put everything away and prepare for the tornado.

"What happened to your leg?" Hazel asked.

He sighed, rubbing it where the break had been. "A really nasty horse."

"Oh?"

"Yeah. I know it might be hard to believe, seeing as how this place is in such stellar shape, but I've only been here a few months. I inherited it from my grandfather, and before that it was run into the ground. I'm trying to build it up into something he would've been proud of – something I can be proud of."

"So you fell off a horse when you first got here?"

He shook his head. "No, I was a professional bronco rider. The last rodeo I did, I was thrown pretty bad after being rammed into a fence. The fence broke my leg in two places; the fall knocked me out." He ran a hand over his mouth and exhaled.

Hazel rested her chin on her knees and met his gaze. "I'm sorry. That must have hurt." Her green eyes were full of compassion.

Dalton's breath caught in his throat. "Thanks."

They sat in silence for a few minutes, listening to the wail of the storm overhead. Dalton's mind wandered to thoughts of the herd, the house, the barn. His pulse raced and he shut his eyes tight. He had to distract himself. "So what about you? Gus said you're a vet working for the breeder, but you don't act like any vet I've ever known."

Hazel didn't answer, but stood and began pacing the length of the shelter. He frowned and raised an eyebrow. "Do you hear that?" she finally asked, stopping to stare upward.

"Hear what?"

"It's quieter, I think. Maybe the storm's passed."

He pushed himself slowly to his feet, making sure to keep the weight off his sore leg. "Yeah, sounds like it." Carefully he pushed the shelter door open and it fell back against the ground with a dull thud. He looked out and moaned. The house, barn and stables were intact, but otherwise it looked like a war zone. Branches, roof shingles, even a paddle pool littered the yard. Debris was scattered across most of the pasture. Big drops of rain landed on his face and ran down his neck, soaking his shirt.

Worst of all, he couldn't see the herd anywhere. Adrenaline pumped through his veins making his heart race. He climbed the steps and stood with his hands linked behind his head.

Hazel climbed out to stand beside him, her hands over her open mouth. "Lord have mercy!"

"You got that right," Dalton muttered.

*H*azel tucked two carrots into her shorts pocket and wandered out the front door. She could see Dalton in the distance, fixing a fence torn down by the tornado the previous day. Already he'd managed to haul a lot of the debris into a big pile beside the end of the driveway near the house. She'd helped as well, carrying what she could and dragging the rest.

She walked past the pile and headed for the field where Charity and Rocket grazed. She'd been grateful to see they were unhurt when she emerged from the tornado shelter. Though Dalton said it was unlikely Rocket would be interested in playing his part for a while, given the scare he'd likely received.

Thankfully, the neighbors had corralled Dalton's herd after the storm had passed, and a few quick phone calls had located them. He'd spent the rest of the afternoon and evening returning them to the Cotton Tree Ranch and erecting a makeshift fence to keep them overnight. He'd been up before dawn as well – she'd heard him go outside just as the first rays of sunshine peeked into her room. He'd been out there ever since.

He might be a pain in her rear, but he was a hard worker, and he truly loved this ranch and his livestock.

She sighed and ran a hand over her eyes. She'd already had to place a phone call to her parents to let them know she was unlikely to make it to Jekyll Island this week. The way things were going, she'd end up blowing her entire vacation on this ranch. She knew she'd have to talk to Jen soon – maybe Rocket and Charity's love affair just wasn't meant to be.

She walked toward the pair, grazing cozily side-by-side. "Now, you two, do I need to play some Barry White, Kenny G? What's gonna get you in the mood? 'Cause Aunty Hazel really needs to get home sometime this century, okay?" She chuckled and pulled the carrots from her pocket, taking one in each hand and holding them out through the fence rails.

Both horses lifted their heads and ambled over, ears flicking back and forth. They nipped the carrots from her hands and munched happily while she stroked their faces. Rocket left first – she'd noticed he never stuck around long for pats – but Charity remained, her eyes half-lidded, enjoying the snack and the attention.

After a while, Charity too wandered off to find a new patch of grass deserving of her attention. Hazel shoved her hands into her pockets and headed back to the house. She'd spent much of the day cleaning up after the storm, and her shoulders, arms and back ached.

A small yelp caught her ear and she looked around, trying to work out where it had come from. When she heard it again, she ran toward the source – the long grass lining the side of the barn, where Dalton's bush hog hadn't been able to reach. She leaned forward and parted the grass with both hands, careful not to move too close in case whatever was making the noise was dangerous. There was really no telling what it might be.

The noise again – it didn't sound dangerous, but small and possibly injured.

As she pushed aside a piece of firewood that had fallen from a nearby stack, she saw it. It was a little black puppy with a diamond-shaped white patch on its chest and floppy black ears. It yelped again, sticking out a tiny pink tongue with blue and gray patches on it. "Well, hello there. Who are you and how did you get here?" She scooped him up against her chest. He was a boy, she saw that right away, and she tickled the top of his head with her fingertips. "You poor little fella, you must have gotten lost in the storm."

She carried the puppy into the house and set him down on a towel on the kitchen floor, rubbing him all over to make sure he was dry. "You must be hungry and thirsty, huh? Let me see what I can find in here." A search of the fridge and pantry uncovered a leftover hot dog and a few cubes of cheese. She cut them up and placed them in a bowl in front of the dog. He stared at them, but didn't move. He looked exhausted.

"Well now, maybe you just want something to drink." She filled bowls with milk and water and set them out.

He wobbled to his feet and tottered over to the bowl of milk, lapping it up. She smiled and squatted to watch him for a few moments, until a hunger pang reminded her that she'd need to eat as well. And

Dalton was probably starving - she'd seen him come in for lunch, but otherwise he'd been out working hard all day. Maybe she should whip something up for both of them.

She foraged for ingredients and found eggs, bacon and pancake mix. It wouldn't be as delicious as the meal Dalton had made earlier in the week, but she loved breakfast for dinner and hoped he would too.

By the time he came in, it was already dark. She heard him tapping the mud off his boots as he deposited them by the front door. He walked inside and headed right for the bathroom, no doubt to wash up. The bacon was sizzling in the frying pan and she had a batch of beaten eggs in a bowl, ready to fry in the bacon grease. She'd even managed to find and drain a can of sliced mushrooms, which she'd sautéed before adding the bacon to the pan. Four slices of bread toasted in the toaster oven on the counter, and she'd mixed the pancake batter.

The sound of the shower filtered through the kitchen walls and mingled with the sizzling of the bacon. She smiled and lifted the bacon out onto a paper towel to drain, then filled the pan with the eggs. She warmed the griddle on the other side of the stove top and placed a dollop of butter on it before pouring out two generous portions of pancake batter.

She was pleased with herself and proud of what she'd managed. She rarely ever prepared meals for herself at home – it seemed almost a waste of time to put effort into a meal for one. Sometimes when Jen was around, she'd make breakfast. But otherwise, with so many good restaurants within walking distance, she'd never really felt the need to learn how to cook.

When Dalton walked into the kitchen, all the food

was done and she was kneeling beside the pup, offering him a small piece of bacon. He'd nibbled it, but otherwise seemed content to lie on the towel and snooze. "What is that?!" exclaimed Dalton, crossing his arms.

Hazel looked up at him. "*That* is a puppy. Surely you can see that for yourself."

He came over and crouched beside the dog, scratching him behind the ears. "Hey there, buddy. You're a cute one, aren't you?"

Hazel smiled. "I found him in the long grass beside the barn. He was crying and hungry. I think he must have gotten caught up in the storm somehow, since there's no way he could have walked here from anywhere. He's still unsteady on his feet – he can't be more than a couple of months old."

"At the most," agreed Dalton, his eyebrows lowering over blue eyes. Her pulse raced. He was so close and smelled of soap and shampoo, his hair falling in wet strands around his face and his tanned arms bulged beneath the sleeves of a white t-shirt.

He angled his head toward the stove and sniffed the air. "Is something burning?"

"Oh! My eggs!" Hazel jumped to her feet and ran to the stove, stirred the eggs frantically and scooped them into a bowl. She flipped the pancakes onto a plate, poured more batter onto the griddle, then set the bowl of eggs on the table beside the bacon, toast and mushrooms.

Dalton stood and combed his fingers through his hair. "What have we got here?"

"I made dinner," she said with a shy smile.

"Breakfast for dinner," he commented. "It smells amazing."

"Well, you've been working so hard all day, I figured you'd be hungry."

"Starving!" He pulled out a chair and sat at the table. "Thank you. You didn't have to do that."

"I don't mind."

He grinned, his gaze caught hers and she felt her heart jump. She quickly turned back to flip the pancakes.

"So what do you plan to do with your dog?" he asked, a grin in his voice.

She sighed. "I don't know. I figured he was yours, since this is your place. And I noticed you don't have a dog – you know, every ranch really needs a cat and a dog. I think I glimpsed a cat in the barn, so all you needed was a dog, and now you have one. At least, that's what I've seen in the movies."

He laughed. "Well, if it's in the movies …"

She chuckled too and felt the tension leave her shoulders. "He really is cute. Maybe we should ask around to make sure no one's lost him."

"Good idea. I'll start doing that tomorrow. But for tonight, I'll see if I can find him a box to sleep in."

Hazel piled two plates high with golden pancakes and set one in front of Dalton, then sat across from him with the other. They each served themselves bacon, eggs, mushrooms and toast. Then Dalton linked his hands together above his plate and bowed his head, closing his eyes. Hazel stared – he looked as though he was going to pray. She hadn't said a blessing over her meal in … well, she couldn't remember how long. She quickly copied his movements.

"Heavenly Father, thank You for this delicious meal and for the hands that prepared it. Thank You for keeping the ranch safe, the livestock and us as well. In Your mighty name, amen."

Hazel's cheeks warmed. There was something very attractive about a man praying over his meal that way. She wasn't sure why – something about being vulnerable, grateful, humble. Maybe Dalton Williams wasn't the man she'd thought he was. He'd certainly seemed different over the past two days, dealing with the tornado and its aftermath – confident and strong, but caring, and not arrogant or obnoxious at all. Maybe she'd gotten him all wrong.

She slathered her pancakes in butter and syrup, took a bite and chewed slowly while watching him eat. She swallowed and patted her mouth with a napkin. "So why are you so intent on turning this ranch into something?"

His eyes narrowed and he finished his bite before speaking. "Well, it was left to me by Grandpa Joe. And I found out it's been passed down through the generations. In the 1800s, my Nana's grandparents, Clem and Della, moved down here from Montana to spend their twilight years in a warmer climate. They bought the place and ran a horse ranch – they'd bred Morgan horses up north, I believe, but down here they took to stock horses. It's been a stock horse ranch ever since. My father didn't have the passion for it – he was a musician, and he died when I was young. So my grandfather hired a property manager who let the place fall apart."

"You want to make it back into what it was for the sake of your family?"

He nodded and cut off a piece of bacon. "Yeah, I guess so, but not just that. It's really all I've got now." A muscle clenched in his jaw. "I can't go back to riding broncs. My leg could be permanently damaged if I take another spill, and the doc said I can't afford another concussion either. Problem is, I've never really done anything else. Honestly, before Grandpa Joe left me this place, I was wondering what on Earth I'd do with myself. I guess you could say the Cotton Tree Ranch saved me." He cleared his throat. "Well, now you know my life story. What about you?"

"What about me?"

"Tell me about yourself. I mean, I know you're a vet. But what about family, friends. Boyfriend?"

Her cheeks flamed, and she pushed the pile of scrambled eggs around her plate with her fork. "Um … well. I live in Virginia-Highland, which is part of Atlanta, close to downtown. It's full of beautiful old buildings and I can walk to dinner, so I pretty much never cook. I have a roommate. No boyfriend. And my parents are currently spending the summer in their summer house on Jekyll Island – I'm planning on joining them as soon as I leave here."

Dalton swallowed a piece of bacon and tipped his head to one side. "Are you close with your folks?"

She shook her head and almost choked on a bite of pancake. "Uh, no. Let's just say they make a Wisconsin winter seem warm."

He chuckled. "Sounds bad."

She nodded with a wry grin. "It's not that bad – I'm exaggerating. But they're not real big on affection, or encouragement …"

The sound of Dalton's cell phone interrupted her. He apologized and excused himself from the table to answer it.

* * *

"HELLO?" Dalton said as soon as he made it into the living room.

"Dalton Williams?" asked a man's voice.

"Yep, you found me. Who is this?"

"Bill Swanson from the Green Peach Ranch. Just wonderin' how it's goin' down there with Contessa's Charity, the mare we sent you."

"Hello, sir – nice to finally speak with you. She's doing just great down here, though I'm afraid we've had a bit of bad weather so Rocket Peak hasn't shown a lot of interest yet. But I'm sure it won't be long."

"That's fine, fine. I'm actually callin' 'bout the young vet I sent down there with Contessa's Charity. Seems somethin' might've gone amiss."

"Oh?"

"Well, Gus told me Jen never showed, but he took someone named Hazel down to Tifton with him. Now mind you, he's never met Jen – wouldn't know her from a bar of soap – but he's sure the woman he met introduced herself as Hazel. It's possible he got his wires crossed, but I just wanted to call and check, make sure Jen's there and everythin's fine."

Dalton tensed and glanced at the door to the kitchen. "Yessir, everything down here is just fine."

"And Jen's doing her job?"

"Yessir, she is."

"Well, that's a relief. I'll let you go, but y'all just holler if you need anythin'. Take care of my girl Charity for me – she's worth a bundle, that one. I'd hate to hear she'd been carried off by a twister or some such – I saw on the news you had one nearby."

Dalton chuckled. "Yessir, I sure will."

"Bye now."

"Bye."

Dalton hung up, slouched onto the sofa in the darkness and rubbed his hands over his face. What was going on? It was possible the woman in his kitchen had some entirely logical explanation for why she called herself "Hazel." But there was also the issue that had plagued his thoughts ever since she arrived in her shiny silver pumps – she didn't look or act like a vet, and she didn't seem to know the first thing about animals.

He stood, tucked his phone into the back pocket of his shorts and marched back into the kitchen.

CHAPTER 6

Dalton rubbed the sleep from his eyes and rolled over in bed with a groan. Everything hurt – every single muscle, joint and ligament.

He sat up with another groan and ran his fingers through his tousled hair. He hadn't been able to get Hazel off his mind, and he still hadn't decided what he would do about Bill Swanson's phone call. He'd returned to the kitchen afterward, determined to confront her with what he'd learned, but she'd greeted him with a smile that made his heart melt and he'd sat back down at the table without a word.

With a sigh, he considered all the work he had to do that day, and the day after, and the day after that. The ranch had a neverending list of things for him to fix, mend, plant, harvest, feed, tend and more. It made his head spin. He rubbed his eyes again and took a deep breath. He needed help.

He reached for his phone on the bedside table, switched it on and dialed, glad it was Saturday morning. Eamon would be at home.

"It's your quarter," the man at the other end grumbled.

"Eamon, it's Dalton. How are you?"

His brother's voice blasted his ear. "Dalton! Bro! I'm great, how are you?"

Dalton pulled the phone from his ear with a grimace, then replaced it. "I'm fine, man, thanks for asking."

"How's the ranch going?"

"It's going okay. We had a big tornado a couple of days ago – it created a lot of work, but we were lucky to miss the worst of it. How's bean counting?"

Eamon laughed. "Oh, you know, still getting them counted. Someone's gotta do it."

"You get sick of it yet?" queried Dalton, looking for an opening.

"Well, I wouldn't turn down a pro bass-fishing contract, if you're offering."

Dalton chuckled, switched the phone to his other ear, stood and stretched his free hand above his head with a yawn. "Sorry to call so early, man. but I knew you'd be up, doing that crazy boot-camp thing in your girly tights."

Eamon burst into loud guffaws. "You know it."

Dalton scratched his head. "I do have a favor to ask you, actually."

"Yeah?"

"The ranch is in a pretty sad state. Since the storm there's so much work to do, I just don't see how I can do it on my own, but I can't afford to hire anyone. I was wondering ..."

"... if I'd come on down there and save my big brother's butt?" Eamon laughed again.

"Well ... yeah. If you aren't busy."

Eamon took a slow deep breath while Dalton held his, then said, "I thought you'd never ask."

Dalton laughed out loud and slapped his thigh. "Woo-ee! Do you mean it? You're gonna come down here?"

"I've been looking for an excuse to do something different – I need some time off. And I sure could do with some big-brother time. When do you need me?"

Dalton grinned and put his free hand on his hip. "As soon as you can get here. And leave your girly tights at home – this is manly country. You'll need your jeans and work shirts, some cowboy boots and a hat. That's about it."

"You got it. I'll put in a request for vacation time and be down there Sunday. How does that sound?"

"Sounds just about perfect, man. Can't wait to show you around the place."

"I can't wait to see it. Bye."

As Dalton hung up, he couldn't wipe the grin off his face. Eamon was coming for at least a little while. He and his brother had always gotten along – a little too well, if you asked their mother. She always said that if there was mischief to be had, the two of them would be in the thick of it, egging each other on.

Now he called the younger of his brothers, Parker. The call was polite and friendly. He told Parker the situation, and Parker said he'd get back to him. He hung up with a frown and a heavy feeling in his heart.

He loved his brothers equally, and longed to have a better relationship with Parker. His youngest brother had always been a bit distant, had lived in his own thoughts a lot. And they didn't always see eye to eye. Parker was serious, determined and focused, where Dalton was lighthearted, spontaneous and scattered, or at least had been when they were younger. He'd hoped that as they got older they'd grow closer together.

But then Parker had surprised the whole family by joining the Army right out of high school. He'd been an above-average student and a track champion, and they'd expected him to take one of the college scholarships that had been dangled under his nose. But instead he chose to defend his country, eventually becoming an Army Ranger, but breaking his mother's heart in the process.

Recently Parker had gotten his honorable discharge, moved back to Chattanooga and their childhood home. The only time Dalton had seen him since was at Grandpa Joe's funeral. They hadn't gotten much chance to talk, but from what Dalton could tell, he was the same as he'd always been, other than a dark shadow behind his eyes that hadn't been there before. Dalton hoped he would see the ranch as an opportunity to move into the next stage of his life. But for now he'd just have to wait.

He headed out into the hallway, pulling a T-shirt on as he walked toward the kitchen. He hadn't bothered to change out of his boxer shorts, expecting that Hazel would be out on her run, as she usually was at this time of the morning.

"Good morning, Dalton," she said from the kitchen table, a spoonful of cereal hovering in front of her mouth. She was still dressed in her running gear.

He stopped and combed his fingers through his hair again, making it stand even further on end. "Morning. Did you sleep well?"

"Fine, thank you. And you?"

He grunted and opened the cabinet, pulling out a

box of Honey Bunches of Oats and setting it on the counter.

"I thought I heard you talking to someone," she queried.

"Yeah. My brothers Eamon and Parker. Eamon's coming here Sunday, and I'm hoping Parker will come as well."

"Oh?"

He poured cereal into a bowl, piling it high up to the edges, then added milk from the carton on the counter where Hazel had left it. "Yeah. There's so much to do around here. They're gonna come and help me out, just to get things going."

"That sounds good. I suppose I'll get to meet Eamon then, since it doesn't seem like I'll be leaving today and perhaps not tomorrow either."

"Maybe." He turned to face her, the bowl in his hand, and leaned back against the counter. She took a bite of cereal and studied the news on her tablet as if nothing was amiss. He should confront her, make her tell him who Jen was, why she was pretending to be a vet when it was so obvious she wasn't. But instead he asked, "Where's the dog?"

She smiled and swallowed a mouthful. "He's in the laundry. He keeps piddling on the floor, so I laid down some old newspapers in there. I'm going to take him for a little walk outside later, but for now he's staying put."

He nodded and took a bite of cereal.

"Then I thought I'd got to town and buy some dog food, maybe a collar and leash." She finished her cereal, took the bowl to the sink and rinsed it out, then turned and left, saying she would tend to the dog and have a shower.

He nodded, chewed, then sat at the table and thought. Why hadn't he said anything? He certainly had reason to be suspicious. For that matter, why had he lied to Bill Swanson on her behalf? He supposed it was because he desperately wanted her to be who she'd said she was, someone he could trust. He wanted to give her the benefit of his doubts. Maybe she had a good reason for keeping secrets, and would open up to him in her own good time.

He knew he was being irrational. If she was lying about who she was, it was unlikely she'd just cave and tell him the truth. And if she didn't set his heart racing every time she walked in the room, maybe he'd be acting more sensibly about the whole thing and wouldn't care so much about whether or not he could trust her. He didn't want to feel for her the way he did. But he could tell, there wasn't much he could do to stop those feelings now.

* * *

HAZEL'S PHONE RANG, and she sighed when she saw Jen's name on the screen. Her roommate had been calling her constantly the past couple of days. Ever since her warning text about the impending tornado, she'd become panicked about something happening to Contessa's Charity on her watch and had phoned Hazel incessantly. "Hello?"

"Hi, Hazel. We have a problem." Jen's voice was strained.

"What is it?"

"Mr. Swanson, my boss, keeps calling me and calling me. He knows something's up, I'm sure of it.

I've put it off for as long as I can, but I'm gonna have to answer his next call. It's stressing me out!"

"You should answer it. He probably just wants to know how his horse is doing. And she's fine, by the way, so you can just tell him that."

"I don't know. I think I should come down there."

"What? How on Earth would we explain that to Dalton, or Mr. Swanson, or anyone? No, we have to finish this. It was a ridiculous idea, definitely one of your worst, and I shouldn't have let myself be sucked into it. But now we're in the middle of it and we have to see it through or we'll both be in a lot of trouble."

"No, no, I think I should come down there. I'm feeling much better now. I'm basically just lying around the house watching TV and hyperventilating into a paper bag thinking I might get fired or go to prison or who knows what else. I have to do something."

Hazel could tell her friend was pacing as she spoke – her breathing was labored. "Okay, tell you what. If you speak with your boss and still think you should come down here, we'll just tell Dalton you're my friend, my roommate, you've just had surgery and didn't want to be alone. How does that sound? You can check on things, then drive into town and find a motel to stay at or something." She sighed and ran her fingers through her hair. This whole thing was getting completely out of hand, and Jen's panicking could bring it all crashing down around them.

"Yes, okay. I'll speak to Bill, and if he's freaking out, then I'll drive down there. That's perfect."

Hazel groaned. "The list of things you owe me for is getting longer and longer."

"I know. I'll owe you forever for this one. I'm so sorry I dragged you into it all."

"Never mind that now. I'll see you tomorrow, okay?"

"All right. See you then." Jen's voice was filled with relief.

"And answer your boss' phone call or he will definitely fire you."

"Yes, you're right. I will. Thanks, Hazel."

Hazel hung up, stood and shoved the phone into the back pocket of her white Tommy Hilfiger shorts, then hurried to her bedroom. It was almost game time and she had to don her lucky jersey and cap before the first pitch.

* * *

WHEN DALTON RETURNED to the house for lunch, he found Hazel dressed in white button-up jersey with FREEMAN 5 on the back in blue-and-red letters, tiny white shorts and tall boots. She must have gotten the boots when she was in town that morning buying dog food. They suited her – and her shapely legs.

She stood in the living room shouting at his TV. "Yes, yes, go, go! Safe at home!" she yelled. She spun around, fists pumping the air, caught sight of Dalton and froze.

He leaned against the wall, his arms crossed, and raised an eyebrow. "I'm gonna go ahead and guess that you're a Braves fan."

She laughed and ducked her head, her cheeks flushed. "Been one since the Maddux and Glavine days."

"I see. Didn't know you liked baseball."

"All right-thinking people do, don't they?" She grinned and turned back to the screen.

"How long 'til it's done?"

"Huh?" She wasn't paying attention to him, just the game.

"Never mind. I'm going to an auction down the way – might be some fine horses there. And I thought, seeing as how you're a big-time city vet, you might be interested in a livestock auction and could help me pick out a few for my herd." He grinned

She spun to face him, eyes wide, but recovered fast. "Why … yes, of course – I'd love to come to the auction with you. Let me just grab my purse." She turned off the game and trotted down the hallway to her room, soon emerging with a purse over her shoulder. "Let's go."

He opened the door for her and followed her out to the truck, helped her up into the cab, hurried around to his side and jumped in. He was anxious to get the auction – it had already begun, and the animals he wanted to take a look at would be up soon. He needed to expand the bloodlines of his stock, and if he could get some well-bred animals into the herd for a decent price, it could make a big difference in how much he'd get for his own fillies and colts the following year.

They reached the auction in half an hour and were soon seated in the arena bleachers. Several different yards were set up within the arena and people milled around each, flashing their auction cards to bid on animals. He and Hazel waited a few minutes until for the stock horse yearlings' auction began, then made their way down to that yard.

In the end Dalton purchased three yearling fillies, then found two mares with outstanding pedigree to add to his breeding herd. The sellers promised to deliver the stock in the next few days. He was more than satisfied with his purchases – he felt as though he could float right up through the clouds. He loved Cotton Tree Ranch already, more than he'd thought possible.

And he wanted to celebrate the next step in its growth. "Wanna grab some lunch?" he asked Hazel.

Hazel nodded and rubbed her stomach, her eyes gleaming. "I would love to – it's three o'clock and I'm absolutely famished. I thought at one point my stomach would outbid you on that last mare."

He chuckled and took her elbow to guide her through the crowd and back to the truck. "Well then, let's find somewhere to eat. I can't have you fainting on me." Her skin was soft, and he found himself not wanting to let go once they'd gotten through the throng.

When he opened the truck door for her, she glanced up at him, her eyes locking on his. His heart skipped a beat and he felt a bolt of adrenaline course through him. He helped her up into her seat, then closed the door behind her, his heart thundering. Hazel or Jen or whoever she was had made him feel things he hadn't felt in a long time. She'd awoken his heart again, and he knew there was no turning back now.

No doubt about it, Dalton thought. *I'm in real trouble.*

*H*azel sat down and Dalton pushed her chair in behind her. She lifted the napkin from the table into her lap and watched him take his seat across from her. He could have taken her to a burger place or a drive-thru for lunch, but instead he'd chosen one of the nicest restaurants in Tifton, with silverware, cloth napkins and soft jazz playing in the background. She wasn't sure yet what food they offered, but she felt nervous about the implication. Did he think this was a date?

He looked nervous as well. She picked up the menu and held it between them, her eyes skimming over the meals on offer. It seemed standard, but the atmosphere suggested more than a meal between colleagues. She selected a buffalo chicken salad and sat back to regard Dalton. He ordered a rack of barbecued ribs and coleslaw, thanked the waiter and set his hat on the table, combing his fingers through his thick hair. She wished for a moment she could run her fingers through it as well.

She shook her head – what was wrong with her? She had to keep her wits about her. Her time at Cotton Tree Ranch was almost over – she just had to withstand Dalton's charms a little longer. But it was getting more difficult by the day.

They talked and laughed over their meal. Hazel suggested calling the puppy Harley, and Dalton tried to talk her out of it, saying it was no name for a ranch dog. By the time they were done, she felt completely at ease. She couldn't believe how badly she'd misunderstood him when she'd arrived – he wasn't a jerk at all, and she'd probably deserved everything he'd said.

"So tell me, why did you become a vet?" he asked, wiping barbecue sauce from his stubbled chin.

She paused to think up a response. Better to stick as close to the truth as possible, so she wouldn't be as likely to slip up. "Well, my whole life that's what I wanted. Or at least I thought I did. I'm starting to wonder now if perhaps it was my parents who wanted it for me and I just wanted to please them so badly I went along with it all." She spoke from her heart, and felt it lurch within her.

His eyebrows arched high in surprise. "Really? Don't you love it?"

She took a deep breath. "I don't know anymore. A year ago, I would have said yes, but now it seems like the passion has gone out of it for me. I was so driven, always striving for the next level of achievement. But I don't feel that way anymore. It's like I graduated, got my dream job and a part of me is thinking 'now what?' Does that make sense?"

He nodded. "It makes perfect sense."

"But if I don't do this with my life, I honestly don't know what I *would* do. It's been everything to me for so long, everything I've worked toward for so many years. I don't know what life would look like without it."

"Maybe it's time to think about that." His eyes were warm.

She blinked and felt a lump rise in her throat. "Yeah, maybe it is."

"Dessert?" he asked with a hint of a smile.

"Hmmm …" She picked up a menu to look at the choices … and Dalton's phone buzzed.

Dalton winced in apology and looked at the screen. "It's one of the sellers – he's on his way over to the ranch now with the mare we bought. We'd better go." He texted a reply, stood and tucked it back in his pocket. "Sorry – no dessert this time. But I'll make it up to you next time."

She nodded and smiled. He was already planning a next time. The thought made her giddy. She visited the restroom while Dalton paid, then met him at the front door to head back out to the truck.

The drive back to the ranch was quiet, each lost in their own thoughts. She stared out the window at the countryside, as they wound their way along the country roads. She'd miss this place when the time came to leave. For the first time since she'd arrived, the idea of leaving gave her a hollow feeling inside. Her eyes narrowed. Dalton Williams sure was getting under her skin – and not in the way she'd expected him to.

When they pulled into the drive, the trailer carrying Dalton's new mare was already parked beside the barn. A man stood next to the truck, his hands on his hips, and waved as they drove up. Dalton pulled the truck to a stop, killed the engine and leaped out to shake the man's hand. Hazel followed slowly, keeping her distance.

Just then, there was a terrible banging as the mare began acting up inside the trailer. Both men ran over and disappeared through a small door in the front. Their soothing, shushing noises carried on the breeze back to Hazel, but still the mare bucked and kicked and cried out in distress.

Hazel inched closer, standing on tiptoe to peer into the trailer. She could see the horse throwing her head around and banging against the sides of the trailer, her eyes wild.

"Hazel!" called Dalton.

"Yes?"

"Can you unclip the rope behind her for me? We want to back her out."

"Sure!" Hazel hurried to the back of the trailer. The tailgate had already been lowered and there was a rope stretched across the opening with a clasp on one end. She climbed slowly up the ramp, anxious to avoid the distressed mare's flying hooves, reached forward and quickly unsnapped the clasp.

As she did, the mare whinnied and pushed backward down the ramp. Her back hoof landed directly on Hazel's foot, crushing it, and she knocked Hazel over as she clambered down the ramp and trotted off into the yard, her head high and eyes wide with fright. The man who'd brought her ran after her.

Dalton careened around the side of the trailer. "Hazel, are you okay? I'm sorry – she bit me and I let go of the rope for a moment ..."

Hazel pushed herself to a sitting position and rubbed her forehead. Her head felt light and she tried to lean forward, putting her elbows on her knees. But when she put her foot down, she yelped in pain.

"Oh no, your foot! Are you okay?"

Hazel's face blanched and she took a quick breath. "It hurts." She couldn't see what shape it was in due to the tall boot, but she knew it couldn't be good.

Dalton nodded, leaned down and scooped her easily into his arms, carried her across the yard and up the front steps. The front door opened easily, and he pushed past it with his back and hurried to lay her on the couch. Once she was comfortable, he disappeared, soon returning with the first aid kit.

"You should make sure the mare is okay," Hazel protested. "I'm fine, really. It's just a bruise, I'm sure."

"We'll see." He knelt beside her and started to remove her boot, but she cried out in agony. He took more care and finally got it off. "You're bleeding." He eased off her now-stained sock, wiped away the blood with a cotton ball, and put on some antibiotic ointment and a bandage. Finally he sat beside her and lifted her foot into his lap. "Are you sure you're okay?" he asked, his hand caressing her cheek.

She smiled. "I'll be fine. Please, go take care of your new horse."

She swallowed hard as he stood, carefully lifted her foot and placed it on the couch. It was still warm from his body heat, and the skin on her cheek goose pimpled where he'd touched her. He walked out, with one last backward glance in her direction.

Once he was gone, she threw her head back against the arm of the sofa with a groan. She was feeling things for him she shouldn't, not when she was leaving soon. Caring for him would only complicate matters, especially since he didn't know who she really was – a violinist, not a vet. And if he discovered the truth … she shook her head and ran her hand over her eyes. *When* he discovered the truth, he'd despise her.

Hazel shut her eyes and took a deep breath. She couldn't let herself feel anything more for him than friendship. Maybe not even that.

* * *

DALTON FLIPPED the pancakes over on the griddle and hummed a tune. It was a fine day and he was feeling good. There was still a lot to clean up around the ranch after the tornado, but Eamon was due to arrive today, he had a new mare with more animals on the way … and there'd been that shared moment with Hazel the previous day. That, most of all, brought a smile to his face as he slapped the cooked pancakes onto a plate and poured two more dollops of batter.

Hazel hobbled into the kitchen with a groan, collapsed onto a chair at the table and stretched her foot out in front of her. It was neatly wrapped – he'd made sure of that – but purple and blue toes poked out from beneath the bandages. She leaned an elbow on the table and set her chin in her hand. "Morning."

"Good morning! Isn't it a wonderful day?" He grinned and winked at her, flipping the pancakes over.

She groaned again.

"Foot hurting?" he asked.

"Yes. Only it doesn't feel like my foot anymore – more like a ski boot or something. Ugh." Her nose wrinkled.

He had to fight the urge to kiss its tip. She looked adorable in her pajama pants and camisole. She usually dressed so stylishly, he was surprised at her informality, but assumed it was because she felt poorly. She obviously hadn't brushed her hair, just pulled it into a messy bun on top of her head, curls spilling loose. Her face was makeup-free apart from a smudge of mascara beneath both eyes. She'd never looked more adorable.

He set the spatula on the counter and knelt in front of her, taking her hands in his and kissing their backs. "Again, I'm so sorry. I feel terrible about what happened."

Her cheeks flushed, and she smiled as she pulled her hands away. "Well, it wasn't your fault. I should have been more careful."

He had to stop himself from asking the question that burned on his tongue: *what were you doing standing directly behind an anxious mare?* She was a vet ... wasn't she? But he bit his tongue. It wasn't the right time for that confrontation, not when her foot was still damaged from an accident he could have prevented. Instead he said, "Well, to make up for it, I cooked pancakes. Want some?" He hurried to flip two more off the griddle and onto the plate, now stacked high.

"Yes, please – who doesn't love pancakes? I can make them from a mix, as you know, but they never taste as good as ones made from scratch – and that, I've never quite figured out." She sat up straighter.

"Well, these are most definitely from scratch and soft and fluffy to boot, if I do say so myself. As you can imagine, I was pretty popular on the rodeo circuit." He grinned smugly, slid a pile of pancakes onto a separate plate and set it in front of her.

She rolled her eyes and poured syrup onto her stack. "I'm sure you were – and not just because of your pancakes."

He chuckled, sensing a touch of jealousy. That

suited him just fine – it meant she might care for him more than she was willing to let on. She couldn't know he'd turned away every woman who'd pursued him on the circuit, having never found one who could match up to the ideal in his head. He wasn't the type to date every pretty face he met – deep down, he was sentimental and loyal. After his engagement was broken, he'd longed to find that connection again, to find a partner, someone to share his life with.

He knew that point of view wasn't fashionable among the other bronc riders. But he didn't care to waste time with just anyone. He wanted to be with *the* one, or no one at all. Let the rest of them have the one-night stands.

"I've set a table out on the porch if you'd like to eat outside. It's a beautiful day." He turned the burner off and picked up the rest of the pancakes, along with a bowl of fresh fruit salad.

She chewed and swallowed quickly, her cheeks flaming. "Oh yes, that sounds lovely."

He laughed and carried the bounty out to the porch table, holding the door open for her to hobble through. She sat, and he helped scoot her chair in beneath the glass-topped table, then went back for her plate, the butter, syrup and silverware. Finally he joined her and poured syrup over his stack of pancakes. "Just so you know, I called Gus – he's coming to get Charity the day after tomorrow."

Her eyebrows flew upward. "Oh. That soon, huh?"

"Yep." He grinned and took a bite of pancakes. "I thought you'd be happy to hear you could go home."

She nodded. "I am, of course. But this place was beginning to grow on me."

He raised an eyebrow. "Really? Even with the injured foot?"

Her cheeks flushed even pinker and she shrugged. "I guess so."

His eyes narrowed. What was she trying to say? He'd been certain ever since she arrived that she couldn't wait to leave. Now that she could, she was acting as though she didn't want to. He took a quick breath and jumped to his feet. "I'll just get the O.J. ...."

"I could use some coffee ..." She stood too and stumbled in front of him, his chest smacking into her. "Sorry!"

He shook his head. "No, I'm sorry." Nervously he ran his fingers through his hair, his eyes on hers. She swallowed and he stepped closer, his thundering heart the only sound he could hear. He lifted his hand and traced her jaw with his fingertips.

She leaned her cheek into the palm of his hand and the corners of her lips curved into a smile. "Dalton?" she whispered.

He leaned forward, his lips hovering over hers. He couldn't think straight, not with her so close, her hot breath on his wrist, her green eyes wide and inviting. His lips met hers and he backed her up against the wall of the house, cupping both cheeks between his hands. She tasted like butter and syrup, and she melted beneath his touch. She moaned against his mouth as her hands crept around his neck, and his body trembled.

A loud beeping sound jolted them both. Dalton lifted his head and turned to peer down the driveway. A Chevy pickup roared into view, horn blaring. He frowned, his hands dropping to his sides. "Eamon ..." With a shrug, he waved a hand over his head.

"Who is it?" asked Hazel behind him.

"My little brother." Reluctantly, he pulled away, headed down the stairs and across the yard.

As he reached the truck, Eamon cut the engine, opened the door and jumped out with a whoop. "Hey there, big brother!"

Dalton grabbed him in a bear hug and slapped him hard on the back. "Eamon! Good to see you, man. I wasn't expecting you until this afternoon."

Eamon laughed, his eyes twinkling. "Yeah, I could see that! But I decided to drive through the night – I wasn't doing much, and I figured traffic would be easier that way. Besides, I had help." He banged a hand on the chassis, and another man slid into view from beneath the dash. He nodded at Dalton and snapped off a sharp salute.

"Parker!" Dalton cried, rushing around to the passenger side. Parker stepped out, and Dalton wrapped his arms around him, then stepped back to study his face. His eyes were ringed with dark circles and his smile shallow and fleeting. "You came. I hadn't heard back from you, so I thought you weren't coming."

"Well, I couldn't let the two of you have all the fun without me, now could I?"

"Ain't that the truth." Eamon slapped Dalton on the back. "Help me with the bags?"

Dalton nodded and hurried to lift two bags from the truck bed. He couldn't wipe the smile off his face. He loved it when the three of them were back together, even if only briefly – it felt as though anything was possible and nothing insurmountable. With the three Williams boys working together, the ranch couldn't fail.

"Tell me now, who's this?"

Eamon's question as he reached the porch made Dalton's heart lurch. His brother had a way with women that couldn't be denied. Any time the three of them went out together, it was always Eamon who ended up dancing with the prettiest girl in the room. He didn't breathe again until he heard Hazel introduce herself and shake his hand. A gentle breeze ruffled her soft curls, and a wave of protectiveness washed over him.

By the time Dalton caught up, they were in the foyer. He set down the bags and crossed his arms. "So I see y'all have met."

Eamon cocked his head, a teasing smile on his face. "Yeah, no thanks to you and your lack of manners. You've been holding back, brother."

Dalton ignored the glint in his brother's eyes. "Well, Hazel's leaving tomorrow, so ...," he replied gruffly.

Hazel just smiled. "I've heard a lot about both of you – though Dalton didn't tell me you were so charming."

Parker blushed. "Pleased to meet you, Hazel. Dalton, do you think I could get settled in my room? It's been a long night and I need some shuteye."

Dalton nodded and picked up Parker's rucksack again. "Of course – follow me. It's not fancy, but it is clean."

Parker chuckled. "I wouldn't know what to do with fancy."

Dalton led the way down the hall and got Parker settled in one of the spare bedrooms. He was grateful for the sheer size of the place now, and how it was fully furnished when he'd arrived. Some cleaning and a trip to Target for linens, towels and pillows had been all it took to complete the guest rooms. Parker immediately kicked off his sneakers and lay back on the bed with a groan.

"Rest up," said Dalton, noting those worrisome dark circles again. "There's plenty of time later for work."

Parker nodded and shut his eyes, his hands laced behind his head.

Dalton quietly pulled the door closed behind him and stood a moment in the hallway listening to the low murmur of Eamon and Hazel's conversation in the living room. He sighed and his heart plummeted. Any feelings he'd thought Hazel had developed for him were likely already scampering rapidly from her mind – Eamon was here, and he knew she'd have eyes only for him. It never failed.

CHAPTER 8

*L*ate that evening, when Dalton and his brothers came in from an afternoon of cleaning up debris and fixing the fence destroyed by the twister, Hazel was making them dinner. She hadn't contributed much to the cleanup, especially with her sore foot, so she felt the least she could do was to feed the men. Or try to. She pushed pieces of breaded chicken around the frying pan, smoke hovering over her like a cloud. When she added another piece, the hot oil spat, sending her stumbling backward.

Dalton pushed the kitchen door open and coughed. "What the …?"

She rubbed her nose with the back of her hand and blinked stinging eyes. "Hi."

"Hi," he replied. "Why is the smoke so thick in here?"

Just then, the smoke detector started keening, drowning out every other sound. Dalton rushed to open the back door and all the kitchen windows.

Hazel turned off the burner, noticing that the breading on the chicken looked a tad dark. "I don't think anything's burned," she cried. "It's just very smoky!"

Dalton grabbed a broom from behind the pantry door, stood on a kitchen chair and used the handle to press the button on the smoke detector. The beeping stopped.

Hazel wiped her forehead in relief. "Thank you."

He glanced at her, and she thought she saw frustration and longing in his eyes. Was he remembering their kiss that morning? She hadn't been able to think about anything else. All day long she'd been on tenterhooks, waiting for him to come in, wondering if he'd say anything about it. He'd barely made eye contact with her since his brothers' arrival, and she wondered if maybe he regretted it all – the moment, the vulnerability, the passion.

He raised an eyebrow. "Need help?"

"Yes, please."

He walked over to the stove, checked the fried chicken in the pan, then moved it piece by piece onto a paper-towel-covered plate to drain. Freed from that worry, she pieced together a salad, set plates on the counter and piled silverware on them, and carried all of that out to the porch to set the outdoor table. Dalton transferred the chicken to a bowl and followed, placing it at the center of the table.

She turned back for the salad dressing, and ran right into his thick chest again with a cry.

"Sorry," he said, stepping to one side and grinning. "We have to stop doing that."

She tried to step aside too, but went the same way and bumped into him again. His hair was still damp from the shower, and he smelled of soap and aftershave.

He chuckled, and her cheeks burned as he lifted her face toward his with a finger beneath her chin. "It looks and smells delicious. I ... guess we should talk about this morning ..." He trailed off.

She opened her mouth to reply – and the front door slammed open. Parker and Eamon fell laughing through the door, and Dalton frowned. "Hey, where's the fire?" asked Eamon, pushing Parker in the back. Parker dropped his shoulder and stepped sideways to shove his brother, who stumbled and thudded into the wall. "Ooomph! Hey!"

"No fire," said Hazel, pulling free of Dalton and walking past him toward the door. "It was just me making fried chicken." She returned to the kitchen and gathered the ranch dressing, hot sauce, salad tongs and a pile of napkins, then came back out to find the brothers all seated around the table.

"I'll get drinks," said Parker, standing back up.

Hazel set everything on the table and sat next to Eamon, across from Dalton. Dalton look sour, but she couldn't imagine why – perhaps the presence of his brothers, though he loved them, made him a little tense. Or maybe he'd just wanted to talk about their kiss when Eamon and Parker came outside.

She'd resented the interruption, but was also grateful for it. If he planned to tell her their kiss was inappropriate and a mistake, she didn't want to hear it. It might be the truth, but her heart slumped at the thought of it. And yet, if he'd told her he cared for her and wanted more, she wasn't sure how that could possibly work. The idea filled her with hope, but the knowledge of the impossibilities involved drained it right back out again.

Dalton said the blessing, then they passed the food around the table and served themselves. Hazel reached for the 2-liter bottle of Coke that Parker had set on the table and poured herself a glass. The men talked and joked, catching up on all they'd missed in each other's lives. She ate quietly and listened, enjoying how Dalton's eyes sparked when his brothers ribbed him, or gleamed when they mentioned home.

Eamon glanced her way, noticing her silence. "Tell me about yourself, Hazel. Dalton said you're a vet, but I don't really know anything else about you. Where do you live?"

Hazel swallowed and dabbed her mouth with a napkin. "Virginia-Highland. It's near the center of Atlanta, right by Piedmont Park."

"That sounds nice. I've been to Atlanta a few times, but don't really know it well. What do you do for fun there?" He had the same dimple in his cheek as Dalton, and she felt her face warm under the intensity of his gaze.

She shrugged. "Same things anyone does. I go out to dinner with friends. There are shows and concerts all the time, so my roommate Jen and I go to a lot of those ..." Her eyes widened as she realized her blunder – she'd mentioned Jen, which she'd been careful not to until that point. Perhaps it wouldn't matter, since none of them knew who she was. She quickly took a bite of chicken and focused on her plate.

But when she glanced up, she noticed Dalton's narrowed eyes on her. He frowned, laid his fork down beside his plate and picked up the bottle of hot sauce, his eyes never leaving her. Her heart plunged into her stomach. He knew – or at least suspected – something.

"So, Hazel, what do you think of this stallion my brother here bought?" Parker's voice was gentle and his eyes crinkled at the edges as he spoke. "He tells me the fella's gonna produce some award-winning offspring, but I'd be interested to hear what you think, considering the pretty penny Dalton spent on him."

Hazel swallowed, and the hairs on her arms stood on end. "Um … well, he's a fine animal …" She took another bite of chicken, her heart racing.

Dalton interrupted her, his voice cold. "Though perhaps we should ask Jen about that instead of Hazel."

She stopped chewing and her gaze met his, her eyes widening. She swallowed hard and set her fork down on the table. "Er …I…?"

"Yeah, I had an interesting conversation with Mr. Swanson from Green Peach Ranch a few days ago. He told me he sent a vet named Jen down here with Contessa's Charity and didn't have any idea who Hazel might be. I thought maybe you had an explanation for it. And now I hear that Jen is your roommate. What gives?"

Hazel broke out into a cold sweat. Of all times, why now? Why here?

"What's going on?" asked Eamon, his head cocked to one side.

"Ask her." Dalton leveled a glare her way. His lips were tight.

She felt tears prick her eyes as her anger rose. "I can't believe you knew all this time and you didn't say anything. And then you kissed me?! How could you do that, knowing what you do?"

Eamon and Parker exchanged an anxious glance.

Eamon stood, picked up his plate and nodded toward the door. "You know, if y'all don't mind I think I'll go eat in front of the TV. I think *SportsCenter* comes on in a minute …"

"Oh, good idea – I want to catch up on the NFL news!" Parker stood as well and the two of them hurried inside the house, the front door slapping closed behind them.

Dalton sighed and ran his hands over his face.

She took a deep breath and exhaled slowly. The heck with it. "I'm not a vet," she began.

"No kidding," he snarled, closing his eyes.

She stood, her chair scraping against the floor. "Well, I'm leaving tomorrow, so I guess there's no point saying any more about the matter." A tear trailed down her cheek and she angrily brushed it away.

He stood as well, and stepped in her way so she couldn't rush inside like she meant to. He lifted a hand and ran it down her arm, making her skin prickle. "You don't have to go."

She blinked, stunned. "I don't?"

"No. Look – I'm sorry. I shouldn't have done that – not then, anyway. I meant to talk to you about it privately, not in front of them."

She wrapped her arms around herself. He still sounded angry. "Do you even want to hear my side of the story?"

"Hazel, not only do I want to, I think you owe it to me. Why would you pretend to be a vet? What do you expect to get out of it?"

She fumed at his insinuation. "I don't expect to get *anything* out of it. You think I wanted to do this? I did it for Jen – she's the vet. Yes, she's a little crazy and she was high on drugs when she asked me … wait, let me rephrase that – she'd just had her appendix removed and was doped up on painkillers. But she's like family to me and she really needs this job and she was sure it would just be a day or two and she *begged* me, so I did it. I know, it's ridiculous, but there it is. I did it for her."

He pinched the bridge of his nose. "So you were just covering for your friend."

"Yes." She sighed. "I was just supposed to babysit Charity up and back, nothing more."

"So what do you do for a living?"

"Third-chair violinist for the Atlanta Symphony."

He laughed, softly at first, then louder until his whole body shook.

She hadn't expected that reaction. "What?!"

"I thought maybe you were a con artist or something. I was terrified you'd murder me in my sleep!" He guffawed again, his eyes tightly closed.

She laughed, offended but also amused. A con artist? A murderer? Wow, he had a much lower opinion of her than she'd realized.

When they both caught their breath, she crossed her arms, feeling more hurt by the moment. "So you thought the best thing to do was to kiss me."

"I was … well …" He took her by the arms and looked deep into her eyes. "I didn't *really* think you'd kill me, though I am relieved to know you weren't trying to pull a scam on me. But …" He shook his head. "Hazel, I kissed you because I couldn't stop myself. You are just so beautiful, and strong, and stubborn …" He couldn't go on, just shook his head again.

This was more than she was prepared to handle. "I think I'll just going to bed early," she said, pulling free of his grasp.

"Don't go. I think we should talk some more."

Her cheeks flamed. "Later – I'm tired." She moved past him and pulled the door open. "Good night, Dalton. I'll see you in the morning." She stepped inside the house and shut the door behind her. Then she leaned back against it and closed her eyes.

The cell phone in her pocket vibrated, and she pulled it out with a sigh. One glance showed it was her boss, the director of the orchestra. "Hello, Harold," she said, her voice strained.

"Hazel! How are you?"

He was always so chipper, it made her wince. "I'm fine, thanks. And you?"

"Wonderful, wonderful. Say, I hate to do this to you, but I have to ask you a favor. Frieda injured her hand – cutting an avocado, I believe."

"Oh no!" Hazel frowned and her hand flew to hover over her mouth. "Is she okay?"

"Well, she will be, but I don't know how long it will take her to recover. You know she was playing for the Ballet. The first rehearsal's next week, but of course she's had months to learn the pieces. I was hoping you might come in tomorrow and we can work together on it to get you ready for the rehearsal. You'd be first chair – I called Damien already, of course, since he's second chair, but he turned it down. You'd be the youngest first chair in the history of the Atlanta Symphony. What do you say?"

She took a deep breath and held it. First chair for the ballet – it was a dream come true, though temporary and not under ideal circumstances. She really hoped Frieda would recover soon – she knew how much the violin meant to her. "All right. I may not make it tomorrow, since I'm out of town. But the day after should be fine."

After they finished the conversation, she hung up and slumped against the door again … just as it opened, landing her on her rear. She rolled onto her back, the phone still her hand.

Dalton stood over her, his eyebrows arched high in surprise. "Hazel, what are you doing? Are you okay?"

She shrugged in embarrassment. "Meditating …?" she offered with the hint of a smile.

He laughed, offering her a hand. She took it, he pulled her to her feet and they stood there, inches apart, gazes fixed on one another. "Hazel … I …"

"Yes?" she whispered, her eyes drifting to his inviting lips.

"I'm sorry."

"You don't have anything to be sorry for. I'm the one who lied. I pretended to be someone I'm not. I forced my way into your life. And I apologize. Could you ever forgive me, do you think?" She stopped, a sob caught in her throat.

He nodded, then pressed his lips to hers, taking her breath away with the intensity of his kiss. There was nothing more than that – that moment, those lips, filled her with joy and tore her apart all at once.

She pulled away and rested her forehead against his. Biting her bottom lip, she pressed her hands against his firm chest. "I still have to leave tomorrow."

"No, you don't. You can stay. I don't mind –"

"It's not that. I wish I *could* stay. That was my boss on the phone just now – he needs me back in Atlanta. I have an opportunity to play first chair, which has been a dream of mine … well, forever. It'll be the first time I've ever done it and it's not likely to happen again for a long time. I have to go."

He took her hands in his and kissed the palms. "I

understand. I don't like it, but it sounds like an amazing opportunity – you have to take it. But … will you come back?" He looked at her expectantly.

She took a slow breath, unable to speak.

His smile faded. "I see."

"I don't know if it's a good idea …" She trailed off.

"Why not?"

"Because my life, my career, my friends – they're all in Atlanta. And you live at the other end of the state on a horse ranch. Would you give up all of this to move to Atlanta for me?"

A muscle in his jaw flexed. "You know I can't. I've sunk everything into this place."

"Well, I can't either. There's no orchestra in Tifton, is there? There's not even a good sushi place. How could we have a relationship if we live hours away from each other? We barely even know each other – I've only been here a week, and under false pretenses. We'd need more time before we could make life-changing decisions for each other. It just doesn't make sense." She sighed and stepped away from him. His eyes were full of pain and she just wanted to escape them.

"If that's how you want it," he whispered, combing his fingers through his hair.

"I just don't see any other way. I'm sorry, Dalton. I'll go back to Atlanta tomorrow and you can get on with your life and forget all about me."

His laugh was ragged and hollow. "Forget you? Hardly."

CHAPTER 9

*D*alton flipped through the channels, unable to find a program that interested him. His mind raced, going over and over his conversation with Hazel earlier in the evening. He'd jumped to so many conclusions about her, even after telling himself he should wait to hear her story. And now she was leaving.

Finally he turned the TV off, ran a hand over his stubble-covered chin, stood and stretched his arms above his head. They'd worked hard that day. It had felt good to have his brothers by his side.

But now, Eamon and Parker were hidden away in their rooms. No doubt Parker was reading, and he could hear Eamon's voice echoing down the long hallway. He was likely on the phone with someone from back home in Chattanooga. He wondered if his brother had a girlfriend – the subject hadn't come up yet. He'd have to find a way to ask soon.

The sound of the front door opening caught his attention and he hurried to peer out through the curtains. Hazel was climbing into the cab of his truck. He frowned – where was she going? It wasn't that late, but Tifton rolled up the sidewalks pretty early. And she hadn't said anything about going out – she'd borrowed his truck to drive to town a couple of days earlier, but that time she'd asked.

He went into the kitchen and scooped himself a large bowl of Moose Tracks ice cream. He didn't care what she did with her time – let her do what she liked. She'd even said Moose Tracks wasn't a "grown-up" ice-cream flavor (whatever that meant), rolling her eyes as if to infer some kind of meaning to his selection. He shook his head and piled the bowl even higher in spite. There was nothing wrong with enjoying delicious ice cream – she was just too uptight. That was her problem. He embraced life.

He carried the bowl back into the living room and sat on the couch, resting his bare feet on the coffee table. By the time he'd finished it, he'd gone back to channel surfing, but the selection hadn't improved. Agitated, he stood and carried his bowl to the kitchen, rinsed it and added it to the dishwasher.

With a deep breath, he peeked through the curtains again. No sign of Hazel. Well, if she could go out after dinner on a Monday night, so could he. It didn't make sense for a single man to be sitting at home alone in his house, when he could be out enjoying what little nightlife Tifton possessed.

He padded down the hallway to his bedroom, threw on a pair of faded jeans, a checked shirt and square-nosed cowboy boots. His motorcycle helmet sat on his bedside table, and he lifted it with one hand, grabbing his wallet with the other and shoving it into his back pocket.

He poked his head into Parker's room and found him nose-deep in a James Patterson mystery. He glanced up and grinned. "Going out?"

"Yeah, thought I'd take a ride. Maybe stop somewhere for a drink. I won't be long."

"Okay. Want company?"

Dalton shook his head. "Not tonight. But Friday, we'll paint the town, okay?"

"Sounds good. See you soon."

Dalton headed down the hall and heard a scratching at the laundry room door. He opened it, knelt down and Harley clambered up into his lap, licking his hands furiously. "Wanna go out, little fella?" he asked with a smile. He took the puppy outside, then returned him to his box in the laundry room and refilled his water and kibble.

Finally he got to the barn, where his Ducati motorbike was stored beneath a blue tarp. He didn't ride it all that often anymore and had been considering selling it. But tonight, Hazel had left him no other option. His leg felt stiff, and he stretched it a little before pulling his helmet on. The growl of the engine filled him with warm satisfaction, and he revved it a few times before maneuvering carefully down the gravel drive.

Once he reached the main road, he let it fly. The bike had always handled like a dream and he felt a thrill of excitement as he gathered speed, rounding gradual bends and sailing down the straights. He pulled up at a four-way stop, lifted his visor and peered for a moment in each direction. There was no traffic at all, not unusual for a Monday night. Which way should he go?

He could see Clancy's up head – a dive bar with

mediocre live music and all-you-can-eat crab legs advertised in bold red lettering on a large sign on its roof. He could do with some crab legs. He flipped the visor down and set off toward the bar.

The parking lot was a bare patch of dirt with a few trucks and SUVs parked in haphazard fashion. One of the trucks was his. He backed the bike up into the space next to it and pulled his helmet off. This is where Hazel had come? Clancy's really didn't seem like her kind of place … but come to think of it, her kind of place didn't really exist in the entire county. She was probably just out of options.

He kicked out the side stand and leaned the bike onto it, making sure it held, then dismounted, wincing as pain sliced through his leg. Usually there was just a dull ache in his thigh and knee, but that movement had made it worse. He closed his eyes, took a long slow breath, then headed into the bar.

Hazel nursed the glass of Bud Light in front of her. She really didn't enjoy beer, but Clancy's wasn't the kind of place that stocked a high-quality Shiraz. Even her request for a Manhattan had left the bartender scratching his bald head. So instead, she'd settled for a beer. She took another sip, grimaced and set it back on the coaster.

The front door swung open and Dalton marched in, looking around – for her, no doubt. She shrunk down in her seat, hoping the tall back of the booth would hide her. She really didn't want to see him right then. She'd walked away from him when he'd asked her to stay, then taken his truck without asking. Their next conversation wasn't likely to be a fun one.

A glance around the side of the booth revealed she'd been caught – Dalton was headed right for her. She rolled her eyes and took another sip, immediately regretting it – her mouth puckered.

He stopped next to her, his hands on his hips. "Fancy seeing you here."

"It's unexpected, I know."

He slid into the booth across from her and folded his hands in front of him on the table. "I wouldn't have thought a concert violinist would be caught dead in a place like this." He grinned.

She tipped her head to one side. "Are you making fun of me?"

"Maybe a little."

"Well, I like it here. They've got my favorite beer …" She took another swig and scowled at the glass. "… ugh. And there are bowls of peanuts on the tables, peanut shells on the floor, a jukebox in the corner. I mean, what more could a fiddle-playin' girl ask for?"

He caught the bartender's eye and pointed a finger at Hazel's beer, then returned his attention to her. "So what would you be doing right now …?"

She sighed and smirked. "You mean, if I wasn't pretending to be someone else?"

"Well, yes." He chuckled as the barkeep deposited a bottle of Bud Light on the table in front of him. He took a sip.

"I'm supposed to be with my folks at their summer place on Jekyll Island. Now that they're retired they spend a good portion of their time there."

His brow furrowed. "I'm sorry you're missing out."

She laughed. "Don't be. It's a good excuse. Don't get

me wrong, I love my parents. It's just that ... they're a little intense."

"Meaning?"

"Well, if I was there right now, Mom would be asking me how long until I got first chair in the orchestra. Dad would be pressing me on why I'd missed the turn around the dock in the sailboat earlier that day. And I'd be wishing I was anywhere else."

"They can't be that bad."

"Oh yes, they can – twenty-four hours a day. Judging everything I do, nitpicking over every little ... oh, maybe I am exaggerating. Isn't that what children do, exaggerate the flaws of their parents?"

He nodded and pulled a corner of the sticker free from the bottle. "I suppose that's true. Although I can't fault my Mom. She's amazing."

"Spoken like a true mama's boy," quipped Hazel, slapping him gently on the arm.

He grinned and grabbed her hand, winding his fingers through hers. "I suppose. Though after Dad died, she had to raise three boys on her own – it can't have been easy. I mean, you've met us." He traced a circle on her palm with his finger.

Her cheeks flushed and her pulse raced. "The poor woman – that must have been really hard. And on the three of you as well, losing your dad like that."

He nodded and exhaled slowly. "Yeah. I still miss him."

A silence fell between them. The jukebox started playing "Friends in Low Places." She relaxed, enjoying the low buzz of conversation at the bar, the hum of the music. And the company. She'd never have believed she'd enjoy sitting in a place like that with Dalton as much as she was. He was really easy to talk to, which seemed hard to believe. With his dimpled cheeks and muscular physique, he would draw attention wherever he went. She'd seen that in the short time he'd been there that night. But he didn't seem to notice the effect he had on women.

His eyes were fixed on her and one corner of his lips curved up. "Care to dance?"

She blanched. Dance? She knew how to waltz and tango from her time on the debutante circuit as a teenager – her mother had made sure of that. But slow dancing was another matter entirely. She couldn't remember the last time she'd done it – she was usually in the band, playing music for others to dance to, not on the floor in the arms of a man who made her heart race and her legs quiver.

He stood, his fingers still entwined in hers, and pulled her along behind him before she could protest. He spun her into his arms, and rested his left hand on the small of her back. His right caressed her hand, and guided her around the small space dotted with couples bound together in an intimate embrace.

She could feel the pressure of his chest against hers. When their eyes met, her heart skipped a beat and her cheeks warmed. She smiled shyly. "I'm sorry – I'm not very good at this."

He laughed. "I could swear that you're nervous, Slick."

She frowned. "Not at all. I'm just …"

He pulled her closer still and softly kissed her forehead, sending a tingle over her skin.

They danced until the song ended. She noticed a small scar above his left eyebrow and soft crinkles around the edges of his eyes, likely from long days squinting into the sun. He grinned, and a sense of well being flooded her. She yawned and laid her head against his chest.

He tipped her chin up with his finger and gazed into her eyes. "You're tired. We should go."

She nodded and let him walk her out the front door and down the rickety steps. Another yawn, and she covered her mouth with her hand.

"I'd drive you home, but I rode my bike ..."

She nodded. "Of course. I'll be fine – it isn't far." Another yawn. "I'm sorry. I don't know what's wrong with me. Ever since I got here I've been going to bed so early and doing all this physical work. I'm sleeping a lot more than I normally would."

He chuckled. "Country living."

By the time she reached the ranch, she was grateful it was a short drive – she could barely keep her eyes open. She parked the truck in front of the house and climbed out just as Dalton rode by on his bike. The roar of the engine echoed over the fields, and she could see Rocket and Charity as dark shadows in the darkened field, trotting away with their tails held high.

She climbed the stairs slowly, and turned with a start when she heard Dalton run up behind her. He caught her in his arms and spun her around to face him, his lips pressing hungrily to hers. Pulling back, she pushed against his chest and turned away. "Dalton ..."

"What? I know you feel the same way. Don't try to tell me you don't."

She covered her face with her hands. "It's not that," she groaned.

"Then what?"

"I'm leaving in the morning. The timing is ... not good." Her voice wavered.

He pulled her to him, his eyes intense and longing. "Why does it have to end? So you go home tomorrow. That doesn't mean we won't see each other again. It doesn't mean we have no future … does it?"

"I just don't see how it could work. Please let me go."

He released her, and she turned and fled into the house, racing to her room and shutting the door quietly behind her. The house was still – Eamon and Parker must have turned in for the night. She threw herself on the bed and rolled onto her back to stare at the ceiling, her hands behind her head.

By tomorrow afternoon, all of this would be a fading memory. She'd be home, ready to begin rehearsals the next day for the ballet. Her dreams were coming true, much quicker than she'd ever imagined. Who knew where this might lead? She could be fielding requests from orchestras all over the world by the end of the year.

She squeezed her eyes shut and groaned. Why didn't the idea bring her the satisfaction she'd always thought it would? She'd worked her whole life toward this moment, this point in her career when everything was falling into place, and all she felt was anxiety and nausea. There was no excitement, no anticipation, no pride in her achievement. No doubt Mom and Dad would be proud, but that wasn't enough anymore.

Pleasing her parents couldn't fill the void inside her that opened whenever she thought of the years stretching out ahead of her. Years of violin practice, striving, looking over her shoulder to see who was vying for her position, travel, hotel rooms, lonely nights eating room-service meals in bed. She'd experienced it for years already, and knew more of the same lay ahead because she'd talked to others about it who'd been doing it for decades. They loved it – it was their passion and filled them with joy. But they'd sacrificed so much. Was she willing to do the same? Would she give up this chance of love to follow that dream? Was it even *her* dream, or just her parents'?

Hazel shook her head, then turned over and buried her face in the pillow.

CHAPTER 10

*T*he sound of a car in the drive pulled Hazel from her bed. She'd been awake for an hour, her thoughts in a jumble, hoping the Williams brothers would be off to work by the time she showed her face. She hadn't seen Dalton since she ran away the previous night and was embarrassed by her behavior.

She hurried to the window and pushed the blinds aside. A Volkswagen Jetta sat beside Dalton's truck, the door hanging open. *Jen!* She'd called her before falling asleep, but hadn't expected her to show up like this. A swell of gratitude swamped her like a wave against a sandy shore. She threw on shorts and a T-shirt and ran out to greet her friend, squealing as she padded down the stairs barefoot and threw her arms around Jen, squeezing her tight.

"Ahh … you're suffocating me," Jen joked. "And remember, I just had surgery."

Hazel quickly pulled away with a sheepish smile. "Sorry, I'm just so happy to see you. Did I hurt you?"

"No, it's fine. And I'm glad to see you as well. I just

had to come down here after your phone call last night. This is all my fault, and I have to clean it up – you shouldn't be shouldering the whole thing yourself." Jen placed a hand on Hazel's shoulder. "Did I tell you how sorry I am?"

"Only a hundred times. It's fine, really. I actually had fun."

Jen's eyebrows arched in surprise. "Really?"

"I know it sounds strange, but it's nice here. Dalton's been so kind to me, welcoming me into his home. And Harley's adorable – you'll have to come inside and meet him. I've even made friends with the horses, if you can believe it?"

Jen shook her head. "That's great. Unexpected, but great. And Contessa's Charity …?"

"She's over there," Hazel pointed her out. "See how happy she looks?"

Jen squinted in the bright morning sunshine and watched the mare grazing contentedly.

Hazel smiled. "Come on inside and meet everyone. They already know everything, so you might as well join us for breakfast."

They went into the house and through to the kitchen, where the murmur of conversation and sounds of laughter floated out to greet them. "Good morning," Hazel chirped. "I'd like y'all to meet someone. This is Jen."

"*The* Jen?" asked Eamon, a spoon poised over his bowl of cereal. "The real one?"

Parker laughed. "Well, it's a pleasure to meet you, Jen. Pull up a chair."

Dalton just kept eating, staring into his bowl. He wasn't his usual cheerful self.

"Thanks," replied Jen, sitting beside Parker at the

table. He handed her a bowl and spoon and she poured herself some Rice Chex.

The only empty seat was beside Dalton and Hazel took it with a bright smile. "Morning, Dalton."

He glanced up at her. "Mornin'. Nice to meet you, Jen – we're glad you're here. I believe Gus is arriving later to take Charity home. I'm assuming you'll be going with him?"

Jen's eyes found Hazel's and Hazel nodded. "Um, yes. I think Hazel's going to drive my car back this morning and I'll ride with Gus later. I have to thank you, Dalton – you've been very welcoming to Hazel. I really appreciate it. And thank you for not reporting us to my boss – I don't think he'd understand. I apologize for this whole mess. I wasn't thinking clearly."

He chuckled and tipped his head toward her, his eyes sparkling. "It's been a pleasure."

Jen fit in well with the Williams brothers – before long, the four of them were laughing and joking like old friends. Hazel carried her empty bowl to the sink, rinsed it and stacked it in the dishwasher. She watched their playful banter with a smile, then slipped out of the room. She had to finish packing and get on the road. There was no reason for her to stay any longer – Jen had everything under control now.

* * *

DALTON WATCHED Hazel sneak out of the kitchen, her eyes downcast, and frowned. He hadn't been able to get through to her the night before, even though he was certain she felt the same way about him that he did about her. He could understand her reluctance – to be together, a lot of things had to work out. He didn't pretend to know how, only that he wanted to try.

He was reluctant to press the issue any harder than he already had. He knew what she was doing – pushing him away so she wouldn't get hurt. He'd done it himself plenty of times, especially after Jodie broke his heart. He'd been determined not to let a woman do that to him again. But now he'd fallen for Hazel, and he didn't want it to stop. Not this time.

He pushed his chair back and went after her. If she'd planned on leaving without saying goodbye to make it easier on herself, he wasn't about to let that happen. He found her loading her suitcase into the trunk of Jen's car, leaned against it and crossed his arms. "I hope you weren't planning on skipping out on us without so much as a goodbye." He did his best to smile.

"No, of course not." She flashed him an unconvincing grin.

He took a long, slow breath. "Hazel, I really don't want this to be it."

She blinked. "Me neither. It's just that … if I stayed, if I gave us a chance, I know I'd give up everything for you. But there's no future for me here. Tifton's a small town – no opera, no symphony orchestra, no ballet. Well, there's Janie's Ballet School, but you know what I mean."

He laughed. "I know."

"So … what would I do? I don't fit down here. If things didn't work out between us … let's face it, it's not like I've ever held down a long-term relationship before. What then?"

He sighed. "I don't have the answers. I just know I

want to see you again. I want to spend time with you, get to know you better. I'll miss you …"

"I'll miss you too. But I'm sorry, Dalton, I have to go."

He hung his head and stepped back from the car.

"Say goodbye to the others for me – I don't think I could face them right now. I already said my goodbyes to Harley. Take care of yourself." She got into the car and slammed the door closed, then backed out and turned down the long driveway.

He waved goodbye, a single flick of his hand, then tipped his cowboy hat. He didn't even know if she saw him. He just watched the small white car until it rounded a bend and was gone, then stood gazing at the empty road.

With a sigh, he wandered back into the house, stopping to remove his boots at the front door. He followed the hoots of laughter back into the kitchen and pulled up a chair across from Jen. She was telling a funny story about a house call she'd made to a jaundiced cat, and his brothers were crying with laughter. She was a born storyteller and he couldn't help smiling at the expression on her face as she wove her tale.

When she finally finished and the laughter faded, she caught his eye. "Is she gone?"

He nodded and drummed his fingers on the table top.

"What?" asked Eamon with a frown. "Hazel's gone? But she didn't tell us goodbye!"

Dalton smiled sourly. "She said for me to tell you goodbye for her. I think she was feeling a bit emotional … you know, at leaving Harley behind."

Parker arched an eyebrow but didn't say anything. "Really? Just Harley, huh?" Eamon chuckled.

Dalton got up and headed for the coffee maker. He poured himself a cup and stood with his back to the countertop, his ankles crossed, as he drank it. Once it was empty, he set it down on the counter. "We'd best get going. The day's well and truly started and we've got a lot of work to do."

Parker carried his dirty plates to the sink, then turned to slap Dalton on the back, his eyes full of warmth. "Sorry, man. I know how you feel about her. But maybe she'll come back."

Dalton managed a smile. "Maybe. Though I doubt it – she made that pretty clear."

Parker shook his head. "Her loss, I guess."

"Thanks, Parker."

"Enough talk about feelings – let's go and do manly things!" exclaimed Eamon, slapping his palms against his chest with a shout.

Dalton laughed and headed for the door. His brothers followed, while Jen stood to carry her dirty dishes to the sink. "Let me know when Gus arrives," Dalton called to her over his shoulder.

"Will do," she replied.

He stepped outside and took a deep breath. It felt different with Hazel gone, like something was missing – a piece of his heart, maybe. But the day was full of sunshine and promise, and he couldn't help feeling a bit of joy in that. He didn't blame her for not wanting to stay. He'd tried to think of what she might do if she remained here, and came up empty.

It didn't matter which way he looked at it, she didn't belong in south Georgia any more than he belonged in Atlanta. If he'd met her before he inherited the ranch, he'd have given it a try, though he wasn't likely to fit in there. But now, he was tied to Tift

County as surely as if he'd been chained to it. He couldn't leave; she couldn't stay. It was an impossible situation and it made his heart ache.

* * *

HAZEL DREW the bow across the strings, and the final note hung in the still air. It wasn't a full orchestra, just a few latecomers who needed to catch up on learning the music before rehearsals began, but it still sounded beautiful. Her eyes were moist and her hand shook as she lowered the bow to her side.

Music always manipulated her emotions. A dirge made her sad, an anthem lifted her spirits and filled her with hope. But today's piece had simply amplified what was already there beneath the surface. She couldn't stop thinking about Cotton Tree Ranch, Harley, Rocket, Charity, Eamon, Parker, and most of all Dalton. His dimpled smile and tanned cheeks, the strong arms that had wrapped around her and held her close …

She nodded goodbyes to the rest of the group as they packed up, a few words about the weather here and brief discussions of dinner plans there. Then they were gone and she was left alone in the small room. She sighed and packed her violin away.

Her parents had been delighted when she'd called them last night to tell them she'd made first chair, however temporarily. She'd skipped over the part about the ranch, blaming her delay entirely on the rehearsals for the ballet. *First chair – well now, isn't that something?* was what Dad had said. Mom had nattered on about how she should take her part seriously and never for a moment take it for granted, how she'd have

111

to up her daily practice from two hours a day to four, and be sure to network and solidify the relationships she had within the orchestral community …

Hazel rubbed her eyes. Just thinking about it all made her stomach clench. She wasn't cut out for schmoozing, or cutthroat competition. Her time at the ranch had brought clarity to that for the first time. She'd gotten to relax, read, listen to the music she wanted to listen to, go out for a drink, laugh with friends – she'd even kissed a sexy man. She couldn't remember the last time she'd had so much fun.

Of course, one of the best things about it was that no one there had known who she really was. She got to play a role - maybe not well, but a role nonetheless. There were no expectations on her, no pressure to perform, no one studying her every move to see if she'd qualify for the next opportunity. And she'd loved it.

* * *

DALTON HAMMERED the nail into the fence post. It was the last one for that post, and he stood to stretch the kinks out of his back with a sigh. He glanced down the length of the fence with pride. It looked good and they were almost done. He'd replaced all the torn-up barbed wire with a rail fence – more expensive and it took longer to build, but it was better for horses. He intended to breed the best stock horses in the South-east, so he figured he should do everything on the ranch with excellence.

"How's it going?" asked Eamon as he piled another load of palings at Dalton's feet.

"Done with this section. Only a few more to go and we're finished completely."

"That's music to my ears, brother."

Dalton laughed, but his smile quickly faded. He bent over to retrieve a paling.

Eamon lifted a post and carried it with a grunt to set in the hole they'd dug for it earlier. "Why so glum?"

Dalton sighed. "You know why. Dang it, I just can't seem to get her out of my head."

Eamon grinned as he brushed the dust and splinters from his shirt. "Sounds to me like you're in love."

Dalton kicked dirt into the hole around the post. "What would you know about that?"

Eamon's eyebrows arched high. "Now, now – no need to get testy. I know enough. You should probably give her a call."

Parker pulled up in the truck and jumped out with a wave. "I brought more palings."

"Thanks," replied Dalton, then told Eamon, "There's no point in calling her. She's got her life there, I've got mine here. She doesn't see a future for herself down here, and frankly, I get that. But getting it still doesn't help the way I feel."

Parker grinned. "Ahh … we're talking about the lovely Miss Hildebrand, I take it."

Eamon nodded. "Yeah, and this dipweed is moping over her, but won't do anything about it."

Dalton leaned an elbow on the fence post and glared at his brother. "Tell you what – if I say I'll think about it, will you leave me be?"

Eamon raised his hands in surrender. "Done. Consider it dropped."

"There's something else on my mind as well."

Dalton rubbed his hands over his face and took a breath. "It's the ranch."

Parker and Eamon stopped what they were doing and listened.

"I'm running out of money. I've got another mare arriving for Rocket Peak today and a few more later in the week, so the stud fees will help. But I'm still just starting to build a name and it's not going to be enough."

Eamon scowled. "How bad is it?"

"The problem is, the ranch isn't properly mine until the end of twelve months – that's only four months away. If I don't make it until then, it'll revert to Nana Dixie."

Parker's mouth fell open. "I hadn't heard that. Grandpa Joe sure had fun writing that will of his. I think he did something similar to our cousins."

"And I've sunk all my money into this place. If it goes, I lose everything – my inheritance, my savings and a year's worth of work, all down the drain."

"I'm really sorry, man," said Eamon with a scowl. "But we'll think of something."

"Yeah, we'll figure it out." Parker rested his hand on Dalton's back. "Eamon and I have to head back north in a couple of weeks, but we'll see what we can come up with before then."

"Thanks." Dalton kicked more dirt into the hole, then stomped it down hard, fixing the pole in place as he did. They'd think of something. They had to. Otherwise he didn't know what he'd do. It was times like these he missed his father. Dad would have known what to do. But he was gone, and Dalton was on his own.

*H*azel walked through the front door and dropped a handful of bills and junk mail on the kitchen table. The house was still and quiet, and for a moment she remembered the rambunctious fun of living at Cotton Tree Ranch. Here there was no puppy licking her toes, no brothers fighting over the last slice of cake. No noise at all other than the rumble of traffic as it drove in a continuous stream past the house.

She missed it.

She hung her purse on the coat rack by the door, then searched through the refrigerator for something to cook. It was obvious Jen hadn't bothered to shop while she was away – the fridge held a half-used bottle of ketchup, another of French dressing and a carton of milk that was turning into a new lifeform. She sniffed it, wrinkled her nose, then poured it down the sink.

The kitchen door flew open and Jen breezed in, her duffle bag over one shoulder. She grinned when she saw Hazel, then grimaced and covered her nose. "Ugh! What is that smell?"

Hazel laughed. "The milk you let spoil."

"Disgusting – it smells like foot!"

"Uh-huh. I didn't realize you'd be home so soon. How'd it go?" She threw the empty jug in the recycling bin and went to hug her friend.

Jen returned the embrace, then hurried to open every window she could find. "It was good. Everything went fine and Gus barely batted an eye when he saw me. I told him I'd been there the whole time, that you'd just ridden down with him to keep him company. I think he bought it. But I'm done with lying – it's exhausting and twists my stomach into knots and makes me want to throw up." She shivered and slumped down onto a kitchen chair.

"I'm with you on that. No more pretending. No more lies. Let me tell you, I'm a terrible actress. If you ever need someone to pretend to be you again, please don't choose me. I'm really no good at it." She groaned and slid into a chair beside Jen.

Jen pulled a packet of Starburst from her pocket and offered one to Hazel. "So how was rehearsal?"

Hazel took one, unwrapped it and popped it into her mouth. "Fine."

"Fine? I thought this was it, the opportunity of a life time, blah blah blah." Jen leaned her elbows on the table.

"Yeah, I thought so too. But I don't know. I'm starting to wonder if it really is all I've ever wanted, or if I followed this path just to please my folks." She leaned her cheek on the table and folded the empty candy wrapper into a tiny square.

Jen sat up straight and lifted her feet onto the lip of

her chair, wrapping her arms around her knees. "Okay, tell me this – if you could do anything in the world, what would you do?"

Hazel chewed the candy. "I don't know."

"What would make you happy, make your heart sing, you know?" Jen frowned and rested her chin on top of her knees. "For me, it's working with animals. I absolutely love it. And I thought it was the violin for you, but if it's not, then what is it?"

Hazel lifted her head from the table and gazed into the distance. What did she love? What would make her happy? She'd enjoyed her time at the ranch – the relaxed atmosphere, clean air, beautiful scenery, and of course the company. And she loved working with the local Junior Orchestra. She'd helped children learn to play as part of an ensemble, their little faces lighting up when they got it right. That definitely made her heart sing. "Well, I love teaching kids ..."

"Really?" Jen grimaced. "Ugh."

With a laugh, Hazel cocked her head to one side. "No, it's great. They're sweet and they listen and try to do what I ask them. And they're so happy when they get it. It's adorable."

"Well, I don't understand it, but if that's where your bliss is, why don't you do that?"

"Do what?" asked Hazel. Working with the Junior Orchestra was a volunteer role – she couldn't do it for a living.

"Teach!" cried Jen in frustration.

"Teach?"

"Yeah, become a teacher. People do it all the time."

Hazel's eyes widened and she sat up straight. She could teach music! Why hadn't she ever thought of that before? She enjoyed performing, but after a while it felt hollow. However, every time she'd taught, she'd loved it. And teachers were needed everywhere there were schools, not just in Atlanta or other big cities. Even in small towns in south Georgia. "Huh. Do you really think I could?" She pursed her lips, considering the possibilities.

"You would kick so much butt at it," Jen assured her.

* * *

I-75 STRETCHED out wide and straight as it headed southeast. Hazel had secured the roof of the convertible to protect herself from the sun burning overhead. She turned the air conditioning up further, until it was blasting the damp curls off her neck. With a deep breath, she reached for the radio dial and turned up the music. Sibelius was playing, loud and dissonant – good preparation for facing her parents.

She was headed to Jekyll Island, and her nerves were already jangling. Her pulse raced every time she pictured the looks on their faces when she told them her decision. She was leaving the symphony to be a music teacher.

Ever since Jen had suggested the idea weeks earlier, she hadn't been able to get it out of her mind. She'd researched it, obsessed over it, had every university she could think of in Georgia and north Florida send her an information packet about their teaching program. She was excited, nervous and happy all at once. For the first time in a long time she felt as though the future wasn't written in stone but ripe with possibility.

An exit sign declared it was her turnoff. She

checked her mirrors and merged into the far-right lane. State Highway 16 would take her most of the way there, while I-75 headed south toward, among other places, Tifton. If she just keep going and didn't take the exit, she'd find herself back in Tifton before nightfall ...

The heck with it.

She stepped on the gas and sailed past the exit. Her parents would be furious when she didn't show up again, but she'd deal with that later – at a comfortable distance. What she really wanted to do right now was talk to Dalton about everything. It made little sense, since they hadn't spent much time together, but it *felt* like she'd known him forever. She really wanted to hear what he thought of her plan.

That, and she missed him. Just the thought of his arms around her, his lips on hers, made her shiver in anticipation. They'd spoken on the phone almost every day in the weeks since she left the Cotton Tree, and she found herself waiting for his calls, even begging off social engagements to make sure she was home when he phoned. They'd spend hours talking about any and everything. But she still hadn't talked to him about this, about leaving the orchestra to teach. She hadn't been able to get the words out. It was something she wanted to discuss face to face.

She changed the radio station, scanning until she found some country music, then leaned back in her seat. She was going to see Dalton and she couldn't get the grin off her face.

* * *

THE SIGN for Cotton Tree Ranch swayed in the breeze

over the gate as Hazel climbed out of her convertible to open it. She drove through, closed it behind her and saw Rocket Peak prancing along the fence line, his nostrils flared. Another mare, a palomino, grazed nearby in his pasture. "Hey, Rocket, you stud," she quipped. "I'll bring you a carrot later, boy."

She was glad she'd decided to wear her cowgirl boots that morning. She'd been feeling nostalgic, and now it was a necessary touch – no tromping through fields in pumps. Denim shorts and a black tank top completed the ensemble, with her chestnut curls pulled back into a messy ponytail. She ran a hand over her hair, wishing she'd made more of an effort.

She reached the house and saw Eamon, Parker and little Harley by the barn. The dog came bounding toward her, still awkward in his gait. His little paws tripped over a tuft of grass and sent him nose-first into a puddle lined with red clay, but he stood up, shook his head and continued toward her.

She climbed from the car with a laugh and caught him in her arms. "Hello there, little one," she crooned, rubbing his tummy with her fingertips. His tail wagged madly and he licked her fingers in excitement.

Eamon and Parker regarded them from a distance, then walked over to greet her. "Hey, Hazel. We weren't expecting to see you again so soon," said Eamon, tipping his hat.

"Yeah, I wasn't planning on coming back so soon. But I needed to talk to Dalton about something. Is he around?"

She noticed the strained look that passed between the brothers. "Ah, no. He's in town for a bit. He'll be back soon."

"Oh?"

"Yeah, he has a meeting," offered Parker, adjusting his hat.

"Okay. Well, do you mind if I hang out for a while and wait for him?"

Eamon grinned. "Sure, come on in. I'll make you a cup of coffee. Or if that's too hot for you, we've got lemonade."

"Lemonade sounds wonderful." Hazel opened the passenger door, retrieved her purse and followed Eamon inside.

In the kitchen, she pulled a stool up to the counter and watched him pour her an ice-cold glass of lemonade, salivating in anticipation. It wasn't often she let herself drink anything sugary, but being back on the ranch made her feel almost carefree. Eamon had removed his hat and set it on the counter, and a lock of blonde hair hung over his forehead and obscured his eyes. He looked like Dalton, only fairer – same mischievous dimples and confident air.

He handed her the drink and she took a sip. Suddenly she felt uncomfortable. Maybe she shouldn't have come. Dalton wasn't even here – how long should she wait for him? *Why* had she come? What did she think would happen – he'd fall into her arms, beg her to stay, confess his undying love? Of course not. She was being ridiculous – they barely knew each other, yet here she was, imagining how their lives might come together.

She'd made a big decision about her future, and now she was trying to fit Dalton into it. But she wasn't entirely sure he'd want her to. He'd said he did, but perhaps things had changed since the last time she saw him.

Eamon watched her in curiosity. "Everything all right there, Slick?"

She ducked her head and her cheeks warmed. "Yeah, fine. How about you? How's ranch life treating you, cowboy?"

He grinned. "It's hard work. But ... you know what? I'm loving it. Back home I'm an accountant."

"An accountant?" she spluttered, spraying lemonade across the counter.

Eamon slapped her on the back as she coughed. "Don't sound so surprised, Slick. Yes, I was a bean counter – still am."

She recovered her composure and took a long, slow breath. "Don't take this personally, Eamon, but you don't seem like one."

He chuckled. "Don't let the boots and hat fool you. I dress in a suit everyday and drive a BMW to work in an office on the sixteenth floor of a high-rise in the heart of Chattanooga."

She raised an eyebrow. "Well, you learn something new every day."

He smiled and poured himself a glass, took a sip and leaned his elbows on the counter between them. "So, Slick, what's the deal?"

"What do you mean?"

"I mean, what are you doing back here so soon? If I didn't know better, I'd think you were sweet on my big brother." He winked and set his glass down.

Her face burned and she twisted the glass in a circle on the tile countertop. "Well, I'm trying to figure some things out."

"Like ...?"

"Like what to do with my life." The words echoed in the room as she spoke them, coming back to her and making her gut lurch. She'd had her life all planned out – every piece in place – but in the space of a few days, a cowboy from south Georgia had her questioning everything. Or maybe it wasn't just him – maybe she'd known for a while that something had to change. Maybe she'd be wrong all along about what she wanted, what she needed, and Dalton had just brought her some clarity.

Eamon pursed his lips. "Well, that isn't a small thing. Have you got it figured out yet?"

She shook her head and took another gulp of lemonade. "Not quite. But I think I know what I want, so I suppose that's a start."

"Yeah." He lifted his glass and tapped it against hers in salute. "Cheers to that."

"Cheers," she agreed with a shy smile. They both sipped their drinks, then set them back down on the counter. "So where did you say Dalton was?"

Eamon's cheeks colored and he combed his fingers through his hair. "I don't suppose he'd mind me telling you … he's at the bank, asking for a line of credit. He can't afford to keep the ranch going more than another two months. But if he's to inherit the place, he has to make it four more months. It's obvious to me that running this place is too much for him to do on his own, but he's stubborn. I worry if he gets this line of credit and keeps going the way he has, he'll lose everything and kill himself in the process. It's a big ranch and it needs a lot of work – and to make it profitable might take more than he's got."

She rubbed her chin and studied Eamon's face. She'd had no idea things were that dire. Dalton always made it seem like he had everything under control – he was so self-assured, so confident. She'd never have guessed the pressure he was under. "Have you talked to him about your concerns?"

Eamon shook his head and scratched his shoulder. "For all the good it's done. He wants it to work out so badly and he's sunk everything into this place."

She nodded. "You're an accountant – this is what you do for a living. Treat him like a client – run the numbers, then sit down and present him with options."

With a sigh, he chewed his bottom lip. "You know, I haven't done *that*." The sound of a truck in the drive caught his attention, and he stood straight, his eyebrows lowered. "That must be Dalton now. I'll go tell him you're here."

She nodded her thanks and waited at the counter, slowly drinking the refreshing liquid. Her purse was still looped over her shoulder, so she set it on the floor, her hand shaking. What was wrong with her? It was just Dalton – the same man she'd shared a tornado shelter with. The same man that had kissed her until her heart felt like it might leap from her chest.

The front door banged, boots slapped across the living room floor ... and there he was, grinning, his eyes gleaming. "Hazel! I wasn't expecting to see you." He crossed the kitchen, pulled her in his arms and kissed her passionately on the lips. Her heart pounded, and she closed her eyes and wrapped her hands around his neck, threading her fingers into his thick hair.

She leaned back, opened her eyes and found his gaze fixed firmly on her. She smiled, her entire body trembling. He didn't release his grip on her and she felt whole in his arms.

"Whatcha doing here?" He grinned and ran a finger

down the side of her face, sending a tingle over her skin.

"I came to see you."

"Oh?" There was a glint in his eyes.

"Yeah. I wanted to talk to you about something."

"Well, that sounds serious. Can it wait until after dinner?" He released her and sat on a stool.

She returned to her seat and took his hands in hers, massaging his scarred knuckles, her body trembling. "Yes, I suppose it can."

He studied her face. "You are staying, aren't you?"

She smiled. "If that's okay."

"Of course. Though I can't promise anything extravagant, like you big-city folks are used to." He winked.

"Sounds perfect," she sighed.

"*I*'ll buy Vermont Avenue." Hazel now had the whole set of light blue properties – next she'd start building houses on them.

The Williams boys groaned. Dalton ran a hand over his forehead and Eamon slapped his thigh. "You're cutthroat!" exclaimed Parker, passing her the card for Vermont.

She grinned. She loved to play Monopoly, and she didn't mess around, buying property as fast as she could. Anyone she played against usually regretted their own reticence. She'd discovered the beat-up old board game in the back of the linen closet a few hours earlier when searching for sheets for the guest bed, since Dalton had convinced her to spend the night. She couldn't remember an evening where she'd been so relaxed and happy – they all laughed over the game more than she'd laughed about anything in years.

"I love that you're a heartless tycoon," said Dalton, his eyes flashing. "Even if you are bleeding me dry with your rent."

Hazel laughed an evil laugh and rubbed her hands together. Dalton's eyebrows arched high and he pounced on her, tickling her sides until she squealed for mercy.

Eamon rolled his eyes and stood, stretching his hands over his head. "That's it, I'm out."

Fighting for breath, Hazel tried to push Dalton away. "No! We're not finished yet …"

"How about some ice cream?" suggested Parker as he followed Eamon into the kitchen.

"Sounds good," Eamon told him. "With chocolate sauce."

As soon as his brothers disappeared, Dalton turned serious and lowered his lips toward hers, his breath quickening, his gaze intense.

"But the game's not done," Hazel pouted.

"I think it is, sweetheart. Enjoy your victory." He laughed softly and kissed her, then righted himself and settled beside her on the couch. "So what did you want to talk about?"

She sat up to face him, tucked her hair behind her ears and gathered her thoughts. "You know, when I was here last, I talked about how I wasn't sure the orchestra was my dream?"

"Yeah …"

"Well, I've had time to really think about it. Jen suggested I consider what I wanted out of life, instead of just taking the path Mom and Dad planned for me to. So I did – I thought about it."

She could see she'd piqued his interest. She paused for a breath, her heart pounding. Would it sound ridiculous? She was a musician performing at the highest level. The world was laid out before her with opportunities galore, and she was about to turn away from it all. Her father used to tell her, *those who can, do; those who can't, teach.* She could just imagine what he'd say when she informed him of her plan. And yet her only worry was, what would Dalton think?

"And?" he prompted her.

"And I think … no, I *know* what I truly want to do is to teach. I want to teach music."

"Oh. Wow."

Was that a "good" wow, or a "you're crazy" wow? She tensed and waited.

"Do you mean you want to teach school? Or private lessons?"

"School," she replied firmly. "Maybe private lessons too, but mainly school."

"Okay."

She frowned. "You know, you could give me a little more enthusiasm. I've just told you something that's really important to me and I'm dying to know what you think."

"Well, I don't want to sway you one way or the other. It's not really my place …"

She grabbed his shoulders in frustration. "Yes, it *is* your place. I'm asking what you think."

"If you really want my opinion … I think it's fantastic!" He smiled and placed his hands over hers, squeezing them gently.

"You do? You don't think it's crazy for me to give up my place in the orchestra, my future as a performer?"

"I don't think it's crazy at all. You should do what makes you happy. If performing does that, be a performer. If it's teaching, then teach. I'll back whatever you decide."

Her eyes widened and her hands dropped back into

her lap. "You must think it's strange I came all the way here to tell you that, considering the last time I saw you I was pretty adamant we didn't have a future together."

His dimples deepened and he cocked his head, his eyes playful. "I knew you'd be back. You can't resist me."

She slapped him lightly on the chest, her pulse racing. "Oh really? You're so sure of yourself, are you? Let me tell you something, buddy. I can resist you."

Without warning, he lifted her feet from the ground and pulled her into his lap. He cupped her cheeks in his hands and kissed her, his lips exploring hers, sending waves of pleasure through her.

When he pulled away, she felt as though he'd taken her breath with him. Her eyes opened lazily and she leaned her cheek against his firm chest. "I guess I was wrong..."

He chuckled and tightening his embrace. "So what does this mean? Are you going back to school then?"

She sighed. "I guess so. I know it sounds strange, but even the idea of studying again is pretty exciting. I've lost my passion for the orchestra – or maybe realized that I didn't have a passion for it, I don't know which. When I think back, I wonder if I ever cared about it, or if my ambition and success was all just because I'm naturally driven and competitive. I mean, I love music, I always have. But I also love being around people, children especially. And the orchestra is a lonely place at times."

He lifted a hand and stroked her hair back from her forehead. "You know, Valdosta State's only about a half-hour from here, and they have a teaching program."

She pulled away and stared at him, her brow furrowing. "Really? It's that close?"

"Uh-huh." There was a gleam in his eyes.

Her heart leaped. "Well! I really should consider all my options …"

"Of course. Though if you were to live close by, I wouldn't object."

"You wouldn't?" Could she live near the Cotton Tree? It would mean she'd have nothing to keep them apart. And she didn't want anything to stand between them any longer, even if the thought of it made her nervous. If Dalton asked her now, she'd stay forever, happily melding her life to his. He'd been right – she couldn't resist him. It'd been futile to even try. She couldn't pinpoint the exact moment she'd fallen for him, but she had – so hard it made her chest ache. She'd fought against it as long as she could, but it was stronger than her.

"You know, Eamon told me about the meeting at the bank today," she whispered.

Dalton sighed, rubbed his face and closed his eyes. "Yeah."

"Did it work out the way you'd hoped?"

He shook his head, then looked at her, a finger tracing the outline of her cheek. "No. I'm not sure what I'll do. The whole thing might be over in a couple of months unless I can think of something."

She looped her hands over his forearm and massaged his arm with her fingertips. "I'm sorry. I know how much you love this place."

He half-smiled and fingered a curl of hair that hung over her shoulder. "Well, I've still got some time."

"How has it been with Eamon and Parker here? Y'all seem to get along really well."

His face lit up. "It's been great. I hadn't realized how much I missed them. We haven't lived together since I left home to follow the rodeo circuit. I've loved having them here. And we've gotten so much more done than I could've on my own. They're heading back to Chattanooga in a few days and I'm dreading it, dreading how quiet the house will be again and having to do everything myself. But that's how it goes."

"What does Parker do for a living?" she questioned, tracing a circle on his arm with a fingernail.

He grabbed her hand and kissed her fingertips. "Well, he was discharged from the Army a few months ago. I think he just does odd jobs here and there. He doesn't seem to know what to do with himself. He was so excited when he joined the Rangers, but it changed him. He doesn't like to talk about it, but I imagine he's seen some things. Anyway, I'm just glad he's back. I was always worried I'd get the call …"

She nodded, considering his words. She'd noticed Parker seemed to keep mostly to himself, and didn't joke and laugh the way the other brothers did. After hearing why, it made sense. "Have you thought about asking him to stay?"

With a furrowed brow, he shook his head. "No. I haven't."

"Maybe he could live here and help you out on the ranch. It's worth finding out if he'd consider it, I suppose."

"I couldn't pay him," he mumbled.

"Yeah, but, what if you offered him a partnership in the ranch? You're worried about losing it – maybe he could buy a share, keep the wolves at bay, and you could work it together." She knew she was overstepping, but she wanted to help Dalton any way she could. And losing the ranch would devastate him.

"A share of the ranch? That's not a bad idea ... though I don't know if he has any money." He slipped out from beneath her legs and stood to pace across the living room.

"Well, there's no harm in asking. He can always say no." She stood as well, lacing her hands together behind her back.

He returned to her in two long strides and scooped her up in his arms, pulling her against his chest and staring into her eyes with a faint smile on his lips. "You're amazing. You know that?"

She laughed, her pulse racing. The electricity between them could almost be felt. "You're pretty amazing yourself," she whispered. She kissed him, sweetly and gently, and craved more.

Dalton set Hazel down, took her hand and led her toward the kitchen. "Let's go and see what my brother has to say about your idea, Slick."

* * *

DALTON RAN his fingers through his hair and whistled. "Seriously? You both want in? Y'all have talked about it?"

Eamon and Parker sat at the kitchen table, legs stretched out in front of them and cans of root beer each on the table. Eamon nodded, tipping his hat back. "Yep. I want to be a partner in the Cotton Tree too."

"But what about your hoity-toity job up in Chattanooga?" queried Dalton, going to the fridge to fetch himself a drink.

Eamon hissed. "Give it a rest – it's not 'hoity-toity'

just 'cause I don't wear jeans to work. I'm bored, that's all there is to it. I've had enough of working for someone else in a big impersonal company, crunching numbers but never really doing anything. I want to work with my hands and build something … meaningful."

Dalton sat down again across from him, popped the top of his coke can and took a sip before it could overflow. "First I've heard. I thought you loved accounting."

"I do, just not the corporate rat race. And I want to do something else with my life as well. I figure here, I'd be able to work with my hands and do the books. I'm assuming you probably need help with those, right?"

Dalton chuckled and slapped his hand hard on the table. "Heck yeah, I sure do! I have to say, I wasn't expecting this. And how about you, Parker – you're in as well?"

Parker nodded, his eyes gleaming. "I'm in. It's the best offer I've had since I got out. And the idea of working with you two everyday … I can't imagine anything I'd rather do."

Dalton felt as though his heart might explode. He didn't know how to express the joy that swelled within him. So he sipped his drink and kept grinning. "I guess I can put up with both of you. Though it'll likely be the death of me."

"I've got money saved," Parker added. "I haven't really had anything to spend it on, being in the desert and all the past four years. So I can afford a share."

"I've been living with Mom and saving for years," offered Eamon. "I'll pay my way in as well. With both of us in, we should be able to keep this place out of trouble. I'll run the numbers soon as I get a chance, just to be sure."

Parker's eyes narrowed and he rested both hands on the table. "You know, with three of us running the place, if we get low on cash we could even do some outside work to bring in the money."

Dalton hadn't thought of that. But Parker was right – one of the three could keep the ranch going if money got tight, while the other two worked for a wage until things picked up. Sharing the load would certainly make it easier to bear. He'd been so disappointed when the bank turned him down for a line of credit, but since 2008 most banks around the state were hesitant to lend money where they didn't see a certainty of return. A rundown ranch, being managed by a green rancher like him, apparently wasn't a solid enough investment for Tifton First Savings & Loan.

"It means so much to me that you'd do this," Dalton told them. "I really think we can make it work, and I love you both."

The men ducked their heads and mumbled in embarrassment. The Williams brothers weren't accustomed to sharing their feelings so openly. But Dalton felt it needed to be said. Lately, he'd been working up to saying what he felt when he felt it. Jodie had left him for another man, in part because they'd never communicated well. She didn't know how much Dalton cared about her, and had found someone who'd had the nerve to tell her just how special she was. Dalton had regretted his silence ever since.

But now he had a chance at a new life, a new love. His future looked bright. And he wasn't going to let the words go unspoken between him and his brothers.

There were a few more words he wished to say before the day was over as well.

Eamon's eyes glinted. "Where's Hazel? You're getting a little too emotional, dude. You should be saving that kind of talk for your woman." He laughed.

Dalton grimaced. "Don't get all squirrelly on me just 'cause of feelings. You're my brothers and you mean the world to me. Hazel's visiting the Valdosta State campus – she wanted to check out the teaching program there before she goes back north tomorrow." He leaned forward, his voice low. "Speaking of Hazel, there's one other thing I need your help with ..."

CHAPTER 13

*H*azel pointed the convertible down the long drive at Cotton Tree Ranch, a packet of flyers and brochures on the passenger seat. The Valdosta State campus had been gorgeous and the program included just the kind of course she'd be looking to start in the fall. She wasn't sure she'd be able to apply this late in the summer, but the admissions officer had assured her they accepted late applications for their Master's in Education program all the time. She was hopeful it would work out.

The sun was setting across the pastures, backlighting the barn and sending shimmering rays of pink and orange over the short-cropped grasses. Horses grazed nearby, the swish of their tails sending flies buzzing off to find evening sanctuary. Peace settled over her soul, and she was filled with a longing to settle in this place, to plant roots here and never leave. The sentiment startled her. She'd never considered herself the kind of person to stay put, let alone on a ranch in the middle of nowhere.

The front door creaked open as she pulled in front of the house, and Dalton sauntered out, a hand raised in greeting. She turned off the car, got out, met him at the foot of the steps and threw her arms around his neck, kissing him hard on the mouth.

He laughed against her lips and stumbled backward, catching her and steadying himself all at once. "How'd it go?" he asked, kissing her forehead and looping an arm around her shoulders so they could stand side by side and admire the setting sun.

"It was great. They have a really good program there, and the campus is bigger than I expected. I like the feel of it too – relaxed and friendly. I can imagine attending there."

He smiled and drew her closer. "That's good. I'm glad."

She gazed up at him, her brow furrowed. "Do you think I should? I mean, would you want me to … I know it's too soon for us to be making plans about the future, but …"

He gazed down at her, his eyes sparkling, and tilted her chin up. The kiss was tender and warmed her to her core. "Come with me," he said, dropping his arm from her shoulders to take her hand.

They walked toward the barn and stables, and she noticed that her hand fit into his as if custom-made. A sliver of moon hung high above the horizon where the sky had deepened to blue-gray, and she looked up to find the first star where it blinked in the dusky light. "Where are we going?"

He just smiled and shook his head.

They rounded the corner of the barn and she gasped, covering her mouth. "Oh, Dalton …"

He laughed a small, satisfied laugh and pulled her forward. "Come on."

The entire external wall of the barn and the overhanging roof were decked in twinkling lights. The chairs and table had been relocated from the porch, the table covered in a white cloth. Lanterns sat on either end, and in the middle were two table settings, a bottle of wine and sparkling crystal glasses. Candles were dotted between the bowls and beside the table.

Parker sat on a stool with an acoustic guitar on his knee. Eamon, beside him, was dressed in a white button-down shirt and black slacks. Both men had combed their hair and were grinning from ear to ear. Eamon pulled out a chair, offering it to Hazel.

She laughed and sat down, and Eamon laid a napkin on her lap while Parker began playing a soft melody. "You did all this?" she gasped, her throat tightening.

Dalton nodded. "Yep. You like it?"

She grinned. "It's beautiful."

"Welcome to the Cotton Tree Outdoor Diner," said Eamon with a smirk. "I'll just get you started with a salad – the main course will be out shortly." He spooned salad into bowls for each of them, then headed for the house.

As Hazel poured vinaigrette dressing over her salad, she fought against the tears that threatened to overwhelm her and took a deep breath. She knew Dalton had feelings for her, but this was the most romantic gesture anyone had ever made her. She knew what her own heart wanted – a future with him, a happily ever after – and he seemed to want it too. Could this be it?

Dalton reached across the table and took her hand. "You asked me a question before."

She cocked her head. "Yes?"

"I think you should go to school in Valdosta. But that's me being selfish – if you want to go somewhere else, I'll support that too. I just want to see you every chance I get."

Her heart was playing a concerto. Her mind whirled like a ballerina. He looked so handsome seated across from her, toying with her fingers. His gaze shimmered over her, taking in every part of her.

"You look beautiful."

She smiled brightly. "So do you."

He laughed and lifted her glass by the stem. "Wine?"

She nodded, and he popped the cork from a champagne bottle, filling her glass, then his own. "What are we celebrating?" she asked.

"New beginnings, Slick," he murmured, handing her the glass.

She took it by the stem and held it up. "To new beginnings."

"Cheers," he responded, clinking his glass against hers. They drank, and the bubbles tickled her nostrils. She rubbed her nose with the back of her hand and blinked.

They ate their salad and chatted about the ranch. He told her how Eamon and Parker were both staying on as partners, and she toasted their new venture. Eamon returned with a steak and baked potato for each of them, setting one plate in front of Hazel, the other in front of Dalton. "Thank you, Eamon," said Hazel.

Eamon gave an exaggerated bow, then left with a chuckle.

"This is all amazing," she continued. "Thank you, Dalton. I feel like a princess."

"You're welcome. I wanted to spoil you – and let you know how I feel about you. This isn't a small thing for me. I haven't wanted to be with anyone ever since my fiancée left me for another man two years ago. I haven't even wanted to talk about it. Until now. Until you came along and changed everything. Now, I want to be with you, all the time. When you're not here, I miss you and wish I was with you. When you are here, I feel like I could take on the world. I don't know if I'm making any sense …" He shook his head with a wry smile.

She reached for his hand and traced a circle on his palm, a lump in her throat. Her words came out a hoarse whisper. "It makes a lot of sense. I feel the same way …and it's as much a surprise to me as it is to you."

He grinned. "Good." He got down on one knee beside her.

Hazel's eyes flew wide, and she put a hand to her heart. Surely he couldn't be …?

"Hazel Hildebrand, from the first moment I saw you I should've known I was a goner. You stole my heart, even while lying about who you were …" He chuckled. "You might be the worst vet in the world, but you're perfect for me. I want to spend the rest of my life with you. I want to be your family, if you'll have me. I love you. I know this is quick, so you don't have to answer me right away, but will you marry me?"

"YES! I love you too!" she yelled, wrapping her arms around his neck. She hadn't known him for long, but she understood, deep down, that he was the one she could spend her life with. The quiet surety of that was enough – she loved him!

So what if it didn't make sense, that she wasn't the type of woman who leaped into things, that she'd always carefully considered every angle? Because here she was, changing everything about her life to commit herself to a man she'd met only weeks earlier. She didn't need a pro-con list for this, just how it felt when she was with him and how it felt when she wasn't. She didn't want to be apart from him, and she couldn't shake that off.

"You sure Slick?" asked Dalton with a grin.

"I couldn't be more sure about anything." She used her lips to block any more questions, and melted into his embrace.

HAZEL CLOSED the door to her dorm room and locked it behind her. Class was done for the week and she was tired. She'd forgotten how intense it was to have a full load of classes, and her eyes were weary from all the reading over the past five days. Now it was the weekend, and she would spend it at the ranch with Dalton. Her fiancé. The thought buoyed her spirits, and she began to whistle as she skipped to her car.

The drive to Cotton Tree Ranch was quick, the sun not yet at the horizon when she pulled up in front of the house. She waved to Rocket Peak, who had a new companion sharing his pasture, then braced as Harley launched himself at her, his tail wagging ferociously. He licked her legs, her hands and her arms, then her face when she squatted. "Hey, buddy. You gonna give me a bath?"

When the front door opened, she stood and ran into Dalton's arms, burying her face between his neck and shoulder. He lifted her into the air and kissed her hard on the lips. "You're a sight for sore eyes." He lowered her to the ground again and his hands caressed her back. "How was school?"

"Great. But my brain is fried."

He chuckled. "Good to hear. Hey, I have something to show you. How'd you like to see the latest addition to our little herd?"

She clapped her hands. "You got the chestnut mare?"

"I sure did. And her foal's only a few months old – a real handsome little fella."

She took his hand and leaned into his side as they walked to the stables together. The first stall they came to housed the new arrivals. Hazel peered over the door and laughed as the golden foal frolicked around his resting mother. "He's gorgeous!" She reached in a hand and brushed his coat as he ran by. He lifted his tail high and bucked, and she giggled. "I spoke to Jen yesterday. She says hi."

Dalton smiled. "How's her new boyfriend? What's his name again?"

"Chris. She sounds like she's completely smitten." Hazel missed her friend, but they caught up at least once a week by phone. And it was only a few hours' drive for her to visit, which she planned to do during the winter break when her parents would be back in the city. They'd forgiven her for putting them off for so long that summer when she showed up on Jekyll Island with her new fiancé. With Dalton there as her buffer, they had to at least pretend to be supportive of her life-changing decisions.

Of course, phone calls since then had proven otherwise, but she was confident she'd made the right choice. She'd never felt happier or more at peace.

They left the stable and Hazel tugged on Dalton's arm. "Let's watch the sunset. It's always so beautiful the way it lights up the ranch just before it disappears." She leaned her arms on the top rail of the yard fence.

Dalton looped an arm around her shoulders and kissed the top of her head. Harley settled at her feet – whenever she visited, he rarely left her side.

"I told my parents we were planning a July wedding – how does that sound?" She raised an eyebrow.

He frowned and chuckled. "Hot. Humid."

"Should we aim for spring break, then?" She'd really wanted a long honeymoon, and summer vacation was the best time for that.

"No, summer is better. You don't want to have to worry about going back to class. Not right away – you'll have your hands full with me." He laughed suggestively and planted a hot kiss on her lips.

"I'm sure I will. Okay, summer it is."

A shout behind them made her turn her head. Eamon and Parker waved from the front porch, then jogged over. Eamon wrapped her in his long arms and spun her around, making her legs fly out. "Hey there, Slick – how's it going?" he asked, setting her feet back on the ground.

"Great, thanks."

Parker hugged her and released her quickly. "Good to see ya, sis." He'd taken to calling her that ever since Dalton popped the question. She liked it.

"Did he tell you?" Eamon asked. "We passed the one-year mark on the ranch and the paperwork was all finalized this week. This place is officially ours." He held up his hand for a high-five.

Hazel slapped it. "That is awesome! Congratulations, you guys."

Dalton took her back in his own arms, planting a kiss on top of her head.

She rested her cheek against his chest as the last rays of sunshine glanced off the bowing heads of grass. "I never would have imagined this is where I'd spend the rest of my life," she whispered.

"On a ranch in south Georgia? Or in my arms?" His breath was warm against her hair.

She lifted her gaze to meet his, and her pulse raced at the look of love in his eyes. "Either. Both."

He grinned and his cheeks dimpled. "Well, I never could have imagined I'd be here with you either. I guess some things are just meant to be." He placed his lips over hers, and the heat of his touch took her breath away.

THE END

EAMON

ABOUT EAMON

Eamon thinks he has love and life figured out. A successful accountant, full of confidence and charm, he's got it all, including the beautiful girlfriend and the high flying job. But when his brother inherits a ranch in south Georgia, he leaves everything behind to help him run it.

Emily Zhu is a driven and ambitious surgeon from Boston. Everything in her life is structured and planned, down to the last detail. When she doesn't get the job she's been promised and has been working toward, it seems everything could come tumbling down around her. Suddenly the future is clouded with uncertainty.

When Eamon and Emily's paths collide at a wedding, they fight an immediate attraction. Eamon could be the only person who can help Emily find her feet in a world where nothing makes sense. The one to show her opportunity where all she sees is failure. But will she be willing to give Eamon a chance to prove he's the one thing she really needs? And what will they do when an unexpected tragedy strikes at the heart of everything they've fought for?

CHAPTER 1

TIFTON, GEORGIA

*E*mily Zhu *hated* weddings.

She hated the pomp and ceremony, the lace and tulle, the sappy speeches and centuries-old rituals. She even hated the new rituals, like when the bride and groom and their entire bridal party would break out in a flash-mob dance during the reception. She'd begged Hazel not to do it – the last thing she needed was a video of her tearing up the dance floor to "Gangnam Style" surfacing on YouTube and have her boss, the Chief of Surgery at Brigham & Women's Hospital, discover it.

She tugged on the low square neckline of her lavender jersey dress and grimaced. Evening gowns didn't suit her, and that's what bridesmaids' dresses really were. It didn't fit her personality to be so … frilly. She stared at the mirror on the wall of the small room, surveying the dark shade of eye shadow above her almond eyes and the pink blush brushed across her prominent cheekbones with a frown. Even the red lipstick looked strange on her usually bare lips.

Her gaze landed on the long white dress behind her and Jennifer Barsby, the maid of honor, standing to one side of the train. The bride turned around. "Em, you have to help me with this - I can't quite get the zipper to ... ugh!" Hazel's green eyes implored her. Her gown was a form-fitting cream with lace overlay on the bodice. It opened up at the back, and fell straight down her lithe frame. A long train draped along the ground behind her. She looked every bit the bride.

Emily turned to help with a smile – even though she couldn't stand the tradition, she had to admit her friend looked amazing. Hazel's eyes sparkled and her cheeks had a natural flush that made her beautiful face glow. With a quick tug, Emily zipped up the side of Hazel's dress. "There you go."

Hazel sighed and ran a hand over her hair, smoothing it back into place.

Emily took Hazel's other hand and squeezed it gently. "Leave it be. Your hair is perfect. *You're* perfect."

"I'm nervous," her friend confided.

"I can tell," responded Emily with a laugh. "I think it's just about time to start – we'd better find your dad. I thought he was going to meet us back here." Her brow furrowed as she scanned the small dressing room tucked behind the chapel.

Hazel's eyes flew wide. "Yes, we should find Dad. Oh, and we need the bouquets – where are they?" She threw her train over one arm and teetered around the room in her cream heels.

Emily raised an eyebrow. She moved a pile of bathrobes – no bouquets. They weren't on the dressing table either. They were nowhere to be seen.

Just then, Hazel's cousin Hannah raced through the

door, puffing frantically. "Have you seen Camille and Jason?"

"What? We've lost the father of the bride, the bouquets, the ring bearer and flower girl as well?" Hazel's face fell and she pressed her hands to her forehead. "We're supposed to be starting the ceremony ..." She turned to Emily, her face betraying her panic.

"It's fine, Hazel. You sit right here and relax – I'll find them. They can't have gotten far – it's a small chapel, there are only so many places they could be. Just breathe, I'll be right back." Emily hurried from the room as Hazel sat, tucking her train carefully around her legs.

Emily scampered down the short hallway on her tiptoes in an attempt to prevent her heels from clacking on the hardwood floors. She pushed the chapel door open slightly, peered in and saw Dalton and his groomsmen standing by the pastor, handsome in black suits.

She'd met all three groomsmen – two were Dalton's brothers and one a friend from the rodeo circuit. She'd been paired with Parker, the groom's youngest brother. Eamon, the best man, stood beside him. From their time together at the rehearsal the previous evening, she could already tell he was more than full of himself. He was handsome, no questioning it, but he seemed to know that a little too well for her liking.

The chapel was filled to bursting with family and friends, and even the mother of the bride was already seated, fanning her face with an order of service. But there was no sign of the flower girl, or the ring bearer, or Hazel's dad. She let the door swing shut and hurried down the hall.

The pastor's chambers were on the opposite side of the building from the dressing rooms. She burst through the door there and searched the cozy space frantically. Where *were* they? A look out the window revealed Hazel's dad smoking a cigarette beneath a large oak outside. She sighed and pushed the door open, feeling the heat of summer flood the cool room. "Mr. Hildebrand?"

He spun around, his eyes wide and his mouth open. He dropped the cigarette, his cheeks turning pink, and stepped on it with the sole of his shiny black shoe. "Yes?"

"It's time, Mr. Hildebrand. Hazel's ready for you."

"Oh, of course – thanks for letting me know. Just enjoying the view, you know, getting some fresh air."

She smiled and nodded. "I understand. It's a big day." She opened the door wider to let him pass. As he hurried down the hallway, she sighed and set her hands on her hips. Now to find the children …

There were several closets in the small chambers and she checked each one. Finally she found them behind the last set of doors, which opened onto a wide square cabinet beneath the narrow staircase that led up to the quaint bell tower. The children had crept inside and shut the door behind them. Dismantled bouquets littered the ground around them, and her eyes widened. "Jason! Camille! Oh my goodness, what have you been up to?"

Five-year-old Jason looked at her with sparkling eyes and a mischievous smile, his hair mussed and one button of his vest undone. Camille, three, bit her lower lip and stared wide-eyed at Emily.

Emily reached into the cabinet, and both children took her hands and allowed her to lead them out of the confined space. Then Camille linked her hands behind her white skirt, her cheeks dimpling as she frowned. "Sorry, Miss Emily."

Jason quickly followed her lead, though his expression was much less contrite. "Sorry, Miss Emily."

She sighed. How could she be angry at creatures with such sweet faces? She squatted to retrieve what was left of the bouquets. Even reassembled, they looked tattered, with petals torn and greenery pulled loose. What would Hazel say when she saw the mess that had been made of her thoughtfully selected flowers? "Never mind, children, what's done is done. Though I imagine your momma will have something to say to you about it afterward. Come on, we have to find your cousin Hazel – it's time to walk down the aisle. Do you remember how to do it? Just like we practiced."

"But will Hazel be mad?" asked Jason, fear creeping into his voice.

"She might, but we can't worry about that now. You both have a very important job to do, okay?"

Jason and Camille exchanged a look, then both nodded at Emily. "Okay."

She laid the bouquets on a nearby table, stood between the children and took their hands. "Let's go."

Jennifer Barsby flew out the dressing room door, her eyes widening when she saw the children holding Emily's hands at the end of the corridor. "Phew, you found them! Crisis averted. Where were they?" She tickled Camille under the chin and kissed her on her ruddy cheek.

"In the pastor's chambers, hiding in a closet."

"Of course they were. Well then, come with me, you two rascals – we've got to go around to the front of the church so we can walk down the aisle with Hazel." She turned and took the children's hands from Emily with a wink.

Emily leaned close to Jen's ear and whispered. "They tore up the bouquets. I put them back together, but they still look it. What should we do?"

Jen blanched and her eyebrows arched. "Shoot. Um … maybe we could pick some flowers from the church garden." She stood on tiptoe to glance out a nearby window.

Emily frowned. "I don't think we can do that. You know what? You take the kids around front and leave the flowers to me. I'll be right behind you."

She watched Jen lead the kids out the door and along the footpath, then went back to the cramped room to retrieve the bouquets. They were a sorry sight, and she stood with her hands on her hips surveying them for a moment. Well, there wasn't time to go for more flowers – but if it came down to it, having no flowers at all would be better than raggedy bunches of torn ones.

She plucked out the most damaged buds, removed the torn greenery and re-tied the ribbons that held them together, then held each of the four bouquets up and studied it, her forehead creased in concentration. Better. Not as impressive as they had been – the white roses had been reduced to only a half-dozen each, and the greenery and baby's breath were cut back – but they looked passable.

She gathered them up and carried them as fast as she could in her high-heeled silver pumps back the way she'd come and along the garden path beside the chapel. When she reached the front of the church, she smiled. The breeze caught Hazel's veil, making it swish around her satin gown. The sun glanced off her chestnut locks that curled around her long neck as she looped her arm through her father's. There was no mistaking it – she was a stunning bride.

Emily's throat tightened. She swallowed the sob that threatened to escape and shook her head. What was wrong with her? She'd never teared up at a wedding before. She must be getting soft. Now that she'd finished med school and didn't have the constant pressure of study hanging over her, at least until she had to sit the exams for her chosen specialty, she'd changed. She wasn't as driven as she had been, as consumed by succeeding. That must be it.

She hurried over to Hazel and handed her friend the bridal bouquet with a smile. "You look amazing." She smiled and felt tears looming again when she met Hazel's gaze. Her friend seemed excited, anxious and happy all at once, and Emily hoped for just a moment that one day she'd get a chance to feel that way.

Hazel took the bouquet and her eyes narrowed. "Does this look different to you?"

Emily raised an eyebrow. "Different from what?"

"How it looked before."

Emily shrugged.

"Time to go," called Jen, waving to them from the top of the church steps.

Emily handed the third bridesmaid, Hazel's cousin Hannah, her bouquet, then followed Hannah up the stairs. She gave Jen the last bunch and Jen arched an eyebrow when she saw it. "Looks perfect!" she insisted with a wink.

Emily lifted her own bouquet with both hands in front of her lavender gown. The dress clung to her figure more than she'd have liked. She was used to wearing scrubs every day to work, and having so much skin exposed made her shiver a little even in the heat of a south Georgia summer day. The church doors opened ahead, and she glanced over her shoulder to see Hazel behind her, her arm linked through her dad's, her eyes glowing. She took a deep breath and forced a smile, even as her lips trembled.

Piano music filtered through the doorway, and as Emily stepped into the chapel her heart seized at the sight of hundreds of onlookers' eyes on her. Jason and Camille were already standing in place beside Hannah at the front of the room. She just had to make sure she didn't stumble in these ridiculously high heels Hazel had insisted she wore.

She sighed with relief when she neared the end of the aisle and the music changed. As the bridal march rang out clearly and powerfully through the beautifully decorated chapel, the audience shifted its attention to the bride. Emily took her place at the front, soon joined by Jen, and the two of them turned to watch Hazel almost float toward Dalton, smiling and nodding to people from beneath her white veil. Then Hazel's gaze focused on her groom and her smile widened.

Emily swallowed the lump in her throat as the couple stood beside Jen, hands linked. Hazel passed her bouquet back to Jen, and Emily saw the glimmer of happy tears in her friend's eyes.

As the service progressed, Emily let her gaze wander over the rest of the bridal party on Dalton's side. Parker stood behind Eamon. His hair and eyes were dark, and from their time together at the rehearsal she knew he was quiet and reserved. He was also better-looking than any man she'd ever dated. But there was something out of reach about him, as though he lived deep inside his head and couldn't quite be persuaded to venture out.

Behind Parker stood Buck, his hands clasped in front of him. He looked awkward in a suit and tie, his hair slicked down against his head – you could tell he'd much rather be wearing jeans and a Stetson. There was a line of sweat across his brow and he stared straight ahead as though he might lose his balance if he didn't.

Then, beside Dalton was Eamon. She wasn't entirely sure what to make of him yet. Hazel assured her he was likable, but when she met him his eyes had flashed with mischief, and he insisted on calling her "Doc." He'd flirted with every eligible female who'd crossed his path at the rehearsal dinner the previous night, including her, and he'd taken every opportunity to flash his heart-stopping dimples, to great effect. Before the night was over, every other single woman in the room had thrown herself at him.

But she wasn't impressed by a cowboy who played the field – she had no desire to be his latest conquest. Besides, with his wavy blond hair, blue eyes and those dimples, she knew she didn't stand a chance with him. He'd have his pick of women – and from their short time together, it seemed he knew it. No, he wasn't her type, not even close.

She realized she was staring when he caught her eye and winked. Her cheeks blazed and her gaze dropped to the floor. Great – now he'd think she was interested in him, just like every other woman he met.

CHAPTER 2

*B*ack at the Cotton Tree Ranch outside Tifton, where Dalton and his brothers lived, Emily changed from her pumps into cowgirl boots beneath her gown. She put on a white beaded shoulder shrug, then hurried outside to join the festivities. The photographer had taken longer than she'd expected, and the wedding reception was already well underway, but there was no way she was dancing at a country hoedown in pumps.

The entire yard at the ranch had been transformed with twinkling lights, strings of hanging lanterns and flowers galore. A square dance floor had been erected in the center of the space, with white cloth-covered tables extending in a horseshoe around it. She reached the dance floor and flashed her boots to Hazel and Jen, who laughed out loud and beckoned her to join them. "Where did you get those?" yelled Hazel above the noise of the band.

Emily struck a pose. "Bought them in town yesterday. Do you like them?"

Hazel grinned. "Love them."

They danced until the sweat dripped from their faces, then sat just in time for the speeches and the meal. Emily couldn't remember the last time she'd had so much fun – or so much wine. She rarely drank, since most of her life was spent working in the hospital. As a surgical resident, she barely had time to go to the gym or cook herself a meal, let alone go out for a drink with friends. And being on call so often, she didn't feel it was right to indulge in case she had to go in to work.

But this was different – she was on leave, nowhere near Boston, and could do as she pleased. She threw her head back and gulped another mouthful of red wine. In fact, maybe she'd be doing a lot more of this – her year as a resident had just ended and she'd been offered a permanent position at the Brigham, where she'd been for the past three years. She couldn't wait to get moving on her career as a general surgeon. It was what she'd always dreamed of.

The food was amazing – Dalton had selected his favorite dishes, so it was nothing like a Boston wedding reception. Steak so tender it melted like butter in your mouth, barbecued ribs that fell of the bone, corn on the cob, cornbread, sweet potato casserole, fried okra, biscuits and gravy, turnip greens, black eyed peas, and the best macaroni and cheese she'd ever tasted. "Mmmm … this macaroni is amazing!" Emily licked her lips, then dabbed them with a napkin.

Hazel, seated beside her, exchanged a loving glance with Dalton, who laughed and leaned in to kiss her full on the lips.

"What?" asked Emily, who had the distinct feeling she'd missed something.

"It's an inside joke, mac and cheese," replied Dalton with a grin that deepened his already pronounced dimples.

Hazel closed the distance between her and Dalton and laid her head against his shoulder. "The first night we met, I tried to show Dalton how independent and competent I was by making mac and cheese from a box."

Emily rolled her eyes. They were adorably disgusting. "Oh, that's cute."

Hazel kissed her new husband gently on the lips, and Emily turned away with a grimace. Ugh. It was true, she wished she had what they did, but they were so sweet it was almost sickening. She stood and took another slug of wine. "Yes, well – you two are beautiful but revolting. I'm going to see if I can get a bowl of that banana pudding – it looks amazing." She strode off, still sipping her wine.

With a fresh bowl in hand, she scooped a large serving of pudding with a smile. She might not have a hunky man to make out with, but she did have dessert. She turned to head back to the table and spotted Hazel's parents standing behind her and Dalton. The conversation looked uncomfortable. She knew about the tension between Hazel and her folks, having lived in the same dorm as Hazel while she was studying pre-med at the University of Georgia. She took a bite of pudding, watching the exchange. Hmmm ... perhaps she should find another table.

She swiveled in her new boots, lost her balance and stumbled sideways, holding her pudding high in one hand and the half-full glass of wine in the other, not wishing to spill either. Her eyes widened as she felt her feet go out from under her and she landed in some-one's lap.

"Well, what a pleasant surprise," said Eamon, his breath against her ear.

Her eyes still wide from the fall and her mouth full of pudding, Emily turned to face him and swallowed. "Safe!" she cried, then burst into giggles. What was she doing, making a baseball reference? She knew nothing about baseball and she rarely joked. Her cheeks flamed.

He raised an eyebrow and smiled. "Impressive – you didn't spill a drop."

She nodded, took another bite of pudding, then realized with dismay that she was still sitting in his lap. How drunk was she? "Oh, sorry." She stood and swayed. "I think I've had a bit too much wine. I don't usually drink, so I'm a bit of a lightweight, and there was champagne before the service and during the photos … well, you know. You were there."

"Yes, I was." He studied her with a lazy grin, then stood and took her arm. "You okay?"

She giggled again. "So chivalrous. I didn't think you were – you seemed so … oh dear, I'm talking too much."

He frowned. "I seemed so …?"

Her cheeks flushed a deeper red. "Um … well, you know. You're confident."

"You mean arrogant."

Her eyes flew wide. "No, of course not, well, maybe. You just like the ladies … oh man, I don't feel so good …"

"So I'm arrogant and a player?" His eyes narrowed.

He seemed to be purposely misunderstanding her. She was sure she hadn't said anything like that. Had she? But her head was spinning and everything swayed. "I'm gonna go dance." She leaned forward and wobbled across the uneven ground toward the dance floor.

When she reached it, she set her wine and pudding down on an empty table and stepped up onto the raised surface. Hannah was there, dancing with Parker. The band was covering a Kenny Chesney song, "Everybody Wants to Go to Heaven," and it blasted out across the ranch as the crowd on the dance floor writhed to the beat.

Emily looked up and watched the stars twinkle overhead. It really was beautiful out here on Dalton's ranch – and now Hazel would be living here too. That was hard for her to imagine – Hazel, an orchestral violinist, living on a horse ranch in south Georgia, married to a cowboy. She shook her head and fixed her eyes on the dancers surrounding her. Hannah smiled at her, her lavender gown shimmering in the dim lighting, and she began swaying along to the music with the rest of them.

She felt her feet slip from beneath her again ... but two strong hands closed around her waist, setting her right again. She spun around to face Eamon, a sparkle in his eyes. "Mind if I join you?"

She shook her head and he lifted her hands one at a time around his neck. She didn't resist, unable to break her gaze from his. His eyes were so blue they were almost irresistible. Her legs felt weak, and he pressed close against her, making her gasp. She tightened her grasp on him, letting her fingers comb through the hair at the nape of his neck.

Then she felt her stomach lurch, and her eyes clenched shut. "What's wrong?" asked Eamon.

"My stomach ... I feel sick." She clutched her abdomen and wrinkled her nose.

"Let's go then," he said. "Everything's finished anyway. I'll take you back to your room." She was staying at the ranch for the night. In fact, Hazel had convinced her to stay for a few days after the wedding. She'd agreed, since she didn't know when she'd get time off again – she expected to start her new permanent position at the Brigham as soon as she returned to Boston.

Granted, since she still didn't have anything in writing, so she could've taken a longer vacation and gone to Florida, or even California or the Bahamas. But none of those places sounded inviting when traveling alone. In the past, she'd have asked Hazel to go with her, but now that was out, and even Jen had a boyfriend back in Atlanta – Chris something-or-other. She was the only one of the trio still flying solo.

She nodded to Eamon, and he put an arm around her waist. As they walked, she leaned on him, grateful for the support. She wasn't entirely sure she could've made it on her own. It couldn't just be the wine – she'd only had three glasses. She was exhausted as well. Through years of studying and working, her entire focus had been on her career, and she hadn't relaxed, really relaxed since ... she couldn't remember when. High school? Maybe not even then.

They entered the ranch house and Eamon helped her down the long dark hallway, the music outside muted by the walls and drapery-covered windows. She stopped outside her bedroom and leaned against the door jamb, then turned to face Eamon with a grin.

"Thank you, Mr. Williams. You're quite the gentleman."

He raised an eyebrow and scratched his chin. "Will you be all right? Can I get you anything ... maybe a glass of water?"

"I've got water in my room, thanks." He leaned closer and she caught her breath. He smelled of after-shave and barbecue sauce and a tremble ran through her body. "Eamon ... I ..."

He leaned in and kissed her, wrapping his arms around her and pulling her closer. She trembled in his arms and closed her eyes. When he pulled away, she opened them and saw him rub his chin as he backed away. "I'm sorry, Emily. I shouldn't have ... I'm sorry." He stumbled down the dark hallway and disappeared.

She covered her face with her hands and sighed. What had just happened? She went inside her room, closed the door and leaned against it, the rise and fall of her chest the only movement in the room. Then she ran her fingertips gently over her still-tingling tips. She hadn't expected that, not from him – or rather, she had, but not his courtliness earlier. What did it mean? Did it mean anything? Did he kiss every woman he was attracted to? Was he intoxicated too?

Without switching on the overhead light, Emily felt her way across the room to the bed, kicked off her boots and lay down. Her entire body felt like lead. As her eyes drifted closed, the beat of the music outside reverberated through her tired brain. And when she slept, it was as though she might never wake.

* * *

EAMON WILLIAMS LIFTED a bale of hay onto his broad

shoulders, carried it to the other side of the barn, dropped it onto the growing pile and brushed his hands together with a sigh. The cleanup from the wedding reception the night before was well under-way, but the bales they'd used for seats were strewn all over the yard and around the outside of the barn.

He scratched absently at the straw poking through his shirt into his skin and stood with his hands on his hips to survey the damage. Parker, Mom and Hazel's folks were picking up trash and tossing it into bags. People from the equipment rental company, all in black, were folding up tents and slipping covers off chairs, stacking them into the back of a large white truck with "Penton Party Rentals" painted on the sides in sloping red lettering.

Even with all that help, it would take all morning to tidy up the place before they could get to the regular work around the ranch. Dalton had left him in charge while he and Hazel were on their honeymoon in Destin, Florida. He'd seen the worry on Dalton's face as he'd said his goodbyes, reminding Eamon and Parker about all that needed doing over the next two weeks, and Eamon didn't intend to let his brother down. He wanted to show him he could be entrusted with the care of the ranch.

He went to pick up another bale and carry it back to the barn. The straw scratched at his neck again, making it itch.

His mind wandered back to the reception – the speeches, the dancing, the twinkle of stars in the black sky overhead. And that kiss. He couldn't stop thinking about it. He'd kissed Hazel's friend Emily from Boston. She'd barely said five words to him before last night, yet he'd found himself drawn to her. It was obvious she was smart and beautiful, but there was something else about her, an inner strength that intrigued him.

Still, he *had* a girlfriend. Sure, he hadn't seen Penny in months – she'd come to see him once since he'd moved to Georgia almost a year ago, and he'd only been back to Chattanooga twice – and three visits in a year wasn't really enough to build a relationship on. But they were still officially involved. He'd intended to break things off before moving south. But he hadn't, and couldn't bring himself to do it over the phone. And now there was Emily Zhu, the mysterious surgeon from Boston ...

He took off his Stetson, ran a hand through his hair and set his hat back in place. Emily hadn't shown her face yet this morning. He wondered if she still intended to stay at the ranch for a few days before returning home. If she did, perhaps he'd get a chance to talk to her about what'd happened. Though he wasn't sure what to say.

Eamon gathered a strand of twinkle lights in his hands, looped it around his arm, then climbed the ladder to the loft and hung them on a peg in the wall. They used the loft to store food for the livestock, tack and other bits and pieces. Hazel had asked him to put the decorations away there until she had a chance to better organize them.

As he returned to the ladder, he heard a voice below. He squatted beside the ladder and stared over the edge of the loft. It was Emily – he could see her back. She was kneeling on the floor, murmuring to Lulu, the black cat who lived in the barn. Lulu circled her, tail raised as she rubbed against Emily's legs. A line of kittens followed her, tumbling, playing and mewling as they went. Emily picked up one of the kittens, a gray one with white mittens, and held it to her chest, whispered in its ears and caressed its soft fur before setting it back on the ground.

The soft sound of Emily's laughter warmed Eamon's heart. He cleared his throat with a soft cough.

Emily spun to face him, her eyes wide. "Eamon. I didn't see you there." She stood and brushed the straw from her jeans.

He turned and backed down the ladder. "They're cute, aren't they?" He walked over to Lulu, squatting beside her to scratch her head. The cat purred in response and rubbed against his leg.

Emily chuckled. "And they know it."

He smiled. "You can have one if you like. We've got to get rid of them anyway – can't have a dozen cats running around the place. They'll eat us out of house and home."

Emily squatted beside him. "Me, own a cat? I can hardly take care of myself – I don't think it would be wise for me to take on anything else. Anyway, my building manager wouldn't be happy if I brought a pet into my apartment." She stroked the gray kitten's head, then picked up a black one and held it against her cheek. Her eyes narrowed and she smiled. "But they're so beautiful, it's very tempting."

Eamon sat down on the barn floor and set his hat in the straw beside him. He picked up a tabby kitten and held it in his lap. Lulu soon followed, stepping daintily onto his leg and letting her claws extend, puncturing his jeans – and his thigh. He frowned and scratched behind her ears. "Okay there, Lulu, pull your claws back in girl. Ouch."

Emily laughed. "Good girl, Lulu." She reached out to pat the cat, but Eamon caught her hand and held it in his . His gaze met hers and a bolt of energy passed between them, making his heart pound.

Emily broke the connection. She pulled her hand back and looked at the ground. "Don't."

He raised an eyebrow. "Why not?"

She frowned. "Because we barely know each other, and I'm leaving in a few days to go back to Boston."

He rubbed his chin, the stubble scratching his palm. "Okay."

She rose to her feet. "I'm sorry."

He stood as well and put his hat back on with a frown. "Forget it."

She lifted the black kitten and kissed its soft fur with a smile. "Goodbye, little one."

He took a quick breath. "I meant it – you should keep the kitten. It could use a good home."

"I'd love to." She set the kitten down on the ground and watched it scamper off to join its brothers and sisters. They were playing with a rope that hung against the wall, the end of it trailing on the ground for little paws to bat. "But there's just no way I can, living in an apartment like I do."

"Yeah, I'm sure glad I gave that up." Eamon set his hands on his hips. It felt awkward standing there, pretending nothing had passed between them. But it had – he'd felt it. And he'd never felt anything like it before – not with Penny, not with anyone.

Emily looked at him, her eyes guarded. "You lived in an apartment? I thought you were a cowboy through and through."

He chuckled. "Nope. I'm an accountant, actually."

She frowned, her brow creasing. "What? An accountant?"

He nodded. "But I left it all behind to help Dalton

out with the ranch. He needed me, and I needed a change, so here I am." He chewed on the inside of his cheek. She looked so beautiful standing there in the barn in her jeans and white T-shirt. A beam of sunlight caught her black hair, setting it alight with a golden glow. "How long do you think you'll stick around for?" he continued, his heart in his throat.

"Well, Hazel suggested I stay a few days, since I haven't had any time off work in ... well, I'm not sure how long. Years, I guess. I don't have to be back in Boston until next week. I hope it's okay if I stay a little while – I promise I'll keep out of the way." She pushed her hair behind her ears and squinted into the morning sunlight.

He swallowed hard. "Yeah, of course – stay as long as you like. There's plenty of room."

"Thank you."

"Well ... I'd best get back to work."

"Can I help with anything?" She lifted a hand to shield her eyes from the glare.

Eamon tipped his head to one side. "I'm sure there's plenty to do. I think Hazel's mom Anne is coordinating it all."

"Okay, I'll ask her." She half-smiled, turned and walked away.

He watched her go, rubbed his eyes and groaned inwardly. He'd never felt so flustered around a woman in his life, and it only seemed to grow in intensity the more he got to know her. He was usually so smooth, so confident. What was wrong with him?

Shaking his head, Eamon went to fetch another bale of hay. If Emily was staying at the ranch for three more days, he'd best get used to feeling out of his depth.

CHAPTER 3

*E*mily rocked the porch swing back and forth, her legs crossed at the ankles in front of her. She straightened them out, lifted one foot to tuck it beneath herself and leaned against the back of the seat. The sun was setting behind the barn, and the colors that illuminated the sky made her heart ache.

She'd been there two days and all the other guests had left the ranch. It was quiet now, with Eamon and Parker out working on something or other. She was all alone at the house and felt as though she could really breathe. She did, filling her lungs with the fresh country air, then exhaling slowly.

She couldn't remember the last time she'd sat and watched the sun set. She'd seen plenty of sunrises, mostly in the car on her way to work, but never had the time to appreciate them. More often than not, she'd simply grunt in frustration at the glare that made driving more difficult. But this sunset truly was beautiful in all the clichéd ways it could possibly be. It filled her heart with a peace she hadn't felt in a long time.

She'd let work consume her, and before that, her studies. Whatever it took to succeed, that's where her focus had always landed. It was what she had to do – she was a Zhu, and the Zhu family always succeeded. If she didn't try hard enough, there was the shame and guilt that her father and mother heaped on to help push her back into line. No doubt her grandparents had done the same thing to them; it was a proud family tradition, one she'd had no intention of upsetting.

Until now. Now she was tired. She'd worked at full capacity for so long, she wasn't entirely sure what rest felt like. She knew sitting curled up on a porch swing was a good start, but it wasn't enough. She let her eyes drift closed and leaned her head back until it rested on the back of the swing.

Where was that email the HR manager had promised her from the Brigham? She'd worked there for two years as an intern, then a surgical resident. And her boss had offered her a permanent position there as a general surgeon. "We're thrilled to have you on the team," he'd said the last time they met. "We'll get the paperwork started ... just a formality, really. There's no one else we'd rather work with."

So where was that pesky contract? It needed her signature to make it official, and from what she understood she was supposed to be starting in the new position in seven days, next Monday. Yet here she was, waiting. Everyone else from her program had joined hospitals all over the country.

Her father kept asking her if she'd signed on the dotted line yet. She recognized the look in his eyes: worry and shame. Shame that his daughter hadn't been scooped up by the best hospital in the country, like he had when he'd completed his surgical residency. She'd disappointed him again. But then, she was used to that – she'd done it her whole life.

She'd already turned down offers from Emory in Atlanta, Northwestern in Chicago and UCLA/Reagan in California. Maybe she shouldn't have dismissed them so quickly, but she loved working at the Brigham. And she loved general surgery – the variety, the challenge, the interactions with the patients.

But of course her father the world-renowned neurosurgeon wasn't impressed. Dr. Ang Zhu expected more from his only daughter. "General?" he'd asked, as if he hadn't quite heard her. "You're choosing *general* surgery? Why not just become a *chiropractor?*" He'd sniffed and stalked out of the room. And she'd felt small and hollow inside.

Never mind – she'd show him. General surgery was a respectable field. And to be a good general surgeon was something anyone would be proud of. At least, that's what she tried to tell herself. But it wasn't quite true. It was something anyone would be proud of … except her father.

She sighed and swung her feet back down against the hard boards. She should relax – she was on vacation. Who knew when she'd next get the opportunity? Perhaps she should take a walk, or a nap … no, it was probably too late for a nap. Maybe she should drive into town and find a restaurant, since it was almost dinnertime. She could buy a tub of ice cream as well, really spoil herself.

A buzz in her back pocket made her jump. She pulled out the phone and checked the screen. It was a text from Hazel: "Em, try to enjoy yourself at the ranch. RELAX, okay?"

She chuckled. Hazel knew her so well. Too well.

She replied and was about to tuck the phone back into her pocket when a thought occurred to her. Why not call the hospital and ask about the contract? The HR manager had said she'd send it through, yet it hadn't come. There could be a mix-up somewhere along the line, and if she didn't bring it to their attention they might never realize it.

She frowned and chewed her bottom lip, then quickly dialed the hospital number. "Yes, can I speak to Milton Andrews please?" Her boss would likely be hunched over a pile of paperwork this time of day. His desk seemed to breed the stuff throughout the workday, and he never got home before nine o'clock. She had no desire to be a chief of surgery – she wanted to do surgery, not administrative work.

"Yes, this is Dr. Andrews."

"Dr. Andrews – Emily Zhu. How are you, sir?" She did her best to smile, even as her heart hammered against her ribs.

"Emily, how nice to hear from you. Are you back in town?"

She laughed. "No, not yet – still down south, I'm afraid."

"And how was the wedding?"

"Lovely, thank you."

"Good. Glad to hear it."

She could hear the rustle of papers – she was losing his interest. "Actually, sir, I was calling to ask you about my contract. I haven't received it from HR yet and I'm supposed to start in about a week. Just wondering if I should call HR myself …?"

Andrews cleared his throat. "Hmmm … ah, no. No need to do that. I thought they'd called you."

"No." Her hand trembled, and she switched the phone to her other ear.

"Yes, well, I'm afraid that position has been filled. I'm sorry about that, Emily. Hopefully you can take one of the many other wonderful offers I'm sure you've received. You're a solid surgeon and we'll miss having you on the team."

She took a deep breath, the air burning inside her lungs. "Filled … what do you mean? By whom?" Her voice sounded lost in the wide-open space of the ranch.

"Ah, well, actually, it was Ben Hudson." Andrews' voice was strained and he cleared his throat again. "You know, the head of cardio, Sam Hudson? His son."

"Dr. Hudson's son? Wow. Okay. I didn't even know he'd applied." Her head felt light and she swallowed hard.

"Yes, well, he fit all the criteria. So … anyway, we wish you all the best. Don't hesitate to call if you need a referral."

"Thank you," she whispered. She wanted to scream. But she knew it wouldn't help. Instead she wrapped up the call as quickly as she could and slumped on the porch swing, her body flaring with angry adrenaline.

How could this have happened? She hadn't even given much thought to her interview, since it had been with people she considered friends and colleagues. Had she not prepared adequately? Had she taken it too much for granted? But everyone, including Dr. Andrews, had assured her the job was hers. Only clearly it wasn't.

Emily slapped her forehead and her eyes widened. Now what would she do? She'd been afraid something like this might happen, especially when she'd turned down the final offer from UCLA/Reagan. She'd been promised. She'd never suspected those promises would be broken so easily.

She stood slowly and stumbled over to the porch railing, which she gripped white-knuckled to steady herself. Now what?

She hurried down the front steps. A walk – that's what she needed. After all, she was supposed to be relaxing. It's what vacations were all about. She exercised all the time at the hospital gym, but that was different – that was feet pounding a treadmill while she stared at a whitewashed wall or the news on her phone screen or the latest issue of the *Journal of the AMA*. It wasn't a wander down a country lane, savoring the landscape and beauty all around her.

With quick steps, she set off down the long, winding driveway, only to trip on a rock and almost land on her hands and knees. She saved herself just in time, but a sob escaped and she clamped a hand over her mouth.

Now what? That question wasn't going away.

She gulped the sob back down and frowned. She was being ridiculous. This wasn't a catastrophe. Flooding in India, or a mother losing her child to a preventable disease, or a tree branch landing on a father on his way home from work during a storm – those were things worth crying over. This wasn't. She'd work it out. It'd be fine. If all else failed, she could ask Father to intervene, call in a favor. No doubt that's what Ben Hudson had done, destroying her hopes in the process.

No. She didn't want to be like Ben Hudson and ruin someone else's dreams. And who knew, maybe he really was the best person for the job.

Emily took a long, deep breath, filling her lungs to bursting. She closed her eyes tight, then slowly exhaled. She'd work it out. It'd be fine.

When she opened her eyes, a horse stood in front of her on the other side of a white paling fence. It looked at her with wide brown eyes, flicked its ears and stepped closer, whinnying, its muzzle quivering.

She cocked her head, examining the animal. It was a stunning creature, dark brown all over with a black mane and tail. It was quite tall and its coat shone in the golden afternoon light. "Hello there." She stepped forward and stretched a hand through the fence toward it, her pulse racing. The animal nudged her hand with its nose, then looked immediately bored and turned away. No doubt it was hoping for a treat, but she didn't have anything edible on her except a pack of breath mints, and she didn't think a horse would appreciate those.

"I'll bet no one ever stole your job out from under you," she whispered, leaning against the fence and stepping up onto the bottom paling to drape her arms over the top. She watched him graze beside her, admiring the muscular curve of his neck and the way his lips grabbed at the grass and pulled.

She stepped down and continued along the driveway, heading away from the ranch. She could see Eamon and Parker in the distance. Eamon's pickup was parked on the grass, and he appeared to be hammering something while Parker fussed with the fence. A black dog followed them back and forth wherever they went.

Her heart skipped a beat as she watched Eamon. His shirt sleeves were rolled up and she could see the outline of sweat around the neck of the checked shirt.

His jeans fit a little too tight and his cowboy hat and boots had seen better days. His sun-bronzed skin almost glowed under the changing light of the setting sun. She felt her cheeks warm and her lips tingle at the memory of their kiss.

She ducked her head and continued on her way. A group of foals frolicked alongside the driveway in yet another field, dashing between their mothers. A chestnut foal nipped at a bay one, while a black one kicked up its heels with a snort. She laughed out loud and stopped a moment to watch them. They were so innocent, so full of life and energy. She missed feeling that way. She'd felt it briefly as a child, until the pressures of school – and her parents' expectations – landed on her small, thin shoulders.

Then she'd bowed to the altar of achievement and never looked back. She'd done everything right, everything she'd been told to. She'd studied hard, gotten good grades, won a place at the University of Georgia, then Harvard Medical, then the coveted internship at the Brigham. And now … now what?

Yes, she'd likely be able to apply again during the next round, or maybe even get something sooner. But the bloom had worn off the rose. She was exhausted. And when did it end? When did she get to stop running on the treadmill and look back on what she'd achieved with a sense of satisfaction?

She sighed, then turned to walk back toward the house. She knew what she should do next – send out resumes and hope for the best. Maybe someone would still have an opening. She just hoped it wasn't too late. In the meantime, she'd have to tell her parents what had happened.

She dreaded hearing what they'd say. Father would

be blunt, telling her exactly where she'd gone wrong, and how it would impact her career and life forever. Mother would passive-aggressively comment on her friends' or cousins' successes while carrying an injured look on her round face that insinuated a great tragedy had befallen the family. She grimaced and wrapped her arms around herself. Well, she wouldn't put up with it this time. She'd done nothing wrong – the system had failed, not her.

Perhaps she wouldn't even call them … at least not immediately. She sighed as a weight lifted. Yes, she'd enjoy her vacation, and worry about the future and what her parents might venture to say on the subject later.

Wrinkling her nose, she started to jog. The ground was uneven, and her knees bumped against each other. She chuckled at how uncoordinated she no doubt looked from the outside, but what did it matter? There was no one there to see her. And anyway, it was high time she gave up caring so much about other people's opinions.

With a whoop, she accelerated her pace until she was sprinting along the driveway. A group of chickens flapped their wings and ran from her path with loud squawks, startled by her sudden burst of speed. She laughed and turned to watch their bobbing heads and disgruntled cries, just as her shoe hit a stone in the path. Her right knee bent awkwardly and her ankle twisted. She fell in a heap on the driveway, clutching her ankle with both hands.

Pain shot up her leg, and she gasped. She hadn't heard a snap and didn't think from the angle of her fall that she was likely to have broken anything. She bit her lip and palpated the ankle and foot, searching for anything out of place. She groaned as she discovered a tender spot just beneath the ankle bone. Likely she'd just strained a tendon. She tried to stand, but cried out with the pain as it flared up the moment she put weight on her right foot.

The pounding of footsteps on the driveway made her look up in surprise. She squinted into the glow of the sun and saw Eamon heading her way. He stopped and knelt beside her. "You okay?" he asked, his blue eyes compassionate.

She nodded. "Yeah, I think I just sprained my ankle. I'll be fine."

The dog nudged her with its nose, then stepped back to study her, panting hard. Eamon chuckled. "Sorry, that's Harley. He's Hazel's dog, but since she's away he's taken to following me around. He's harmless." He rested a hand on her arm. "Let me help you."

Her skin tingled beneath his work-worn palm. Why did he have to be so *hot*? She'd made up her mind to steer clear of him, but here he was, making her quiver with just one touch. She'd never met anyone like him before. All the doctors, nurses and physiotherapists she'd dated in the past were good men – intelligent, committed to their work. Good matches. But they'd never made her feel like her heart might burst from her chest if they came any closer, like Eamon did. "Um … no need. I'm sure I can limp back to the house."

He grinned, the lines at the corners of his mouth deepening and his eyes sparkling. He always seemed to be laughing at her, in a teasing kind of way. "Okay. Well, I'm here if you need me." Even his voice made her pulse race.

Her eyes closed, she tried to stand again … and the

pain landed her on her rear, grimacing. "Yeah, I think I do need you, actually," she replied, gritting her teeth at more than just the pain.

Eamon raised an eyebrow. "Seems like you've hurt it pretty bad. Here, lean on me."

With a long, slow breath she looped an arm around Eamon's neck. When she stood, he stood with her, bearing the brunt of her weight on his shoulders. She hobbled forward on her left foot, the right one lifted just off the ground.

"You always like to be in control, huh?"

His question caught her off-guard. "What?"

"You didn't want me to help you. You act like touching me is the same as touching a leper. You don't like needing anyone, is that it? Or do you just dislike me specifically?" His eyes were narrowed, the earlier light-hearted banter gone.

"Well, you just have me all figured out, don't you?" she snapped, hobbling forward with more resolution than before.

He frowned. "Sorry. I guess it's a sensitive subject."

They stopped at the foot of the stairs leading up to the porch. She loosened her grip on him and took hold of the railing with both hands, her cheeks burning. "It's not a *sensitive subject* – I just don't like when arrogant cowboys think so highly of themselves that they believe their own press! Just because you're sexy and tanned and everyone loves you, you think you know everything. It ticks me off, that's all …"

Eamon's grin widened with each word from her mouth. She frowned, her eyes widening in anger, then turned and hopped up the stairs, pulling herself forward using the handrail. His laughter behind her spurred her on, and she muttered under her breath the entire way down the hall until she slammed the bedroom door shut behind her and collapsed onto the bed with a sigh.

Okay, perhaps she'd overreacted just a little bit. She was already so upset by the news about her job at the Brigham that she'd found herself in a rage before she even realized it was coming. She rubbed her eyes and groaned. What would he think of her now? She'd just made an absolute fool of herself over one little comment, as though she couldn't handle criticism. She sighed again and stared at the chipped paint on the ceiling above the bed.

There was a knock at the door. She sat up, her eyes wide, and smoothed her hair back into place. "Yes?"

The door opened. Eamon leaned against the jamb with that mischievous look on his face that never entirely went away. He flashed his dimples at her, then stepped into the room, holding his hands out in front of him. He held a bag of ice and an elastic bandage. "I come in peace," he said with a chuckle. "I thought you might need a bit of first aid."

She rolled her eyes and took a long, slow breath. "Thank you. After the way I yelled at you, I'm surprised you're even speaking to me."

"Is that an apology?"

She took the ice bag from him and pressed it to her ankle. "Yes, I suppose it is. Though, you did start it." She grinned and blushed as she met his gaze, then quickly returned her attention to ministering to her rapidly swelling ankle.

"You're right. I'm sorry as well – I shouldn't have said you were controlling. I mean, clearly you're nothing of the kind." He frowned and folded his arms.

Her eyes narrowed as she studied his face. Was that

his attempt at sarcasm? It sounded like it, but his expression seemed sincere. "I'm not. I'm just ... independent. Thanks for the ice and bandage."

"You're welcome." He came closer and squatted beside the bed, laying a palm on her ankle and covering her hand as it held the ice bag. "You sure you'll be all right?" His voice was soft, caressing and his eyes locked on hers.

"Yes, of course. I'm a doctor, after all ..."

He laughed. "Yes, you are. But, even doctors need help now and then." He stood and walked out, but as he was closing the door, he winked at her.

Emily's heart leaped into her throat. It was about time she went back to Boston, or else she might find herself in serious danger of falling for a cowboy from Georgia. She couldn't even imagine what her parents would have to say about *that*.

CHAPTER 4

*E*amon parked the tractor, turned it off and jumped to the grass below. He was finally done slashing hay. Dalton had decided to rotate grazing fields, leaving some to rest. He grew crops in a few of them and left others alone, giving them a chance to refresh for when the herd rotated back into them. Parker was still gathering the hay into stacks and would ride the three-wheeler back while Eamon finished up with the chores in the barn.

With Dalton gone, there was plenty to do around the place: chickens, hogs, cats and dogs to feed; foals to tend to; expectant mares to check on. And even though he was tired, Eamon felt exhilarated. A year earlier he'd been a bored accountant in a high-rise in Chattanooga. Now, he was helping run a large working ranch that he and his brothers hoped would soon be one of the most successful horse ranches in Georgia.

He finished up feeding the foals and their mothers sheltering in the stables, then wandered back to the house. He was proud of what they'd achieved with the Cotton Tree Ranch – and of himself for managing while Dalton was away. He knew how nervous his brother had been over leaving him and Parker in charge, but already they were showing they were fully capable of doing what needed to be done.

He took off his hat and paused on the front steps, still unable to get the conversation with Emily earlier that day out of his mind. She'd been clear about the disdain she felt for him. He wasn't sure what he'd done to deserve it – perhaps it was that kiss after the wedding. Well, he couldn't take it back now, and in all honesty, he didn't want to. She might regret what happened, but he hadn't been able to think about much else while driving the tractor up and down the field.

It was a sign of the effect it had that the day after the wedding, he'd called Penny and ended things between them. Finally. He didn't think it right to have one woman invading his thoughts while he was still tied to another. Penny had taken it well – she told him she was just on her way out the door with Jed, his childhood best friend. Not that he could blame her – he should've known she wouldn't wait around for him to come back. He only wished he – or she – had broken it off sooner.

But even without Penny, it still didn't make sense for him to pine over Emily Zhu. She was leaving for Boston soon, and he'd likely never see her again.

Hmmm … when was she leaving? He'd expected her to be gone already. She didn't seem to be enjoying herself all that much at the ranch, so she'd probably leave sooner rather than later. He'd been under strict instructions from Hazel to take care of her friend and make sure she relaxed and had a good time, but it sure was difficult with her tendency to keep people at arm's length.

He grimaced, closed his eyes and took a deep breath. Well, there was nothing for it now but to go inside and face her. He took off his muddy boots and padded inside in his socks.

The drapes were drawn over the windows, leaving the living room in darkness save for the flash of the widescreen television Dalton had hung on the wall soon after he'd arrived. The house might be in dire need of a paint job, but he'd sure wasted no time investing in a state-of-the-art TV. Eamon grinned. There were some things the brothers agreed on without need for a discussion, and a good screen for watching sports was one of them.

When his eyes adjusted to the dim light, he saw Emily curled up on the couch, her cheek against the cushioned arm. She wore frayed jean shorts, a pink T-shirt, and the Ace bandage he'd given her wrapped tightly around her ankle. Her shiny black hair was pulled into a messy topknot, and instead of her usual frown, she looked relaxed, rested – cute, even.

His eyes narrowed and he crossed his arms over his thick chest. She seemed very comfortable there and he hated to disturb her. He grinned as she laughed at something on the screen, and even from across the room he could see the gleam of unshed tears in her eyes. He raised an eyebrow. What was she watching that would make her react like that?

He shifted to see the screen – it was a *Friends* rerun, apparently the one where Monica and Chandler were married. He loved the show himself, though he'd never admit that to anyone. His brothers wouldn't let him live it down. What he couldn't comprehend was how a hardened surgeon with a perpetual scowl could be laughing and crying over a decade-old rerun. She must be softer than she let on. His heart warmed as she rubbed her eyes, then wiped her cheeks with her fingertips.

A bang from the kitchen pulled her from her reverie, and she sat up with a gasp when she spotted Eamon watching her. He waved one hand and offered her a half-smile. *"Friends,* huh?" He wandered over to the couch and sat beside her.

In reaction she pulled her feet in, tucking them beneath herself. She ran her hand over her cheeks again, seeming embarrassed by their dampness. "Yeah, I can't help it. It's still the best show of all time, but it's been so long since I've seen an episode. There's a marathon on today, and since I can't really get around, I thought I'd just sit and watch. I hope that's okay."

She looked so vulnerable, with her moist brown eyes trained on him. "Of course. *Mi casa es su casa,* or something like that."

She laughed, and the sound warmed his heart. "Thanks."

Eamon grimaced. "So Parker's cooking in there, is he?"

"Yep."

He chuckled and rubbed his stubbled chin. "Oh. We may be ordering in, then." She smiled and let her legs relax, resting her feet against the side of his thigh. He liked how it felt, and gently laid a hand on her good foot. "How's the ankle?"

She didn't shrink away, but met his gaze. "It's sore, but I think it'll be okay. Thanks for asking."

"Are you heading back to Boston day after tomorrow?"

Her eyes clouded over and the frown returned. "Um ... I suppose. Do you mind driving me to the airport?"

He wondered what her reaction was about – was she upset he'd asked about her plans, or about the trip itself? Either way, he was curious. He wanted to know everything about her – especially why she'd stayed behind after the wedding. She didn't really know him or Parker, she wasn't from the area, and she had a big fancy surgeon's job up in Boston. No doubt she could afford to vacation anywhere she wanted. It seemed odd that she'd stay with strangers on a horse ranch.

But what did he know – when was the last vacation he'd taken? He really should think about having some time off when Dalton got back.

This was the first vacation Dalton had taken since he'd inherited the ranch. Eamon had teased Dalton before they left, saying they'd run out of things to do spending three weeks in a sleepy beachside town like Destin, Florida. With a wink, Dalton had assured him they'd manage somehow.

He grinned at the memory. He certainly envied his brother the opportunity to spend time in a beachside resort with the woman he loved. It sounded like paradise to him. Eamon had been a confirmed bachelor before he moved to Georgia – dating casually all over Chattanooga. He always told his brothers that he didn't have a type, all women were beautiful in his eyes, so he intended to spend time with as many as he could. Then he'd met Penny, and tried to make it work. But deep down he'd always known it wouldn't.

But over the last year with Dalton and Hazel at the

ranch, Eamon had come to appreciate what they had –
much more than the simple attraction he usually felt
for the women he dated. They had a partnership,
chemistry, love – they were a team. He wanted that,
wanted a soulmate to spend his life with. The thought
almost made him laugh out loud – he'd never considered himself such a romantic. Who'd have thought
Eamon Williams would be looking for true love?

Another clang in the kitchen made his eyes narrow.
"Um … I think I should check on Parker before he
burns the place down." Reluctantly he stood, his hand
still tingling from her touch.

She nodded and turned back to face the TV screen.

Eamon took a slow breath as he traced the outline
of her profile with his eyes. True love might be real, or
it might not – he still hadn't decided one way or the
other on that matter. But if it was real and it was
something he could aim for, he sure would do his best
to find it.

EMILY'S EYEBROWS rose as banging and laughter
emanated from the kitchen. Ever since Eamon went in
there, it had sounded like the brothers had joined the
circus and were rehearsing their act rather than
preparing a meal.

Eamon's head popped through the swinging door.
"Supper's ready," he announced with a grin. A dish
towel was slung over his shoulder and the front of his
shirt was spattered with something red. She hoped it
wasn't blood.

She lurched to her feet with a groan. "Everything
okay in there?"

"Yep. All good." He hurried to help her, slipping his arm around her waist and sending a flash of electricity through her.

With a good deal of hobbling she made it to the kitchen table and sat down, setting her wounded ankle in front of her with a grimace. "So what's all the noise been about?" she asked, eying the messy kitchen with suspicion.

Parker hurried toward her with a bowl, his face flecked with what looked like tomato juice. "I made Brunswick stew," he said. He placed the bowl in front of her with a flourish.

"Oh? What's Brunswick stew?"

"It's a Southern dish," Eamon explained. "You never had it when you lived in Athens?"

"No. I didn't … I mostly stuck to the college basics. You know, pizza, Chinese food, burgers, sushi."

"Well, you're in for a treat. Brunswick stew is a Southern specialty you have to try at least once in your life," said Eamon.

"Well, it's my first attempt, so don't let it put you off trying the good stuff," added Parker, his hands on his hips and eyes glowing. "There's a joint down town called *Oinkers* – we'll have to take you there for the all-you-can-eat ribs before you fly home."

Emily studied the bowl of what looked like some kind of meat, corn, onion and tomatoes all mixed together. "Thank you."

Parker nodded and returned to the counter to get stew for himself and Eamon, then set their bowls on the table and hurried to open the oven with a mitt.

"What's that?" asked Emily.

"Cornbread."

"Did you get jalapeños?" asked Eamon.

Parker nodded. "In the fridge."

"Jalapeños?" Emily couldn't imagine how they might compliment stew and cornbread.

Eamon grinned, his dimples deepening and eyes sparkling with mischief. "Of course. Jalapeños make everything better."

Emily rolled her eyes. "Shoot, could you guys get any more masculine?" she asked with a chuckle.

Eamon leaned forward, his eyes flashing. "I'm sure I could arrange for a demonstration."

"Now, Eamon, behave yourself," admonished Parker, setting the jar of jalapeños on the table. "Don't mind him, Emily. He was raised by a wonderful Southern lady, but never seemed to learn any manners."

Eamon sniffed and set his elbows on the table. "I've got manners coming out my –"

"Would you look at the time?" interrupted Parker. "I guess we'd better bless this food and get to eatin'."

Eamon tipped his head to the side, studying her and her cheeks warmed. She wasn't going to let him intimidate her. She returned his stare with confidence, only betrayed by her ever-reddening cheeks. Finally, he grinned and broke their connection to close his eyes. "Father in Heaven, thank You for this food and company. Thank You for the cook, and we pray Your protection and blessings over Dalton and Hazel. In Your holy name, amen."

Emily watched him throughout the prayer, her eyes widening. She hadn't realized Eamon had a faith, though she supposed she shouldn't be surprised – they were in the Bible Belt, after all. When it was over, she took her first taste of the stew. It was too hot to discern any flavors, but the second sip danced across her taste buds, awakening them with vigor, and she grinned. "It's delicious, Parker."

He smiled and offered her the cornbread. "Try it with some of this."

She took a piece and watched Parker dunked his in his stew. She followed his example, bit off a piece, and her eyes widened. It was earthy and tasty and comforting at the same time.

"Sure was a hot one today," said Eamon, turning to Parker. "We'll have to check on the new foals and their mommas in the barn, make sure they have enough water to last through the night before we turn in."

Parker nodded. "Yep. Summer has definitely arrived."

"Thank goodness for air conditioning," added Emily, dunking her cornbread in her stew again.

Eamon and Parker nodded their agreement, both chewing thoughtfully. "Hey bro, don't forget the vet is coming in a couple days to check out the new foals," Parker continued.

"I know, I know. Dalton reminded me three times as well."

Parker chuckled. "He sure seems convinced we're gonna destroy the place while he's gone. Doesn't seem to have much confidence in our abilities."

Eamon raised an eyebrow. "Yeah. Well, let's just make sure we do everything even better than he would've if he was here. The last thing we need is for him to come back sayin' *I told you so*. We can run this ranch – I mean, heck, we've been here a year already. It's about time he trusted us with it."

Just then, the usual whir of the air conditioning fell silent. "What just happened?" asked Parker, looking toward the ceiling.

Eamon frowned. "That was the HVAC. Dalton said it was on its last legs, and I guess that was its final breath. Must have heard us say its name and gave up the ghost." He continued to eat, seeming unfazed.

Emily frowned in puzzlement. What was he saying?

"So no more air, then?" asked Parker with a shrug.

"No more air," replied Eamon. He grinned at Emily, then reached for another piece of cornbread.

"For how long?" she asked, her eyes widening. The thought of spending a swampy Georgia summer day without A/C on top of everything was almost too much.

"I guess until this number cruncher figures out how to fix it," replied Parker with a chuckle, jerking a thumb at Eamon.

"Is the HVAC that big gray boxy thing by the back door?" asked Eamon, his brow furrowed.

"What?" gasped Emily.

Parker dramatically slapped a hand to his forehead. "We're doomed."

But Eamon laughed. "Just kidding."

CHAPTER 5

*E*mily tossed and turned on top of her covers, sweat running down her face onto her already-damp pillow. She'd barely slept a wink all night, it had been so hot. Humidity was a killer in south Georgia – she'd only managed it so far by mostly staying inside the house. But with the A/C broken, she was experiencing the full effects – nothing between her and 96% humidity. Ugh.

She groaned and sat up on the edge of the bed, her ankle throbbing when her foot touched the ground. She'd had no Tylenol since the previous afternoon, and she could feel it. But it didn't hurt too badly, so she knew the swelling and bruising would go down soon enough and that she hadn't done any long-term damage. Much to her relief – since surgeons had to spend hours a day on their feet. An ankle injury could cause no end of pain and discomfort in her field.

She dressed slowly, grimacing as she pulled on a pair of khaki shorts. Her entire body was coated in sweat – perhaps she should take a cold shower after breakfast. She'd had one before bed, and it seemed to be the only way to beat the heat – that and ice cold drinks on the porch when there was a hint of a breeze, which was rarely.

A glance at her laptop on top of the bureau beside the bed reminded her of her jobless state. She really should spend the day sending out resumes, perhaps somewhere in town with some air conditioning. Maybe she'd even purchase that tub of ice cream she'd been craving.

She brushed her hair, massaging her weary scalp with each stroke. It felt good to take her time with small tasks – she hadn't done that in so long. Even brushing her hair had been a rush, usually pulling it out of the way into a tight ponytail. It was getting long, almost to her waist, since she rarely visited the hairdresser.

She stood and limped down the hall and into the kitchen. Eamon and Parker were already there, empty cereal bowls in front of them. Both had iPads in their hands, and Eamon's feet were resting on the chair across from him. He saw her and sat up straight, setting his feet back on the ground with a grin. "Mornin'. How'd you sleep?"

She grunted and headed for the coffeepot.

"That good, huh?" asked Parker, with a chuckle.

"It's just so stifling," she complained as she poured herself a cup. She was going to need caffeine.

"Welcome to the South," murmured Eamon, using a finger to scroll through whatever he was reading.

"Did you hear about the earthquake out in California?" asked Parker, setting his iPad on the table.

"Yeah – not too bad, I guess," Eamon replied.

"Doesn't seem like anyone was hurt. 'Course, the wild-fires around L.A. can't help the situation."

Parker shook his head. "Why anyone would live in California is beyond me."

"Nicer weather," Emily grumbled, reaching into the freezer to grab a few ice cubes for her coffee – there was no way she could drink it hot. If the brothers didn't get the A/C fixed soon, she might be tempted to crawl into the freezer herself.

* * *

EAMON TURNED THE KEY, and the pickup's engine rumbled to life. He set his hat on the center console and secured his seat belt, then turned to look over his shoulder, preparing to reverse. He jumped at the sound of a bang on the hood, and threw the truck back into park with a frown. "What the …?"

Emily came to his window with a smile that made his heart skip. "Where are you going?"

His eyebrows lowered. "Just into town to get a few things."

"Can I come?" She hobbled around the front of the truck and opened the passenger door, sliding onto the seat before he could respond.

"Uh … okay. What exactly do you plan on doing in Tifton?" He waited while she buckled her seatbelt, then resumed his reverse turn onto the long driveway.

"Buy some ice cream. Plus I have to get out of that house – I'm going stir crazy. I never stay in one place that long, ever! Back in Boston, I went to work every day, and on my days off I went out with my running group, had coffee with friends, or attended conferences and seminars. I mean, I've been sitting around for four days now, and with my ankle the way it is I can't even go for a run. I have to do something! Not to mention this heat – I'm dying." She screwed up her face, her nose wrinkling.

He chuckled. "All right, then – ice cream it is. We can't have you losing your mind. Hazel would kill me." He was silent for a moment, watching her squirm. She glanced at him twice, then looked away with a sigh both times. What was going on with her?

Just as he was about to ask, she leaned forward and flicked on the radio. She fiddled around, switching between stations until she found one playing experimental jazz. To Eamon, it sounded like a bunch of instruments being thrown against the wall, but she laid her head back on the headrest and closed her eyes, a smile lingering on her full lips. He raised an eyebrow as a saxophone leaped between notes, seeming to hit every one but the right ones. This was how she relaxed? No wonder she was so tense.

"You like this stuff?"

She glanced at him, then nodded as her eyes drifted shut again. "Yep. Isn't it amazing?"

"It's … wow," he responded. "But if you really want to relax, you should try something like this." He switched to his favorite radio station, Hometown Country 107.5, and cranked up the volume. The sound of a banjo filled the truck.

Her eyes flew open and she clamped her hands over her ears. "Argh – too loud!" She reached for the volume and dialed it down.

Eamon laughed and winked. "Now, *that's* music." They halted at a four-way stop, and he grinned when he saw Emily bobbing her head along to Keith Urban. He pushed his sunglasses back up the bridge of his nose – even with the air conditioning in the truck blasting, it wasn't exactly cool.

Up ahead he saw the faded sign of Clancy's Bar, a few dusty cars already littering the gravel parking lot. Emily straightened in her seat and peered at it as they rolled past. "What's that place?"

"Clancy's, the local dive bar. Good crab legs, though." He combed his fingers through his hair, feeling the sweat soaking his scalp.

"Stop! Let's go there – I need a drink."

He frowned. "Isn't it a little early for a drink? Besides, I thought you wanted ice cream."

"No, it's the perfect time for a drink, actually. Maybe I'll see if they have some ice cream to float in it." She laughed.

He thought he heard an edge of hysteria in her voice, and didn't want to be the one to send her over the edge. Whatever was on her mind, maybe she just needed a chance to cut loose a bit. "Okay – we'll stop, then." He pulled over to the side of the road, then U-turned and drove back to the bar.

He parked the car, studying Emily's face with concern. What was she so worked up about? He didn't know her well yet, but he'd spent enough time with her to recognize when something was on her mind. Hazel said she was usually very calm, collected and driven, a surgeon who never let anything stand in the way of her success. So why was she still hanging around the ranch with no sign of leaving?

He put on his hat, stepped out of the cab and hurried around to her side of the truck. She'd already opened the door by the time he reached it, but he took the handle and pulled it all the way open anyway. "Howdy, ma'am." He touched his hat brim and grinned.

She raised an eyebrow and frowned. "I'm perfectly capable of getting out of a truck on my own."

His eyes narrowed. "I know, but this is the South. Down here we're expected to act like gentleman and treat ladies with deference. It's not an insult, it's a sign of respect." He offered her his hand, and she hesitated but took it. As he helped her from the truck, he noticed she flinched when her tender ankle touched down, and she kept her hand in the crook of his arm as they walked up the stairs and into Clancy's.

When they were seated at a booth, Eamon set his hat on the table, reached for a bowl of peanuts and cracked one open as he scanned the room. It was almost empty, of course – it wasn't even close to noon yet.

He noticed Emily studying him intently. "I'm sorry," she finally said, leaning back against the cushion behind her and crossing her arms. "I'm not used to men being gentlemen. Not just because I'm from up North, but because I've always worked hard, so the men I usually meet are colleagues. I also grew up in a Chinese-American household, and our culture is very different. I shouldn't have snapped at you."

He nodded. "Thank you. I appreciate the apology, and the explanation. Seems society doesn't want us men to be ourselves anymore. There's little room left in the world for cowboys these days."

Her eyes softened and she leaned forward, setting her hands on the table near his. "Well, if you ask me, the world would be a better place if there were more cowboys in it." She almost whispered the words and he felt his heart slam against his ribs.

The waitress, a woman with a short black pageboy and a nose ring, sniffed beside them. She held a notebook in one hand, her pencil poised above it. "What can I getcha?"

Eamon bit his lip. "Um … Coors in a bottle, please."

The woman turned to Emily with bored disdain. "And you?"

Emily's eyebrow arched. "Can I get a Beefeater martini?"

Eamon shook his head, suppressing a grin. The waitress sighed heavily.

Emily nodded. "Got it. I'll have a Bud Light, then."

The woman turned without a word and disappeared toward the bar, where the bartender stood polishing empty glasses with a towel. "Well, she was a barrel of laughs," said Eamon with a chuckle.

"My goodness – imagine if I'd asked for a Cosmo or a Long Island iced tea." Emily laughed – and in that moment she was the most beautiful woman he'd ever seen. Her face lit up and the worry disappeared from behind her eyes.

But by the time their drinks arrived, the anxiety was back, hooded behind a facade of cool. Eamon recognized it now – she couldn't hide it from him, not anymore. He took a swig of beer, reached for her hand and held it as he watched as her cheeks flushed. He softly stroked the back of it with his fingertips, but she pulled away to grip the bottle in front of her. "What is it?" he asked. "What's on your mind?"

She sighed deeply and let her eyes drift shut for a moment. "It's … ugh."

"What?"

"I hate even talking about it. I feel like such a failure, and if I say it out loud, that'll make it real. I don't want it to be real." She covered her eyes and rested her elbows on the table.

"Now you're making me nervous. What's going on?"

"You'll think I'm overreacting."

He twisted the beer bottle around in front of him. "Just tell me."

"I was supposed to start my new job in a week – general surgeon at the Brigham and Women's Hospital. But they gave the job to someone else – a department head's son, actually. They told me it was mine, then suddenly it wasn't, and I'd already turned down every other offer. So basically I'm unemployed."

She stopped, dropping her hands to the table and looking at him as if searching for some kind of confirmation of her failure.

He frowned and leaned forward to take her hand again, this time more firmly. "That stinks. It really does. But it's not the end of the world." She tried to pull away again, but he didn't let her. "No, really. Listen, it's going to be okay. You'll get through this, you'll find another job, you'll be fine."

"You don't understand. By now, all the good jobs are taken – and my father … I haven't even told him or Ma Ma yet – I just can't deal with …" She groaned and squeezed her eyes shut. "Oh, I'm so screwed."

His heart ached for her. "Emily, look at me." She did, and the hurt he saw in them made the ache grow. "You're not a failure. Is it a setback? Yeah. But no one who ever succeeded at anything did it without some kind of setback along the way. Usually more than one. You can handle this."

She frowned. "Did something like this ever happen to you?"

"Absolutely. I don't think you can have a career in any field without somebody leading you on, giving you false hope or passing you over for a relative or friend. It happens all the time. What really matters isn't what happens to you, but how you react to it. Leastways, that's what *my* dad used to say. Remembering his words always seems to help when I'm feeling low about something like that." He let his fingers wander over her hand, his own trembling at the contact.

She made a face, seeming to consider his words. "You're right. I can get through this, I'll be fine. In fact – I can't believe I was so upset over it. I mean, it hurts, don't get me wrong, and I still dread telling my parents. But maybe this is my chance to take a break and reassess. And I need a break, you know? I've been working so hard for so long, I don't even know what to do with myself. I mean, I'm going crazy after four days with nothing to do. That's nuts, right?" She laughed and shook her head.

He noted with concern that the hysteria was back. "That's right. You sound like you could really use a rest – a vacation even. Maybe this is exactly what you need."

"Yes, I think so." She seemed to be trying to convince herself.

He sighed. At least he knew what had her so worked up. She'd done her best to hide it, but she was wound tight as an eight-day clock. "How about we finish our beers and go get that ice cream?" He drained his bottle, stood and threw a few bills on the table.

She finished her drink and stood as well. "Ice cream sounds perfect."

Eamon looped his arm around her shoulders and together they walked back to the truck. But his mind was racing with what she'd just told him. He couldn't help it – whenever someone he cared about was in trouble, he wanted to do something for them, wanted to make the problem go away. But this was one thing he knew he couldn't fix.

* * *

EMILY LIMPED DOWN THE HALLWAY, her stomach full of butter pecan ice cream. Eamon walked beside her, steadying her as pain shot up her leg with each step. They'd had a lovely time eating dessert downtown and soaking up air conditioning, and now she wanted to take a nap. She felt like she'd stepped into an alternate universe – drinking beer in the morning, eating ice cream for lunch, taking afternoon naps – and almost giggled at the thought. Who had she become?

She stopped at the door to her room and leaned against the door frame. "Thanks for the beer … and the ice cream."

He nodded. "You're welcome. Feel any better?"

"Actually, I do. I'm almost relaxed … though it's been so long, I'm not sure I recognize the feeling." She laughed at her own joke and stepped back, awkwardly bumping into the wall. She felt like a nervous teenager. Would he kiss her again?

He leaned closer, and she could feel the heat of his body against her skin, smell the beer on his breath.

"Well, I guess I'll see you later."

She nodded, her breath caught in her throat.

He turned and walked back down the hall and out the front door.

She exhaled and collapsed back against the wall. Why hadn't he kissed her? He'd been holding her hand, caressing her arm and flirting with her all day long.

Then he just walked away as though there was nothing between them.

She'd never understand men.

It was true, she hadn't dated much, and usually grew bored with the men she saw after only a few dates. But Eamon was different. Instead of being tired of him, every moment she spent with him seemed only to intensify her feelings. It was unexpected and intoxicating. And she hadn't thought about her job once since they left Clancy's.

Something had changed, and Emily was beginning to think that it had everything to do with a certain handsome cowboy.

CHAPTER 6

The HVAC unit looked like it was older than Eamon was. He sighed, lifted the lid from the unit and studied the engine, then reached for his tool belt. He didn't really know what he was doing, but he wasn't about to tell Parker or Emily that. A man had his pride.

The afternoon sun beat down on his head, and he wiped the sweat from his brow with the back of his gloved hand and squinted across the field behind the house. The horses were gathered beneath the few large shade trees on the other side, tails swishing at flies and heads hanging low. He grinned at the sight of them. Even when things got hard around the ranch, the beauty of the animals they cared for each day always brought a smile to his face.

There was something so special, regal, about horses. He'd always loved them and couldn't believe he now got to spend his time raising them on a ranch he owned with his brothers. It was more than he'd dreamed possible. Even though their first year

209

together had been tough and margins were tight, he could see that before long they'd be on their way to profitability.

He turned back to the task at hand, just as Parker appeared around the corner of the house. He knelt beside him and rested a hand on the engine with a frown. "How's it going?"

Eamon managed a sardonic smile. "Oh, great."

Parker laughed. "You have no idea what's wrong with it, do you?"

"I'm sure I can figure it out. After all, we can't let Dalton think we couldn't handle things, can we?" He peered into the open unit, examining various coils and wires.

"No, we can't. But maybe we could hire someone to help us out – you know, a professional?"

"But where's the fun in that?" Eamon chuckled. "Seriously, though, we might have to, but I'm hoping we can save the expense by doing it ourselves."

Parker nodded, then rubbed his face with a groan.

"What's wrong?" asked Eamon, one eyebrow up.

"Nothing … it's just … I've got to tell you something."

Eamon took a deep breath. It seemed everyone wanted to come clean to him today. "Yeah?"

"Well, you know how I … I'm not sure how to say it."

Eamon sat and leaned his back against the HVAC unit, stretching his legs in front of him and crossing his feet at the ankles. "I've got all day. Take your time."

Parker half-smiled and sat beside him, sighed and let his eyes drift closed. Only now did Eamon see the large black circles beneath his eyes, and his chest ached at all his brother had likely been through but never spoken of. He'd been so excited about becoming an Army Ranger, but Rangers had to do and see things most people didn't – and no person should have to.

Parker's eyes opened again and he focused on the herd in the distance, pinching the bridge of his nose. "I've decided to see a psychologist." His voice was solemn.

Eamon's eyes followed his brother's gaze, and he watched the horses laze beneath the shade trees, the younger ones nipping playfully at each other. "Oh yeah?"

He'd wanted Parker to get help for whatever was bothering him for so long, he felt like cheering with relief. Instead he bit his tongue and waited for Parker to go on.

"Yeah. It's been hard, being back stateside. And the things we did … I need to talk to someone about it."

Eamon picked a blade of grass and rolled it between his fingers. "You can always talk to me."

"No, I can't really, not yet. You and Dalton – you're home to me, and I don't want to bring that stuff home. Does that make sense?"

Eamon nodded and took a long, slow breath. He wished he'd realized the reason for his brother's reticence sooner. He'd been worried Parker didn't feel comfortable enough with him to really talk, and it was a relief to know that wasn't it. "It makes a lot of sense."

"So anyway, I called the VA this morning and made an appointment with her, the psychologist. And I think it's going to be good … helpful. I don't know if I'll ever be back to normal, but she told me I can find a new normal, whatever that means." Parker stood slowly and lifted his arms over his head with a yawn. "I haven't been sleeping well since I got back. I really hope this'll help with that, and some other things …"

Eamon stood as well, put his hands on his hips and faced his brother. "I'm glad you're doing this, Parker. You've got your whole future ahead of you and I'm on your side. So's Dalton. We both just want to see you happy again. I hope you know that." He grinned. "We miss that high-pitched girly laugh of yours."

Parker did laugh then, and Eamon caught a momentary glimpse of the brother he used to know. The sight made his eyes water. Parker stepped over and threw his arms around him, thumping him on the back with one fist. "Thanks, bro."

Eamon returned the bear hug, his throat tightening. "Anytime."

Parker headed toward the house, but before he turned the corner, he glanced back over his shoulder. "Beer on the porch tonight?"

"You got it."

Eamon watched him leave, his head spinning. He loved his brothers more than anyone else in the world – except Mom, of course. Seeing Parker struggle had been difficult for him, and he knew Dalton felt the same way. They'd often talked about it, especially when Parker retreated to his room for hours on end or was particularly morose. They'd both wished he'd open up to them, but hadn't wanted to push the subject, afraid he might not take it well. They weren't sure just how precarious a place he was in emotionally.

Eamon smiled to himself and turned back to the HVAC unit, frowning as he squatted beside it. Now if he could just figure out how to fix that contraption, his day would be complete.

* * *

EMILY TUGGED on the end of the stick. Harley tugged back, sitting on his haunches, his eyes gleaming. She laughed and pulled again, but, tail wagging, he shook his head, yanking the stick from her grasp. Happy with his victory, he trotted off toward the barn with his prize between his teeth. "Hey, you cheated!" complained Emily, setting her hands on her hips and chuckling as the dog disappeared around the outside of the building.

She'd always loved dogs but had almost forgotten after living of years in condos and apartments and working such long hours. Spending time with Harley these last few days had reminded her. When she was a girl, her parents had brought home a cocker spaniel she'd named Goldie, and she'd enjoyed feeding her, grooming her and taking her for walks down the streets of their neighborhood. She'd loved that dog.

Maybe she should get a dog. She didn't know where she'd be working or living yet, but wherever she settled she could surely find space for a small one. They brought her so much joy, and she was sick of living alone – it was too quiet. She hadn't spent much time at home in recent years, so it hadn't really mattered. But she hoped now that she'd finished her residency, perhaps she'd find a job that gave her more time off, and maybe she could manage a pet. And a roommate. Perhaps even a social life. She shook her head and laughed as she walked toward the barn.

A whistle made her spin around to see Eamon and Parker on horseback, rounding up horses. The animals snorted, necks arched, and trotted forward in a group. A few tried to make a break for it, and a dark brown one kicked up its heels and shook its head at Parker before returning to join the rest of the herd. Eamon rode his golden mount around the herd, waving his hat behind them and whistling.

Emily walked to the paling fence by the barn, climbed up onto the bottom rail, leaned her arms on the top one and watched them with a wide smile. Horses were such graceful creatures, the way they moved, the muscles rippling beneath dazzling coats in the brilliant sunshine ... she couldn't take her eyes off them.

She'd never had much to do with horses before – her entire previous experience had been at Susan Wallerford's birthday party when she was eight. Susan had insisted they go riding, but Emily's horse had turned around halfway and galloped back to the stables, Emily clinging to the saddle for dear life. That scraggly, dull-coated beast had looked nothing like these magnificent creatures, their heads held high above strong necks.

Before long, all the horses were shut into the yards beside the barn, milling around the hay bales, buckets of molasses and salt licks. The air was full of the musky odor of horseflesh and manure, and the whinnies, snorts and the clomping of hooves in the dry dirt sang in Emily's ears. As one chestnut horse ran by where she was perched, Emily reached out and let her fingers skim the animal's satiny back. Its coat was hot beneath her hand, and she laughed as it shied away from her touch.

The pop and crack of wide tires on the gravel drive made Emily turn her head, and she raised a hand over her eyes to shut out the sun's glare. A black pickup crawled toward the house, bumping and jerking over the uneven ground. It stopped behind her, and a man stepped out, wearing a scruffy goatee, jeans and a button-down red-and-white plaid shirt. He smiled and waved.

She waved back and stepped down from the fence. "Hi."

"Hello there, I'm Will." He strode toward her, his hand outstretched, and she took it, shaking it firmly. "Ah, there's Eamon and Parker." He slipped between the fence rails and headed for Eamon, who tipped his hat. She heard them exchange pleasantries as Eamon dismounted to shake Will's hand.

Eamon took his horse by the reins and left the yard, making his way to where Emily stood. "Who's Will?" she asked.

"He's our vet. He's here to check out the foals for registration and do some immunizations." Eamon wrapped the reins around the fence and rested one foot on the lowest paling.

Harley trotted out of the barn and sat beside Emily, his head tipped to one side, one ear standing tall and the other cocked forward. "That dog is stalking you," said Eamon with a chuckle.

"Awww, he's so sweet." Emily scratched Harley's head and ruffled his furry ears. "He misses Hazel."

"Yep." Eamon removed his hat and combed his fingers through his sandy blond hair. "Do you have any pets? I mean I know you said *no way* to the kitten, but I thought maybe you had a goldfish or something."

"No, definitely not." She laughed.

"Why not?"

"Well, like I said before — I live in an apartment, and I'm never home."

"But you like animals, right?" His tone was casual,

but she could sense a deeper meaning behind his questions.

"Yes, I love them, actually. But I think it would be cruel for me to own any with the schedule I keep." She bent to pat Harley's side, and his tail wagged furiously. "This guy would be so lonely if he lived with me." Her heart ached at the thought. Had she chosen such a lonely path that even owning a pet was too much of a commitment?

Eamon smiled at her. "Sounds like you're a busy lady."

"Probably too busy." She laughed, and it sounded hollow, jaded. "I don't know … I've given so much, sacrificed everything for my career. And now I don't even know where it's headed. I was angry before, but now I just feel disappointed and tired."

She stood and stretched her arms over her head with a yawn. "See, I'm yawning."

"Do you like it? Being a surgeon?"

"I love it – it's the best thing in the world – but I'd really love if I could have a life as well. Maybe I'm asking too much." She chuckled and leaned back against the fence.

"I don't think that's too much. Might be just about right." Eamon's voice warmed her soul and she imagined for a single moment how it might feel to hear that voice every day of her life.

Emily smiled at her own imagination, wondering how she'd changed so much in such a short amount of time that she could daydream about spending her life on a ranch with a cowboy. But it felt like a dream she'd long forgotten. She felt a peace deep inside for the first time in so long it seemed strange. Her heart was ticking along at a normal rate, her veins weren't quivering with adrenaline, her mind was clear. Would it be so bad to live this way?

* * *

EAMON AND PARKER waved goodbye to Will, his black truck kicking up dust as it rumbled toward the main road. Parker opened the latch on the corral gate and Eamon ushered the herd back out into the field. They left in a rush, glad to be free again.

The men wandered to where Emily now sat, beneath the shade of the large oak that spread a canopy of branches over one side of the barn and part of the yard. She had a book in one hand, the other behind her head against the rough bark of the thick trunk. Harley lay at her feet, his head resting on his paws. His tail thumped the ground as Eamon grew near. "We thought we might go to town for lunch to celebrate," said Eamon, tipping his hat back. "Care to join us?"

Emily laid her book on the ground. He looked so handsome, his tanned face split by a wide white smile, his blue eyes sparkling beneath his black hat. Sweat made his shirt cling to his muscular chest. She grinned. "Sounds good. What are we celebrating?"

"We made it through foaling and registration. Will says we've got a great crop of foals for our first lot. Dalton was so worried we wouldn't be able to handle things while he was gone, so we're celebrating success and smooth sailing."

She raised an eyebrow. They still had two weeks to go before Dalton and Hazel returned – celebrating might be a bit premature.

"Okay." She stood and dusted the dirt and twigs from her shorts. "I'll just go freshen up."

After showering, changing clothes and fixing her hair, Emily found Eamon and Parker waiting for her by the pickup. They'd both changed into fresh shorts and T-shirts and combed their hair. She wondered if they'd usually do that to go into town, or if they were making a special effort.

In Tifton, Eamon parked in the street.

"I've got to get something at the pharmacy," Parker mentioned. "I'll meet you at *Oinkers* after." He wandered off.

Eamon nodded and turned to Emily.

"Actually, I need to go to the livestock store down yonder – do you mind? Oinkers is just there on the corner. You can come with me, or take a look around and meet us there, it's up to you."

Emily stuffed her hands in her shorts pockets with a shrug.

"Actually, I think I'll wander around a few minutes. I haven't spent much time in town."

As Eamon disappeared around the corner, she set off down the street, her hands linked behind her back. She stopped to peer in through store windows or wandered inside to check out their wares. Everywhere she went, people nodded or said hello, curiosity in their eyes. She smiled and responded in kind, soaking up the atmosphere. Tifton wasn't really a small town – but compared to places she was used to, it was sleepy and quaint in that charming way only small towns could manage.

She paused at a glass door next to a long-closed Blockbuster Video. The lettering on it read Tifton West Medical Center, General Practitioners," followed by three doctors' names. Inside was a cozy waiting room – a television hung just below the ceiling soundlessly played a cartoon. A few plush chairs lined one wall across from a reception desk where a woman with a red bob held a phone against her ear with her shoulder.

Then she spotted the sign – black marker on white printer paper – taped to the front of the desk. HELP WANTED – GENERAL PRACTITIONER.

Her eyes narrowed. She was looking for a job, but she wanted to be a big-city surgeon in a hospital with a stellar reputation, not a GP in a small-town practice in south Georgia. Still, her curiosity was piqued. She frowned, then pushed the door open.

An electronic bell chimed overhead and the woman behind the counter glanced her way, still speaking into the receiver.

The woman finished the call, and Emily walked up to the desk. She was suddenly aware of how casually she was dressed: no makeup, her hair in a ponytail, wearing khaki shorts and a plain T-shirt. She probably looked like she was twelve years old. Oh well.

"Hi."

The woman smiled and wrote something on a ledger in front of her before looking up at Emily. "Can I help you?"

"Yes, I was just wondering about the Help Wanted sign."

The woman arched an eyebrow skeptically. "Are you a GP?"

"Actually, I'm a general surgeon – I just finished my residency up in Boston. I came down here for a friend's wedding. And, well, I saw the sign and it made me curious. I'm not really trained as a GP and it's not what I was looking for, but …" She shrugged.

The woman smiled again. "I'm Jocelyn, but most people call me Joss."

"I'm Emily Zhu. Nice to meet you, Joss."

"You too, Emily. Well, let's see … the position *is* still available. It's only part-time – all the GPs here actually double-up at the hospital – but it's a paid position, and after twelve months the partners plan to review things to see whether or not it's still a good fit and whether you want to buy into the partnership. The partners are Joe Hamilton and Maria Suarez. Dr. Ramachandra just accepted a position in Atlanta, so he's selling them back his share. Does that answer your questions?"

"Yes, it does, thank you."

Emily pursed her lips. It sounded flexible, and there was a possibility of doing surgery at the local hospital at the same time. She loved the quiet feel here – she hadn't been this relaxed in years. What if she could live this way? What would Eamon think about her sticking around.

Then her heart lurched. What would her parents think?

"Here, why don't you take my husband's card, just in case? It's got our e-mail address and fax number on it, so you can send us your resume. It's a pretty great place to work, if you ask me, but then I'm probably biased since I'm married to the boss." Joss laughed.

Emily looked at the card, which belonged to Dr. Hamilton."Well, thank you. I appreciate it."

She headed back out onto the street, her pulse racing. What was she doing? Was she actually considering moving here? She didn't know anything about the place other than that it was quaint, hot and sleepy, and you could find a dive bar open at ten in the morning. But if she really needed a taste of the city once in a while, Atlanta and Jacksonville were only a few hours away …

She was getting ahead of herself. They might not even consider her for the job. She wasn't a GP, which would likely disqualify her … though Joss hadn't said so. She barely remembered her General Practice rotation – she'd been studying up on her surgical knowledge the whole time and hadn't paid as much attention as she should've. Still, it wouldn't take much to get her licensure as a GP. What would it hurt to apply?

She pondered it as she walked toward Oinkers, a seedy-looking establishment with a large faded sign of a cartoon hog swinging over the door. It declared itself a barbecue restaurant, and she remembered Parker saying it the best one around. She entered and frowned at the dirty floor, mismatched furnishings and dim lighting. This place didn't look like it would serve anything good. Then she took a sniff, and her mouth began to water.

The server led her to a corner booth where Parker and Eamon waited, each cradling a half-full Mason jar in one hand. Eamon nodded to her with twinkling eyes and an impressive display of dimples that made her head spin as she sat beside him. "Thought we might have to come looking for you, but Parker reminded me that it'd be hard for anyone to get lost in Tifton." He chuckled and took a sip of his drink.

The waitress, who looked to be seventeen at most, appeared by her side. She smacked gum between her teeth and rubbed her nose with the back of her hand. "Would you like a drink?"

Emily frowned. "Hmmm ..." She reached for one of the menus that lay piled in the center of the table.

Parker laughed. "No need for that – you have to try the sweet tea in a place like this."

"Okay, I'll have some sweet tea."

The girl nodded, then disappeared. "What did you get up to?" asked Eamon.

"Not much, just looking around. It's a cute town." Her pulse raced. He was so close to her, she could feel his warmth against her arm, could sense his nearness through the fabric of his shirt. She picked up a menu and began flicking through it, not even seeing the words in front of her. Her drink arrived and she hastily took a gulp. It was so sweet, her eyes bulged.

Eamon laughed. "Good. Huh?"

She took a second mouthful. "Very good, but I'm sure I'll go into a sugar coma before I finish the glass."

"Well, it wouldn't be Southern sweet tea if you didn't." His eyes flashed and she felt her cheeks burn.

"So are you heading home tomorrow?" asked Parker.

She blinked. Was she? She hadn't thought about returning to Boston in days. She didn't want to go, not yet. She had nothing to go back to, save an empty apartment with a dead potted plant on the counter. No Harley to wag his tail and follow her around. No noisy roommates. No family. And no job. "Um ... actually, do you mind if I stay a little longer?" She glanced sideways at Eamon.

His expression didn't change. "Yeah, of course. You're welcome to stay as long as you like." He exchanged a look with Parker.

Her face burned. "I'm sorry, that's an imposition. It's fine, I'll leave – you've got things you have to do."

"No, stay, please." Parker's voice was warm and sincere.

"Okay, thank you. I promise, it won't be much longer – I just have some things I need to work out." Emily could feel Eamon's eyes on her, as though he was trying to drill into her head to find out what she was thinking. Good luck to him – even she wasn't sure what she was thinking, except that she didn't know what she wanted. And until she did, she couldn't talk about it. She had to go home to Boston sometime, but perhaps she could postpone it a little longer and give herself a chance to think. Maybe even dream a little more.

*E*amon sipped the ice-cold glass of Coke and set it back down on the outdoor table. The afternoon sun warmed his back, and he scooted his chair forward into the shade of the porch roof. He leaned over the table, his finger running down a printout of the ranch's profit and loss statement, and sighed. Things were tight. Tighter than he would've liked.

The back door swung open and Emily stepped outside, wearing a long, flowing midnight-blue dress covered in small pink and yellow flowers. Her hair, freshly washed, hung damp down her back and her face glowed with health and vitality. She looked so much more alive than she had when he'd first met her, as though she was transforming into a confident, vibrant woman in front of his eyes. His body tingled at the sight of her. "Nice shower?" he asked, internally chiding himself over his lack of creativity.

She nodded and sat in a chair across from him. "What are you doing?"

He ran his hands through his hair and grimaced. "Looking over the accounts."

"Oh. That bad, huh?"

He chuckled. "Bad enough."

She smiled wryly. "Well, if it makes you feel better, I hate doing paperwork as well. I much prefer having a scalpel in my hand."

He feigned horror. "Not sure how I feel about that!"

She laughed, and slapped his arm. A bolt of electricity ran down his arm, and through his body, as her hand stopped and rested gently in place where it landed.

She'd seemed so frail, so lost, when she'd first arrived – beautiful but troubled. Now, though, she was almost a different person. He knew she'd lost her job and it was natural she'd be torn up about it, but maybe it was just what she needed.

"Emily, I …"

Parker banged through the back door, the screen whacking against the wall of the house. "There you are," he said, his face drawn.

Eamon stood and reached for his hat beside the paperwork on the table. "What's wrong?"

"Did you fix that boundary fence where the oak branch fell yet? We've got to get that done before nightfall."

"Uh, no – I was gonna do that after I looked over this paperwork."

Parker shifted the strap of his shoulder bag. "I totally forgot I have to head up to Macon to pick up a mare to be covered by Rocket Peak. I'm already running late – can you take care of everything else?"

"I've got it. You head on to Macon – we'll see you when you get back."

Parker ran down the steps and headed for the pickup, Eamon close behind. He helped his brother hitch up the horse trailer to the back of the truck, then waved goodbye as Parker rolled down the long drive. He'd forgotten about the mare as well … and the fence, to be honest. Too much of his mind was on a certain black-haired doctor. He had to get it back on making sure that the ranch ran smoothly until Dalton got back.

He walked toward the stables to fetch the three-wheeler. He had to fix that fence before dark, or the herd, which was all the way at the other end of the property now, might find the opening and get loose. Within a few minutes, he was racing toward the western fence line, the growl of the engine drowning out every other sound.

Afternoon shadows crept long across the grass as the sun headed toward the horizon. And Eamon's mind wandered back to Emily – the touch of her hand on his arm, the feel of her lips against his, the way her smile lit up her dark eyes …

He found the big oak, and the long low branch that had fallen in a thunderstorm the previous night and landed on the fence. It was the longest fence on the property, covering the entire western and south-western boundary lines. It was also one of the few remaining stretches of barbed wire on the property, and he shuddered at the thought of how much work it would be to replace it all with paling, the way Dalton planned for them to do. He pulled the three-wheeler to a halt and slid to the ground.

The branch was a big one. It would take a while to cut it up and remove it from where it lay, obstructing the fence line. Worse still, when he stepped around the tree's wide trunk, he saw Sassy, one of their mares, lying tangled in the fence. She raised her head to look at him, the whites of her eyes showing, then lay back on the ground with a long sigh, exhausted.

His heart fell – how long had she been there? He'd checked the fence early that morning, looking for damage from the storm – that's when he'd found the fallen branch. But she hadn't been nearby. At some point in the day she must have wandered away from the rest of the herd and gotten tangled. He'd kept a close eye on the horses to make sure that exact thing didn't happen, but somehow she must have evaded him.

He ran to her side and knelt on the ground, surveying the damage.

"There, there, Sassy, I've got you now. We're gonna get you out of here in no time. Hold on for me."

The wire was tangled around her legs and had punctured the skin, leaving a trail of blood across her limbs, chest and belly. He couldn't tell yet how badly injured she was – it might just be a few nicks, or it could be worse. He ran a hand over her side, murmuring words of encouragement all the while.

She raised her head again with a snort and thrashed around for a few seconds. Then lay still once again. While she moved, he stepped back out of the way, his face stricken. "Come on, girl, stop that. You're just making it worse."

When Sassy stilled, he hurried back to the three-wheeler and grabbed rope and wire cutters. He marched back to her side and knelt beside her with the cutters. He looped the rope into a makeshift halter, fixed it around her head, then set the loose end of it down. "Shhhh, now. I'm just going to cut this wire off you. Hold still …"

She kicked, catching him in the thigh with her hoof. He winced, took a deep breath, then continued working on the wire. Every time a barb dug into her flesh, she struggled again, but after the first kick he was ready and leaped out of the way.

Within moments, she was free. He pulled the wire back and she lurched quickly to her feet, eyes wide, snorting and gasping. He reached her in two strides and took hold of the rope dangling beneath her neck. With pats and more words of encouragement, he led her over to the tree, tying the rope around its thick trunk.

He sighed deeply and tipped his hat back to scratch his head. Now what? It was times like this he could really use Dalton's help. But he had to show himself – and Dalton – that he could handle whatever the ranch threw his way. Yes, he was an accountant by trade, but he was a rancher too now, and ranchers didn't always have the luxury of turning to someone else when things got tough. They had to act on their own.

Her wounds didn't look too deep, but you never knew with horses – their legs could be problematic. He remembered that from his youth spending time on a hobby ranch in Tennessee. His father hadn't ever wanted to run a working ranch, but they'd had property with horses, a few cattle and chickens. He hadn't spent all his time outside with the horses like Dalton had, but he'd picked up a few things.

And he knew this mare, like all their breeding stock at the Cotton Tree Ranch, was valuable. He couldn't risk her being injured or developing an infection.

He chewed his lower lip. Should he leave Sassy there? If her legs were badly injured, it wouldn't do her any good to walk her all the way back to the barn. And she was safe now.

He patted her again, then hurried to the three-wheeler. The engine started right away and he accelerated across the field, standing high over the seat to avoid being jostled too badly as he went.

When he reached the ranch, he ran past Emily, still seated on the porch. She was reading a book, and glanced up at him in surprise when he bolted past. He hurried to the kitchen, grabbed the phone and dialed the number for the vet, which was stuck to the side of the fridge with a Domino's Pizza magnet.

Will's receptionist informed him that the vet was out on a job and wouldn't be back in the office that afternoon. If it was an emergency, she said, he could call the vet over in Ocilla – they had a reciprocal arrangement. Eamon sighed and wrote down that number, thanked her and hung up. He rubbed his chin and closed his eyes.

The creak of the kitchen door made them fly open again. "Is everything okay?" asked Emily, resting her hands on top of a chair back.

"A mare's been injured along the western fence line – her name's Sassy. I'm trying to find a vet who can come check her out. I don't want to walk her back to the barn if something's wrong – it could make things worse." He put one hand on his hip and breathed deeply, his heart still racing from the exertion of getting back to the house.

"Can I help?"

He considered her offer. She was a doctor – maybe there was something she could do.

"But you're not a vet."

She shrugged. "True, but I could assess the damage, apply first aid, that kind of thing."

"Hmmm … you don't mind?" It would save time and money if she was able to take care of it. Even if they could just get the animal back to the barn, it would make things simpler. He'd still get the vet out, but wouldn't have to sweat the hefty emergency fee. And the way the ranch's accounts looked, every saving counted.

"No, I don't mind at all. It's not like I'm doing anything." She laughed and pushed her hair behind her ears.

"Okay, great. I've got some first-aid supplies for the horses in the barn. Just follow me." He left the kitchen, Emily close on his heels. He glanced back over his shoulder, realizing as he did that she was barely even limping now. "And thank you."

"You're most welcome." She grinned up at him and his insides melted.

* * *

SASSY STOOD STILL beneath the sloped branch of an enormous oak shadowing the fence line, her dark coat shining in its shade. Emily got out of the pickup, grimacing as her sore ankle touched down. The mare's head hung low, glancing their way as she and Eamon hurried over, but otherwise not moving. She looked to be favoring one of her hind legs.

"Hello there," she said, sliding a hand gently down the horse's shoulder.

Sassy stamped her front foot and turned to sniff Emily's hand. Emily had grabbed some carrots that were kept in a bucket in the barn as treats for the herd, and handed the mare one. The horse snapped it up and chewed eagerly.

Emily squatted beside the mare's injured leg and ran her fingertips down it. There were multiple lacerations on both hind legs and her hindquarters, but particularly the left leg. She pressed gently along the length of it, then examined the horse's front legs, and belly and found several other cuts, but nothing bleeding too badly.

She stood and pressed her hands to her hips. "I'll bandage up that hind leg and just put some antiseptic cream on the other lacerations. She was lucky – it doesn't look like she hit any major veins or arteries. And nothing seems to be broken, although you'll probably want to make sure with the vet when they come."

Eamon scratched his chin, then strode to the truck for the first-aid supplies. Emily was grateful he and his brothers kept such a good stock on hand for times like this. She helped Eamon carry the items over to Sassy, and then ministered to the animal's wounds as best she could. "Some of these cuts need stitches, but I can fix them up back at the barn. I've got my medical bag with me – I'll need to sterilize my instruments, but I'm happy to do it if you'd like me to."

He nodded enthusiastically. "Thanks, that'd be great."

Emily drove the pickup back to the barn and began preparing everything she'd need to finish working on the mare while Eamon slowly walked the mare back. As she watched them approach the barn, she was relieved to note that the mare no longer appeared to be limping or favoring the injured leg as much as she had at first. The anesthetic cream must have taken effect.

By the time she'd finished stitching up the wounds, Emily's back ached and her neck was cramped. She wasn't used to working in a hunched-over position like that. She stood and stretched her arms high, rolling her head from side to side to loosen her tight neck muscles.

Eamon patted Sassy's side affectionately. "All done?"

"Yes, all done. I've stitched the lacerations that needed it and bandaged them. Other than replacing the bandages regularly, she should be all taken care of."

Eamon stepped closer. "Thank you."

"You already thanked me." Emily swallowed. It suddenly felt hotter in the barn.

He took another step forward, making her shiver. "I'm thanking you again."

"No need ..." She cleared her throat, her eyes locked on the small patch of blond hair sprouting just above his top shirt button. Her gaze drifted upward and over his full lips, slightly parted, finally resting on blue eyes that were flecked with gold and brown. He was staring at her. She swallowed again as her heart thudded.

His hand brushed against her arm, setting the small hairs on end. Then his fingers closed around her hand and he raised it to his lips, his eyes still fixed on her.

"What are you ...?" She didn't get to finish, as he closed the gap between them and pulled her to him, his eyes full of fire.

His lips met hers, and sent a bolt of heat through her. Her eyes closed and she moaned. She hadn't been kissed like that ... ever. Her hands found his hard back muscles and worked their way up to his neck as she stood on tiptoe to lean deeper into the kiss.

The world spun around, every thought in her over-active mind dissolving. She didn't want to think, only to be. And to feel like this forever.

*E*mily rested her elbows on the kitchen table and rubbed her tired eyes. For the past two hours she'd been sending resumes to every hospital she could think of, and now she could barely see straight. She was used to hours in front of her laptop after so many years of study, but had barely touched it in the two weeks since she'd arrived at the Cotton Tree.

Was it really two weeks already? She smiled at the realization – she could already see a difference in herself. When she'd looked in the mirror that morning after her shower, she'd seen plumper cheeks, brighter eyes, skin fairly glowing with health. She felt more like herself than she had in years. It seemed all she'd needed was some rest and good old Southern cooking.

She snapped the laptop shut and stood with a yawn, stretching and letting the tension of being seated in a hard chair so long work its way out of her neck and shoulders. With a sigh, she carried her empty water glass and crumb-covered breakfast plate to the sink, rinsed them off and set them in the dishwasher. After drying her hands, she wandered out to the porch. Her ankle was back to normal – she could walk comfortably without even a twinge, and had gone for a short jog the previous day with no ill effects.

Parker was in the pasture with the prize stallion, Rocket Peak, whom she'd taken to visiting with a carrot or handful of oats every morning. A new mare had arrived that morning and Parker led her into the field, then slipped the lead from her halter before stepping back toward the gate. Rocket high-stepped over to greet her, his muscular neck arched and rippling in the bright morning sunshine. She laughed as the mare snorted at the approaching stallion, then turned her back on him and made a display of kicking a hoof at the green grass. He shied away, then moved toward her again and stretched out his nose to touch hers.

Emily skipped down the porch stairs and across the yard to where Parker stood, his arms leaning on top of the gate to watch the interaction. She climbed up beside him and rested her arms on the gate as well. "Morning, Parker. How's it going?"

He glanced her way with a smile, then tipped his hat back further. "Good morning Em. It's going well so far, I think. He's got his work cut out with this one." He chuckled as the mare nipped at the stallion, sending him into retreat once again.

Harley trotted out from behind the house, his nose and one side of his body coated in mud. He ran over to Emily and pressed his nose against her leg, leaving a dirty trail across her thigh. "Ugh! Harley!" She jumped back, but the dog followed. Thinking it was a game, he leaped up with bright eyes to press his feet on her shirt, his tongue lolling out the side of his mouth.

"Harley, down!" commanded Parker, suppressing a laugh as Emily tried desperately to brush the mud from her shirt and thigh. "You spoil him. He'd never get away with doing that to Hazel."

Emily sighed, but couldn't help laughing at the same time. No matter what he did, she just couldn't stay mad at that dog, with his floppy ears and mischievous sparkling eyes. She could swear he was grinning at her too.

"Hey, thanks for your help the other day with Sassy," Parker continued. "The vet says she's all good, and he admired your handiwork with the stitches – said he'd never seen better." He looped a rope around his arm, tying the end around the loops to hold them in place, and set off toward the barn.

Emily fell into step beside him. "You're welcome. Actually, it was kind of fun. It's been a while since I've enjoyed medicine – even if I was treating a horse. I've been so stressed that I'd forgotten how much I like it. I'm actually looking forward to getting back into my scrubs. Whereas before …"

"You just wanted to hide?" asked Parker, eyebrow raised.

"Yeah. How did you know?"

"Oh, I recognize the feeling." He smiled ruefully.

Emily heard tires crackling on the gravel driveway, turned to see Eamon's pickup curving toward the house, and her heart skipped a beat. She shoved her hands into her shorts pockets and hunched her shoulders as she wandered over to greet him. Just being near him made her pulse race and her ears buzz with adrenaline. She swallowed hard and tried in vain to calm her breathing.

Eamon parked the vehicle, climbed out and pulled

two bags of groceries from the bed of the truck. She waved, and he nodded in response, setting the groceries on the ground. When she reached him, he put his arms around her waist with a hint of a smile, then leaned forward to kiss her. When he pulled away she grinned, her cheeks burning. "Can I help?"

He grinned too, leaned down and handed her a bag. "Thanks."

Over the past two weeks, things had changed between them. The intensity of her attraction to him had grown each day, and he'd taken to walking with her hand in his, holding her and kissing her whenever he felt like it. She wasn't sure where things were headed between them, but each day felt like an adventure she didn't want to miss.

She still hadn't booked her return flight to Boston. It was always on the edge of her thoughts – she had to go home, had to face her parents sometime. They were currently in Europe on vacation, so they might not have noticed her lack of communication. In truth, she was avoiding them – avoiding everything.

Including telling Eamon about the job in Tifton. She knew she should, but the timing never seemed right. She'd sent them her resume too, even while thinking nothing would come of it – but they'd had her in for an interview and offered her the position on the spot. Dr. Hamilton, the senior partner in the practice, was a man in his fifties with kindly eyes and an open, friendly face, so different from the department heads at the Brigham. She'd asked for a few days to think it over, and he'd agreed.

She wanted to accept the position ... but her stomach churned at the thought of having to tell Eamon, Hazel and most of all her parents. And she'd kept sending out her CV hither and yon – once again, avoiding.

Her thoughts spinning, Emily followed Eamon inside and set the groceries on the kitchen counter. While he brought in the rest of the bags, she stowed his purchases in the fridge and pantry. It felt good to be doing something simple that didn't require any thought. It made her heart sing that she could allow herself to just be without focusing on achieving. She knew that sooner or later she'd have to make some decisions, but right now she was happy to leave it until later.

"I thought I might get started on dinner," he said, setting the last bag on the floor. "I was going to work on the HVAC, but it's too late really …"

She laughed. "You mean, you don't want to work on the HVAC."

He rolled his eyes and flashed his dimples. "Yeah."

"Maybe it's time you called in help."

"What, you don't believe in me? I'll fix it … I just have to …"

"Figure out what on earth the big gray box is for?" She smiled and set a jug of milk in the door of the refrigerator, then pushed it shut.

"Hey! I know what I'm doing … or at least I will as soon as I sort out just what the spring thingy is supposed to do." His eyes twinkled and he pushed himself up to sit on the counter, his feet swinging free beneath him. He reached for Emily, caught her by the waist and tugged her closer until she stood between his hanging legs. With soft fingertips he looped strands of her hair behind her ears and caressed the side of her face.

"All joking aside, I do believe in you. I also believe

there's no shame in bringing in an expert when you're in over your head." She kissed him boldly on the lips.

He laughed, his eyes full of intensity. "Okay, okay, I'll call someone. I just hope it's something easily fixed – and cheap. Hey, come back," he groaned in complaint.

She pulled back anyway and pinched the bridge of her nose to clear her thoughts. "Eamon, there's something I have to talk to you about. You know how I lost that job at the Brigham?"

He nodded, watching her closely. "Yeah …"

"Well, I found another job."

His eyes lit up and he smiled brightly. "Awesome! I knew you would. Where is it?"

She paused. What would he say when she told him? He'd think she was moving here to be with him, no doubt, and probably freak out, thinking she was the clingy type who'd move across the country because of a few stolen kisses. But that wasn't it … or not entirely. She wanted this job because being here made her feel warm, at home. Peaceful.

"It's in Tifton."

His eyes narrowed in confusion and his smile wavered. "What do you mean?"

"I've been offered a position as a GP at a practice in town. I'll be working as a surgeon at Tift Regional Medical Center as well – they tell me I can split my time between the two."

His eyes widened and he slid from the counter, his hands landing on his hips. "Oh wow! I didn't know you were looking for something like that."

"I wasn't – I sort of tripped over it, the morning before we ate at *Oinkers*. There was an ad for the position at the GP's office, and I sent my resume in. I wasn't serious at first – I mean, I still haven't told them I'll take the job. But being here has given me time to think, and I know I don't want to go back to working the way I was – constantly, no breaks, no vacation, no rest. I was stressed all the time – you saw the way I was when I got here …" She laughed nervously.

He nodded and combed his fingers through his hair. "Yeah, you were wound pretty tight."

"And I don't want to be like that again. I want to take time to smell the roses. I can't remember the last time I enjoyed life before coming here, and I hadn't even realized it until I got here and slowed down and gave myself a chance to think. I promise, I'm not stalking you …"

He frowned and studied her face. What was he thinking? It was so hard to tell.

But finally he grinned, stepped forward and wrapped his arms around her. With his lips hovering just above hers, she could smell his musk and admired the crinkles at the corners of his eyes. He took a long, slow breath before saying,

"I don't mind you stalking me. Just an FYI – you can stalk me any time."

She threw her head back and laughed as her fears dissipated, then rested her cheek against his chest as he stroked her hair. She could hear his heartbeat though his shirt, and the sound flooded her soul with peace. "So you think I should accept?"

"Of course I do. Are you gonna be living in Tifton, then?"

She nodded. "I should probably start looking for a place this weekend."

"Would you like me to help."

She leaned back to see his face. Counting the tiny

freckles across his nose could become her new hobby. "That would be great. I could really use your local insights." She chuckled and raised a hand to brush his cheek, reveling in the feel of day-old growth beneath her fingertips.

"Well, you don't want to pick something down by the river, trust me. Midges are not your friend."

"See, that's the sort of advice I need – real estate agents are likely to sell me on something with midges, rats and backing onto a construction site, and I wouldn't even know it."

He laughed. "That wouldn't do." He kissed the tip of her nose. "Hey, how about we get started on that supper."

She frowned. "What? I thought you were cooking supper. Now it's we? What are you trying to do – make me learn how to cook?"

"I hadn't considered it. Though of course it would be nice if my girlfriend could cook me a meal occasionally, not just the other way around. I mean, what if I get sick, or injured? Who would feed us?"

Girlfriend. The word sent a shiver of delight through her. Never had such a simple word sounded so delicious.

Her cheeks flamed and she ducked her head with a chuckle. "Well, in that case … hand me an apron."

He laughed and reached into a cabinet to get one for each of them, while she pulled her phone from her pocket and scrolled through it for some music to play while they cooked. She connected it to the Bluetooth speaker in the kitchen, and within moments Taylor Swift's "Shake It Off" blared through the room.

Eamon flinched, smacking his head on the top of

the cabinet door as he pulled two aprons out. "Ow!" He rubbed the back of his head ruefully.

She took one apron and put it on, tying the string carefully around her waist. "You okay?"

"Yeah, it's just that awful noise."

"What? Come on…"

"I'm sorry – my kitchen, my music." He lunged for the phone.

She struggled to keep hold of it, but his arms closed around hers, holding her in place while he attempted to wrench the device free of her grasp.

"Hey, stop that! You're out of line, Mr. Williams!" she shouted between giggles.

Finally, he yanked it free and raised it high in victory, his eyes shining. He turned his back to her and the music stopped, soon to be replaced by Trisha Year-wood. "That's better."

She groaned and slapped a hand over her eyes as she realized which song he'd picked – "She's in Love with the Boy." "Come on, really?"

He faced her grinning, his hips gyrating to the beat of the song. He laughed as he faced her and offered her his hand. When she took it, he spun her beneath his arm and she collided into his chest with a gasp. They danced in a slow embrace as the country song surrounded them, aprons pressed together and eyes connected in an intense and unbroken gaze.

"What did you think of the last one?" asked Eamon, glancing at Emily as he shifted into third gear.

She didn't want to say that she'd felt like bursting into tears three apartments ago. That would sound hideously spoiled. So instead she forced a smile. "It was … okay."

She pressed the button to roll down the window and let the hot breeze blow against her face. It felt like an oven out there, and the air-conditioning in the truck couldn't keep it at bay. She rolled it back up and leaned her head against the headrest with a sigh, her temples pounded with the beginning of a stabbing headache and her throat was parched.

"Well, this is the last one, so I hope you like it. Otherwise we're gonna have to get you a double-wide out at the Golden Sunrise Trailer Park." He chuckled and rubbed a hand over his hair, which was springing free without his usual Stetson or ball cap to keep it in place.

Her heart fell. She wasn't a snob, but why did every property they'd inspected so far have to smell like wet dog, cigarette smoke, motor oil, or have mildew on the ceilings? Was it so much to ask that her new home be free of dangerous toxins and wretched odors? She sighed again and massaged her forehead gently.

"Don't worry," assured Eamon, resting a hand on her shoulder. "If all else fails, you can stay at the ranch until the perfect apartment comes along."

She looked at him in gratitude. How had she managed to discover a man who not only made her body quiver with one touch, but also seemed to genuinely care about her? And why hadn't she ever found such a man before in her life? Were they all hiding in rural Georgia?

"Here we are." Eamon turned the steering wheel, guiding them through a large wrought-iron gate next to the sign saying "Stoneleigh Apartments." Emily straightened to look at the sprawling buildings with interest. Already it looked much better than anything else they'd inspected. "This one's also close to the doctor's offices – you could walk there in about fifteen minutes if you wanted."

"Yeah?" She leaned forward and studied the picturesque kudzu vine that crept up the front wall of a red brick building. Fifteen minutes to walk to work … that would be a nice change of pace from the hour-long commute in heavy traffic to the Brigham each day. The gardens were well-maintained and there was a security keypad at the entrance – likely they shut the gates at night. Not as necessary in such a small town, no doubt, but it still made her feel a little more secure.

They met the building manager in the reception area and she showed them several units. The rooms were spacious, clean, mildew-free and smelled like a home should. Emily preferred living on the upper floor, and within thirty minutes she'd signed a lease for number 215. She was officially moving to Tifton, Georgia for at least a year – and she had a lease contract to prove it.

While they'd inspected the property, marveling at the size of the gym and the swimming pool, Eamon had held Emily's hand, lacing his long rough fingers through hers. He grinned at her and pulled her close while they wandered through the apartments. For a few minutes she caught a glimpse of everything in life she desired. It was within her grasp – all she had to do was reach out and take it.

* * *

EAMON PUT the tip of the straw in his mouth and tasted the delicious chocolate milkshake. *Aunt May's Southern Grill* was just one of the eateries on Main Street – most were chain restaurants, but this one was small, and family-owned. He loved their oversized burgers, thick-cut fries and milkshakes. They made him feel like he was a boy again.

So did Emily – he'd laughed more in the past two hours than he had in years, something he never would've thought possible with the dour, serious woman he'd met at Dalton and Hazel's wedding rehearsal. There was no doubt about it – she'd undergone a transformation in the time she'd stayed with them, and he liked it. He was beginning to think there might be a future for them together. The idea made his gut churn and his heart race at the same time.

He chewed a fry as he listened to Emily talking

about her new job. She was excited to begin and candid with him about how much that surprised her. She'd always gone for the most challenging roles, the ones that would elevate her career to the next level. Now she was just looking forward to making a difference. Already, her employers were calling her daily to talk about patients, excited about what she'd be bringing to the community in terms of patient care, expertise and skill.

He smiled as he listened – he could see she felt appreciated, and it brought out a warm glow in her cheeks. He let his hand drift toward hers, took her fingers and played his own across them, the thrill of her touch making his skin spark with pleasure. "Hey, I was wondering something ... have you ever been fishing?"

She laughed, as though she'd been expecting him to ask anything else, then shook her head, her long dark locks swaying. "No, I haven't."

"I love fishing. I used to go with my Dad before he died, so every now and then I like to take my pole out to a lake in the area and just sit, waiting for something to bite. Gives me a chance to rest and to think." He took another slurp of milkshake.

She tipped her head to one side and frowned. "That does sound nice. I'm not sure about the worms, though."

He chuckled. "If I handle the worms, would you like to come fishing with me this afternoon? I usually take Saturdays off from the ranch and I thought I might go, but ... I'd also like to spend the afternoon with you. Why don't you come? It might be fun."

Her eyes narrowed. "You'll bait the hook?"

He nodded.

"Okay, it's a deal. I should probably change first …"

"Me too. Let's head back to the ranch, we'll change and I'll grab my poles and tackle and meet you back at the truck. Okay?"

"Okay."

BY THE TIME she'd put on the cutest fishing outfit she could muster, torn denim shorts and a button down checked shirt that tied just above her navel along with white converse slip-ons, she could see Eamon through the window, already waiting by his pickup. She reached for a straw hat, and shoved it on her head as she skipped out the front door.

"Ready?" he asked, leaning back against the door of the truck, his ankles crossed and his cap tilting lazily over his eyes, throwing them into shadow.

The sight of him, all tanned muscles, shorts and t-shirt, made her palms damp and she rubbed them down the sides of her shirt with a quick intake of breath. She knew she should take things slow with this cowboy from south Georgia -- shouldn't dive head-first into anything without thinking it through. But her head and her heart seemed to have lost their connection.

Eamon opened the passenger door for her, and she slid into the seat, her arm brushing up against his and making her skin goose pimple. Slow things down? It'd take everything within her not to leap into his arms right now.

She pushed her hands beneath her rear, and sat on them. If that's what it took - she'd just have to stay that way until she could trust herself around him. She sighed. The drive to the lake might be a longer trip than she'd bargained for.

The lake wasn't much more than a large pond. It was nestled against some evergreens, and a sloping rise. Shaped almost like a figure eight, Eamon had lovingly dubbed the place the *Magic Eight Lake*. He swore it was the best place around for catching large-mouth bass, because the man who owned the property, Bill Pullen, stocked it annually with fingerlings. So, the fish were practically begging to be caught. She'd laughed when he said that, and he'd offered her a grin that made her legs weak.

True to his promise, Eamon baited her hook for her. He couldn't resist shoving the wriggling worm in her face before he did it, but she managed to shoot him a look of disdain worthy of a renowned surgeon, and much to her relief he soon gave the game up.

They stood side-by-side, two poles bent warmly over the still, glasslike pond. Emily's heart was full, and she smiled without thinking as she watched minnows darting in the shallows by her feet. The grass was full of the hum of bees, and the occasional rap of a wood-pecker in the trees nearby blended with the call of a family of wood ducks who were foraging in a bed of reeds across the water.

"So, what do you think?" asked Eamon.

Emily slapped at a midge on her arm. "Of what?" She squinted at him through the glaring sunlight.

"Of fishing."

"Oh... it's good so far."

"Hmmm..."

She chuckled. "If I'm understanding it correctly, it

involves a lot of standing and staring at the water. Have I got it right?"

He grinned. "Yep. That about covers it."

"Well, it's beautiful here." She sighed, and then drew in a long slow breath of hot air laden with the musty, sweet smells of the outdoors. "I feel more relaxed already. And hot. But I've kind of gotten used to the heat, now that we don't have AC at the ranch anymore."

He frowned. "Anymore? I just have to fix it, that's all..."

She sniffed. "Yeah, like I said..."

Emily watched with one arched eyebrow as he carefully pushed the handle of his pole into a holder he'd set up on the bank. Then, he stepped over to her and lifted her pole from between her hands, and set it in another holder. She frowned.

"Hey? What are you...?"

Just then, his face erupted into a grin, and he grabbed her, tickling her ribs with his fingertips. "You're just full of feisty today, aren't you?"

She laughed out loud, as the tickling made her sides clench. "Stop it!" she cried between fits of laughter. She couldn't catch her breath. "I'm sorry. Yes, you can fix it. You will, I'm sure of it. You're the best HVAC technician in the south. Stop!"

By this time she'd crumpled to the ground, and the relentless tickling continued as Eamon followed her down. She lay on her back, writhing from side to side. He wouldn't stop. She had to do something. She reached up and poked him in the ribs with both hands, making him flinch. Good, he was ticklish too. She set about tickling him as hard as she could, still overcome by paroxysms of laughter. Soon he was laughing hard too, and the two of them rolled about on the ground caught up in the fun of the moment.

When finally she couldn't take any more, they stopped, both of them breathing hard. She had somehow ended up on top of him, and let her head drop against his chest, her cheek pressed to his shirt. She could hear his heart hammering against his ribs.

She pushed up onto her elbows, still resting on top of him, a half-grin playing around the corners of her mouth. With one hand, she stroked his cheek, her fingertips grazing against day-old stubble.

"How did we get here?" she mused, her gaze focused on his full lips.

"Well, you kind of took advantage of me when I was down..." He chortled.

She slapped him playfully on the chest. "No, I mean here - as in, this thing that's happening between us. I would never have guessed it could happen. That I could..."

"Fall for a cowboy like me?" He filled in the blank, and her cheeks flushed with warmth.

"Well, I wouldn't put it that way. But yeah. I guess so. It was unexpected."

He raised a hand to tuck a strand of hair behind her ears. "Unexpected can be good. Right?"

She smiled. "Yeah. I wouldn't usually agree, but in this case…"

Reluctantly she pulled away, and sat on the ground, her knees against her chest, and her arms wrapped tightly around them.

He sat as well, and lay his legs out straight in front of him, crossing his ankles. Strong arms took his weight as he leaned back, and she resisted the urge to run her fingertips over them.

"What's wrong?" he asked, one eyebrow arched.

"Nothing."

"No, it's not nothing. What is it?" He turned to face her, and gently stroked her hair with the palm of his hand.

"My parents."

"Oh." He chewed the inside of his cheek. She knew he didn't understand.

"What's your Mom like?" she asked.

He leaned back again, and stared off over the lake. "She's Mom, you know? She's always there for me. Loves me unconditionally. Just wants to see me happy, I guess."

She sighed, and let her eyes drift shut for a moment. "Yeah, that's nothing like my parents. Oh, don't get me wrong — I'm sure deep down they want me to be happy. But the most important thing to them is that I bring honor to the family. That I work hard, get a good job, make money, buy a nice house, marry a successful Chinese doctor, or judge, and have at least one, possibly two perfect little babies, who will grow up to do the same."

She pressed her fingertips against her eyes with a groan. When she opened them again she could see him watching her with interest.

"What you mean is, they won't approve of me." He stated, as though he finally understood.

She nodded. Unable to find the words.

He let out a short sigh, then offered her a smile. "Okay. That's fine. We'll just have to prove them wrong. Won't we?"

She nodded, but she knew that was impossible. Her parents were never wrong, at least not in their own eyes. And they'd never approve of Eamon Williams as a match for their little girl. And that's how they saw her, as their little girl. As if they still had a say in every aspect of how she lived her life. Her heart sank at the thought of it, but she continued smiling as Eamon helped her to her feet, and they went back to the business of fishing.

CHAPTER 10

*E*mily crunched a mouthful of Shredded Wheat and read the back of the cereal box. Her phone sat beside her, and she glanced at the black screen – still no response to the dozens of resumes she'd sent out. She'd received the automated "thank you for your application" responses, but nothing about an interview or the possibility of an opening.

Granted, she already had a job – she'd called Dr. Hamilton when she returned from her fishing trip with Eamon and accepted his offer – but she wasn't applying for now, it was for the future. She had to think of her future … at least that's what her mother would say. She had no idea what her father would say.

She hadn't spoken to either of them since she'd lost the position at the Brigham, but she'd received a text from them while she was still asleep in bed that morning - they were on their way home from Europe. They'd spent the summer in London and Paris, Copenhagen and Rome. And right at that moment, they were scheduled to arrive stateside. The text made it clear they expected to see her tomorrow night for dinner at their place in Cambridge, near Harvard.

She swallowed the mouthful and looked at her phone again. There was no getting around it – she'd have to speak to them. She'd at least give them some time to go through customs, get home, unpack and take a shower before she destroyed all their plans for their only child.

She ran a hand through her hair, took another bite of cereal, then unlocked her phone and typed a quick response to her mother: *Ma Ma, so glad you're home. Looking forward to seeing you. Can't do tomorrow night, as I'm still in Georgia for Hazel's wedding. Love, Emily.* She hit "send" as her gut twisted into a knot.

She got one more bite in before her mother's reply made her phone ding: *CALL ME.*

Two words, and her heart fell. With slow deliberate bites, she finished her cereal, then rinsed the bowl and spoon and deposited them in the dishwasher. If she called back, it might end in a fight and her day would be ruined. If she didn't, Mother would keep hounding her until she did. She just wanted to enjoy a lazy Sunday in Eamon's arms, his tender kisses on her lips. She shivered at the pleasant thought, even as she stared in dread at her phone.

The door swung open and Eamon wandered in, his sandy hair standing on end. He wore loose fitting shorts and a tight white T-shirt, and his eyes were still half-closed as he yawned. He spotted Emily, smiled and scratched his chest as he made his way over. "Morning."

She smiled. "Good morning."

He kissed the top of her head, then went to pour

himself a cup of coffee from the percolator. "You look tense."

She chewed her lower lip – did he already know her so well? "My parents are back in the country. They want to see me."

"Oh. Is that so bad?" He sipped his coffee, his free arm over his chest, his blue eyes twinkling.

She couldn't help the way her lips curled up at the edges when he looked at her. "I guess I'll call them ... later. Ma Ma's already agitated because she knows I'm not in Boston. The longer I can put off that conversation, the better for everyone involved." She chuckled, then sobered.

"So what's on your agenda for today?" asked Eamon.

"I don't have anything planned."

He sat beside her and rested his elbows on the table. "Parker and I usually go to church, but we've missed the past couple of weeks trying to keep up with everything on the ranch. Want to come with us?"

She frowned. She'd never been inside a church building before except for a museum trip – her family was Buddhist, so who knew what they'd say about her attending a Sunday service? Well, she was sick of doing everything they expected. It was her life. She could do as she pleased. "Sure, I'll come."

But while Emily showered and dressed for church, all she could think of was the impending conversation with her parents. As they drove to town, music blaring over the radio and Eamon singing off-key, the only thing running through her mind was how little he and she had in common, how she'd rushed into a relationship with a man she barely knew. And what kind of answer she might give to her father when he asked her why.

* * *

EAMON TOOK a sip from the glass of sweet tea and set it on the side table next to the sofa. His eyes were glued to the flat-screen TV on the wall, but his mind was elsewhere.

"Hey, where's Emily?" asked Parker, tossing a handful of Fritos into his mouth.

Eamon glanced down the hallway at the closed bedroom door. She'd been quiet all through church, and as soon as they'd gotten home after lunch at the local Chinese restaurant she'd retreated to her room and shut the door. He was pretty sure it had something to do with her parents. Ever since she'd heard from them that morning, she'd seemed distant and tense. The noise of the baseball game on the screen filled the room as he reached for a handful of chips.

"Braves are goin' down today!" Parker teased.

Eamon frowned. "No way. You and your smack talk … I still can't believe you'd pull for the Nationals over the Braves. Where's your loyalty, man?"

Parker laughed. "The Nats are better. That's where my loyalty lies, with the best team."

Eamon huffed. "Everyone's better than the Braves this year. Proves nothing except you're a fair-weather fan." He usually loved talking smack with his brothers over anything competitive – and they were competitive about everything. But today his heart wasn't in it. He couldn't get Emily out of his mind – it was like she was pulling away from him already, before they'd even given their relationship a chance.

He sighed and took another sip of tea as Freddie Freeman drove a ball into the outfield. "Suck on that, Strasburg," he grumbled at the Nats' pitcher.

"Yeah, yeah" Parker conceded. "Watch your boy get stranded on first. Again."

Eamon glanced again at the closed door, and made up his mind. He set his drink down, stood and walked down the hallway to knock on the door.

Emily answered from inside. "Just a moment." Thirty seconds later, the door opened and she stood there in the white dress with lace trim she'd worn to church that morning, one that set his pulse racing. "Hey."

"Hey." He waited for her to continue, and when she didn't, he asked, "Can we go for a walk?"

She nodded, pulling the door shut behind her, and he followed her onto the front porch. What should he say? Was she having second thoughts? He didn't want to tell her it was too late for him, his heart was already lost. He was afraid of what she might do with it.

She stopped at the porch railing and leaned against the top plank. He stood beside her and felt the gentle afternoon breeze caress his face. "How are you?"

"Fine. You?" Her voice was clipped, her face tightly drawn.

"Em, what's going on? You're pulling away from me and I don't know why. Please, talk to me."

She ducked her head, her eyelids lowered against her golden cheeks. "I don't know … I just feel like we've rushed into things. I mean, we barely know each other, and we're so different. We come from different worlds, really."

"We do?" He frowned. What was she talking about? Did she mean Boston versus Tifton, or something else?

259

She sighed and ran her fingers through her hair. He could see a red blotch forming at the base of her neck. "I'm not sure I can explain it any better than I already have. My parents have always had this plan for my life – they sent me to the best schools, pushed me into med school, dragged me along with them to cocktail parties and events as networking opportunities. They've set me up on a hundred blind dates with successful eligible men whose families come from Beijing or Shanghai, good Buddhist families with summer places in the Hamptons …"

"So I'm not good enough for you because I don't have money?" His cheeks felt hot and his gut twisted.

Her eyes, full of pain, met his. "It's not like that!"

"What's it like then?"

She groaned, covered her eyes with her hands and took a deep, slow breath. "Eamon, I really like you, more than you can imagine. But I just don't know if this can work."

He crossed his arms, anger rising in his chest. "I don't see why not."

"My parents …"

"… don't run your life," he interrupted.

She sighed. "You don't understand."

"I understand plenty. I understand that you're scared. I understand that you stall when you're scared, and you're hiding behind your parents as an excuse to stall longer. They've never even met me. They might actually love me, you have no idea. Just like you had no idea about Tifton, or about that job in town, or about me, and each time you ran and hid until you couldn't any longer. Well … well, come get me when you're tired of hiding – I'll be around."

"Eamon …"

"You heard me." He turned on his heel and marched down the porch steps and across the yard. She kept calling his name, but he didn't stop. He couldn't bear to hear any more. Besides, the property line needed checking and now was a perfect time. Let Parker have the ball game and his stupid Nationals. Let Emily stew in her fears.

He hated how her words had cut him — as though she liked him against her better judgment. He hadn't expected that from her, not after how things had been between them in recent days. She'd finally seemed to relax and just be herself – calm, happy, vivacious, even funny at times. But he could see all of that disappearing behind a veil of uptight apprehension and excuses, and it made his heart ache. Was that who she really was after all?

He went to the barn, saddled and mounted a bay gelding named Pensacola, and trotted him briskly around the fields, steering him as close to the property line as trees, creeks and hollows would allow. Everything looked to be in order, and he knew he'd already checked the entire fence line after the last storm and the incident with Sassy. But he needed to be out and about, and the task gave him an excuse.

That was odd … he spotted a single mare beneath a birch tree, nowhere near the rest of the herd. It was Maggie, the oldest mare in the group, but she had a foal and he couldn't see it anywhere around her. He frowned and urged his horse into a canter.

When he reached Maggie, he spotted her small brown colt nestled at her feet. She stood over him like a sentinel guarding her richest treasure. Her brown eyes followed their approach and she nickered warmly at Eamon as he dismounted and stroked her neck.

"What's going on, Maggie?" he asked, squatting beside her foal. She followed his descent with her head, leaning low to sniff her baby.

The colt's breathing was labored, but he couldn't see any obvious injuries. He rested a hand on the animal's side, feeling the rise and fall of each breath. When he listened to the foal's heart, his ear against its side, the beat was rapid and weak. He stood and set his hands on his hips. This colt was in trouble – he'd have to get the animal back to the stables and call the vet.

He leaped onto his mount and galloped back to the ranch house to get the pickup truck, ducking in the back door and filling Parker in when he arrived. By the time he returned, bumping and weaving over the uneven ground, the colt was in worse shape than before. As gently as he could, he lifted the foal to its feet and maneuvered the horse into the back of the truck. He raised the tailgate and hurried to get back into the cab.

The mare trotted anxiously around the outside of the vehicle, her head and tail high, whinnying in concern. "It's okay, Maggie," he called out the open window of the cab as he nudged the accelerator, inching the truck forward. "Just come with us – everything's fine."

When he reached the barn, he saw Emily still on the porch where he'd left her. Parker waited by the barn door. She was sitting in the porch swing, one leg tucked beneath her, the other pushing the swing slowly back and forth. "Everything okay?" she called, her voice soft and distant on the breeze.

He pulled the truck to a stop close by the stables and jumped out. "Sick colt!" he yelled back as he ran around to open the tailgate. Maggie trotted up behind him, snorting, her eyes wide. He slipped his arms beneath the foal's body, all long legs and downy hair, carried him into the stables and laid him on a clean pile of straw. Parker bent to check the animal's pulse. Maggie stayed outside the fence that separated the corral from the stable, watching through the fence rails, her tail swishing at the occasional fly.

Emily reached his side. "What's wrong with him?" she asked, kneeling beside Parker and placing a hand gently on the foal's neck.

"Not sure. He's not breathing well and his heart rate's erratic." He rubbed his chin and drew a slow breath. "I've got to call the vet. Be right back." He stood and hurried out of the stables, taking his cell phone out of his pocket as he did. He watched Emily with the colt while he spoke to Will. She was so gentle, and the smile that lit up her face made his heart ache. She'd smiled at him that way before, and when she did, he couldn't think of a single thing he wouldn't do for her. Harley wandered into the stables and licked Emily's face, making her laugh.

Eamon smiled and hung up the phone. "He's on his way," he said.

Parker jumped to his feet. "I'll go and open the gate." He ran down the drive with long strides.

Emily nodded and continued to stroke the foal's side. Harley slumped onto the straw, panting, and Eamon sat beside him.

She looked up at Eamon. "I'm leaving for Boston tomorrow morning."

His heart lurched. "I thought you were staying. You, you just signed a lease on an apartment."

She nodded slowly. "Yes, I did, and I am. But all my stuff is in Boston – I've got to go back there to pack it up and ship it down here. And I need to deal with my parents, talk to them face to face about what's going on."

He ran a hand over his eyes. "That makes sense. How long will you be?"

"Just a few days. I start at the GP's office on Monday, so I'm planning on getting back Friday to unpack and get settled beforehand."

He couldn't stand the distance between them."Make sure you give me a call. I can help."

"I'll just get movers. Thanks for offering, but you have so much to do around here …"

She stood and smoothed her shorts with both hands. "I don't think there's much you can do for this colt. I'll wait for the vet with you if you like."

He shook his head. "No need. He said he'll be here in fifteen. Thanks."

She smiled tightly, her eyes were filled with sadness. "Okay. Well, I'm going to go pack. I know Dalton and Hazel get back tomorrow, and I'd really like to tell Hazel about my new job and apartment myself if that's okay with you. Ideally on Friday, when I get back."

"I promise I won't say anything."

She left, and Eamon's heart dropped into his stomach. She was leaving him – and from the way she was acting, she might as well have already left.

* * *

EAMON JOLTED awake as the sound of a car on the gravel drive disturbed the morning silence. The sun hadn't yet risen, but he could see a glow on the horizon through the open doors of the stable. The foal lay on the straw in front of him, its breathing labored and even more shallow than the previous day. Parker, propped up against the stable wall, was gently snoring.

Eamon stood with a groan and stretched the kinks out of his neck, back and legs. Spending the night on the cold hard earth of the stable floor had left his body stiff and sore. He stumbled through the stable doors and blinked.

The lights of the taxi idling in front of the house illuminated a patch of the yard and the side of the barn. The front door opened and Emily stepped out, pulling it quietly shut behind her. She crept down the front steps, lifting her luggage with both hands, then passed it to the driver who stashed it in the open trunk. She didn't see Eamon watching as she climbed into the back seat of the cab.

The taxi left as quickly as it had arrived, only the crunch of tires on gravel announcing its departure. She was gone.

He ran his fingers through his hair and glanced around. Maggie stood still beside the fence, one hind leg resting with its hoof tipped forward. He shook his head – Emily would be back on Friday. It wasn't long, and it would give them both some time to think about what they wanted. He knew what he wanted: her. But she still had doubts. Maybe some time apart would help her realize she didn't want to live without him.

He smiled ruefully at his own wishful thinking and returned to the foal's side. He knelt and frowned. Will had said it was some kind of heart condition, likely congenital. Unless they intended to spend thousands of dollars on risky surgery, he couldn't do anything more for the horse.

He touched the foal's side. It was still, cold. The colt

was gone. He rocked back on his haunches and rubbed his eyes, his heart aching. What would he tell Dalton? He reached out and tapped Parker on the arm. "Parker."

Parker groaned, rubbed his eyes with his knuckles and blinked at his brother. "Huh?"

"The colt's gone." As he said it, Eamon felt the grief he'd been suppressing well up inside him. He loved these horses – they spent every day caring for, loving, protecting, feeding them. He'd watched as this foal was born only a week earlier. It'd been an amazing experience, one he wouldn't soon forget. Every foal that had been born since he arrived was special to him, every one precious. And now one was gone.

"Oh man." Parker squeezed his eyes shut and took a quick breath. "Poor little buddy."

"Let's head inside," grunted Eamon. "This floor ain't made for sleeping on. We'll deal with the colt later."

Parker nodded and they trudged back to the ranch house. Eamon's heart ached as though it was filled with heavy stones. Two losses this morning – and one definitely wasn't coming back. What about the other?

CHAPTER 11

*E*mily stared at her phone. It blinked on with a buzz as the plane pulled to a stop at the gate. She was home.

She'd texted Ma Ma before she left to let her know what time the plane was meant to arrive in Boston. Her mother hated to wait for delayed flights. Her reply had been terse – they'd pick her up at the airport. She replied that there was no need – she wanted to head back to her apartment, and a taxi would be just fine. No response.

She didn't stop at baggage claim – she'd only brought carry-on luggage, something she'd taken to doing after an airline lost her checked bag on the way to an important conference in San Jose. It was her first time presenting, and she'd packed her presentation, her outfit, jewelry, everything she needed in that bag. They found it and got it to her, but barely an hour before her presentation. No more checked bags for her, not unless the trip was going to be longer than a week.

She hurried through the throngs of people, through duty-free shopping, past clusters of cafés and fast food restaurants. A man dressed in a black suit stood by the exit with a sign in his hands – EMILY ZHU.

Emily glanced around. There was no sign of either of her parents anywhere nearby. She sighed. They hadn't come to get her, just sent a driver. She wasn't surprised so much as disappointed; they hadn't seen her homecoming as important enough for them to make the effort, after not seeing her for three months. Even though she dreaded hearing their thoughts on her current life situation, she missed them in her own way and had looked forward to seeing them again. She'd hoped they'd feel the same way.

She raised a hand, indicating to the driver that she was who he was looking for. He smiled and led the way to the car. All too soon, they pulled up in front of her parents' expansive house. She took a deep breath and squeezed her eyes shut. Time to face the music.

* * *

THE FAN in the living room turned slowly overhead. Emily tipped her head back against the plush sofa back and watched it spin. The only sounds were the ticking of the grandfather clock against the far wall and the whir of the fan, but they were soothing to her frayed nerves.

"So you are saying there is now no position at the Brigham for you?" barked her father.

She lifted her head and met her father's gaze. "That's right, Ba Ba." She'd called him "Ba Ba" ever since she was a child, but the name didn't seem to fit anymore.

"What about Reagan?"

"As I said, I turned them down because I thought I had the job at the Brigham."

He shook his head and put his hands on his hips, a purple flush creeping up his neck. "And Emory?"

"Same."

He took a quick breath, his nostrils flaring. "So you have no options left?"

Here it went. "Well, I've accepted a job in Tifton, Georgia …"

He interrupted her. "Where?"

"It's in southern Georgia. There was a practice there that needed a GP …"

His voice sounded strangled. "A GP?!"

"Yes, Ba Ba, a GP. I know you don't approve, but I'm really looking forward to it. I think it will be good for me to get some general skills, improve my bedside manner, my diagnosing. And I'll still be doing some surgery at the local hospital, so I won't get rusty. I know it's a setback, but I don't think it's the end of the world."

His eyes widened and his lips formed a thin, straight line. "You don't? How you can stay calm about this? This is your career! Don't you understand that?"

Emily's mother Julie bustled into the room. "Now, now … let's keep our voices down. We don't want Kimberly and Harold to hear us yelling at one another."

Emily rolled her eyes. Heaven forbid the cook and the butler hear the family arguing. Her mother would sooner have her hair plucked out one strand at a time than find the help gossip about them.

Her father walked over to the fireplace and rested his hands on the mantle, staring into the cold hearth.

When he spoke again his voice was measured. "So what are you going to do about it, then? I assume you have a plan."

"Yes, I do. The GP position is only for a year, and meanwhile I'm applying all over the country for next year's intake. I'm hopeful I'll get a more favorable position. In fact, I think it will look good on my resume to have such a diversity of experience."

His eyes narrowed and he studied her as though he didn't recognize her any longer.

"Ba Ba, I'm happy about this. I want to do it. Why isn't that enough for you?"

He slapped the mantle, hard. "I have given you everything," he intoned in a deep rasp. "The best schools, the best of everything. I have worked so hard with the purpose of giving you the best life possible. And now I find that you are squandering it."

Now she frowned. "I'm not squandering anything. I've done my best. It isn't my fault that …"

"Have you seen Lee lately?" Mother interrupted, as though she and her father weren't having a heated argument at all.

"What?" Emily's mind raced to make the connection. What was her mother talking about? Surely she couldn't be referring to the pediatrician she'd set Emily up on a date with four months earlier?

"You know, Lee Ng. The two of you went on a date before your father and I left for London." She smiled and sipped the glass of champagne she'd been nursing since Emily arrived at the house from the airport an hour earlier. "Have you seen him again since then?"

"No, Mother, I haven't seen Lee. We had one date, we didn't connect and that was it. He called a few times, but I didn't call him back. He was a nice man, but not for me."

Her father strode from the room, and flinched at the sight of his ramrod straight back. She hadn't seen him so angry in a long time. Hopefully he'd calm down with a bit of time and distance. Her heart pounded and her armpits were drenched with sweat. She knew it would be tricky explaining her situation to her parents, but she hadn't imagined just how badly they'd react. And now her mother had jumped directly from conversations about her career meltdown to asking about her love life. Could it get any worse?

"Really?" Mother continued. "I thought the two of you would be perfect together. You should give him another chance. After all, the clock is ticking." Her mother pointed to the clock against the wall and forced a smile.

Emily swallowed. She should make some kind of excuse, and head to her bedroom.

"No, Ma Ma, he just wasn't right for me. I want someone genuine, fun, strong and considerate. I want him to be exciting, adventurous, handsome and good."

Her mother rolled her eyes. "You live in a fantasy world, Emily. Where do you expect to find someone like that?"

Emily grinned, as a dawning realization welled up inside her. "Actually, I already have. His name's Eamon and he's all those things and more. I think he might be The One."

Ma Ma tipped her head to one side and studied her daughter. "Eamon? Who is this Eamon? Where did you meet him, at the Brigham?"

She shook her head. "No, I met him at Hazel's

wedding. He's Hazel's brother-in-law and works on the horse ranch he and his brothers own down there."

Mother's eyebrows arched and her eyes widened. "He's a rancher? A … cowboy? You're seeing a *cowboy* in *Georgia?*"

Emily nodded, bracing herself.

"I forbid this. You cannot do it! You will break your father's heart. First you toss away your career and now you throw yourself at a cowboy? What do you intend to do, live on the ranch and cook and clean while he rounds up cattle?" Her mother's tone was loaded with contempt.

Emily felt tears welling in her eyes. She cared for Eamon and wanted to be with him, and her mother was working hard to make her feel ashamed of it. "I already told you what I intend to do," she replied angrily before she could stop herself. "You should try listening."

Ma Ma reacted like she'd been slapped. "Don't you *dare* talk back to me!"

"Why do I bother talking to you at all?" Emily ran from the room, taking the stairs two at a time to the second floor. The staircase wound upward, regal marble with a cedar banister that shone in the morning sunlight. With a sob, she burst through her bedroom door, flung it shut behind her and launched herself onto the soft queen-sized bed in the center of the room. As she cried into her pillow, she remembered the warmth of Eamon's embrace, and the softness of his kisses. She'd been so happy. And now, that feeling was well and truly gone.

EAMON LAY on his back in bed, staring up at the ceiling. He'd slept only two hours since stumbling out of the stables and into the house, without even the energy to change out of his soiled jeans and shirt. At least he'd thought to kick his muddy boots off by the front door. The heat of the day was already permeating the house, and a trail of sweat trickled down the side of his face. He really had to get someone out to look at the HVAC before Dalton and Hazel arrived home today. Otherwise, Dalton would think he was slacking.

As he lay there, the memory of what took place that morning before sunrise hit him once again and he groaned. He rubbed his face and sighed deeply. Emily was gone. And so was the colt.

The phone in the kitchen began to ring and he groaned again in response. With a grunt, he lurched to his feet and ran out of the room in his socks, reaching the phone just as the answering machine kicked on. "Hello? Hello?" he heard Dalton call.

"Hey, Dalton," he responded sleepily, rubbing his eyes again and attempting to focus.

"Eamon?"

"Yep. It's me."

"Are you seriously still sleeping? It's eight in the morning."

Eamon rolled his eyes and frowned. "No, I'm not sleeping, I'm answering the phone. What's up, bro? How's the honeymoon?"

He could hear Dalton's smile through the line. "It's great – we've had the best time. We're looking forward to getting home and starting our lives together, but we decided to stay in Destin a few more days. I just wanted to let you know we'll be home Tuesday instead of today. Is everything okay there?"

Eamon frowned. He was glad his brother was so happy – and that he had more time to deal with the HVAC – but he didn't want to answer that question. "Yeah, of course. Everything's good …"

Dalton's tone changed. "What's going on? You sound upset about something."

Eamon sighed and settled into a kitchen chair. He never could hide anything from his big brother. "Um … well, we lost Maggie's colt this morning. I'm sorry, Dalton – Parker and I did everything we could."

On the other end of the phone, Dalton whispered something to Hazel before coming back. "I'm sorry to hear that, Eamon," he finally said. "But it's not your fault – I'm sure you did your best. Did you get the vet out?"

"Yeah, Will said it was a heart defect – nothing he could do that made sense. So I made the call to just let him go."

"You did the right thing, Eamon."

Eamon took a breath as relief washed over him. He hadn't realized just how much he'd wanted Dalton's approval. "Thanks, Dalton. And the HVAC unit finally went – I made a couple runs at it myself, but I couldn't make heads or tails of it, so I guess we'll just have to call in a pro."

"Smart move – some things have to be left to the experts. Anything else?"

Eamon wasn't sure if he should bring up Emily. He'd promised her he wouldn't tell Hazel about her new job or apartment, but she hadn't said anything about keeping their relationship secret. And he could really do with some brotherly advice. Parker had been no help – he'd just shrugged and mumbled about women being a mystery. "Actually, I met someone …"

"Oh? Who is she?"

"Emily Zhu. You know, Hazel's bridesmaid –"

"Woo-ee! Ha ha – I knew you two hit it off. I told Hazel, but she didn't believe me. So – what happened?"

"We spent some time together while she stayed here and we got on really well. We had fun together. But now she's telling me that we can't keep seeing each other because her parents – they wouldn't approve, or think I'm good enough for her." Eamon choked on the words, his chest tightening. Just saying it out loud made it hurt even more.

"I'm sorry, man. Would you like some advice?"

Eamon nodded, then pushed out a single word around the lump in his throat. "Yes!"

"She'll come around. If she really cares for you like you think she does, in the end she won't worry about what her folks think. She'll follow her heart. At least, that's been my experience ... you know, watching all those Dr. Phil episodes in my spare time."

Eamon felt the lump in his throat shift as he laughed along with his brother, the tension broken. "You really think so?"

"Yeah, I do. And if she doesn't, she's not right for you. Because you're a great guy and she should know that."

Eamon blinked hard. Sometimes his brother really knew the right thing to say. "Thanks, Dalton."

"You're welcome. Now get an A/C guy out there – I don't want to come home to an oven."

* * *

THE MUSTY SCENT of hay and horse manure greeted Eamon. The stables were his favorite place to spend time. He even loved mucking out the stalls, which Parker and Dalton hated. The physical activity gave him something to do, but the mindlessness of it allowed him time to think. He took the pitchfork off its hook on the wall and set it end down on the floor with a clang.

"Eamon?" Parker called through the side door. The stables had been tacked onto the side of the old barn, almost as an afterthought, and a single door joined the two buildings.

"Yep?" Eamon replied. What was Parker doing? He'd thought his brother was still asleep in the house. They'd both been exhausted after spending the whole night with the colt. Parker walked in, a grin on his face, one cheek smudged with mud or dirt and his dark brown hair standing on end. "What have you been up to, brother?"

"Just working on Dalton's motorbike – thought I might take it out for a ride, but it wouldn't start." He rubbed his chin. "Any ideas?"

Eamon chuckled and shook his head. "Sorry, wish I could help. But I'm still trying to figure out that dang HVAC, and I'm running out of time. Dalton'll be back next Tuesday."

"Tuesday? I thought they got back today." Parker leaned against the wall, and crossed his arms over his chest.

"Yeah, I guess they're having too good a time. Dalton called a few minutes ago to say they're staying on."

Parker leaned against the wall and crossed his arms. "Must be nice. Hey, I see Emily left."

Eamon frowned and stabbed the pitchfork into a mound of soiled hay. He tossed the muck out into the yard, then dug the fork back into the hay for another load.

"Where's she headed?" asked Parker.

"Boston. But she's coming back Friday to move into her new place."

"Oh, so it's not over?" Parker's eyes narrowed.

"Honestly, that's up to her. I don't want it to be, but …"

Parker grimaced and ran a hand over his face. "Sorry about that, bro."

"Yeah, well, apparently I'm not what her folks had in mind for their daughter. So she's running scared." Eamon shoveled another forkful of hay into the yard, grunting with the effort. He didn't want to think about Emily. He needed a distraction.

Parker seemed to sense it. "There's a monster truck rally tomorrow night in Albany. I was thinking I might go. Wanna come?"

Eamon set the pitchfork on the ground and leaned against it, one foot balanced on the curve of metal. "Yeah. Actually, that sounds perfect. I really need to get out and have some fun."

"That settles it, then. We'll go see some really big trucks crash into each other."

The new apartment was smaller than she remembered. Emily stood in the center of the living room and turned around, her eyes narrowed. Or maybe it was just that all her things filling the space made it seem as though it was closing in on her.

She set her hands on her hips and surveyed the boxes and furniture. Thankfully the movers had pushed the furniture against the walls so she was able to move between rooms. But there was a lot of unpacking to do. She started with the kitchen, unpacking plates, bowls and silverware. She set a vase on the kitchen counter, recalled she'd seen some flowers in the garden downstairs and wondered if she could sneak a few once she was done unpacking. There was nothing like fresh flowers for making a place feel like home.

While she worked, she thought about her parents in Boston. After telling her mother about Eamon, she'd hidden in her room the rest of the night, sobbing into her pillow. But the next morning her parents seemed ready to put their differences aside. They didn't say anything about her career or love life all day, and even took her to lunch at her favorite restaurant, which was owned by her father's cousin. They always ordered traditional Chinese food, stuff not listed on the menu, and it was always delicious.

That night, however, it was as they'd decided to team up against her. They'd started out sweet – appealing to her sense of family, to reason and logic. She couldn't move to south Georgia, it wouldn't be good for her career. She had so much potential, it would devastate them if she was to give that up for a man. It didn't make any sense. When she told them she wasn't sure if it would work out with Eamon anyway, so they might not have anything to worry about, they were relieved. Her mother hugged her, something she rarely did, and her father smiled.

But when they began making plans for her return to Boston, she had to stop them. "I'm not moving back – I told you, I have a job in Tifton. I'm going to be working there for at least a year. I have a contract – I'm not going to back out on them."

Ma Ma covered her mouth with a hand and squeezed a single tear from her closed eyes. Her father's smile faded fast and his eyes narrowed. "You still insist on making this mistake?"

She nodded. "I don't think it's a mistake. I feel really good about it, Ba Ba. I know it's a bit of a detour, but I think it'll be good for me."

He shook his head and stormed from the room again, the same as the previous night – and many other nights in the past. Always running out on arguments, because he couldn't stand his daughter standing up to him. She knew what he was thinking – in *his* culture, that just didn't happen. He found it hard to swallow that a daughter of his would not only defy him, but do so openly in his own home.

"We only want what's best for you," Mother insisted, teary-eyed

Emily hadn't wished to confront her parents this way, but they'd given her no other choice. She swallowed hard. "I know, Ma Ma, but this is what I think is best. I hope you and Ba Ba will understand that in time."

When her taxi pulled out of their long drive, they'd waved goodbye, standing apart, a world of space between them, looking old and tired. Her heart lurched at the sight.

* * *

THE SMALL OFFICE space she shared with Drs. Hamilton and Suarez was cozy and noisy. It seemed that when the building was erected, no one had bothered with insulation or sound-proofing. And in a clear lapse of judgment, the interior designer Dr. Hamilton hired had given the place a polished concrete floor that amplified every normal office sound.

A nice carpet could easily have dampened the din, but Joss wouldn't hear of it. She liked to fling herself around the place on her wheeled office chair, often crashing into the filing cabinet under the reception desk, which only added to the noise. Both her knees were covered with scars, but it didn't seem to stop her careening or dim her smile. Emily decided she'd just have to get used to it. It was different from her Boston office, but sometimes being different was a good thing.

She opened every cabinet door in the small kitchenette, finally discovering a pile of mismatched coffee mugs. The pot on the coffee maker was almost full and she poured herself a cup, but one sip revealed a bitter flavor that made her grimace. It took her three sips for her taste buds to grow accustomed to it.

"How are you settling in?" Dr. Maria Suarez was a curvaceous forty-something Cuban woman with long thick hair that fell in waves around her shoulders, who wore her white coat as if it were a fashion statement. She had a warm smile that immediately set Emily at ease.

"Not too bad. I started unpacking when I got back from Boston on Friday, and by last night I only had a few boxes left. So I did them and went to bed early. I didn't realize how tiring it can be to unpack boxes and make a thousand decisions about where everything you own should live." She laughed and spooned sugar into her coffee cup, hoping it would cut through the bitterness.

Maria grimaced. "I know just what you mean." Her voice was smooth as silk, her accent softening the edges of words. "We moved here five years ago, and I vowed never to move again."

Emily nodded. She'd be happy to go a long time before moving interstate again. And after having to organize the entire procedure in just a few short days, all she wanted to do now was curl up in a corner somewhere and sleep.

She wondered what Eamon was doing. Ever since she'd climbed into the taxi and left for Boston a week ago, she'd regretted the way she'd left things between them. The arguments with her parents had helped her realize her feelings for him were stronger than she'd thought – all she wanted was to see him again. But had he washed his hands of her entirely? He hadn't called her, and every time she picked up the phone to call him, fear stopped her. She couldn't bear the idea of having him hang up on her, or worse, act cold and distant.

She took a deep breath. No time to think about him now – it was her first day at a new job and she had patients to see. Butterflies swirled in her stomach. What if she didn't know what to do? What if she overlooked something important and failed to diagnose a serious illness? She'd never worked as a GP before and diagnosis had never been her strong point. She was a surgeon – after someone else settled on a why, she implemented the how. Now, she'd be doing both between the GP's office and the hospital.

She followed Dr. Suarez out of the kitchenette and down the hall to their offices, each with a sign on the door. Hers read, "SUNDEEP RAMACHANDRA, M.D." She paused in front of the door and frowned – they'd have to take care of that. She headed to the reception area. "Excuse me, Joss?"

Joss looked up from her computer screen with a smile. "Yes?"

"I was wondering when I might be able to get the sign on my door changed?"

Joss blinked. "Oh, of course – I'll change that directly. By the way, the boss wants to see you at ten, so I've left you an open slot then. Okay?"

Emily nodded, smiling at how she referred to her husband, Dr. Joseph Hamilton, as "the boss." Emily always liked to arrive extra early on her first day, and that morning she'd beaten everyone else to the office. She'd had to wait outside until Joe and Joss arrived to open the place. The quaintness of it all made her smile – yes, this was far more relaxed than the Brigham. She thanked her and headed back to her office.

The first four patients flew by in a blur of questions, smiles and answers. She was happy with how she'd handled them, and the nerves began to fade. She could do this. At ten, she finished keying notes into the computer and hurried to Joe's office, where he was waiting for her in a worn leather armchair. The nerves returned and her stomach clenched – what did he want? Had she already made a mistake? At the Brigham, the boss never asked to meet with you unless you'd done something wrong.

"Emily, good to see you. Have some cake." He pushed a plate covered in slices of fruitcake toward her, just as Joss bustled in with a hot cup of coffee.

Emily nodded her thanks and took the cup and a slice, holding it carefully on a napkin to avoid spilling crumbs. "Thank you."

Joss left and Joe leaned back in his chair to sip his coffee. "So how're you doing?"

She could almost feel his sincerity, like a warm blanket. "I'm doing well."

"Finding your way around?"

"Yes, thank you."

"Well, I just wanted to meet with you to make sure you have everything you need. Oh, and we're all going to Oinkers for lunch – kind of a welcome to the team. You been there yet?"

She nodded. "That sounds lovely, thank you." She kept waiting for the other shoe to drop. Everyone in the office seemed kind, polite, hard-working and considerate. It felt too good to be true.

He smiled warmly. "Wonderful. Well, you just let

me know if you need anything or have any questions. We're all family here."

She couldn't speak, just nodded again. By the time she made it back to her office, she felt like she might cry. She sat down with a sigh and took a deep breath.

Joss knocked on the door with a grin. "I made pumpkin scones last night – care to try one before your 10:30?"

Her eyes smarted with tears.

* * *

THE APARTMENT FELT like home already. At 5:30, Emily was seated on the couch, with a glass of iced tea in hand and the evening stretching out in front of her with nothing in it but the television. She had no idea what to watch, though – she'd rarely had time before.

The clock she'd hung on the kitchen wall ticked loudly. She set up her Bluetooth speaker, searched her phone, and soon Adele echoed off the walls. She sat with a sigh on the couch, flicked on the TV, surfed through the channels and turned it off again – there was nothing on. What did regular people do, the people who knocked off work at five and had no peak-hour commute to contend with – how did they spend their evenings?

She carried her empty glass back into the kitchen and opened the refrigerator. She hadn't had time to go to the store yet. Perhaps that's what she should do. At least it would fill time. She grabbed her purse and headed out the door. She'd purchased a used Toyota hatchback on Saturday – it waited in her designated parking space outside, red paint dull in the golden afternoon light.

She passed Kroger a block away and slapped her forehead when she saw she'd missed the turn. She glanced in the rearview mirror and thought about what to do - keep going and do a U-turn further along the road, or look for another grocery store? But then she saw the turnoff to the highway up ahead. She recognized it as the highway that led to the Cotton Tree Ranch.

Her thoughts returned to Eamon. Likely he and Parker were doing their evening chores, or maybe they'd already finished and were cooking supper. The memory of the warm, cheerful kitchen made her heart ache. Parker would be stirring something on the stove top while Eamon chattered on about something one of the foals had done. Parker would nod or grunt in response, and Eamon would grin, those dimples casting shadows in his cheeks.

She sighed and turned the wheel. What was she doing? How did she know Eamon would want to see her after the way she'd treated him? But she couldn't help herself – she had to see him, to find out if there was still a chance for them.

Within minutes she'd reached the gate, and she took a deep breath and exhaled slowly. There was no turning back once she drove through – likely Harley would see her and begin barking, announcing her arrival to all and sundry. She stepped out of the car, the cool evening air brushing over her skin and raising goosebumps. The gate swung open easily, and she drove through, shutting it behind her car.

Sure enough, she heard Harley's urgent calls. Looking toward the distant ranch house, she saw him standing at the end of the drive, his tail held high, his head raised. He didn't know her car, since she'd only just bought it. By the time she reached the house, his barking had become urgent and drew Eamon from the barn. She didn't see Parker – he must be out on the property somewhere.

She parked the vehicle and stepped out, noting with a grimace the new layer of mud on the car's wheels and fenders. Well, she did live in the country now.

"Harley," she called softly, and the dog raced toward her, tail wagging. He licked her legs, then turned to let his tail thump against her calves. She laughed and ran her hands down his sleek sides. "Happy to see me, boy? I sure am glad to see you."

"So you came back." Eamon's voice startled her. It was a statement, not a question.

She could hear the tension in his voice and straightened, letting Harley continue to pummel her with his tail. "I told you I would."

He pushed his hat back with his finger, his eyes narrowed. "Yeah," he replied.

He wasn't going to make this easy. "Eamon … I'm sorry. I shouldn't have pushed you away like I did. It's hard to explain to someone who's never been there, but my parents don't exactly encourage standing up to them. I wasn't allowed to argue with them – that's how I was raised, and I knew they wouldn't approve of us, and I got scared. But when I saw them … I found I didn't care what they thought any longer."

His eyebrows arched skyward, and his eyes widened in surprise.

"I told them everything, and they were furious. I mean, not just about you, but about the job as well. And suddenly, I didn't care. I stood up to them, for the first time in my entire life. And it was amazing, and horrible, and gut-wrenching all at the same time - but I did it. I did it. And I'm free. I feel free anyway. Like for the first time, I'm not worried about pleasing anyone else. I can make my own decisions, the decisions that are right for me. And my parents don't have to be happy about it, and that's okay." She laughed. She was babbling. Was she losing her mind? Yet, she felt a clarity she'd never experienced before, and joy bubbled up from deep within.

"I'm happy for you." He tipped his head to one side, his eyes dark with concern. "Are you sure you're okay?"

She nodded. "I'm great. Wonderful, actually. And it's so good to see you."

Emily stepped forward, and reached out a hand to lay on his forearm. He glanced down at her touch, and a spark shot between them that made her breath catch in her throat. When he caught her gaze, his mouth curved into a lazy grin, and his dimples flashed making her heart thud.

"I was just about to head out on Maggie for a ride. She's been moping around the stables a lot ever since her colt died, so I'm trying to keep her distracted. Do you want to join me?"

She frowned. "I'd love to, but I don't know how to ride."

"I'd be happy to teach you. Dexter's an old gelding we keep close to home just for riding – he's gentle as a lamb. I'll saddle him up for you." He took her hand and led her toward the barn.

She fell into step beside him. "Well, okay … but just so you know, I've seen lambs and that metaphor isn't really working for me. They might look gentle, but they do a lot of jumping, bucking and lurching, so …" She was babbling again – the thought of climbing on

Dexter or any other creature that weighed ten times as much as her made her nervous.

He laughed and stopped. "Don't worry so much." Time stood still as their gazes locked. His eyes were the deep blue of the ocean in a storm, and she could read his desire in their depths before he set off again toward the stable.

She fell back into babbling. "See, saying 'don't worry so much' isn't very comforting. I mean, statistically speaking the number of horse riding accidents that result in death is quite high compared with other sports. Not to mention permanent disability ..."

He laughed again and shot her a look out of the corner of his eye. "You'll be fine."

She chewed her bottom lip. Sure, she'd be fine – he'd make certain of it, wouldn't he? She trusted him. Even though she wasn't sure about that Dexter creature.

CHAPTER 13

*W*hat was that saying about falling off a horse? Emily tried to remember. What do you do if you fall off – throw out your arms? Tuck and roll? No, it was something about getting back up again, wasn't it? Not that helpful – she didn't want to fall, and if she did, she certainly wouldn't get back up on this gigantic horse. Eamon had failed to mention that Dexter was really tall. She shivered and clutched tighter to Dexter's reins, looking down at the ground that suddenly seemed very distant. "Are you sure he's okay?" she asked shakily.

"He's docile as a sloth, old Dexter." Eamon rode beside her on Maggie. The mare was tall as well, but not as tall as Dexter. Maggie held her head high and stepped regally, sometimes skittering sideways as though she wanted to go faster and he wouldn't let her. "Don't worry, he'll take care of you just fine."

After plodding along for ten minutes, Emily finally began to relax, and she loosened her tight grip on the reins, letting them hang between her fingers. As she let the tension ease out of her shoulders, she saw the gentle waving of leaves in the pecan trees lining the southern fence line. The soothing call of a flock of ducks as they took flight from the creek banks and flapped up into the sky made her smile. Darkness came slowly in summer, and she was grateful for it. This kind of beauty couldn't be seen in the bright light of day, it was reserved for the dimly lit twilight hours, with lengthening shadows and the brilliant colors of a sunset that warmed the pastures around them.

"So you told your parents about me?" asked Eamon.

She smiled with a quick bob of her head. "I told them we were seeing each other. And that you were just the kind of man I was looking for."

He tugged on Maggie's reins and waited for Emily to catch up to him, then reached for Dexter's bit to make him stop. "I am?"

"Yes, Mr. Williams. You are."

He stood tall in his stirrups, grabbed her around the waist and pulled her from her saddle onto his own. She gasped as he sat her facing him, the two of them squeezed between the rear and horn of the saddle. She wrapped her jean-clad legs around him and looped her arms around his neck with a smile. "I'm sorry," she whispered against his neck.

He tilted her chin up until her eyes met his, and she felt his longing reaching into her soul. "Emily, you must know how I feel."

She looked away, unsure of how to respond. She didn't know how he felt, not really. It was obvious he liked her, but she was in love with him. Since she'd met him, her whole life had been turned upside down – actually, it felt more like right side up. Everything she'd thought was real and true didn't seem all that important any longer. She'd once thought love was just a connection with someone. Not now, not once love knocked her from her feet and left her gasping for air. Not when she felt Eamon's arms around her.

This, this was love. She knew it in the depths of her soul despite never experiencing it before. Love was an all-consuming life upheaval, with the knowledge that nothing would ever be the same again, that a life lived without the other person was no life at all. She'd thought she was content before she met him, but now she knew she'd had no idea. The only question that remained was: did he feel the same way?

"I don't want us to be apart ever again," he simply said.

She sighed in relief and kissed him, hard. He cupped her face in both hands, gently at first, then more passionately. Her mind emptied of every thought other than that she loved and was loved. There was nothing else.

* * *

EAMON SLICED potatoes and lined the bottom of the pan with them in preparation for his special *pommes au gratin*. Hazel and Dalton were due to arrive home any moment, and he never thought he'd be so happy to see them. He and Parker had managed to run the ranch without their older brother for four long weeks, but they hadn't realized just how much of the load their brother carried until he was gone.

He glanced up at a blast of cool air from the vent above his head and smiled. He'd finally figured out how to fix the HVAC, and just in time. He'd spent all morning working on it, determined not to let it beat him. He'd used Google, and the instruction manual, and finally he'd figured it out. The achievement gave him a sense of satisfaction that couldn't be bought, and he grinned, remembering when he'd switched the unit back on and felt the sweet cool air on his skin.

He sliced the cheddar, popping a long piece of it into his mouth and chewing happily. His stomach growled – he hadn't eaten since breakfast. He'd been too busy with Parker, getting the ranch into top shape for the inspection they fully expected their brother to make the moment he stepped out of the cab.

The slam of a car door caught his attention as he was about to start on the green onions, and he wiped his hands on his apron before untying it, flinging it on the counter and leaving the kitchen. Harley barked a few times, then quiet.

He opened the front door with a smile and saw Emily patting Harley. The reclusive Lulu, their black barn cat, had wandered outside with her litter, tail weaving from side to side in curiosity. The kittens romped around her, pouncing on each other and rolling through the dust and dirt. "Hey, Emily." He hurried to greet her, catching her up in his arms and kissing her, feeling her body tremble beneath his touch.

"Hi," she laughed, her eyes gleaming.

They both peered down the driveway at the same time as another vehicle approached. Eamon rested an arm across Emily's shoulders while they waited. By the time Hazel and Dalton stepped from the cab, Eamon could see Emily's cheeks had turned bright red. He grinned, knowing she was nervous about what her friend would think of their budding relationship. But he wasn't worried – he knew Hazel would be delighted. Emily was just so used to the people in her life judging her choices, she didn't yet realize that Hazel wouldn't.

Hazel ran to embrace Emily, her eyes wide. "Emily, what are you still doing here? I wasn't expecting to see y–" She stepped back, her eyes narrowing at Eamon and Emily. One eyebrow slowly rose. "Ohhh. Dalton told me the two of you were seeing each other, but then you'd gone back to Boston and …" She chuckled. "… so what's going on?"

"Well, for starters," Emily began, unable to keep the silly smile off her face, "I've moved here. I have a job as a GP in Tifton, and I've already found an apartment in town."

Eamon grinned too – and covered his ears when Hazel screamed in delight. Yeah, nothing to worry about.

* * *

DIRTY DISHES LAY SCATTERED over the countertop and kitchen table. Emily leaned forward in her seat, listening intently to a story Dalton was telling about his and Hazel's honeymoon. She glanced around the table, her heart filled to bursting with happiness. Eamon and Parker were hooting with laugher, and Dalton's eyes lit up as he recounted a particularly funny incident involving a rainforest-themed restaurant and Hazel's reaction to a realistic plastic snake on the wall beside her seat.

By the time their stories were finished, the hands on the clock were both pointing north and Emily was yawning into her fist. "I think I need to head home," she said around another yawn. "Sorry – full day at work. Learning a new role is hard. Plus I'm studying for my GP licensure."

Hazel smiled. "Yeah, we've been staying up late every night too, so I'll have to get back into the habit of going to bed at a reasonable time before school starts in the fall."

"I'll drive you, Em," said Eamon. "You do look tired."

She yawned again, even as she protested. "You don't have to do that. I drove here …"

"I don't mind." He stood and offered his hand.

She took it gratefully and, after saying her good-byes, they walked out to his pickup hand in hand. She leaned her cheek against his arm, savoring the feel of his skin against hers and the warmth of his hand, their fingers intertwined. They were quiet on the drive. The night was lit up by a blanket of brilliant stars twinkling overhead, not a single cloud to obscure them or the half moon low on the horizon, casting a golden glow over everything.

"Would you like to stop by the lake?" asked Eamon. "You know, the one where we went fishing? It's beautiful on nights like this with the moon reflected in the water."

She nodded and stifled another yawn.

He turned soon after onto the small dirt road that led to *Magic Eight Lake*. They wound slowly through the darkness of the woods, emerging onto the bank of the lake bathed in the brilliant moonlight. When she stepped out of the truck, she didn't feel tired any longer. The air was cool against her face, a gentle breeze lifting her hair from her neck.

Eamon took her hand again, pulled a blanket from the back of the truck and led her to the water's edge.

He laid the blanket on the ground, then sat down and patted the space beside him. She sat as well, and they both lay back on the rug to stare up at the sky. She sighed. It was so beautiful. The stars blinked overhead, the sky was clear and dark yet full of the brightness of the evening lights. The moon shimmered on the surface of the lake. "Look, a shooting star!" she cried, pointing directly overhead. "Did you see it?"

Eamon chuckled beside her. "Yeah, I saw it."

"It's just so amazing. I can't remember the last time I stopped long enough to stare up at the sky. And even then the sky in Boston doesn't look like this – it's nowhere near as clear or bright. The stars look so big, so close, it's as though I could reach up and touch them." She raised a hand skyward, as if to pluck one from the heavens.

"Yeah, it's pretty great."

"Thank you for bringing me here." She turned onto her side and rested her head on her hand, leaning on her elbow. He did the same to look directly at her, only inches separating them. Her heart skipped a beat and, feeling bold, she lifted a hand to trace the line of one dimple.

He smiled, making it deepen. "How are you feeling about the new job, the new apartment ... everything going on with you?" He tucked a lock of her hair behind her ear.

She smiled. "The job's more challenging than I'd thought – just learning all the ways they do things there. It's different, but I'm really enjoying it. They seem to actually care about me, and go out of their way to help me whenever I need it. The patients are grateful for my help, and I've already got a couple of regulars who ask specifically for me. The hospital's smaller than I'm used to, but I can see how I'll really be able to contribute. And I'm loving my apartment – it's so cozy it already feels like home. Only ..."

He frowned. "Only what?"

"It's too quiet. I mean, I'm used to being at work all the time and just coming home to sleep, but now I have all this time to myself. I feel a bit lost, lonely. I was thinking maybe I should get a pet."

He chuckled. "A pet?"

"It's an apartment, so I don't think I can get a dog or anything. But maybe a fish or an iguana or something."

"You want a pet iguana?" Eamon guffawed, his eyes wide.

"I don't know ... maybe."

He stroked her face. "How about we spend more time together? Then you won't be lonely."

"You want to see even more of me than you already do?" she teased, pushing playfully against his chest. "Won't you get tired of me?"

His eyes flashed. "I think I could spend every moment of every day with you and never get sick of you." He cupped her cheek and leaned forward to kiss her lips. "I know you still have some questions about us, but I want you to know I don't – I'm crazy about you. I don't have any reservations about us. I'm all in." The lines around the outside of his mouth deepened with his smile.

Her chest tightened and she leaned over to kiss him back, her heart beating wildly in her chest. Her throat ached with the intensity of her emotions. She laced her fingers in his hair, pressed deeper into their kiss and let go of every inhibition, every fear, every anxiety and doubt in the strength of his arms.

CHAPTER 14

he foals leaped and played, tossing dainty heads and flicking tiny hooves. The sun heated the rain-soaked grass at their feet and sent a cloud of steam rising through the air. The early morning shower had brought some respite from the heat wave, but the last gasp of summer returned in all its glory.

Eamon laughed and adjusted his hat. He looped Maggie's reins around the branch of a small tree and crept slowly toward the herd. He didn't want to startle them – they were all used to him by now, but foals could still be skittish and he wanted to make sure they were all healthy and well. He'd begun doing that daily after they lost Maggie's colt – he couldn't bear the idea of losing another, though the vet assured him the chances were slim. Still, he couldn't help checking, just to be sure.

A movement caught his eye, and he raised a hand to shield his eyes from the sun's glare. Dalton was cantering toward him on Sassy, his favorite chestnut mare who had recovered nicely from her accident with the barbed wire. No doubt his brother was enjoying his first ride after so long away from the ranch. One thing he knew about his older brother – he loved the ranch. "Morning, Dalton," he called, setting his hands on his hips

Dalton dismounted. "How're the foals doing?"

Eamon chuckled – that was Dalton, straight down to business. "They look good."

Dalton grunted and let his gaze wander over the herd, pride in his eyes.

"Man, I'm sorry about Maggie's colt. We did everything we could …"

Dalton looked at him with narrowed eyes. "I know – we've talked about it, bro. There's nothing you could have done differently, nothing I would have done differently if I was here. You and Parker did a great job looking after the place while I was gone. I couldn't have asked for a better team to help me here."

Eamon ducked his head, a lump in his throat. He wasn't used to such high praise from Dalton. Marriage seemed to agree with him. He swore his brother had looked almost giddy since he'd returned from his honeymoon. "Thanks, Dalton, that means a lot. I didn't realize just how much of the load you carried until you weren't around." He chuckled. "I'm glad you're back."

Dalton smiled – but there was a sadness behind his brother's eyes Eamon hadn't noticed there before. Was he about to tell him he was leaving? Walking away from the ranch? His heart lurched. He didn't know if he wanted to manage the place without Dalton. The thing he loved most about the Cotton Tree was that he got to work with his brothers every day. It was something they were growing and building together. "What's up, bro?" he asked, stepping closer.

Dalton swallowed hard, coughed, and now Eamon could see fear in his eyes. "I wanted to talk to you alone for a minute. There's something I ... it's hard for me to get the words out."

Sweat broke out across on Eamon's forehead. What was going on? Nothing ever fazed his big brother – he was tough as nails and never let anything get him down. "Okay ..."

"We had a great honeymoon. But there's a reason we stayed longer ..." Dalton paused and ran a hand over his face. "The day before we were supposed to return, Hazel fainted."

"What?"

"We were on the beach, taking a walk before dinner, and she just passed out. I was the most scared I've ever been in my life. I carried her up to the road and flagged someone down to call an ambulance." He paused again, crossing his arms as he took a deep breath.

"Man, is she okay?"

"When we got to the hospital, she'd woken up, and the doctors did all these tests and scans to try to figure out what was wrong with her. It's ... breast cancer." Dalton sobbed, his eyes filled with tears.

Eamon threw his arms around Dalton and hugged his brother tight. "I'm so sorry, man. That's horrible." He took a quick breath. He had to be there for Dalton, to comfort him. He had to be strong for his brother.

Dalton pressed his face into Eamon's shoulder for just a moment, then pulled away, rubbed his eyes and inhaled slowly. "The doctors say we caught it early. They don't even know why she fainted – apparently it had nothing to do with the cancer. Maybe it was the heat and she was dehydrated or something … but if she hadn't fainted we wouldn't know. So that's a blessing …"

Eamon nodded. "Yeah, that's good."

"Anyway, she starts treatment over at the hospital first thing tomorrow. We stayed in Destin longer to finish up the tests. We're determined not to let it spoil our happiness, you know? And Dr. Nimrez down in Destin said she has a good chance of beating it, so we're just trying to stay positive."

Eamon thumped his brother affectionately on the back. "I'm sure she'll be okay. She's young and strong and we'll all take care of her …" His voice broke.

"Thanks, Eamon."

THE CHURCH WAS a small nondescript building off Elm Street – only the small cross beside the front door and the sign on the street that read "New Life Church" gave any clue to its purpose. Emily parked in the dusty parking lot, wiped the sweat from her brow with a handkerchief and shoved it back into the pocket of her black-and-white polka-dot skirt. No doubt it'd take a while before she got used to the Georgia heat, but she still couldn't believe how much it felt like a sauna just to walk outside.

With her purse swinging from her shoulder, she walked into the building. The worship music had already begun – two vocalists, one with a guitar, stood in front of a small band, singing a quiet, lilting song. The swell of the congregation's voices rose to greet her and the sweet sound made her eyes smart with tears for a moment.

She could get used to coming to a place like this every Sunday. Already she'd made friends with several regulars and every time she stepped through the door she felt warmth, love and peace wash over her. She wasn't sure why, she just knew that she liked it and had never found anything like it outside those four walls.

Eamon, Parker, Dalton and Hazel were standing in their usual row, eyes forward, singing along to the music. Eamon's arms were crossed. Parker swayed nervously toe to heel and back again. Dalton stood with his arm looped through Hazel's. They were pressed against one another and she thought she saw the sparkle of a tear on Hazel's cheek. She slipped into the pew beside Eamon and he flashed her a warm smile, slipping his arm around her waist and squeezing gently before releasing her again.

Hazel caught her eye and waved, then slid by Eamon and whispered in Emily's ear. "Have to talk to you."

Emily nodded, her brow creasing. They walked out of the building, back into the heat, and she reached into her skirt pocket for her handkerchief again. Hazel guided her toward a bench seat beneath a tall oak on the edge of the parking lot, sat and smoothed her dress over her knees. Emily noted that her collarbone was protruding more than usual – she wondered how anyone could lose that much weight on their honeymoon. She sat beside her friend and turned to face her, one eyebrow raised.

When she saw the look on Hazel's face, a knot formed in the pit of her stomach. Whatever her friend had to say, it didn't look as though it brought her any pleasure. She held her breath while she waited for Hazel to speak.

"Em, a few days before we got back to the ranch I fainted. I went to the hospital and they ran some tests …"

"What? Were you dizzy? Did you injure yourself? What happened?"

Hazel laid a hand on her arm and chuckled. "Whoa, I'm getting to all that. I have breast cancer."

Emily took a deep breath and pressed her hands to her forehead. "Oh Hazel, I'm so sorry."

Hazel smiled palely. "Thanks."

Emily switched to patient-care mode, unable to comprehend that she could lose her friend. "What's the prognosis?"

"It's good. The doctor down in Destin, Dr. Nimrez, said it's in the early stages."

"Well, that's good." Emily took Hazel's hand.

"Yeah, we're staying positive. That's what Dalton said we should do – stay positive. He's been so great about it all. He's determined that I'm going to be okay. I don't know … I'm so scared." A stray tear wound down her pale cheek and she dashed it away with her free hand.

Emily squeezed her other hand. "You'll be fine. Do you have a local doctor yet?"

Hazel blinked and sniffled. "Actually, I was hoping you might be."

"Yes, absolutely I'll take care of you. You'll need an oncologist, of course, but I'll be your GP. Does that sound okay?" She patted Hazel's arm.

"Thank you, Em. I think it'll help me feel better

about it to know you're on top of it." She sniffled again.

"You bet." Emily leaned forward to embrace her friend, squeezing her eyes shut as if to shut out the fearful thoughts.

They walked back into church together, and Hazel immediately sang along with the rest of the congregation as they made their way to their seats. But Emily couldn't bring herself to sing. Her head was in a whirl, going over every possibly scenario, thinking through treatment options and running down lists of things to do. Hazel was about to go through what would likely be one of the most challenging times of her life – and she could help. She would help. She'd do everything possible to take care of her friend. They'd get through this.

They had to – otherwise, she didn't know what she'd do.

* * *

EMILY PULLED the door shut behind her. The entire office was dark – the rest of the team had left hours earlier, but she'd stayed after her last patient to pore over journal articles and research papers, investigating the latest advancements in the treatment of breast cancer.

Hazel had already found and met with her oncologist. Dr. Simpson seemed very capable when Emily sought her out at the hospital and shared her concerns over her friend's wellbeing. The doctor had even offered to have coffee with her to talk through the case. Their conversation had given Emily a lot of confidence in the treatment plan Dr. Simpson was recommending for Hazel. Since then, Hazel had started radiation therapy, but it was still too early to tell how successful it might be.

Emily trudged toward her car, yawning. After seeing twenty patients and researching for three hours straight, she was tired. Her stomach growled – she'd forgotten to eat dinner and had only a simple salad at her desk for lunch. She climbed into the car and turned the key in the ignition. The air-conditioning took a while to kick in – it blasted hot air directly in her face, making her cringe and blink dry eyes.

In her purse, her cell phone buzzed. She pulled it free and swiped the screen. "Hello?"

"Hey, sweetheart. You coming over tonight?"

Eamon's voice sent a wave of warmth through her. She smiled. "I'm on my way. I'm starving and *so* tired."

"Why don't you just spend the night, then? The guest bedroom's all made up. I've said you can use it anytime you like."

She yawned again. Perhaps she should stay at the ranch, but she didn't want to be an inconvenience. There were already so many people living there and she did enjoy the peace and quiet of her apartment. But she couldn't ignore the thud of her heart at the thought of seeing Eamon. "Okay, I'll drop by my place first to pick up a few things. See you in a bit."

Emily set the phone on the passenger seat and shifted into reverse to back out of her space. It felt good to have someone in her life, someone who knew when she got off work and was waiting to spend time with her. She smiled and drove toward her apartment.

When she arrived home, she hurried upstairs to find Eamon outside her door, a bouquet of red roses in his hands, his cowboy hat tipped low over blue eyes.

Her heart leaped. Every time she saw him it struck her again just how handsome he was. She grinned and ran into his arms, jumping up to wrap her legs around him. She kissed him hard on the mouth and linked her hands behind his head.

He chuckled against her mouth as she slid to the ground, landing softly on her feet. "I'm glad to see you too."

"What are you doing here?" she asked, unable to wipe the grin from her face.

"You sounded so tired, I didn't want you driving out to the ranch on your own."

She cupped his cheek with her hand. "Really? Has anyone ever told you that you're quite the catch?"

His cheeks reddened and he frowned. "Once or twice."

"Well, you are. Thank you – I'm exhausted."

After she grabbed a few things and packed them into an overnight bag, they climbed into Eamon's pickup and drove out to the ranch. The sky was clouded over and Emily heard a crack of thunder in the distance. Soon, forks of lightning lit up the western horizon. "Looks like it's headed this way," said Eamon, glancing out through his side window.

She nodded and watched the sky silently. She didn't particularly like storms – she knew it was childish to be afraid, but she still jumped every time thunder cracked nearby. By the time they pulled into the long drive at the Cotton Tree, her head lolled against the side door – she could barely keep her eyes open. Eamon leaped out to open the gate, and when they reached the house he carried her bag inside. She followed, shaking her head to try and clear the sleep from her thoughts.

Inside the house, Hazel, Dalton and Parker were lounging in the den listening to music and talking. She heard their laughter before she saw them, and it brought a smile to her face.

"Emily!" cried Parker, standing up to welcome her.

"Em, good to see you." Hazel smiled, waving a spoon. A bowl of ice cream rested in her hands, and she sat nestled in Dalton's lap.

"Hi, everyone."

"We were just about to go for a walk – care to join us?" asked Parker.

Emily yawned, then nodded. "Sure thing."

Eamon laughed. "I don't know – she might fall asleep and just keel over on us."

Hazel stood and headed for the kitchen. Emily followed her, wrapping one arm around her friend's waist. "How are you feeling?"

"Pretty good. A bit sick earlier, but I'm okay now. And Dalton's waiting on me hand and foot, so it's not too bad." She giggled.

"You're doing great."

Hazel put her half-finished bowl in the freezer. "Thanks. I really appreciate all your help. I don't know what I'd do without you, Em. Have I told you lately how glad I am that you moved down here?" Her eyes gleamed with tears.

Emily embraced her. "I'm glad I'm here too."

* * *

OUTSIDE, the storm drew closer. They could hear the rumble of thunder and see the lightning snaking in a long curve toward them. Emily huddled beneath Eamon's arm, pressing close against him as they walked side-by-side, following in Dalton and Hazel's footsteps. The newlyweds held hands and talked between themselves in hushed tones. Parker hung back, wrestling with Harley over a piece of rope the dog was particularly fond of. Even Lulu and the kittens stalked them from a distance. One big happy family.

Emily glanced over her shoulder and grinned at the sight of the black cat sneaking behind a shrub in the darkness, only the light from the porch behind her giving her location away. She giggled.

Eamon glanced at her. "What?"

"Nothing. Just laughing at Lulu hiding back there."

Eamon chuckled. "Yeah, she does that. Otherwise Harley rolls her. He thinks it's a great game, but she's not convinced." He stopped and turned to face her, resting both hands on her arms and staring into her face. It was so dark, she could only see an outline of his smile. "Are you happy?"

She breathed in deeply. "Oh yes."

"Because you know, I'd understand if you weren't. I mean, you've made a lot of changes in your life recently, and you missed out on your dream job. I know working in Tifton doesn't really make up for that. So I guess ... I just wanted to ask." He ran a hand through his hair.

She put her arms around his waist and rested her chin against his chest, looking up at him. "I am happy. Actually, I love my job – it's interesting and challenging, and I really enjoy working with patients all day. I enjoy diagnosing, and I still get to do surgery at the hospital a few days a week as well. I have a pretty great boyfriend too, so there's that."

He sighed. "I'm glad. I didn't want you to feel like

you were missing out on something, or settling for less than you deserved."

"I don't feel that way at all. It's strange, but I really couldn't ask for more. Who knows what the future holds, but for now I'm happy with what I have." She stood on tiptoe to kiss him.

When she pulled away, he spoke again. "The reason I ask is … I want to spend my whole life with you. I know it's soon and you can take all the time you need to think it through, but I know what I want – and it's you." He dropped to one knee and took her hand. " Emily Zhu, I love you with all my heart and can't imagine spending another day without you. Will you marry me?"

She sucked in a quick gasp and her heart thudded, as her free hand flew to cover her mouth. It was all so sudden – she hadn't even considered marriage yet. But now that he'd opened his heart to her, she knew what her answer would be. "Yes! Yes, I'll marry you. I love you too."

He jumped up with a shout and caught her in his arms, kissing her in a way that made her heart pound in her chest.

"What's going on?" called Dalton, concern in his voice.

"She said yes!" Eamon cried.

Dalton and Hazel hurried back to them, and while Dalton shook Eamon's hand, Hazel threw her arms around Emily with a sob of delight. "Oh, that's wonderful! I'm so happy for you both!" Parker soon joined them and congratulated the newly engaged couple.

Emily held Eamon's hand through it all, and her throat tightened with each passing moment. She couldn't believe how much her life had changed for the better in just a few short weeks. And she couldn't ask for anything more. Her heart felt as though it might burst with happiness.

When the rest of the group finally headed back to the house, Emily wrapped her arms around Eamon and gazed up into his face. A fat rain drop landed on her forehead, followed by another on her cheek. She blinked and Eamon chuckled. A loud crack resounded close by, making her jump, but he held her closer and leaned forward to kiss her softly. His lips explored hers, and she forgot everything in his arms. Her body trembled at his touch and her legs felt weak as the rain fell harder, soaking her upturned face.

"So, Doc, do you think you could stand living in the country, married to a cowboy?" Eamon shouted over the storm.

"It's like a dream came true that I never knew I wanted." Emily kissed him again, melting into his embrace as rivulets of rain ran down their faces, soaking their clothes and drowning out every other sight and sound, leaving them all alone in each other's arms.

THE END

PARKER

ABOUT PARKER

When bumbling veterinarian Jennifer Barsby's friend Hazel falls ill, she doesn't hesitate to take action. After quitting her job in Atlanta, she packs up her life and moves to the Cotton Tree ranch in South Georgia to take care of her sick former room-mate. But when circumstances change, she wonders what she should do with the rest of her life.

Handsome and brooding cowboy, Parker Williams, is just another pal — at least that's how Jen sees him. A former Army Ranger, he's found renewed purpose as part-owner of the ranch. But he's given up on the idea of ever moving on or finding love. That is until Jen moves in.

She's fun-loving, accident-prone, earnest and caring. But could she ever see him as anything more than a friend?

CHAPTER 1

*J*ennifer Barsby clenched the steering wheel with both hands, blinked, stifled a yawn, blinked again. Surely she was close to arriving at the ranch – she didn't remember it being this far off the highway. She flipped on the radio, grimaced as static boomed through the speakers and spun the dial to the left.

She was on her way to the Cotton Tree Ranch to see Hazel. Her former roommate had been diagnosed with breast cancer only weeks earlier, on her honeymoon with the ranch's co-owner Dalton Williams. Jen was determined to do everything she could to help her friend. She knew she had no control over how things would turn out, but at least she could be there for Hazel during the most difficult time of her life.

Her eyes smarted as the memory of their phone conversation replayed in her mind. She still couldn't believe Hazel was sick. The last time she'd seen her, at the wedding, she'd glowed with health. She shook her head and yawned again, one hand over her open mouth.

There it was – the sign for the Cotton Tree Ranch. Tapping on the brakes, she slowed and turned onto the long winding drive.

Once she was through the gate, she smiled at the sight of Harley, Dalton and Hazel's black dog with the floppy ears, standing rigid beside the ranch house, barking furiously at her approach. The occasional tail wag betrayed his friendly nature. When she parked out front, he bounced beside the vehicle. She laughed, opened the door and before she could even set foot on the grass, he'd climbed into her lap and was licking her face, his ears back against his head.

"Harley, stop!" she giggled, shoving him away. His tail wagged hard against the car door, thudding in a steady rhythm, before he launched himself at her again, wetting her arm and cheek with his long tongue. He was still just a puppy, but he'd grown so much in the short time Dalton and Hazel had owned him. Now he was a lanky bundle of floppy ears, pink tongue and long legs.

She stroked his back and scratched his rump. "Oh, you're such a sap, aren't you, boy?" She scratched his head and tugged him back by his collar with another laugh, then stepped out of the car and stood as he pressed against her, peering up at her with wide brown eyes full of love.

The ranch house was a long single-story structure. A wide porch adorned the front of the house, and fresh paint gleamed in the afternoon light. She smiled at the hanging plants on the porch – no doubt Hazel's touch. In the short amount of time her friend had lived there, it had definitely benefited from her good taste.

The last time she was there, the house had a bachelor-pad feel to it. Dalton lived there with his two brothers Eamon and Parker, and though the men kept the place clean and tidy, its sparse furnishings and lack of decor made it clear there were no women living there. But things were different now – Hazel had moved in and made the place a home, and the ranch house looked cozy and inviting.

The front door flew open and Hazel stepped onto the porch with a grin. She waved and laughed at the sight of Harley bouncing in excitement beside Jen. "I think he's as happy to see you as I am."

Jen skipped up the stairs and threw her arms around Hazel. Her throat tightened and she held onto her friend, unwilling to let go. Hazel felt thin. Too thin.

Hazel chuckled. "You okay?"

"Uh-huh," she mumbled against Hazel's auburn curls. "It's just good to see you. I've missed you. Are you feeling all right?" She pulled back and studied her friend with concern.

Hazel tipped her head to one side and smiled weakly. "Not too bad. And I've missed you too. But you know, you really didn't have to come. I mean, you quit your job and moved to south Georgia just because I'm sick? You shouldn't have done that."

Jen swallowed around the lump in her throat and shook her head. "Yes I should've. You're my best friend and you need me, so here I am."

Hazel hugged her again. "Thank you."

"You're welcome."

"But what about your amazing veterinary job that you didn't want to lose? What will you do?"

"Don't concern yourself with that." Jen linked her arm through Hazel's as they walked into the house together. "I'll figure it out. Besides, I've got some money saved, so it won't hurt me to take a little time off. You just focus on getting better."

"Oh dear, Harley's followed us inside." Hazel stopped and faced the dog, who looked at her with his head cocked to one side and one ear standing on end. "Back out you go, Harley. You know you're not allowed in here."

"I'll take care of it – you sit down and rest."

"I'm not an invalid, you know," muttered Hazel. "Not yet, at least," she said as she sat on the couch.

Jen turned, clucked her tongue and shooed Harley back toward the porch. He didn't budge, so she grabbed him by the collar and ran with him through the door. He darted to one side and she tripped over the lip of the door and fell – directly into a thick, hard chest. She crumpled to the ground, landing in a heap on a set of mud-encrusted cowboy boots and whacking the back of her head on the hard porch.

"Jen?" the owner of the boots asked.

Jen squinted up at him, rubbing the back of her bruised head with one hand, and smiled. "Hi, Parker."

* * *

JEN TOOK the ice pack Parker offered her and put it to the back of her head with a sigh. Hazel hovered over her, a worried expression on her pretty face. "Really, I'm fine. It's not that bad – it doesn't even hurt," she complained. "I should be taking care of you, not the other way around."

Hazel handed her a tall glass of iced tea and sat beside her on the edge of the couch. "Never mind that. I'm happy to help."

"Are you sure you're okay?" asked Parker, crossing his arms.

"Yes, I'm fine. Thanks."

"Well, I'll just stash your things in the guest room for you, then head back out to work. Dalton will be wondering what happened to me." He chuckled and headed for the front door.

"Thank you!" called Jen at his retreating back.

"I'm sure glad this house is so big," said Hazel, tucking a cushion behind Jen's head lovingly. "Dalton and I have the master suite, and Parker and Eamon each have their rooms. Even with you here, we have another empty guest room we're using as a storage space and office. If someone else comes, we'll be packed to the rafters." She laughed and folded her hands in her lap.

Jen noticed the dark circles beneath Hazel's green eyes. "I could always stay at a hotel or something in Tifton, if it gets too crowded ..."

"No, please stay here. I'm going to love having you around. We were roommates for so long, I miss living with you."

"Me too," said Jen with a smile.

"I mean, here there's no one to leave expired cartons of milk in the fridge, or blast their bizarre dance mixes on full volume through the house." Hazel winked at her and chuckled.

Jen made a face. "Yeah, yeah. I kept things interesting, didn't I?"

"Yes, you did. Especially when you called me from your hospital bed begging me to fill in for you and impersonate a vet at a ranch in south Georgia!"

Jen laughed. "That *was* beyond the pale, but I'd say it worked out pretty well for you."

"Yes, it did." Hazel patted her arm gently. "Thank you. And thank you for coming down here when you heard I was sick. I really appreciate it … you're a good friend …" Her voice broke.

Jen leaned forward to embrace her. "We'll get through this together," she whispered.

"Yes, we will."

Both women pulled back, wiped the tears from their eyes, laughed and sniffled. Hazel grabbed a box of Kleenex from the side table at the end of the couch and handed it to Jen. "Here."

"Thanks." Jen took a few and handed the box back. "So how are Eamon and Emily doing?" she asked.

Hazel grinned. "They're sickeningly happy," she said with a laugh. "Do you remember how any display of love used to make her grimace? Well, now she's the one being all lovey-dovey, and it's beautiful."

"That's good to hear." Jen pulled the ice pack off her head and set it on the coffee table, then stood with a yawn.

"Tired?" asked Hazel.

"Yeah, for some reason driving makes me sleepy."

"It does that to me as well. Never mind – you can hit the hay early tonight if you like. We generally go to bed pretty early around here, since work on the ranch starts at dawn for Dalton and his brothers. And I've been sleeping a lot more lately. My doctor wants me to take care of myself and give my body the best chance it has of fighting off the cancer."

Jen nodded. "That's a good idea."

Hazel stood as well and ran her fingers through her hair. "Come on, I'll show you to your room and you can get settled before dinner."

Jen followed her down a long hallway to a door on

the right-hand side. The door opposite it was shut. "That's Eamon's room. I'm not sure when you'll see him – he left on a business trip of some kind a few days ago."

Jen raised an eyebrow. "A business trip? I thought he worked here on the ranch."

Hazel nodded, her brow furrowed. "Yeah, he does. He was very cryptic about the whole thing – something about investigating some blood lines. And Emily left for some kind of surgical conference a day after Eamon."

Jen frowned. "I thought she was supposed to be performing *your* surgery."

"Oh, she is. She'll be back in plenty of time. I think she's only gone for a few days."

"Hmmm …" Jen wasn't pleased to hear that Hazel's surgeon and future sister-in-law was out of town. But she supposed she could overlook that, seeing as how Emily was planning on saving Hazel's life when she got back.

Hazel pushed the guest room door open and waved inside. "Here we are – this is your room. If you need anything, just let me know."

Jen's brow furrowed. "I'm sure I can find my way around. Don't you worry about me – I'm not here to cause you extra work, I'm here to help take care of you." She didn't want Hazel to fuss over her or see her as a guest – *she* wanted to be the one to do the fussing.

Parker appeared in the hallway with the last of her luggage, holding her veterinary bag up in the air. "Where do you want this one?"

Jen smiled and held out her hands. "I'll take it, thanks. It's full of my medical supplies. Hey, just so you know, I'm happy to take care of any sick animals free of charge while I'm here. Since Hazel won't let me pay rent."

Parker arched an eyebrow. "That'd be great, thanks! I'll tell Dalton – I'm sure he'll really appreciate it."

"No problem at all. I'm happy to do whatever I can to help. Besides, as of yesterday I'm unemployed, so I'll need something to do with my time." She laughed.

He passed her the black bag. "You really quit your job, huh?"

"I did. My boss told me I could come back anytime, so that's good – if I run out of money before I find something else, I may have to take him up on that."

"I'd be happy to give our vet Will a call for you," Parker replied. "See if he's got any work available."

"Would you? That'd be great, thanks. I'd like to get some part-time work if nothing else, just to keep me occupied. There's only so much coddling Hazel will put up with, if I know her as well as I think I do."

Hazel laughed and rolled her eyes. "You've got that right."

"Okay, I'll call him tonight." Parker set the rest of Jen's luggage in the guest room, then headed back down the hall with a wave over his shoulder. "See you in a few. Dalton and I just have to finish up the chores and we'll be in for dinner."

Jen walked into the room and set her medical bag down on the floor beside her rolling suitcase. She sighed and slumped onto the bed, rubbing her eyes. "It's good to be here. It's been such a flurry of activity getting everything ready to come. I'll be glad to get some rest!"

Hazel tapped her fingers on the door frame and smiled. "Well, you'll have plenty of time for rest now.

I've already made dinner. I've taken to making easy meals these days, so it's pot roast tonight."

"Wow, that sounds delicious," marveled Jen with a grin. "You're like a regular Martha Stewart these days."

"If only," laughed Hazel. She turned to leave, then grinned back over her shoulder. "Welcome to Cotton Tree Ranch, Jen. If you're not careful you may end up like Emily and I and never leave." She laughed as she walked away.

Jen blinked. It was true. Hazel came here for only a few days, and almost two years later she was back living on the Cotton Tree Ranch. Emily arrived a couple of months ago for Hazel's wedding – she ended up moving to Tifton to be close by, and before long she'd be married to one of the Williams brothers and perhaps living at the ranch as well.

She swallowed hard. Well, that wouldn't happen to her. She and Chris were happy in their relationship and she could imagine them getting married one day. She couldn't say for sure yet, since they'd never discussed the possibility, but they both got along well and enjoyed each other's company. He was a great guy, good-looking, a successful junior lawyer with a big Atlanta firm. And he seemed to care a lot about her.

Anyway, the only eligible Williams brother left was Parker, and even though he was strikingly handsome in a mysterious, melancholy kind of way and they always had a lot of fun together, theirs was more of a brother-sister relationship. They teased each other and laughed together, but there was no flirting, not that she'd picked up on. She was glad to have his friendship, but it'd never be anything more than that.

She lifted her suitcase off the floor and set it on the bed. As she unzipped it, the thought crossed her mind that she should probably call Chris to let him know she'd arrived safely. He hadn't been thrilled when she told him she was moving to south Georgia. It was only temporary – she'd been very careful to stress that. But still, his jaw had clenched in the way it did when he wasn't happy about something. And he'd gritted his teeth when she said she was quitting her job to care for her sick friend. He didn't say she shouldn't go, but he'd made it pretty clear he didn't want her to.

Still, she couldn't fault him for a lack of support – he'd told her she should do what she had to do and he'd wait for her to come back to Atlanta. She smiled at the memory of their kiss goodbye. It had been hard to leave. But in her mind the decision was made the moment she heard Hazel's diagnosis. She'd missed Hazel, and once she knew she was sick, she couldn't let her go through that alone. She had to be with her and support her, or she'd regret not doing it for the rest of her life. If something should happen …

No. Jen couldn't think about that. Hazel would beat this thing – she had to. And Jen would do everything she could to help her.

CHAPTER 2

*P*arker Williams settled his hat more firmly, planted his feet, raised the rope over his head and spun it around and around. He let it fly through the air, and it landed with a soft *thwap* around the fence post. He tugged it tight and smiled in satisfaction. He'd been part-owner of the Cotton Tree Ranch for almost two years now, and had just about perfected his lassoing technique.

In all fairness, he'd learned the skill as a boy back in Chattanooga. He and his brothers had been raised on a hobby ranch by parents who loved horses and everything to do with them. They'd grown up around the animals and had free rein to run around the property as they liked. He had good memories of those times.

But when Dad died, everything changed. Mom couldn't, or didn't want to, manage the ranch on her own, and had bought a place in town. By that time, Dalton had already decided on a career in the rodeo as a bronco rider. So when Eamon went off to college to study accounting, Parker felt lost and alone. He'd gone from living with three strong male role models in the house – encouraging, teaching and leading him – to none. It was too quiet.

He knew when he signed up with the Army that Mom wouldn't be happy about it. He was a straight-A student, and she'd made it pretty clear she expected him to follow in Eamon's footsteps to the University of North Carolina. But his feet itched to travel and his heart desired more. He knew he didn't want to go to college, at least not yet, and the camaraderie of the armed forces appealed to him.

The rope whistled through the air again and landed squarely around the fence pole. This time, he heard a slow clapping from outside the yard. He turned his head to see Jen, one foot perched on the lowest fence rail. She'd donned a cowboy hat and boots, and her blonde hair hung in long wet tendrils around her tanned face. "Nice roping, cowboy," she said with a laugh.

He chuckled and meandered over to the post to retrieve his rope. "Thanks. You ever tried it?"

She shook her head and opened the yard gate. "No, I never have. And given my coordination or lack thereof, I'd likely never lasso anything but my own head."

He laughed and pushed his hat back. "I'd be happy to teach you if you like."

She frowned. "Um … okay. It's probably a waste of your time, though. Just warning you – I've never been any good at sports. Or anything requiring hand-eye coordination."

He snickered and handed her the coiled rope. "Well, let's give it a shot anyway. Here, hold this bit. There, that's it … then you swing it around over your head. That's the way … ouch!" He blinked as the rope whacked him in the side of the head. "How about I stand safely over here?" he joked, chuckling as he stepped back.

Jen grimaced. "That's probably a good idea." She frowned, stuck her tongue out of the corner of her mouth and set the rope spinning above her head again. She let it go, sailing toward the fence post, but it fell short and landed with a thud in the dirt.

"Hmmm … not bad, you're on the right track," encouraged Parker with a wink.

She laughed. "Okay, I'll try again." And this time the rope almost made it to the post. She gasped and faced him with a grin. "Did you see that?"

He laughed at her enthusiasm. "Yep, sure did. I think you're a natural. You'll be the best roper in town before long."

The ranch had a small herd of cattle on hand for milk and beef, a mixture of Herefords and Guernseys. The colorful group grazed quietly just outside the yard. Jen watched them, the rope looped in her hand, then started for the gate to that field. "Hey, where you going?" asked Parker, one eyebrow arching in concern.

"I just want to try …" She didn't finish her sentence.

But Parker had already guessed what she had planned. "Jen, no." He hurried after her, ducking through the fence railings into the yard. By the time he reached the other side, she was already near the herd, gently reassuring the cattle. They'd stopped grazing and raised their heads high to watch her approach. "Jen, I don't think that's a good idea …"

Jen set her feet apart and twirled the rope high above her, then let the loop fly toward a pair of young

Hereford steers. The rope settled atop the head of one of them, around the stubs where one day horns would grow. She pulled the rope tight … and the steer shook his head and took off.

"Jen!" Parker yelled.

She squealed in delight. "Look! Look, I did it – I roped a steer! Can you believe AAAAAGH!" The rope went taut, and even though Jen braced herself and pulled back, holding it firmly with both hands, the steer had momentum and weight on its side. Parker watched in dismay as Jen fell face-forward into the dirt. The steer paused a moment in his flight at the sudden dead weight on the end of the rope.

Parker ducked through the fence rails and sprinted toward Jen. But just before he reached her, the steer took off again, bucking and tossing his head as he dragged Jen with him. "Let go, Jen, let go!" he shouted after her.

He saw her fumble with the rope, but she wouldn't let go. The steer set off toward the western fence line with Jen skidding through the pasture behind him. Her hat flew off as she bounced across the field. Parker stared after her in dismay, his hands on his hips and his eyebrows drawn low.

Finally she released the rope after about fifty yards and lay still on the ground. Parker ran to her, squatted beside her and checked her vitals. When he heard her sigh, his eyes drifted closed for a moment with relief. "Jen?"

She rolled over onto her back, scratches across her cheeks from the grass and thistles she'd been dragged through. "Yes?"

He chuckled. "Are you okay?"

She grimaced. "I think so."

He sat back on his haunches and rested his arms on his knees, the adrenaline filtering from his bloodstream. "What were you thinking? And why didn't you let go? You could have been really hurt."

She grinned at him and sat up with a groan. "I don't know what I was thinking. I guess I didn't think. And I tried to let go, but the rope was caught around my arm somehow. Ugh – that really was a bad idea."

"I mean, really! You're a vet, Jen. Surely you knew better than to rope a steer like that – he weighs about eight times as much as you!"

She grimaced as she flexed her hands. "Knowing better and wanting to try something are sometimes two very different things. I guess I didn't really believe I'd actually get the rope over his head like that. I mean, what are the chances?" She laughed and winced, pressing a hand to her side.

Parker laughed as well and ran his hands over his face. "I'd say pretty slim, but somehow you managed it. You sure get yourself into a lot of scrapes, Jennifer Barsby. Come on, let's get you back to the house and patch you up." He guided her gently to her feet and helped her hobble back to the ranch house.

When they went inside, Hazel rushed over with a scream. "What on earth? What have you done to yourself this time, Jen?"

Jen shook her head. "I roped a steer."

"You what?" Hazel frowned at Parker. He shrugged as if to say, *not my idea*.

"Yep, I roped a steer. Didn't I, Parker?"

He nodded. "You sure did – and hopefully got enough sense knocked into you to regret it."

Jen laughed, then grimaced again.

"All right, let's get you on the couch," Hazel admonished. "Please, no more injuries after this – you're going to give me a heart attack, and that's the last thing I need right now."

Parker watched them, trying hard to hold back his laughter. He couldn't help it – there was something so adorably ridiculous about Jen. She was beautiful and intelligent and accomplished, and yet hopeless and vulnerable and clueless at the same time. He couldn't help wanting to laugh, even though he knew it wasn't right with her in so much pain. He went to fetch the ice pack from the kitchen again, wondering if it had even had time to refreeze since Jen's mishap the previous evening. With her around, they might need to invest in a second one.

When he got back, Hazel, having retrieved the first-aid kit from the bathroom, had pulled Jen's shirt up and was dabbing at a graze on her side. "Do you want me to call Chris for you, let him know what's happened?"

Jen shook her head. "No. He's working and I wouldn't want to interrupt him. Besides, I'm fine, really. It's just a few scrapes and bruises." She watched Hazel's ministrations, grimacing with each wipe of the cotton ball.

"Who's Chris?" asked Parker, crossing his arms.

"Jen's boyfriend back in Atlanta," replied Hazel.

"Oh." He didn't know Jen had a boyfriend. Of course, it made sense – she wasn't the kind of woman to be single. "And you left him behind in Atlanta?"

"Uh-huh. He understands — I need to be here with Hazel. Once she's well, I'll go back and everything will be just the way it was before."

"That's right," added Hazel with a wink.

"If you survive that long," muttered Parker.

"What was that?" asked Jen, her brow furrowed.

"Nothing." Parker chuckled, and Jen's eyes narrowed.

* * *

JEN STRETCHED her arms over her head and waited for a shooting pain to charge through her torso, but there was only a dull ache. It had been three days since the incident with the steer and her injuries felt mostly healed, though her right side was covered in purplish-yellow bruises and red scratches. The marks on her face had faded, but the skin where the rope had caught around her arm and hand was still red and swollen.

She set her hairbrush on the dressing table and took one last look in the mirror. With her clothes on, she didn't look too bad. The worst injuries were mostly hidden by the flannel shirt and jeans.

Outside, Harley barked. The barking grew louder and more intense, then faded to nothing. She cocked her head to one side and listened as a car engine shut off — someone had arrived. She hurried down the hall and out the open front door.

Hazel, Dalton and Parker had beaten her outside. They'd likely been having breakfast in the kitchen – she had been about to join them when Harley began his ruckus. She stood on tiptoe to peer over Parker's shoulder, but he was so tall it didn't help.

Then he headed down the porch stairs and she smiled. Eamon and Emily had arrived together in Eamon's truck. But weren't they away on separate business trips? She didn't think they were expected back yet, and certainly not together.

"You're back!" cried Hazel, hurrying to greet them

with Dalton and Jen trailing behind. "What's going on? Why did you drive home in Eamon's truck? Did you leave Em's car at the apartment?"

Emily hugged Hazel, then Jen. "Let's go inside and we'll tell you everything. We're famished – is there anything to eat for breakfast?"

Jen frowned. What did that mean, everything? She could tell something was going on by the shrill tone of Emily's voice – Emily was never shrill.

Eamon thumped his brothers on the back and laughed. "Good to see you. Dalton, Parker. Hope you didn't let the ranch fall into ruin while I was gone."

They all went up the stairs and into the house, joking and laughing. Jen followed them into the kitchen and began filling the coffee pot while she listened to their conversation.

Emily sidled up to her and smiled. "I heard you were coming down here to help Hazel. That's really sweet of you, Jen. She'd never admit it, but I think she'll need you. Her parents are on vacation in Belgium right now, and even though she told them about her diagnosis, they didn't want to change their travel plans. I think they were so shocked they couldn't process it, but she took it pretty badly. I think she hoped they'd get on the next flight back to the States and insist on coming and taking care of her, but they didn't. So it's good you're here."

Jen's throat tightened. She knew Hazel's parents weren't exactly the warm and fuzzy type, but she thought they'd be a bit more concerned about the health of their only daughter. She swallowed around the lump in her throat and flicked the switch to set the coffee pot to brewing. "I'm glad to be here as well. She hadn't told me about her parents. I can't imagine mine doing that."

"Are you and your folks close?" asked Emily.

"Yeah. We talk pretty much every day. They live in Birmingham, so it's not too far away. Though I don't go home as often as I probably should."

"That's nice," said Emily with a frown. "My parents and I aren't really talking at the moment."

"I'm sorry to hear that. What happened?"

"Eamon," responded Emily with a chuckle.

"Oh. But Eamon's wonderful – what's not to like about him?" Jen asked, her eyebrows pulled low.

"He's not exactly who my parents wanted me to marry – he's not Chinese, for one thing. And they blame him for me giving up my dream – more their dream than mine, really – of practicing at some top-tier hospital. Even though I'm happier doing general practice, plus part-time surgery at Tift Regional." She chuckled again and leaned her back against the kitchen counter, watching Eamon laugh and chat with his brothers at the kitchen table.

"Maybe they'll come around in time for the wedding," suggested Jen. "They can't cut you out of their lives forever. You're their daughter."

Emily shrugged. "Too late now."

"What?" asked Jen, her brow furrowed.

Emily nodded at Eamon over Hazel's head. He smiled, stood and clapped his hands loudly. "Hey, listen up everyone!" he shouted.

The kitchen grew quiet as everyone turned toward him. Jen frowned, her gaze flitting from Eamon's face to Emily's and back again. They were up to something.

"Emily and I have something to tell y'all. Neither

one of us was really on a business trip the last few days."

Hazel cried "Ha! I knew it!" Dalton grunted.

Eamon laughed. "Yeah, yeah – well, the truth of it is, we got married!"

Emily wandered over to him, put her right arm around his waist and raised her left hand high to reveal a sparkling ring. "That's right," she added with a grin. "We eloped to Savannah."

"What? Oh, that's wonderful!" Hazel leaped to her feet and hugged Emily, then examined the ring with continued exclamations.

Jen smiled as she joined in congratulating the couple.

Once the noise faded and everyone was seated at the table again, Hazel spoke up. "But why did you elope? I was so looking forward to a big wedding and seeing Emily in a puffy white dress."

Emily smiled weakly. "That's one reason we did," she said sardonically. "Also, there was your surgery …"

"No!" Hazel cried. "You can't …"

Emily shook her head. "It's not your fault. We didn't feel like having a big celebration, not until you're out of the woods. But we didn't want to wait to get married. We hate being apart." She leaned over to kiss Eamon on the lips.

"And with the rift between Em and her folks, we knew they wouldn't come to the wedding anyway," Eamon continued. "Likely none of her family would've come for fear of upsetting her dad. So it just made sense for us to elope. I didn't want the happiest day of my life to be a sad one for my wife."

"Anyway," added Emily. "It's done. We're married.

We're Mr. and Mrs. Williams." She laughed and kissed Eamon again.

Jen's heart skipped a beat. They were so in love. She couldn't help the little flash of jealousy that flitted through her.

CHAPTER 3

*C*offee dribbled noisily into the pot, and Jen rested her elbows on the countertop while she waited, her chin in her hands. She stared out through the kitchen window at the herd of horses grazing in the nearby field and let her thoughts wander.

Today she was taking Hazel to her oncologist.

Jen hadn't slept well at all, and her heart almost leaped from her chest when her alarm went off at six. She'd wanted to get a run and shower in before they had to leave. And now it was time to go, and Hazel still hadn't emerged from her bedroom.

She sighed and straightened, stretching one arm over her head and to the side, then the other. She'd been running further and further every morning. It must've been the country air that made her want to extend herself. Or the beautiful vistas, especially on mornings like today when a soft fog enveloped the rolling green fields.

Hazel came through the swinging kitchen door and

waved a hello. Jen understood her roommate's desire not to speak until she'd had her morning coffee. She hated noise first thing in the morning as well – it was one point the two women agreed on.

She pulled two mugs from an overhead cabinet, poured the steaming black brew into each and added a dash of milk. She handed one to Hazel, who took it with a grateful smile and sipped as she lowered herself into a kitchen chair. She picked a magazine up off the table and browsed through it, pausing to read an interesting paragraph here and there. "Sleep okay?" she finally asked, her voice husky with sleep.

"Hmmm … not great." Jen pulled out the chair beside her friend and sat, resting her elbows on the table with the mug between her hands. The chill of the morning air still hung in the kitchen, even though heat pumped out of the vents with a monotonous hum. "Are you worried about today?" she asked, one eyebrow raised.

Hazel grimaced. "I guess. I'm just thinking …"

"About what?"

"Um … well, at the last appointment the doctor laid out my options. She said if I had to go through chemo, I might not be able to have children for five years. If at all."

"Yeah, you told me that. I'm sorry, sweetie." Jen covered Hazel's free hand with hers.

"But I don't want to wait five years – I want to have babies sooner than that. And what if I can't? What if I'm sterile. What if …?"

"Okay, stop. Don't borrow trouble that way. We don't know what's going to happen, but whatever it is we'll take it as it comes, okay?"

Hazel sighed and ran her hands over her unruly auburn curls. "Yes, you're right, okay."

"It's time to go. Are you ready?"

She nodded and took another sip. "Ready as I'll ever be."

"Okay, let's go, then."

The kitchen door opened and Dalton walked in, Parker right behind him. "Good morning, ladies," said Dalton with a grin. He wrapped his arms around Hazel and kissed the top of her head. "Ready to go, sweetheart?"

"Ready."

Jen pulled two to-go cups out of the cabinet and filled them with coffee and vanilla-flavored creamer. "Coffee?" she asked the men.

Parker took one with a grin. "How did you know?"

"Oh, I just had an inkling. It's that kind of morning."

He laughed. "Yeah, I guess it is."

"What are you doing this morning?"

"Actually, I'm coming with y'all. There're a few things I need to get in town. Anyway, I wouldn't be able to focus on work with everything that's going on." His eyes met hers and she noticed for the first time just how intense they were. A dark chocolate brown, they made her spine tingle a little.

"I'm driving," called Dalton, heading out through the kitchen door with Hazel beneath his arm.

Parker laughed. "We'll definitely be late with Slowpoke at the wheel."

"Mind your tongue there," replied Dalton. "You young whippersnappers think you're all that. It's wisdom and maturity that make all the difference in a man, you just wait and see."

Parker gently kicked Dalton in the ankle, making him stumble. Dalton let go of Hazel, spun around and grabbed Parker with one arm around his neck, rubbing his knuckles back and forth on top of Parker's head.

"Oh, now you've asked for it," Parker laughed. He shifted his weight to grab Dalton around the waist in a tight wrestling hold.

"I give in, I give in," cried Dalton with a chuckle. "You win this round, whippersnapper."

Parker released him and thumped him good-naturedly on the back as they all climbed into the truck. Dalton took the driver's seat and Hazel sat up front with him. Parker and Jen took the bench seat in the back. A saddle filled up the far right space, leaving Jen with barely enough room in the center.

"You okay there?" asked Parker. "Got enough room?"

She frowned as she pulled the seat belt into place. "I think so. Sorry if I'm crowding you out."

"Doesn't bother me at all."

THE WALLS of Dr. Simpson's office in the west wing of the Tift Regional Hospital were covered in chipped white paint, making the office seem old and dirty, but Jen reassured herself that it was likely hygienic enough. But her stomach churned for an entirely different reason: she hated hospitals. The last time she was in one was for emergency surgery to have her appendix removed, and since then she'd avoided them as best she could. There was something about the sounds and smells of a hospital that made her want to flee.

Hazel picked up a magazine from the table in front of them and flicked through it. "You don't have to come in with me if you don't want to – I know how these places make you feel," she whispered

"No, really, I'm fine. I want to be here. I don't have anywhere else to be. Besides, it's time I got over my fear of hospitals, right?"

"Right." Hazel smiled nervously and reached for Dalton's hand.

He enclosed her hand in both of his and grinned. "It's gonna be fine, Slick. You'll see."

Hazel nodded and leaned her head back against his shoulder.

Parker stood and stretched his arms over his head. "I've got a few things to do down at the saddlery and the feed lot. I'll be back in an hour, okay?"

Dalton nodded and handed Parker the keys to the truck. "See you then, bro."

Parker shot a look at Jen before turning to leave. She watched him go, her thoughts racing. She closed her eyes and prayed for the first time in years, for God to take care of Hazel. Then her eyes flicked open as the receptionist told Hazel to go in, the doctor was ready to see her now.

The three of them stood at the same time and shuffled into the office. A sign on the door read ALICIA SIMPSON, M.D., F.A.S.C.O. Hazel sat on the examining table, leaving the chairs opposite the doctor free for Dalton and Jen. Dalton looked nervous, wiping his palms repeatedly down the legs of his jeans. Jen smiled at him sympathetically.

Dr. Simpson entered, her black hair bobbing as she

nodded. "So, Hazel, how are you feeling since we finished radiation treatment?"

"Much better than I did during the treatment. Though I'm still pretty tired."

The doctor nodded again. "Yes, that's to be expected. I've just finished going over your charts and X-rays with the head of oncology, and we agree on the next course of action. We recommend surgery."

"Surgery?" Hazel's eyes widened, and Jen reached for her hand to squeeze it.

"Yes, a double mastectomy." Dr. Simpson's eyes were kindly, but her words were firm.

Jen felt a tremor run through Hazel's hand. "A double …"

"Yes. We might be able to get away with trying to remove the tumor and operating only on the affected area in the left breast. But it's possible the cancer cells have already spread to the right and we just can't pick it up on our scans yet. I don't think the risk is worth it – I really think we should remove both, just to be safe."

Hazel's hand shook steadily now, and Jen could see her eyes fill with tears. Her own throat tightened and she held back a sob. She had to be strong now, for Hazel's sake.

Hazel looked at Dalton, and Jen noticed the stricken look on his face. "I … I don't know. Dalton?"

He nodded sadly. "We should do what the doc says, Slick."

"But I won't have any … I'll be … oh!" Hazel shook silently, tears rushing down her cheeks.

Dalton stood up, kissed her on the cheek and hugged her from behind. "None of that matters, Slick. Just so long as you're here and you're well."

"Now, if you have the double mastectomy and your

tests afterward are clear, you may not have to go through chemo," the doctor continued. "And just so you know, we can do an immediate reconstruction while you're in surgery, if that's what you decide you want." She tipped her head to one side with a compassionate smile. "I know it's not what you wanted to hear, but this really is the best way forward for you."

"An immediate reconstruction ... does that mean she'd have breasts right away, like they are now?" asked Jen, wide-eyed.

"That's right. Hazel, you'd get to choose from a selection of photographs for how you'd like them to look, and we'd make that happen while you're on the operating table."

Jen faced Hazel with a half-smile. "How about that, Hazel? You could finally have that cleavage you've always wanted."

Hazel's tears were interrupted by a brief giggle.

"I mean, you know how we've always been jealous of those women who throw on a push-up bra and all of a sudden they're Kate Upton? You could be that now! And since they're plastic, they'll never droop. Now that's a silver lining if I ever heard one!"

Now even Dalton and the doctor were guffawing.

Finally Hazel took a deep breath and wiped the tears from her cheeks with the back of her hand. "Okay, doc. We'll do it." She glanced at Jen and squeezed her hand. "I'll pick out my new boobs, and next summer I'll strut them in a bikini."

"That's the spirit," laughed Dr. Simpson. "I'll get the book."

* * *

PARKER CHANGED gears and stepped on the accelerator. He glanced at Jen in the passenger seat, her chin resting glumly in her hand. "Rough morning, huh?"

She nodded and forced a smile.

"You don't have to meet with Will today, you know. You could postpone it for another time. I'm sure he wouldn't mind."

She sighed. "No, I want to do it today. I need something to occupy my mind."

"Okay, then." He turned into a short driveway leading to a red brick two-story house set back in a peach orchard. Will Hart stood in his driveway, hosing down his truck. He waved at them as they approached, and a pair of golden retrievers ran over, barking fiercely with tails wagging.

Jen stepped out, patted the dogs on the head, then walked over to shake Will's hand with a smile. "I'm Jennifer Barsby. It's a pleasure to meet you."

"Pleased to meet you too, Jennifer. I'm William Hart, but folks around here just call me Will. I hear you're looking for some vet work?"

She nodded, resting her hands on her hips while Parker shook Will's hand. "Yes, that's right. I worked for the Green Peach Ranch up in Atlanta, but when I heard Hazel was sick I came down here. Part-time work is fine – just something to keep me occupied and pay the bills until Hazel's back on her feet."

Will nodded and went to the faucet to turn off the hose. "Sure, I understand. As it so happens, I've got more work than I can handle at the moment. If you're up for it, I'd love to have you help me out, say, three days a week for now. But it's solid work with a decent paycheck. You'll be doing mostly large animal work – are you okay with that?"

"It's what I love most," said Jen with a grin.

"Good to hear – that's what you get out here in the country. There'll be some cats, dogs and the like, but most of our patients are horses, cattle … you know, the heavier variety. And the majority of our work is call-out, so you won't be in an office."

"Fine with me."

Parker watched the exchange in silence. Jen handled herself well in a business setting. She seemed so much different from the bumbling woman he'd known so far. She was confident and mature, and he was glad to see her melancholy lift as she conversed with Will.

She shook Will's hand. "Okay, that sounds perfect. I'll see you Monday." She headed back to Parker's truck, a smile lingering on her lips.

"That went well," Parker said as they pulled out of the driveway.

She caught his gaze and nodded. "Yes, it did."

"You must love your work to be that happy about starting."

She laughed. "Yeah, I do."

"I guess your folks are really proud of you."

Her face clouded. "They are … though they wanted me to do something else entirely."

"Oh?"

She sighed. "The family business. After I graduated, they just expected I'd join them – they wanted me to run it someday, I suppose. But I had an entirely different plan for my life. I mean, I love my parents and I know they love me, but I wanted to make my own way. They never understood that. Of course, we've put it behind us now, but I know they still harbor a bit of resentment over me being a vet."

He arched an eyebrow. "I'm sure they think you're amazing. At least I do. It's not an easy thing to study as long as you did and take care of sick animals the way you do."

She grinned at him. "Thanks. Maybe you should talk to them."

He laughed, changing gears as they slowed to go around a corner. "I'd be happy to. But what about Chris – can't he talk to them? I'm sure they must love him – they get a lawyer as a potential son-in-law."

She grunted. "Well ... I haven't exactly introduced them to Chris yet. They had this idea that I'd marry my high-school sweetheart Ben Gwinnett. He works for them, and I think they still hold out hope that one day I'll come home, join the business and marry him. Never mind that he's already married to someone else – no one ever lives up to Ben in their minds." She laughed and smoothed her hair back from her face.

He frowned. "Sounds like your folks have all kinds of plans for you."

She nodded. "They sure do. Though they seem to tolerate my rebelliousness now. We get along great."

"That's good to hear. So are you planning on taking Chris home for the holidays?"

She frowned. "I haven't thought that far ahead. I don't feel like I can plan for anything until I know what's happening with Hazel. Thanksgiving is only a few weeks away – I can't imagine I'll be going home for that."

He nodded and clenched the steering wheel. She was right – Thanksgiving wasn't far away. He wondered what his mother would do this year with all her boys down south. He had an idea she just might make the trip, not wanting to stay in Chattanooga without them. They'd all gone home last year, but with everything going on with Hazel he knew Dalton wouldn't want to head north for the holidays. And what about Eamon – had he even told Ma he was married yet? He couldn't imagine how she'd react to that.

"What about you?" Jen asked. "Is there someone special in your life you might take home for the holidays?"

He shrugged. "Nope."

"Why not?"

He frowned. "That's a bit of a loaded question."

She laughed. "Come on, you're a great guy – smart, funny, good-looking, successful. I'm sure women are lining up to date you. Don't you have a girlfriend or three?"

He ran his fingers through his hair. "They're definitely not lining up to date me. I think I would've noticed." He chuckled. "I guess I haven't found someone I *want* to date. And I'm not ready – not sure I'll ever be ready, really."

She cocked her head to one side. "What do you mean?"

He felt his face warm. What was he doing? He never opened up to anyone the way he was with Jen, not since he got out of the Army. But there was something about her that made him want to share, to tell her everything. "I don't know why I said that. It's just that … since the military, I haven't felt like I could share my life, myself, with anyone. And you have to be open and vulnerable if you want a relationship. So they say."

Her lips pursed. "Yes, that's usually recommended. Though I bet *you* could get away with being closed off

– a lot of women would just think you were mysterious. They'd love it, trust me."

He chuckled. "I'll take your word for it."

"Oh yeah, some of them will eat that up. If you want to, we could go out sometime and I'll help you – I'll be your wingman, tell them how dark and brooding you are."

He shook his head with a laugh. "Thanks, but I think I can manage on my own."

"Doesn't seem that way," she murmured.

"Excuse me?"

"Oh, nothing."

"I'll date when I'm ready," he insisted. "And besides, I have to find someone worth opening up to. If those two align, I promise, you'll be the first to know."

Jen's eyes sparkled at him. "I'm holding you to that."

Parker couldn't help laughing. She always made him laugh. Even when she was prying into things that were none of her business and driving him crazy with her advice.

CHAPTER 4

*J*en smiled at the sound of Chris's voice on the phone. She'd missed it, missed him – though not as much as she'd thought she would. In fact, she'd done really well pushing thoughts of Chris from her mind over the past couple of weeks since her arrival. She frowned and threw herself back onto her bed, anxious to give him her full attention. "So what have you been up to?" she asked, rubbing her closed eyelids.

"Jen ..." He paused. "... we need to talk."

Her eyes flew open and she sat up straight. "What? What is it?"

He sighed into the receiver. "I haven't seen you in weeks. And even when we talk, you're completely distracted. I don't know ... I guess I didn't realize how hard it would be. And I didn't think you'd be gone this long."

She frowned. "Chris, Hazel hasn't even had her surgery yet."

Another sigh. "Yeah, I know."

She took a quick breath and her pulse raced. "So what are you saying?"

"It's not working. Not for me. And ... I met someone."

She couldn't speak. It felt like something heavy was pressing on her chest. She took a long, slow breath. "You ... what?"

"We don't see each other. We hardly talk. And ... Emma is here. She's available. And she's on the same track as me. You know what I mean?"

She shook her head silently. What did he mean, *the same track*? "But ... you said you'd wait for me. That you didn't mind spending time apart. I thought you understood what I was doing here."

"Yeah, well ... I guess it's harder than I thought it'd be. I'm just not the long-distance type of guy. I'm sorry, Jen. You're a great person and I enjoyed spending time with you, but let's be real – it wasn't going anywhere. So there's no point letting things drag out."

Her heart fell into her gut and a cold sweat broke out across her forehead. "I didn't think it was going nowhere. I thought we wanted the same things. I ..."

"Like I said. I'm sorry. Look, I have to go. Maybe I'll see you when you're back in the ATL, okay?" His voice was distant, as though he was already pulling away from the phone.

She nodded slowly. "Okay. Bye." The phone line went dead. She let her hand drop to the bed, her cell phone falling from her grasp. How could he end things like that? He didn't even have the decency to come to south Georgia and break up with her face to face?

She stood and rubbed her hands over her face. She needed to get out of there. She wasn't sure if anyone else was up – they'd finished dinner a couple of hours earlier, and after a brief chat around the fireplace in the den, everyone had headed for their respective bedrooms. She'd probably have the place to herself, which suited her fine. Usually, she'd seek out the company of others – she loved spending time with people – but not tonight, not after that conversation. She needed to be alone.

She pushed her feet into a pair of soft slippers, wrapped her plush bathrobe around herself, then peeked out the door before tiptoeing down the dark hallway. Just as she'd suspected, no one else was around. Someone had banked the fire in the hearth, and the remaining embers glowed in the blackness. She put on a knit cap, unlocked the front door and snuck outside.

The night was well-lit by a wide silver moon and a canopy of twinkling stars. She could clearly see the outline of the cattle herd beyond the barn, and the horses stood quietly in the field, only an occasional swish of a tail to show they were awake. With a quick tug, she pulled a chair out from beneath the outdoor table and sank into it with a sigh. She rested her elbows on the tabletop and her chin on her fists and stared out across the fields.

The hoot of an owl overhead startled her, and she watched as a bat sailed by, a dark shadow on silent wings. Cicadas filled the quiet with an unbroken chorus and she smiled at the lowing of a few restless cattle even as tears wet her cheeks.

A silent black figure emerged from the darkness and ran up the stairs, making her gasped. "Jen?"

She exhaled with relief. "Parker, you scared the life out of me!" she hissed. "What are you doing?"

He chuckled and settled into a chair beside her. "Just taking a walk. It's hard to get privacy around here sometimes. I like to go out at night when it's dark – I can just walk by myself and think about things. It's nice."

She raised an eyebrow. "I know what you mean. I came out here for the same reason. It's so peaceful."

He tapped a rhythm on the table with his fingers. "So what's going on?"

She spoke before thinking. "Chris just dumped me. Ohhh …" She sobbed, slapping her hand over her mouth.

She couldn't see his face, cloaked in shadow, but he tipped his head to one side and his voice was filled with compassion. "I'm sorry to hear that. Are you all right?"

She nodded through the darkness. "I'll be fine. I'm probably more angry than anything. He broke up with me over the phone, said he'd already met someone else. I really thought he cared about me, but it was so callous the way he did it. I guess I didn't know him as well as I thought."

He exhaled loudly and went back to tapping on the tabletop. "Yeah, that's pretty rough. I'm sorry." He leaned toward her.

She swallowed another sob as he wrapped his long arms around her and pulled her close. She nestled into the crook of his neck. He was warm, and his scent was a mixture of musk and cologne. She let her eyes drift shut to breathe it in. Already she felt better.

As he pulled away, she smiled through a sniffle. "Thanks, Parker. You're a real friend."

He nodded and stood. "How about we go out for a drink tomorrow night to celebrate?"

"Celebrate what?" she asked with a frown.

"Your freedom from Chris the Idiot."

She chuckled. "That sounds like a good plan."

"We'll see if the others want to join us."

"Perfect." She stood and followed him into the house.

Just before she headed down the hall to her room, he spun to face her. "You're better off," he whispered.

"What?"

"You're better off without him. He doesn't deserve you, Jen. You're amazing – beautiful and smart and sweet and kind and a lot of fun. He didn't see that or he'd never have broken up with you like he did. He'd have hung onto you forever." Parker saluted in the darkness and strode away.

She stared after him, her mouth ajar. She couldn't believe what he'd said. Did he really think that about her? Regardless, hearing it warmed her heart – and made her head spin. She padded down the hall to her room and shut the door behind her. She'd seen light beneath his door. No doubt he was reading – Hazel always said he was a voracious reader. She'd never met a man who read that much, not even in vet school.

She leaned back against the door and breathed deep the cold night air, marveling just how much everything could change in such a short time.

* * *

THE DIM LIGHT of Clancy's Bar and the smell of beer and stale peanuts assailed Parker's senses the moment they opened the thick oak doors. That was something he'd learned from his Army days: the world over, every dive bar felt pretty much the same.

He smiled at Jen and led the way to a booth. As he sat, she slid in beside him, scooting over the red fake leather seat to press against his thigh. She looked even more beautiful than usual tonight – her blonde hair glowed in the neon light, and she'd set it in curls that looped around her pretty face. Her blue eyes sparkled when she laughed. And he couldn't help admiring the curve of her jeans when she walked.

What was he thinking? She was a friend and he had no intention of changing that. Even if he'd wanted to, he didn't think she saw him that way. He was Hazel's brother-in-law and nothing more than that to Jen. Which suited him fine – he wasn't at a place in his life where he was ready for a relationship. And with Jen, it would be a *relationship*. She wasn't the kind of woman he'd be able to casually date.

Dalton and Hazel squeezed into the other side of the booth, followed by Eamon and Emily. The entire group barely fit, cozy and snug. Emily picked up a menu and looked it over. "What's good to eat here?"

Eamon chuckled. "The wings are pretty good. Or the cheese fries."

"I like the crab legs," added Parker with a wink.

Emily frowned. "What about the salads – any good?"

Dalton laughed. "I wouldn't risk a salad in this place."

"But everything else is so … unhealthy," she complained.

Eamon kissed the tip of her nose. "How about we share a grilled buffalo chicken burger with sweet potato fries? Would that work for you?"

She nodded and smiled. "It'll do."

Parker adjusted his seat, conscious of Jen flush

against him. There was no more space in the booth, so he ended up with her tucked under his arm as it lay across the back of the seat. She didn't seem to mind, just smiled up at him and reached across him for a menu.

"I'm gonna put something on the jukebox," said Hazel, then realized she was boxed into the booth.

"I'll do it," Jen replied. "You sit and relax."

"I can play a tune on the jukebox, Jen. I'm really not as incapable as you think." Parker could see Jen shrink back at her friend's harsh words. But then Hazel crossed her eyes and stuck her tongue out at Jen, breaking the tension.

Jen laughed and shook her head. "I know you're capable. I just want to take care of you. Besides," she added as she stood, "I can actually get up without forcing half the group to move."

"Okay, okay," Hazel conceded. "You know what I want to hear."

Jen nodded and hurried across the room to the jukebox. Soon the crooning of Michael Bublé filled the room, and the men rolled their eyes while the women smiled. "I love Michael Bublé," said Jen with a grin as she returned.

"Of course you do," responded Parker sourly. "All women do."

"Speaking of Michael," continued Jen, "I have a funny story to tell ya'll."

Hazel grinned. "Do tell – I love your stories."

"I was over at Doc Salvatore's the other day – he's started breeding hogs, you know? Well, he has two hogs called Michael and Bublé! Apparently his wife named them."

"Prissy Marge?" asked Dalton.

She nodded. "And since he's just begun raising hogs, he doesn't know a lot about them. So when Bublé started acting lethargic, he called me just to come out and check on her, make sure she was okay." She grinned at the group, all eyes on her. "I went into the barn and Doc and Marge introduce me to Bublé. She did seem a bit out of sorts and was butting the door of her pen with her head – things like that. Just seemed agitated.

"So Marge opened the pen and stepped inside, softly talking to the hog, encouraging her. She bent over to scratch her head – and just then, Bublé rams right into Marge's legs! Marge crumpled like a house of cards and landed in a pile of dirty hay. Doc ran into the pen, helped Marge to her feet and dusted off her floral print dress ... and that sow came behind him and rammed him in the butt! Both of them went down, face first in the slop troughs."

Hazel laughed and Dalton, Eamon and Parker hooted with delight. Parker slapped his thigh and chuckled.

"Oh, that would've been a sight to see – Old Doc and Prissy Marge's faces covered in pig slop," chortled Eamon.

Jen chuckled. "Yeah, it was quite the spectacle. But I had to keep things professional, so I sucked it up and rushed to help them – Jen to the rescue! I hurried in, got them upright and scraped off the worst of the slop so they could see ..."

"I see where this is going," Emily interjected.

"So then, Bublé came after me. She tried to hit me from behind, but instead went *between* my legs. So now I'm seated on her shoulders!."

The entire group erupted into raucous laughter and Dalton slapped the table.

"Well, the momentum knocked me off my feet and before I knew it I was riding a hog around her pen with nothing to hold onto! I clenched tight with my knees around her shoulders and prayed for her to stop, her squealing the entire time – squeeee! And Doc and Marge just stood and watched me in shock! It lasted a good minute or two, then Bublé stopped, let me off and wandered away, Without so much as a goodbye kiss."

Parker's laugh rang out above the rest, and Jen smiled up at him with a wink.

"What about the hog?" asked Hazel. "Was she all right?"

Jen chuckled. "She was fine. Just expecting. Go figure – a pig with pregnancy brain."

Parker arched an eyebrow and studied her as she laughed with her friends. She was a born storyteller, that was for sure. And for some reason, those kinds of ridiculous incidents seemed to follow her around. As he sat there, chortling along with the rest of them, he suddenly realized he hadn't laughed that hard since before he entered the service.

He inhaled deeply and set his elbows on the table, bowing his head over his hands. He hadn't known how much he missed it – laughter. What was that saying – "laughter is the best medicine"? Maybe it was true. All he knew was that for the first time in a long time, he felt good. Really good.

Outside on the porch, Jen set her book on the table and watched Emily park her car beside the ranch house. Harley bounded around, tail wagging. Even Lulu the cat emerged from the barn to stalk toward the vehicle, her tail flicking back and forth.

Jen smiled and waved as Emily got out. Eamon climbed from the passenger seat and held high a white plastic bag that looked as though it might burst at the seams. "We brought dinner," he shouted.

Jen nodded. "Sounds great!" She followed them inside, and the smell of Chinese food filled the room. Her stomach growled – Chinese food was her favorite type of take-out. She especially loved the beef and black bean from the Wok Inn in Tifton. She always made a point of checking out the best Chinese restaurants in a new town so she could satisfy her craving whenever it arose. And the Wok Inn was the best she'd found in the area.

Hazel was sitting in the den in front of a crackling fire, a blanket over her legs. Dalton sat with her, newly emerged from a shower after a hard day's work. They stood to welcome Eamon and Emily, then joined them in the kitchen and found seats at the table or counter. Emily passed plates and silverware around, while Eamon opened the boxes of food and set them in the center of the table.

"I'll go tell Parker dinner's ready," offered Jen. She jogged down the hall and knocked on his closed bedroom door.

"Just a minute," came a muffled reply from within. The door opened and Parker stood there, dripping wet with a white towel wrapped around his taut waist.

Jen's mouth fell open, all thoughts vanishing from her head. "Um ... hi."

He grinned and ran a hand through his wet hair. "Hi."

"Hi."

His eyebrows arched and he leaned against the door frame. "Did you need me for something?"

"Oh ... ah ... yeah. Um ... dinner. Dinner's ready. Eamon and Emily brought Chinese food." Her heart hammered.

He was still smiling. "You okay there, Jen? You seem a bit flushed."

She frowned in embarrassment. "Yeah, I'm fine. Great, actually. It's just really hot in here ... you know, with the fire going and everything."

"Oh, okay. I'll get some clothes on and be with you in a minute, then."

Jen nodded, frozen in place.

"I have to shut the door, Jen."

"Oh yeah. Sorry." She stepped back so he could close the door, then sighed deeply and leaned against the opposite wall, her legs trembling. That was Parker. Her friend. Mmmm.

She blinked and rubbed her eyes. So he looked great in a towel – that didn't change their friendship. He wasn't her type. And she was certain she wasn't his. Though really, she didn't know anything about his type – she'd never seen him with a girlfriend and Hazel hadn't mentioned anyone …

She hurried back to the kitchen and slipped into her chair without a word.

"Is Parker coming?" asked Hazel, spooning chow mein onto a plate and passing it around the table.

"Uh, yeah. He is."

Hazel frowned and reached for another plate. "Your cheeks are all red. Are you feeling okay?"

Jen blanched. "Oh yeah, I'm fine. I just got a little shock, that's all."

Hazel's eyes narrowed. "What? What happened?"

Jen leaned closer to Hazel and whispered into her ear so no one else at the table could hear. "Parker was in a towel. *Just* a towel."

Hazel almost choked trying not to laugh out loud. "Well, that explains it," she whispered back. "Are you okay? Can I offer you a fan, or some ice?"

Jen rolled her eyes. "Very funny." She reached for the snow peas.

* * *

PARKER SCOOPED the last spoonful of sweet and sour pork into his mouth and chewed slowly. The noise of the group chattering and laughing soothed his nerves. He'd begun to relax, enjoying their company more with each week that passed. Jen had a lot to do with that. With her here, he felt as though he had a friend he could talk to, spend time with, who seemed to understand him without pressuring him to share too much of himself before he was ready.

"… So as you all know, my surgery is scheduled for just before Thanksgiving. But there's something I wanted to discuss with y'all first."

Everyone quieted down and focused on Hazel.

She faced Emily with a hesitant smile. "You can say no, but I'd like you to perform my surgery."

Emily's eyebrows flew up. "Really? I mean, we talked about that a while ago, but then you seemed to have things under control without me. Are you sure?"

Hazel nodded. "There's no one else I'd want to do it. I know you'll take good care of me. You're probably the best surgeon in the whole area, anyway. So it makes sense."

Emily frowned. "Thank you." She glanced at Eamon, who raised an eyebrow. "Well, I'm happy to do it if you want me to. But remember, every surgery has its risks and I won't be at all offended it you choose to go with someone else. Please don't feel as though you owe it to me."

Hazel shook her head and put her hand in Dalton's. "We've discussed it, and it's what I want. We know there are risks involved and Dalton has promised me he won't blame you if things go wrong." She laughed uncomfortably and Dalton squeezed her hand. "So as long as you feel good about doing it …"

Emily smiled. "I'd be honored."

Hazel threw her arms around Emily, and tears glistened in her eyes.

Parker picked up a spring roll and munched on it as casual conversations started back up around the table. He pondered what had just happened, his thoughts in a whirl. Was it sensible to have a friend perform her surgery? It was Hazel's call, but as Emily had inferred, if something went wrong it would be easy to place the blame on her shoulders. That was a big responsibility for her to carry. Though from what he knew of Emily, she seemed fully capable of carrying it. He'd never met someone as tough and resilient as her.

He finished eating, took his plate to the sink and retreated to his room. He needed some alone time. The older he got, the better he understood that when he felt squirrelly, it was time to lose himself in a book, or go for a walk alone with just music for company.

Parker threw himself on his bed with a huff, crossed his ankles and reached for the book on his bedside table. He smiled at the cover – even though he was glad to have left the service behind, he still enjoyed reading a good military thriller. It let him remember without having to go through the stress and heartache all over again. He settled himself against the pillows, one arm behind his head, and jumped back into the story.

But just as he was getting started, his cell phone buzzed on the bedside table, spinning around in a circle. He sighed and reached for it. "Hello?"

"Hello, darling. How are you?"

"Not bad, Mom. And you?"

His mother laughed. He knew right away what that meant — she only laughed that way when she was feeling uncomfortable or about to confront someone she cared about. He couldn't help smiling.

"Oh, I'm okay, I guess. Though I'm a little put out

that none of my boys has invited me for Thanksgiving this year."

Parker rubbed a hand over his eyes. "Oh yeah, Thanksgiving. Sorry, Mom – we've just got a lot going on here at the moment."

She sighed. "I understand. It's just that I'd like to be part of it all. I mean, Eamon and Emily got married and didn't even tell me until afterwards! I'm still smarting over that one. I haven't met Emily yet. Hazel is sick and I'm stuck here in Chattanooga unable to do a thing to help. And I'm worried about you too."

He frowned. "Why are you worried about me, Mom?"

"I'm always worried about you, darling. You're my baby."

Parker rolled his eyes. "I'm not a baby anymore."

"Yes, but you're always *my* baby, six-foot-four or not."

"Well, you should come and visit sometime, Mom. But I'm not sure about Thanksgiving. Hazel's having her surgery just before the holidays and the house is pretty full." He grimaced as he sat up.

"I don't care if the house is full – I'll sleep on the couch. I miss you boys, and I want to be there. You know what – I'm coming. You can tell everyone else to expect me, okay?"

He heard the hurt in her voice and nodded slowly. "Sure, Mom. It'll be great to see you."

* * *

PARKER LIFTED the horse's hoof and filed it back. Perfect. He set it down and shifted positions until he was in place to shoe it.

He heard a car pull up the drive, then footsteps coming toward the barn, and glanced up. Jen stood there, scratching Harley behind the ears. "Hi, Parker."

"Hey, Jen. You're home early. Can you come have a look at this? Penny here's been limping a bit." He nodded at the horse's rear hoof he held in his hands.

She walked over to him. "Sure. I'd be happy to. I only had a couple of calls to do today, so Will let me finish early." She examined the hoof quickly and frowned. "Looks like the frog is bruised – it's pretty warm right here. See?" She took his hand and put it on the affected area.

He nodded. "It is warmer, I can feel it. What do you think caused it?"

"She probably stepped on a stone or something – it doesn't look like her hoof has been overtrimmed. But I'd keep an eye on her, make sure there's no underlying cause. I can check her over for you now if you like – I just have to get my bag from the car."

"No need. So she should just rest, then?"

"Yeah, stall rest or small-paddock rest. You could also try soaking her hoof in warm water with Epsom salts. Let me know if it doesn't improve."

"Thanks. I'll take care of it."

"You're welcome." She stood and turned to leave.

Parker set the horse's hoof gently on the ground and straightened. "Hey, there's something else I wanted to talk to you about as well."

She turned back and smiled. "Oh?"

"Yeah." He shoved his hands into his pockets and stared at the ground. This was hard – he wasn't sure what to say. He hated when people made a fuss over him, and this was the epitome of a fuss. "I've been invited over to the Ranger Memorial at Fort Benning.

They're giving awards to some of the guys I served with, and I'd like to go – you know, to support them. But I hate all that ceremony, and I'd have to wear my parade uniform … plus I'm not sure I really want to remember the stuff that went down. What do you think – should I go?" He glanced up at her.

She smiled. "Of course you should go. Sounds like it'll be great – you get to see some old friends and honor them, and it's not far away. I mean, I don't know anything about what you went through. But it happened – you can't pretend it didn't or try to erase the memories. I think all you can do is remember what happened and honor those involved the best you can."

He frowned. "I don't know …"

"You'll regret it if you don't. These opportunities don't come along all the time. You think they do when it's happening, but they really don't."

He cocked his head. "How'd you get to be so wise?" he asked with a chuckle.

She shook her head. "I don't know. My parents always told me that I should seize the moment, not say no to good opportunities, because they may never come along again. And I think they're right."

His brow furrowed. "Well, if I do go … would you come with me?"

She smiled. "Sure. When is it?"

"This afternoon," he replied. "That's why I haven't told anyone. It's really bad timing."

She nodded. "It'll be a good distraction for us. I'd love to go with you."

He sighed with relief. "Well, I'm almost finished here. How about we go inside and get some coffee before we leave? We can grab lunch on the way," he said, picking the horse's hoof up again and securing it between his thighs.

"Sounds good to me."

Once he was done fixing Penny's shoe, they wandered inside, laughing over Jen's antics that day on a beef stud farm an hour out of town. His spirits had lifted – instead of dreading the ceremony as he had since he received the invitation, he'd begun to believe that maybe it wouldn't be so bad after all.

Jen stopped and stared at a pair of suitcases by the front door. Parker frowned. He'd forgotten Hazel was leaving for surgery that afternoon. Well, not so much forgotten as pushed it from his mind – he didn't *want* to think about it.

Jen ran her fingers through her hair, sighed then stepped inside and he followed. They found Hazel and Dalton in the kitchen, Hazel in Dalton's lap, sharing a cup of coffee. "Oh, sorry for interrupting," said Parker, backing out of the room.

"No, please come in – we're about to leave." Hazel stood and rubbed her red eyes.

"I wish you had let me help you pack, at least," said Jen, wringing her hands together.

"No, I wanted to do it myself. And I wanted to spend one last afternoon with my handsome hubby."

"Last?" asked Dalton. "I don't think so."

Hazel chuckled. "I meant before the surgery. And before I come home with plastic Barbie boobs."

Dalton laughed and stroked the side of her face. "You're perfect with or without Barbie boobs."

Jen chuckled.

Then tears began to run down Hazel's cheeks and she buried her face in her hands. "Oh baby, come on now," Dalton said, taking her into his arms. "We're done with the tears. Everything's going to be fine."

"I know … it's just that … I can't believe Mom and Dad aren't going to cut their trip short and come home. Their only child is having surgery and they just don't seem to care …"

Dalton cupped her face in his hands. "Firstly, I think they do care – they just don't know how to express it. And secondly, it doesn't matter – you've got a big ol' family right here who care more than you'll ever know."

"That's right," added Jen, wrapping her arms around Hazel from behind.

"Definitely," Parker agreed, encircling Jen and Hazel in an embrace. The four of them stood there, wrapped up in love as the minutes ticked by on the kitchen clock and Hazel's tears dried.

Finally she pulled away, sniffed and wiped her nose on her sleeve. "Thank you, guys. It means so much to me. I'm so grateful for all of you."

Jen wiped her eyes and Parker heard her hiccup. They untangled and said goodbye to Dalton and Hazel, who climbed into Dalton's truck and headed off down the long winding drive. Harley stared after them, his tail hanging limply between his hind legs.

Parker and Jen wandered back to the kitchen and he poured them each a cup of coffee. "When's the surgery?" he asked.

"First thing tomorrow morning. You know, you should tell Dalton and Eamon about the Ranger ceremony. They'd want to know."

He shook his head and turned the coffee cup around in his hands. "No. They have enough on their minds. I'll tell them some other time."

CHAPTER 6

*J*en stared at her reflection in the mirror over the dressing table in her room. Was a little black dress and a blue shawl a bit much for an afternoon Ranger ceremony? She'd never been to anything like that before – should she dress up or down? Parker hadn't told her, and after their sad farewell to Hazel she didn't have the heart to ask him. She picked up the curling iron and wound a strand of hair around it. One final curl and she'd be done.

While she waited for the curling iron to do its work, she couldn't stop her mind wandering to Hazel. Where was she now? Had she settled into her room at the hospital already? Or was she sitting in some waiting room?

She pulled on the curl and it bobbed back into a tight ringlet. With a sigh, she turned off the iron, picked up her purse and headed down the hall in search of Parker. It was odd, going on a date with a man who lived in the same house. But this wasn't really a date, she reminded herself – she was just keeping him company since everyone else was busy. If it had been a date, she'd be much more nervous than she was, but this was Parker, and she never felt nervous around Parker.

Correction: she didn't feel nervous around Parker *when he was fully clothed*. Wet and wrapped in a small towel was another matter entirely. She chuckled and adjusted the purse strap where it hung over her shoulder. Where was he?

She found him waiting by the front door, reading something on his phone. When she walked over, he glanced up and his eyes widened. "Wow."

She smiled, her face burning. "Thanks."

"You look so different. Beautiful – that's what I meant. You look beautiful." His cheeks flushed pink.

"Thank you. You look pretty flash yourself." Gone were the jeans and cowboy boots, the Stetson and the T-shirts. In his forest green uniform and matching beret he looked not just handsome, but sophisticated and masculine in a way she hadn't noticed before. This was a man who knew who he was and what he had to do.

"Ready?" he asked, offering her his arm.

Jen nodded and put her hand through it, smiling at him as he led her out to his truck, her heart pounding in her chest.

* * *

JEN LEANED against the truck door, her chin in her hand. The hum of the engine was a monotone drumming through her high heels and up her spine. They still had an hour to go, and after a half day of work and the emotional toll of telling Hazel goodbye, she was getting sleepy. She leaned back on the headrest and tried to pry her eyes as far open as she could with her fingers.

Parker laughed. "What are you *doing?*"

"Trying to stay awake." She slapped herself gently on the cheek.

He chuckled. "Sorry – is the company so boring?"

She shook her head. "No, driving always makes me sleepy."

"Feel free to doze if you'd like. I don't get sleepy driving, so no need to stay awake for my benefit."

"No. If I do that, I might end up at your event with drool down one side of my face, flat hair and mascara rings around my eyes."

He laughed again. "Now that would be a sight."

"So where exactly are we going again?"

"Fort Benning, near the Alabama border. There's a memorial there for the Army Rangers and they like to give out these awards there. It shouldn't take too long to get there. The ceremony's at four o'clock, so we should arrive with plenty of time to spare."

"We'll be able to get good seats," she chuckled.

He laughed. "Maybe. And we can grab a bite to eat afterward if you like."

"That sounds good. I'm already starving – I barely had any lunch. Too worried about Hazel, I guess."

Parker's jaw clenched. "Yeah. Sorry this is such bad timing. I know you'd probably rather be at home."

"No, it's good. I want something to distract me. I'll go crazy if I just sit around thinking of all the things that might go wrong."

"True. My psychologist says I should learn more strategies to distract myself from my blue thoughts, and …" His voice faded.

"You have a psychologist?"

He nodded and frowned.

Jen watched his reaction. He seemed to regret opening up, and had clamped his mouth shut. "I think that's great."

He glanced at her sideways. "You do?"

"Of course. You're admitting you need help and you're willing to go get it. Do you know how far ahead of the game that puts you? Most people don't even realize they *have* a problem until it's caused them all kinds of pain." She ran a finger over the edge of the door frame, studying the curve of the molded plastic.

"Yeah, I guess that's true."

"It definitely is."

"Anyway, all I'm saying is distraction is something I'm trying to learn."

"Well, it's a good thing we're friends. Because I am the queen of distraction." She laughed and threaded her fingers together, feigning a smug knuckle-cracking.

"Good to know."

"Oh … I've got a great idea. Let's play Truth or Dare."

He grimaced. "I don't know about that …"

"Have you ever played it before?"

"Yes, and it never ends well for me. I can't imagine it'd be a good driving game." He shook his head.

She laughed. "Good point. I promise not to dare you to do anything that endangers our lives, okay?"

"Deal."

"All right – truth or dare?"

He shook his head slowly from side to side. "Ah … truth."

"Good choice," said Jen, rubbing her palms

together. "Okay, let me see. Have you ever been in love?"

He laughed and his cheeks reddened. "Ah ... no, I haven't."

"Interesting ... your turn."

"Hmmm ... Okay. Truth or dare?"

"Dare," she responded with a smirk.

He chuckled. "Let's see. I dare you to burp the Star-Spangled Banner."

She stared at him with wide eyes. "Excuse me? Do you see the way I'm dressed? I am a *lady*. Just in case you were confused."

"Oh yeah? Well, I guess that's just too bad. You chose 'dare,' so you have to follow through, Barsby. Or are you chicken?"

She laughed. "Oh, I'll follow through – I was just making sure you realized I'm a lady."

"That's abundantly clear," he quipped, with an exaggerated leer at her dress that made her blush.

"Here we go then." Jen concentrated, then burped out the tune as requested. When she finished, she grinned proudly.

Parker nodded. "Well, color me impressed. I didn't think you could do it, but you proved me wrong. Where did you learn to do that?"

"Remember me talking about the family business? Well, my parents own Barsby Enterprises. You know, 'Alabama's #1 John Deere dealer'?"

"What? You're one of *those* Barsbys?" Parker glanced her way with arched eyebrows.

She chuckled. "Yeah. I don't like to tell people, since it usually changes their opinion of me. And I've tried to build a life for myself away from all of that."

"No kidding."

"Anyway, they work with a lot of farmers. And I spent many hours at the office as a kid. One day when I was bored, one of the regular customers taught me to burp on command."

He laughed and ran a hand over his hair. "You continue to surprise me, Jen."

She grinned and tucked her dress around her legs. "See? Queen of distraction. Now, truth or dare?"

* * *

JEN CROSSED her ankles under the white folding chair and watched the pretty sunset behind the memorial statue. Folks puttered around the lawn, taking their seats and chatting in hushed tones.

Parker returned and sat next to her, handing over a plastic cup filled with pink punch. "Here you go."

"Thanks. This is really nice. There are more people here than I thought there'd be. This is kind of a big deal, huh?"

He shrugged and sat straight in his chair as he sipped his own punch. "I guess so."

A man in a Ranger uniform sat beside him and slapped him on the shoulder. "Hey, Blue. You ready to go up there?"

Parker laughed. "Trigger! Good to see you man. I didn't know you'd be here."

Jen wondered what the meaning was behind Parker's nickname.

"Same goes for you."

Two more men in the same uniform approached. "Hey, Gadget, Millsy." Parker shook hands with them, and they grinned in reply. ""Everyone, this is Jen." He leaned back to let the men shake hands with her.

She smiled. "Pleased to meet you. How do you know Parker?"

Trigger spoke first. "We served together in Syria. You haven't told her much, huh?"

Parker frowned. "Uh, no. Not really."

"I don't tell anyone nothin'," responded Gadget, leaning back in his chair.

"Me neither," Millsy added. "Best not to. No one understands anyhow."

"Why do you call him 'Blue'?" asked Jen with a frown.

"Because he always has that solemn look on his face," said Trigger with a chuckle. "Even in the middle of a battle." He laughed uproariously, and the others joined in.

Parker grinned. "Yeah, well, at least I didn't have a hair trigger like you."

Trigger laughed again. "Fair point."

An elegant-looking man with a long row of medals pinned to his chest stepped up to the podium, tapped on the microphone, then leaned toward it. "Good afternoon, ladies and gentlemen. Please take a seat. We'd like to get started."

As the rest of the audience sat down, Jen scanned the crowd. She saw wounded and elderly veterans, some seated alone, others with a group. And several young men with families. All with that same intense look on their faces that Parker often got.

Lost in thought, she missed most of what the speaker said, until he announced Parker's name. She jolted as Parker and his friends all filed out of the row and headed for the podium. With a frown, she listened as the man read from a sheet of paper he held between shaking hands. "... the Presidential Unit Citation for extraordinary heroism to the battalion, for their combat actions in Syria ..."

When the medal was pinned to Parker's chest, Jen stood with the rest of the audience and offered her heartfelt applause. Her eyes filled with tears, and she wished she'd thought to bring tissues. She didn't know she'd cry. Parker had told her it was an event to honor his friends, not him. She sniffled into her shawl and continued to clap her gloved hands. The chill evening air made her breath look like puffs of smoke in the dimming light.

She waited after the ceremony was over for Parker to finish speaking with his friends. He joined her and they walked arm in arm back to the truck in silence. He opened the door for her and she slid into the seat.

Once he'd settled himself in the driver's seat, she cleared her throat. "You didn't tell me," she croaked.

He rested his hands on the steering wheel. "I didn't know what to say."

"How about 'I'm getting a medal for bravery'?"

He ran a hand over his eyes. "I don't deserve it."

She took his hand. "Parker." He glared straight ahead, so she put her free hand on his chin and turned his head to face her. "Parker. How can you say that? You deserve it."

His eyes clouded over. "No. I don't. I didn't do anything special. I was there, I did what I had to do, and now I'd rather forget the whole thing."

Her eyes filled with tears. "I can't imagine how hard it was for you. But you shouldn't forget it. Because I'm proud of you. You fought for your country, for your family, for me. You are one of the brave soldiers who keep us all safe and free. And that's worth remembering."

His eyes glimmered in the twilight. "It was ugly. There wasn't anything good about it. We tried, we did. But war just isn't good. And we couldn't make it good."

She smiled gently and took his hands in hers. "But you're good. I know you are. And you took that with you into a horrible war. You carried that goodness with you. And you made a difference – and those people out there, they know it. That's why you got the award. Because you were good, you saved the lives of other people and you made a difference. You should be proud of that, even if it hurts to think about it."

He nodded and closed his eyes. "Thanks, Jen," he whispered.

"Now, let's go get something to eat before I shrivel up and die of starvation." She chuckled and released his hands.

He nodded again and started the engine. "Yeah, let's go."

CHAPTER 7

*P*arker watched Jen out of the corner of his eye as he drove. After dinner at a local diner just off State Highway 520, she'd fallen asleep. They were only five minutes from the ranch, but he wanted to soak up every last moment with her before they got back.

He wasn't sure he wanted to go to the ceremony that afternoon, but he was glad he did. And it was all because of Jen. She'd talked him into it, literally held his hand through it all, and given him a pep talk when he was about to slip into a dark place afterward.

He took a quick breath. He knew she saw him as a friend, but after today that had changed for him. He wanted more than that. The feelings he had for her had been percolating for a while, he knew, but before today he'd been able to ignore them. Now there was no denying it. He'd never felt this way about anyone before. It was as though his heart was in pain whenever he looked at her or thought about her. The sudden intensity of his feelings overwhelmed him, and he began drumming on the steering wheel with his fingers.

Now what? He didn't know what he should say or do. If he spoke to her about it, maybe it'd ruin their friendship. Was it worth the risk?

He pulled into the darkened driveway of the Cotton Tree Ranch and jumped out to open the gate. As the truck rumbled into the yard, he spotted his mother's green Volkswagen parked beside Hazel's hatchback and shook his head. She wasn't going to be happy with him. He leaned across the seat and gently woke Jen.

She rubbed her eyes and yawned widely. "We're home?"

"Yep. A heads up, though – my mom's here."

"Oh? That's great. I've been looking forward to meeting her."

He shrugged as he parked. "She may not be real happy about me going to the ceremony without her. So …"

"Gotcha." She got out of the truck and followed him up the stairs into the house. He led the way, hoping to protect her from his mother's prying.

Susan Williams barreled out of the kitchen and wrapped her arms around him in a bear hug. "Parker, there you are! I've been here all alone, wondering where everyone is!" She peered around Parker and noticed Jen standing quietly in the background. "And who is this?"

No dodging it now. "Mom, this is Jennifer Barsby, Hazel's friend. She moved here to help take care of her."

Susan hurried to hug Jen. "Hello there, Jennifer. How nice to see you."

Jen smiled and returned the embrace. "Thank you, Mrs. Williams."

"Please, call me Susan." She spun to face Parker again. "And why are you dressed that way, darling?"

He frowned and ran his fingers through his hair. "Uh … well, I had a thing over at the Ranger Memorial this afternoon, so …"

Susan arched an eyebrow. "A *thing*?"

"He got a medal for bravery," Jen interrupted.

Susan glanced at her, then back at Parker, nostrils flaring. "You did?"

He nodded. "Sorry, Mom. It's just … I wasn't even sure I was going until the last minute."

"Darling, I'm so proud of you!" Another hug. "Now if you'll just excuse me. I'm tired after the drive down here. There's supper in the kitchen if you're hungry. I'm off to bed – see you in the morning." Susan bustled out of the room and down the hall to the guest room, quietly shutting the door behind her.

Parker sighed and put his hands on his hips, his head down and his eyes clenched shut. He felt Jen's hand on his shoulder. "I'm sorry, Parker – maybe I shouldn't have told her. But she'll find out …"

"It's not your fault, it's mine. I should've invited her. Honestly, I didn't think I'd go at all. And I didn't want her pressuring me about it."

"Well, nothing can be done about it now."

"I'm going to talk to her. Thanks for coming with me – it meant a lot." Parker smiled at Jen and his eyes sought hers for some kind of signal that it had meant as much to her.

But she only smiled faintly and patted his arm. "I'm heading to bed. Thank you for taking me with you. It was really special." Her heels swinging from her hand, she padded down the hall.

Parker drew a deep breath, then followed her, passing her door on the way to the guest room his mother had disappeared into. He knocked on the door, and after a brief pause she opened it. She was dressed in a robe and slippers, her blonde hair pulled up into a loose bun on top of her head. "Yes?" she asked, her eyes rimmed with red.

"Mom, can I come in, please?" He rested a hand against the door frame.

She nodded and pulled the door wider to let him in, then wandered to the bed and slumped onto the edge. She put her hands in the pockets of her robe and stared at him.

"I'm sorry I didn't tell you Mom. It wasn't because I didn't want you there. It's just that until today, I didn't really want *me* there."

She sniffled and pulled a tissue from her pocket to wipe her nose. "Then why'd you go?"

"Jen convinced me I should. She said I'd regret it if I didn't."

"Well, she's right," she huffed. "You would've."

"I know. That's why I went in the end. I didn't tell Dalton or Eamon about it either – they've got enough on their plates at the moment. Jen's the only person I told. So please don't be upset." He sat beside her and put an arm around her shoulders. She buried her face into his arm and sobbed. "Aww, Mom …"

"Eamon got married without telling me. Hazel's sick and I've barely heard anything. And now you didn't even think to invite me. I …" She burst into a fresh round of tears.

He sighed. "Mom, it's not because we don't love

you. You know we do. We're just thoughtless idiots sometimes. Eamon and Em didn't tell any of us they were getting married. We're all a bit annoyed at them, to be honest."

She perked up a little. "Really?"

"Yeah, really. They just came home and said, 'ta-da – we're married!'"

She chuckled. "Nice surprise, huh?"

"Yeah. I wanted to be a groomsman, but that's not an option now. I know Hazel wasn't happy about it either. But they didn't want to wait, what with Hazel's illness and everything. And … you may not know this, but Em's folks aren't speaking to her at the moment. It would've broken her heart to have all our family at the ceremony and none of hers. So they eloped instead. Nothing to do with you – it's just what they decided was best for them."

She sniffled again and wiped her nose. "I guess I can understand that."

"Please don't be upset, Mom. We love you. I'm sorry."

She nodded and put her arm around his waist, squeezing gently. "I love you too, Parker. And I'm so proud of you. Now let me see that medal."

* * *

JEN OPENED HER EYES, yawned and lifted her arms above her head to stretch out the kinks. Hazel's surgery was this morning. She'd heard another alarm go off down the hall a few minutes before hers. Time to get up and get moving. She clambered out of bed, gathered her things and headed for the bathroom.

The sound of the shower already running made her

grimace. Oh well, no time to wait – she'd just have to make do with a splash of water on the face this morning. She did just that in the kitchen, then returned to her room and dressed quickly, pulling her blonde locks still curled into ringlets from the previous evening into an odd-looking ponytail. She applied some basic makeup – tinted moisturizer, blush, mascara. She didn't know why she felt the need for it, since she was just going to visit her friend in the hospital.

But then, it wasn't for Hazel, was it? It was the thought of seeing Parker that made her pulse race. Something had changed between them on the drive to the awards ceremony the previous day. But she didn't have time to analyze that now. She had to get ready.

She checked the contents of the bag hanging from her bedpost – chocolate, magazines, a romance novel and breath mints, all the things Hazel wanted on hand when she had some downtime. Likely she hadn't thought of them, given the stress she'd been under lately. But Jen knew she'd need things to do once the surgery was over.

Jen yanked the strap of the bag over her arm, grabbed her purse, headed out the door – and smack into Parker's chest. Again. She looked up at him, rubbing her nose. "We have *got* to stop meeting like this," she quipped.

He grinned. "Morning, Jen. Sorry about that. I was just coming to see if you wanted breakfast. I'm making pancakes."

She nodded. "Thanks, that sounds perfect. Though my stomach's in knots."

"Yeah, I know what you mean."

She followed him to the kitchen and found Susan

already there, buttering a stack of pancakes. She handed a plate to Jen as she walked in and set a cup of freshly brewed coffee on the table in front of her. "Here you go, dear. I hope you got some rest."

Jen nodded. "Thank you, Susan. I slept okay. I'm just worried about Hazel."

"Of course you are." Susan sat beside her and took a bite of pancake from her own plate. "These are delicious, Parker. You've become quite the chef." His cheeks colored under her praise.

Jen smiled. They seemed to have talked through the incident the previous night. She admired that in a man – the ability to resolve relationship issues like that. Especially with his mother. So many men would just push it down and live with the pain rather than deal with it. And in the end, family issues always came to the surface again, whether you wanted them to or not.

* * *

THE WAITING ROOM smelled of flowers and antiseptic. Jen's nose wrinkled and she stood to stretch her legs. They'd been waiting for four hours already. Emily had assured them the surgery wouldn't take much longer than that, so Jen was hopeful they'd soon see her come through the swinging doors that led to the rabbit warren of rooms beyond.

She stood on tiptoe and peered through the Plexiglas in the top half of one of the doors. No sign of her yet. With a sigh, she returned to her seat beside Parker, picked up a magazine and flicked through it, unable to focus on any of the articles long enough to read them.

"You okay?" asked Parker, looking up from a thick Jack Reacher novel.

She nodded. "I just can't sit still. Surely it won't take much longer."

He half-smiled. "Yeah, must be nearly over. Don't worry, I'm sure everything's fine."

Emily burst through the double doors, letting them swing shut behind her. She pulled the surgical mask from her face and set her hands on her hips with a smile. "She's in recovery and it all looks good."

Susan whooped and threw her arms around Dalton. Eamon stepped forward to kiss Emily on the lips. Jen jumped up and down, faced Parker with her mouth wide open in a cry of relief, and he caught her up in his strong arms, lifting her feet off the ground. "She's gonna be okay," she cried against his ear.

"Yes, she is." He set her back on the ground, then tucked a strand of hair lovingly behind her ear.

"What about chemo?" asked Dalton.

Emily smiled again. "I think we got it all, so it's unlikely she'll need any. Of course, we'll have to do some tests to make sure, but ..." Before she could finish, Dalton picked her up and hugged her tight. She grimaced, as though he were squeezing the breath from her lungs, then laughed as he released her. "Okay ..."

"Thank you, Em," he said, his voice breaking.

She nodded. "You're welcome. She's in recovery now, but if you stick around until she wakes up, someone will come and get you." She faced the group. "But only Dalton. Sorry, the rest of you will have to head on home and see her tomorrow. She needs her rest."

Jen was disappointed, but content. Hazel had made it through the surgery – the hardest part was behind her.

* * *

JEN SET the mustard on the table beside the slices of fresh multi-grain bread, ham and cheese and the bowl of salad. She sighed, her hands on her hips. There sure was a lot of food preparation involved when so many people lived in one house. She felt like the day just skipped from one meal to the next, with only enough time in between to clean up and prepare all over again.

She pushed the hair from her eyes and tucked it behind her ears. Perhaps she should get a hotel room. She wouldn't need to stay much longer if Hazel's post-surgery tests came back all clear. And the house was getting so crowded – every single room was full. Even though Eamon had moved into Emily's apartment, his room was still cluttered with all his things, though he was gradually moving them over.

Jen worried it wouldn't be quiet or calm enough in the house for Hazel's recovery. Granted, Jen herself was gone most days now – her veterinary work for Will had picked up in the last couple of weeks. But still, it made sense for her to find her own space. And it would give her a chance to think about the future and what she wanted to do with her life.

Now that Chris had broken things off, did she want to go back to Atlanta? She really enjoyed her time at the Cotton Tree Ranch. Being with friends made her heart sing. And she loved her new job – Will was a fantastic boss. He let her do things her own way, yet also served as a mentor, giving her kindly advice whenever she needed it.

And then there was Parker, though she still wasn't sure what part he should play in her decision. He was a friend, a good friend. But was he more? Perhaps she'd been imagining things had progressed further than they really had. Nothing was definite, nothing she could quite put her finger on, but she could've sworn there was a moment between them after the Ranger award ceremony, and again at the hospital.

It didn't make sense for Parker to feel the same way about her that she was beginning to feel for him. He was a serious ex-soldier and a very attractive man. She was a scatterbrained, accident-prone veterinarian. Could two such different people ever make it work?

But perhaps she should stick around. For a while at least.

Parker and Eamon burst through the kitchen door in their ranch work gear. They'd spent the morning at the hospital, but there was always so much to be done around a property as big as the ranch. They'd told Jen they intended to spend the afternoon working for as long as there was light enough to work. There was an atmosphere of relief among the group, and they chatted happily as Parker walked to the fridge for a jug of sweet tea and Eamon placed napkins and a bag of chips on the table.

Susan said a blessing and they all filled their plates. Jen put together a ham sandwich with mustard, cut it in half and took a large bite. She hadn't realized just how hungry she was. Now that the anxious knots were gone from her stomach, she felt it growl in antic-ipation.

"So," Eamon said between bites, "I guess we can plan out Thanksgiving now that Hazel's surgery is over."

Susan nodded and swallowed a mouthful of sand-wich. "Yes, I was thinking that I'd make turkey and sweet potato soufflé ..."

"I make a mean stuffing," added Parker with a chuckle.

"Perfect," added Susan.

"I could do potato salad," Jen said. "And I was thinking – it might be time for me to get a hotel room. It's getting so crowded here at the ranch, and with Hazel coming home soon she'll need some peace and quiet. This is your home, and I've invaded your space for long enough."

Susan shook her head. "No, you should stay. I'm heading back to Chattanooga after Thanksgiving, and Eamon's moved in with Emily. It won't be so bad."

"And I think Hazel would want you to be here when she gets home," added Parker.

Eamon nodded. "Yeah. Stay for a while longer, Jen, just until she's recovered. I'm sure it would mean the world to her."

Jen took a quick breath. "Okay … well, if you think I should."

Eamon nodded. "Definitely. Anyway, we'll need your help to make Thanksgiving happen – Hazel's usually the cook around here. But between us I think we can pull something together that'll make her proud."

Jen frowned. "Okay. If you insist, I'll stay. But I promise I won't put y'all out for too much longer."

"Doesn't bother me at all," offered Parker with a grin.

Jen took another bite of her sandwich as her heart skipped.

*P*arker hit the ignition button and the tractor's engine roared to life. He shifted into reverse, looked over his shoulder as he backed across the yard, then pulled to a stop and shifted into first. He needed to plow the southern field – Dalton wanted him to plant oats to harvest next summer. The crop would feed the horses through an entire winter, saving them money. And what the horses didn't eat they could sell for a nice profit.

Movement in front of the ranch house caught his attention. Dalton's truck pulled down the long drive and onto the highway, tires squealing. He frowned. Dalton was barely getting any rest since the surgery – he was at the hospital all hours of the day and night, taking care of Hazel. He only came home for a few hours' sleep and to look over the ranch accounts, then back to the hospital again. He'd burn himself out in no time at this rate.

Parker stepped on the accelerator, reached for his phone and tugged an attached pair of earphones from his pocket. He always listened to music when he rode the tractor. He'd tried audio books, but they were too hard to hear over the engine's roar. He put the earbuds in, turned up the volume and, with Kenny Chesney blasting, pushed down harder on the throttle.

* * *

JEN PUT the stethoscope to the prize bull's side and frowned. She moved it around, listening as the beast's ragged breathing punctuated the still air. "Well, Bob, he doesn't seem to have an infection. His lungs are clear, his heart is beating normally. Likely it's a virus that'll pass soon enough. Just keep an eye on him and make sure he's well-hydrated, and if it'll make you feel better I'll come and check on him tomorrow."

Bob pushed his hat back on his bald head. "Okay, thanks, Doc. It'd sure help me feel more at ease if you could swing by tomorrow."

"No problem – I'll come by after my morning appointments. Can't be too careful when it comes to this big fella, can we?" She slapped the bull gently on the shoulder through the rails of the cattle chute. His tail swished and he tossed his horned head.

"No, ma'am, we can't. He's worth a mint to me and the missus – we'd sure be devastated if we lost him." Bob put his hands on his hips and stared out the barn door. "Looks like a storm's brewin'."

She peered out that way as well and chewed the inside of her cheek. Purple and black clouds roiled on the horizon, flying across the sky in their direction. "Hmmm … well, I'd better get moving, then. Those clouds don't look too good. And I'm done for the day – I'm gonna head home and curl up in front of the fire with a cup of coffee." She grinned and shook Bob's hand, then hurried to her car.

Inside the car, she switched on the radio, searching for a news station. It was only a few days until Thanksgiving and she was excited to spend it with the Williams family. When she'd told her parents she wouldn't be coming home for the holiday, they hadn't been too pleased. She thought they'd finally under-stood her reasoning when she told them how well Hazel was doing.

But they'd made it clear they hoped she'd be returning to Birmingham rather than Atlanta once Hazel was well. "There's nothing in Atlanta that you have to get back to now, is there, dear? And we'd so love for you to come home. We can pull some strings and make sure you get a good job. Just come home and we'll work out all the details."

She smiled and bit on her lower lip. It was nice to be loved, and maybe it wasn't a bad idea. She could take her time finding work, stay with her parents a while, look up old friends and catch up with what was going on in their lives. It did sound appealing. And now that she and Chris were no longer an item, and Hazel lived in south Georgia, she really didn't have any need to return to Atlanta.

She felt a pull inside to stay where she was, but was it sensible to stick around just because she'd made some friends? Good friends, friends that cared about her and gave her a reason to smile ... okay, perhaps she could stay a little longer and see how things went.

As her car rattled down the long winding track that served as Bob's driveway, she listened to the news-caster who warned of a severe thunderstorm with possible hail and high winds. She frowned and downshifted to pull onto the highway, then stepped on the accelerator – she'd better get home before the storm hit.

* * *

PARKER FROWNED AT THE SKY. The clouds were overhead now and he could hear the patter of rain beginning on the tractor's roof. He'd plowed almost half the field and had hoped to push through and get it all done. If it just rained, it wouldn't matter much to him in the cab of the tractor, but it look like more than rain in those clouds.

A great gust of wind buffeted the cab, making the tractor sway gently. That wasn't good. He turned the vehicle around and headed for the barn, the wind whistling and howling through the gaps in the cab, making the vehicle shudder. He'd have to finish plowing tomorrow – it didn't make sense to stay out in a storm like this one was fast becoming.

By the time he reached the barn, the rain was already pouring down. The wipers didn't make much impact on the sheet of water that covered the glass. He got it inside, cut off the engine and sat still for a moment, inhaling deeply. A crack of thunder made him jump – that was close! The wind's howling filled the musty air as he jumped down from the cab.

Eamon hustled in through the barn door, soaked to the bone. "Hey, there you are," he called, wiping rain from his face.

"Looks like a bad one," replied Parker, staring out at the storm with his hands on his hips.

"Sure is. I already tucked all the foals and mares

away in their stables, secured the outdoor furniture and anything that wasn't nailed down."

Parker nodded. "Thanks."

Eamon took off his hat and shook it. "Did you get the field plowed?"

"Less than half," replied Parker.

Eamon frowned. "Well, I guess we'd better head inside. Not much we can do out here for now."

Parker scratched the stubble on his chin. "Yeah. Have you seen Jen?"

Eamon shook his head. "Nope. I guess she's still at work."

Parker's brow furrowed. She was out in this weather somewhere, perhaps on her way home. Or maybe she'd decided to ride it out at one of her clients' homes. He'd try calling her when they got inside. "Dalton's at the hospital."

Eamon shrugged. "I figured. He's living there at the moment."

"You think he's all right?" asked Parker, rubbing his hand over his face.

"Yeah. He's worried about our finances – insurance only covers so much and Hazel's medical care is costing a bundle. You know how tight our margins are at the moment – we're still building the business. So he's stressed about it all."

Parker frowned. "That's why he comes home from the hospital every night and pores over the books?"

"Yep." Eamon grimaced. "Not sure what we can do about it right now, but once Hazel's home we should probably all get together and discuss a way forward. We might have to start doing outside work or something. I could probably get a few accounting clients.

Anything we can think of to keep the lights on, you know?"

Parker nodded and scratched his stubbled chin. He didn't like the sound of that. He'd sunk his life savings into this place, just as Dalton and Eamon had. If the ranch went under, they'd lose everything they'd worked so hard for. They'd have to do whatever it took to make sure that didn't happen.

He couldn't, wouldn't let his brothers lose their savings. Both of them were married now and he knew they'd likely want to start families before long. No, between them they'd come up with something to help get the ranch through this rough patch. No one could have predicted Hazel getting sick the way she did. They'd planned as best they could for every other contingency, but that one had hit them out of nowhere.

The two men sprinted across the yard to the house, the rain pummeling them all the way. On the porch, they shook off excess water, removed their soggy boots and set them by the door. Parker took a look around. Everything was secured and put away. Eamon had moved all the vehicles into the barn in case of hail. It seemed he'd thought of everything, and Parker felt a swell of gratitude toward his brother. It made all the difference working with Dalton and Eamon – he always knew he could rely on them to get things done.

But there was still no sign of Jen's car.

Just as that thought crossed his mind, there was a pinging sound on the porch roof, then another. Soon it became a racket that drowned out every other noise. Parker frowned as he watched as golf-ball-sized hailstones bounce across the ground, then settle in the green grass. He linked his hands behind his head and watched in dismay as they battered the barn and porch. Before long the entire yard was covered in white, as though it had snowed. He didn't even know it could hail this time of year, though it had been unseasonably warm the past few days and especially that morning. Perhaps the inclimate temperature had triggered the storm.

"I'm heading inside," said Eamon behind him.

Parker nodded and followed his brother. The foals and their mothers were settled safely in their stables. The rest of the animals were likely sheltering beneath the large shade trees that dotted the property. There was nothing else they could do now except wait out the storm in the warmth of the ranch house.

Inside, they found their mother in the den watching the Weather Channel. She faced them with wide eyes when they walked in. Parker set his hat on a hook by the door and padded through the den in damp socks. "Hey, Mom."

She gestured toward the TV screen. "Have you seen this?"

Eamon laughed. "Seen it? We were just in it!"

His mother hurried to the window, pulled aside the drapes and peered outside. "Is that *hail* making all that noise?"

Parker nodded. "Yep. Big as golf balls."

"My car!" she exclaimed, a hand flying to her mouth.

"Don't worry, Mom, I moved your car into the barn," Eamon assured her. "I couldn't find you to ask, so I just took your keys. I think you were in the shower or something." He headed down the hall to his old bedroom and pulled the door shut behind him.

"Thank goodness for that," sighed Susan.

They couldn't hear the television above the noise of the wind and hail on the tin roof. Susan picked up the remote and turned up the volume, but it didn't make much difference. She finally hit 'mute' and switched to closed-captioning.

Parker leaned against the window frame and watched the hail pile up all over the yard and against the barn walls. Then a flash of color on the drive caught his eye as Jen pulled up the drive and headed for the barn. There was just enough room for her hatchback under the overhang. He came out onto the porch as she ran across the yard, a large black umbrella swaying above her head. Hail bounced off the umbrella and scattered around her as she ran. He frowned and reached for her hand as she hurried up the stairs.

"Phew!" she exclaimed, setting her umbrella on the porch. "That hail is crazy!"

He sighed. "Sure is. I'm glad you made it – I was getting worried."

She smirked at him. "You were?"

His cheeks burned. "Yeah, I was."

"Well, I'm fine. Though I can't say the same for my poor car – it just took a major beating."

He stared at her, unable to look away from her face. Her cheeks were flushed, her blonde hair drifted in loose curls around them and her blue eyes sparked. He took a quick breath. He wasn't sure how much longer he could pull off the "just friends" bit with her. Surely she could see the effect she had on him. Parker cleared his throat, but still couldn't release her from his gaze.

She smiled and her cheeks grew pink. "So what have you been up to today?"

"I was out on the tractor when the storm hit. Since then, I've just been waiting for you to get home."

She ducked her head with a grin. "Oh?"

He stepped toward her, his heart racing. Then spun around when the front door banged open behind him. His mother stood there, arms crossed over her chest, smiling. "You made it home, I see," she said to Jen. "I'm glad you're okay. I've made hot chocolate – would you two like some?"

There was nothing like being interrupted by your mother to temper a man's ardor. Parker rubbed his face ruefully. "Sure, Mom, that sounds great. Thanks."

She smiled and let the door swing shut behind her.

Jen headed inside, her hand brushing against Parker's as she passed him. He held his breath until she was gone, his eyes wide. Had she done that intentionally? He pressed his eyes shut, and leaned against the porch railing with a sigh. He'd wanted to hold her, kiss her and tell her how he felt about her.

His heart thundered and his breath was ragged. All this from one small touch? He couldn't believe how much he was affected by his feelings for Jen. He swallowed hard, then inhaled deeply in an attempt to slow his pulse and followed her inside.

The Weather Channel played silently in the background as Jen took a sip of hot chocolate. It scalded the tip of her tongue and she set the mug on the coffee table with a grimace. It was still too hot to drink – she should've waited. Susan was chugging it down like it was nothing, but she'd never been able to drink boiling-hot beverages. She frowned and leaned back on the couch.

The hail had stopped, but the wind had only grown stronger, and sheets of rain lashed against the side of the house. She couldn't help thinking about the animals around the ranch and hoped they'd found shelter in time, though in her experience animals were pretty good at taking care of themselves that way. Harley was nowhere to be seen, but likely he'd hunkered down in the barn or stables. Lulu would've ducked inside at the first hint of moisture in the air with an angry flick of her tail – she grinned at the mental image.

She stood with a yawn, stretched her arms over her

head and wandered to the front door. She loved to watch storms, to stare out into the rain as it fell. There was something soothing about watching nature unleash its fury.

A crack of thunder overhead, lasting two to three seconds, made her jump, and she closed her eyes, her pulse jittering. It had certainly grown stronger since she went inside. She'd never seen a wind like this before. Another rumble, and she stumbled backward through the open front door, right into a hard chest and strong arms. "Whoa!" said Parker against her hair. "You okay?"

She spun around in his arms and looked up into his face. He gazed down at her, something deep and intense in eyes, something she didn't quite understand. Her heart thundered in her chest. He shut the door behind her. What was going on? "Parker, I ..."

He took her hand and looked as though he was about to say something. But as he opened his mouth, a sound deeper and longer than thunder filled the room. There was a screech of metal on metal, followed by a bang, then the whistling of wind. The lights and television set flickered and went dark, and the sound of the heater hissing through the vents faded into silence. Jen's eyes widened. "What was that?"

He let go of her hand and ran down the hall, with her close behind.

Eamon came tearing out of the kitchen, half a sandwich in one hand and a determined look on his face. He caught up to them by the bathroom and looked up – only to get a face full of rain. He cursed and Parker's hands flew to rest on his head.

The roof was gone!

Jen's mouth fell open as she crossed her arms and

stumbled backward down the hall. Half the house's roof had been blown off by the storm; the bathroom and Eamon and Parker's bedrooms were exposed to the elements, their belongings being soaked with each passing moment.

"What was that noise?" asked Susan, coming up behind her. Then she looked up. "Oh dear."

Eamon and Parker raced past them and out the front door. Jen hurried to the window and watched them pelt across the yard to the barn, then return laden down with stacks of folded blue tarpaulins. She ran out to help them. "What can I do?" she yelled over the wind.

Parker handed her a stack of tarps. "Hold these!" His face grim, he hurried off again, coming back a minute later with a ladder over each shoulder, He and Eamon set them up and climbed, Jen handing each of them a tarp.

The wind whipped the tarp from Eamon's hands. "We need something to hold them in place!" he shouted.

"There's some two-by-fours by the back door," suggested Susan. Jen nodded, and the two women ran to the back door, shuffling inside again with armfuls of boards.

After half an hour of the men wrestling with flying tarps and the women ferrying loads of wood and nail guns to the men balanced precariously overhead on the ladders, the rooms were adequately sheltered from the storm. The four of them retreated to the kitchen and slumped, tired and wet, around the kitchen table. Jen rested her chin in her hands, staring glumly at the table top. Hazel was due to come home in a couple of days – how could she get the rest she needed in a house with half a roof? She frowned. "Still no power, huh?"

Parker shook his head, water running down his forehead. "And there won't be."

She lifted her head from her hands and raised an eyebrow. "Why not?"

"Because this is an old house, which means over-head power lines. And they were attached to the roof directly over the main bathroom." Eamon closed his eyes and pinched the bridge of his nose before reaching for his cell phone where it sat charging on the kitchen counter. "I'm calling the power company. We'll need them to come and make sure the power lines are off the ground and safe."

"We won't have power until we can fix the roof and get the line reattached," Parker told Jen. He shrugged and leaned back in his chair. "So we're in the dark for now."

* * *

THE STORM LEFT a lot of wreckage in its wake, but everyone had stepped up to help clean and fix it all as best they could in the last two days, in preparation for Hazel's return and a Thanksgiving they were all grateful to share with her. Jen still had to book her car in for an assessment. She hoped they'd be able to fix the hail damage – small craters all over it meant that while it still worked fine, it looked terrible.

She poured sweet tea into tall glasses, set the jug back in the bucket of ice and took the glasses into the dining room. They rarely used the formal dining room in this house – in fact, this was probably the first time since she'd arrived, other than for card games. They preferred eating together around the big kitchen table – there was something so warm and inviting about the kitchen.

But it was Thanksgiving, and that meant a special meal in a special room, according to Hazel. Now that she was home, everyone was happy to do whatever Hazel requested. Despite the missing roof and lack of electricity, the atmosphere around the ranch was abuzz with happy excitement. Delayed tests had meant Dalton had barely brought her home in time for the Thanksgiving meal.

"I'm sorry there won't be any turkey," Susan confessed contritely.

Hazel, seated at the table, smiled and shook her head. "I don't mind one bit. I'm just so glad to be home with all of you." She looked pale, but otherwise seemed to be recovering so well that Jen couldn't help feeling happy.

Susan leaned over to hug Hazel around the shoulders and kiss the top of her head. "We're so excited you're here as well, my dear."

"Never mind about turkey," added Jen as she set the glasses at each place setting. "We've got pork ribs, chicken kebabs and steak. Dalton's got the grill fired up and it smells good out there."

Hazel closed her eyes a moment. "Ah...ow!"

"Does it hurt?" whispered Jen, resting a hand on her friend's shoulder.

Hazel covered Jen's hand with hers and nodded. "Just a little. Not too bad, considering."

Jen smiled, then hurried to the kitchen for the rest of the glasses. Dalton, Eamon and Parker had insisted on making most of the food. Susan made her promised sweet potato soufflé, plus potato salad, squash casserole and honeyed carrots. That left Jen with the sweet tea and pumpkin pie for dessert – no oven, so she paid a visit to a local bakery. Emily had promised to bring a box of chocolates after her shift at Tift General – she was due to arrive any moment – but Jen doubted any of them would have room for even the smallest treat after the meal they were planning on eating.

Eamon and Parker's rooms no longer had a roof, Eamon had just slept at Emily's apartment. Parker ended up on the floor in Dalton's room, but now that Hazel was home, she wondered what he'd do. She should offer him her room – she really couldn't force Parker to sleep on the couch or in the barn. Even with everything that was going on, no power, or turkey, this was the best Thanksgiving she could recall. She had so much to be grateful for this year.

Once she'd finished with the tea, Jen hurried to the bathroom. Using that room had become an adventure with no roof or lighting, just a faint blue glow of sunlight filtering through the tarpaulin. She grimaced at the tarp and washed her hands, then returned to the kitchen, rinsing off dishes and adding them to the dishwasher, wiping down counters and putting ingredients away.

"You know the dishwasher won't work without power, right?" laughed Parker, as he backed through the door, a full tray of chicken kebabs and steaks in his hands.

She rolled her eyes and slapped her forehead. "I can't believe I forgot that. Here I thought I was being so helpful, filling it up. Ugh!"

He chuckled and set the tray on the counter, his eyes twinkling. "You're very helpful."

She laughed and slapped him playfully on the chest. "Stop it! I try …"

"Just as well you're so stunningly beautiful. That way people don't mind when you fill a dead dishwasher."

Her cheeks flamed. Did he really mean that? She didn't think anyone had ever called her "stunningly beautiful" before. "Cute," sure – she'd been called that more times than she could count. "Airheaded" and "klutz" came up a lot. But never "stunningly beautiful." She caught him watching her with one eyebrow arched, his expression pensive. "Thanks," she whispered, then opened the dishwasher to unload it again.

"Don't worry about that now," said Parker. "Dinner is ready." He winked, pulled a platter from beneath the counter and began setting the meat on it.

She reached for a pair of tongs and leaned across him, setting them beside the meat.

"Thanks," he said, his breath warm against her cheek.

She flushed with heat and pulled away from him until her back bumped the cabinets. She met his gaze, her heart pounding.

He stepped toward her and lifted a hand to tuck her hair behind one ear. "Listen, Jen, there's something I wanting to talk to you about …"

Dalton burst through the back door, a tray of browned ribs in both hands. "Ribs are done!" he called.

Parker turned on a dime, picked up the platter and followed Dalton into the dining room. Jen shrugged and followed.

She sat in her place at the table opposite Parker. Dalton stood at the head, leaning his hands on the table top. "As y'all know, this has been a hard year for us. A wonderful year, but also a difficult year. We got married ..."

Eamon hooted and Parker pounded the table with his palms. Jen laughed and clapped along with them.

"... thank you, thank you." Dalton chuckled. "And it was the best day of my life. I was so happy to marry this wonderful woman. Then to find out on our honeymoon that she was sick ..." He faltered, his voice breaking with emotion.

Hazel rested her hand on top of his and whispered something in his ear.

He smiled and continued. "But thanks to our beautiful sister-in-law Emily ..." More hoots and hollers. "... Hazel is now cancer free. We know there are more tests to be done, but we have faith they'll be clear. So we have much to be grateful for. We have each other, we have more time and we have our health." He lifted his glass of tea high, his eyes never leaving Hazel's face. "So I'm thankful for marriage, family and good health."

"Hear, hear," chimed Parker, raising his glass high as well. Everyone drank to that, and Jen wiped happy tears from the corners of her eyes as her throat tightened.

Then Parker stood. "I want to say how thankful I am as well. I'm thankful for my family and for Dalton inviting me into his home to be part of his ranch. I'm thankful for Mom always being there for us boys. And finally, I'm thankful for Jen – she may not realize it, but she's helped me see the light after many years of darkness. She's shown me how to be happy in spite of what's going on around me, to seize the moment and enjoy what life brings. So thank you, Jen."

Jen's eyes widened in surprise, her mouth hanging open. She hadn't been expecting that. As everyone around the table raised their glasses to her, she almost choked on the lump in her throat. She looked at him, tears in her eyes, and he smiled back, his head tipped to one side. He raised his glass with a nod, and she grinned through the tears.

CHAPTER 10

*P*arker picked up the pizza boxes, burning his fingers on the hot cardboard as he worked to keep the stack steady. He hurried up the porch stairs and inside with a grimace, dropping the boxes on the kitchen table. Well, he thought as he rinsed his hands under the tap to cool them off, there was no concern about whether the pizzas would still be hot enough for the party.

Also on the table were paper plates, cups and napkins, and he and Dalton had stocked a cooler with ice and sodas. It wasn't fancy, but it was the best they could do on short notice and without electricity. Mom had been determined to celebrate Eamon and Emily's wedding, and she'd helped to throw a party together in only a few days.

He glanced out the back window and saw Jen stringing solar powered twinkle lights over the bushes outside while Hazel watched, sitting on a chair with a warm blanket tucked around her on every side. He chuckled. Jen had lived up to her vow to take care of her friend. From what he'd seen so far, she wasn't letting Hazel do anything for herself since coming home from the hospital.

Mom flew into the kitchen, velcro rollers still in her hair and sporting a bright smile. "There you are – and good, you got the pizzas!" she said in her shrill organizer's voice. He remembered it well from childhood, and it still made his hair stand on end as though someone had run their fingernails down a chalkboard.

He frowned. "No problem at all. They're still hot."

She nodded. "Good – people will be arriving soon. I hope no one's late. I ask you, what's the point of a surprise party if you're gonna be late and spoil the surprise? But I've seen it happen more times than I care to say." She opened the back door and peeked outside. "Looking beautiful!" she shouted through the opening.

Parker began opening the boxes of plastic knives and forks to set out on the table.

"Where's Dalton?" asked Mom.

"Setting up the fire pits so they'll be ready to light when everyone's here."

"It seems to me everything's in order. You'd better go and get dressed, my boy."

He nodded and hurried out of the room. When she was in party mode, the only thing you could do was whatever Mom told you to, and pronto. He threw on a change of clothes, ran a comb through his hair and hurried out back.

The guests had begun to arrive, and as requested had parked around back in the field behind the house. Dalton was directing traffic while Jen and Hazel greeted the guests – neighbors, colleagues, friends, doctors from Emily's office, men from the stockyards, anyone who could make it on such short notice. Even Jen's boss Will was there.

And Jen ... Parker had to admit, she looked amazing in her little black dress with a long red coat and black stockings. Her hair was piled loosely on top of her head. She even wore red lipstick – the first time he'd seen her with lipstick on since she was a bridesmaid at Dalton and Hazel's wedding. It suited her.

By the time Emily and Eamon pulled up in front of the house, all the guests were well-hidden behind the bushes out back. Mom was inside to meet the couple and come up with some excuse to get the two of them out the back door. Parker crouched in silence, musing over how strange everyone looked, hiding quietly behind bushes and shrubbery.

The kitchen door inched open. Eamon came out first, followed by Emily, both looking confused by the twinkle lights. Emily murmured something about how pretty it was just before everyone jumped out and shouted, "Surprise!" Eamon's eyes widened and Emily's hands flew to cover her mouth.

Parker hurried to greet them. "Finally, congratulations on your wedding!" he said, shaking Eamon's hand and kissing Emily on the cheek. The other guests followed his lead and soon the couple was surrounded by well-wishers.

Parker sidled up to Jen and nudged her with an elbow. "Wanna dance?"

She looked up at him with a half-grin, her eyes glimmering with unshed tears from watching Eamon and Emily. "There's no music."

He shrugged. "A minor detail."

She nodded and he put his hand over hers and led her toward the house. He reached inside the kitchen door and grabbed his Bluetooth speaker, hoping it had enough charge to make it through the evening. In a few moments he had it positioned on the end of one of the folding tables Dalton had arranged along the back of the house for the food, blasting Toby Keith at full volume. Then he pulled her to an open space away from the rest of the party-goers and drew her close, his other hand on her back.

As they moved in time to the music, his eyes locked on hers. She didn't look away as they danced in silence. His pulse raced at her touch, and he fought the urge to kiss her. A few other couples soon joined them on the makeshift dance floor, including Emily and Eamon.

Parker grinned at them. "You gonna show us how it's done?"

Eamon dipped Emily, and she grimaced, then laughed. "Careful now, I'm not a rag doll."

Eamon chuckled, pulled her back up and quickly kissed her.

Parker raised a hand to spin Jen. She stumbled over her own high heels, and he caught her just before she hit the ground. He laughed and pulled her close. "I guess we showed them, huh?"

Her cheeks reddened, but she grinned widely. "We sure did. And that's just the beginning – I've got moves you've never seen."

He threw his head back and laughed. "Julia Roberts in *My Best Friend's Wedding?*"

She nodded. "I didn't think you'd get the reference. I love that movie. It's sappy, but just the right amount, don't you think?"

He chuckled as he pulled her close again and led

her around the dance floor. "Do you think it's possible, though?"

"What?" Her brow furrowed.

"For two friends who think they're nothing more to realize they love each other and make it work. Do you think that could happen?"

She frowned. "In the movie they realize they're *not* right for each other ..."

"Yeah, but still – it could happen, couldn't it?"

She smiled. "Sure it could. I think when it comes to love, anything's possible."

He arched an eyebrow. "Now, that's sappy."

She laughed.

"But just the right amount." He pulled her closer, and her head fit perfectly beneath his chin as they moved.

Emily's phone rang in her jeans pocket. She released Eamon's hand and pulled it free, glowering at it before taking the call. "Hello?"

Eamon's eyebrows arched. "Who is it?" he whispered.

She shook her head and mouthed something Parker couldn't make out before she spoke. "Ba Ba, it's hard to hear you. We're having a party ... to celebrate our wedding. I know, I know you didn't agree I should marry Eamon. And I'm sorry you're disappointed. But we love each other and I hope you'll come to realize he makes me happy. Don't you want me to be happy?"

Eamon set his hands on her shoulders and rubbed them gently as tears began to pour down her cheeks.

"... But Ba Ba, it's not that I don't respect you ... please, can't you just be happy for me?" She wiped her cheeks with the back of her hand, then nodded. "That's

417

all I want. I promise, I didn't do this to hurt you. I fell in love, that's all ..." She was silent for a while, then hung up and fell into Eamon's arms, sobbing against his shoulder.

Parker released Jen and shuffled his feet, shoving his hands into his pockets. He hated to see Emily hurting so much. What kind of parents treated their only daughter that way, just because she chose to marry someone they didn't like? Come to think of it, he was sure they hadn't even met Eamon yet, so it really didn't make sense for them to disapprove.

Eamon led Emily to one of the chairs set up around the party space. She sat down and he crouched in front of her, stroking her cheek and whispering to her. Jen followed and sat beside Emily, wrapping her arm around her friend's shoulders. Parker wandered over, though there likely wasn't anything he could say or do to make things better. But he felt as though he should at least try. "Are you okay, Em?"

She glanced up at him with tear-filled eyes as Eamon took a seat beside her. "Yeah, I'll be fine. Thanks, Parker." She turned to Eamon, who was staring at the ground in front of her. "They don't know you. How can they treat us this way?"

Eamon shook his head, took her hand and squeezed it. "Don't worry about it – they'll come around sometime. I mean, look how lovable I am. They won't be able to resist this level of charm for long." He grinned, and she laughed at him, then hiccupped. "What did your Dad say?"

"That he was disappointed I'd chosen to marry you against their wishes. That Ma Ma wouldn't even come to the phone to talk to me. He wants to mend things between us, somehow. He said he'd like to come and visit. But ..."

"Well, that's good, isn't it?"

She nodded and sniffled into her sleeve. "Well, it's definitely a step in the right direction. I can't believe he was the first one to break and call me. I was sure he'd never do that. But he still sounded like he just wanted to come here so he could talk me out of it …" She sobbed again, and Jen pulled a tissue from her pocket and handed it to her. She thanked Jen and wiped her nose. "He said he'll try to convince Ma Ma to visit after Christmas. They want to see where we live and where I work …"

Eamon smiled. "See, it's all going to work out."

She sobbed again, then burst into a fresh round of tears. "I hope so."

* * *

PARKER HUNG his towel on the rack in the bathroom and grimaced at the condensation on the mirror. He had to remember to switch on the exhaust fan before he stepped into the shower. Hazel hated it when he fogged up the entire bathroom.

He flicked the switch, hoping to clear out the steam before she took her shower. He'd forgotten how much he appreciated electricity until it was gone. Of course, he'd taken many a cold shower in the military, but now that he was out he'd grown used to home comforts. So when Dalton hooked up their new generator so they could get the water heater going for awhile, he'd almost danced for joy.

He'd been showering in Dalton and Hazel's en suite since the roof was blown off the main bathroom. It was small but worked well enough, though he hated invading their privacy that way – having to sneak through their bedroom past a sleeping Hazel with his towel over his arm and a toiletry bag in hand. After sleeping all night on the couch. He was ready for the roof to be repaired so things could get back to semi-normal.

In the kitchen, he nodded to Dalton and reached for the box of Honey Bunches of Oats. He set it on the table, found a bowl and spoon, poured himself a generous portion and added milk from a portion sized long-life carton. As he ate, he browsed the latest news on his iPad until a grunt from Dalton gave him pause. He glanced up at his brother with a frown. "What's wrong?"

Dalton was glowering. "Insurance company. They're saying they won't cover the cost of replacing the roof *or* redoing the bathroom and bedrooms." He ran his hand through his hair and sighed. "I can't believe it. We've paid premiums all this time, and now when we finally need them to step up they're trying to weasel out of paying."

Parker shook his head and frowned. "Typical." He took another bite of cereal, his thoughts swirling as he munched. "I mean, they have to pay. That's what we have insurance for."

Dalton shook his head. "Doesn't look like it. They've found a loophole – something to do with water damage. Apparently our policy doesn't cover it."

Parker swallowed. "So what do we do then? We can't live like this permanently. I don't know how long those tarps will keep the weather out, and if we get another storm they won't. Not to mention it's freezing cold at night. Thank goodness for the fireplace, or I'd probably be frozen solid on the couch by morning." He scooped up the last of the cereal from his bowl.

Dalton closed his eyes and inhaled deeply. "I don't know what we'll do. We don't have the money to fix it, and we can't leave it the way it is."

Parker's heart sank. "Yeah, Eamon mentioned that. I guess I didn't realize it was that bad."

Dalton sighed again. "With Hazel's medical bills stacking up and the ranch running on fumes, we don't have any wiggle room. I'm pretty well tapped out, and the ranch accounts aren't fat enough to take on any major projects. I'm going to get Eamon to take a look at the books when he gets here, but from my perspective it's not looking good."

Parker stared at his brother, unsure how to respond.

Dalton must have noticed his shock. "Don't worry about it too much just yet. We'll figure it out somehow."

Parker's chest tightened. "But it might mean we have to sell the ranch."

Dalton nodded. "It might."

"But we've poured everything we have into this place, and it's just starting to get going – we've finally got the herd we want. Rocket Peak's beginning to get a reputation in the breeding world and is in more demand than ever. We've fixed everything up, painted anything standing still, installed miles of fencing – we've worked so hard!"

Dalton shrugged. "I know. I'm just not sure it'll be enough. "

* * *

PARKER SHIFTED the truck into second as it rumbled and bumped down the winding track toward the lake.

Magic Eight Lake was a place he liked to go when things overwhelmed him. It gave him a chance to think, to calm his mind and to get some perspective. His psychologist had encouraged him to come up with some strategies for managing his stress, and visiting the lake with a fishing pole was one of them.

He pulled the truck onto a grassy rise and set the handbrake, then stepped out of the truck and gazed out across the lake. A flock of geese flew in formation overhead. Ducks paddled serenely on the water's glassy surface, heads dipping between reeds near the swampy edges. He pulled his pole and tackle box from the back of the truck and hiked over to a fallen log he used as a makeshift seat, set the tackle box down and dug through it for a lure.

Before long the float on his line bobbed gently on the water, and he settled on the log and hunched his shoulders. He knew it wasn't the right time of year or best time of day to catch anything, but that wasn't why he was there anyway. He hoped to find some perspective, some insight that would help keep the dark cloud hanging over his thoughts at bay.

The ranch had been his dream for a fresh start. When Dalton asked him to partner in the venture, he'd jumped at the chance. Leaving the military had been the right thing to do, but it had left him with an emptiness he wasn't sure how to fill. Mom had dragged him to church, which helped. Reconnecting with God filled the hole, but he was still left at loose ends. What to do now with his life?

So when Dalton inherited the ranch from Grandpa Joe, he and Eamon both decided they wanted to visit and help their brother out. When he called them, they'd been ready and willing to drop everything –

which for Parker was really nothing at all – and head south. When he asked them to invest, they'd both agreed without hesitation. But if the ranch went under, what then? Everything he'd saved during his Ranger stint would be lost unless they got a good price, which with the current climate in real estate wasn't a given.

The crunch of gravel signaled the arrival of another vehicle. He squinted in the afternoon light to see Bill Pullen, their neighbor and the lake's owner pull up beside Parker's truck. "How's it going, Bill?" he called when Bill exited his pickup.

Bill meandered over, his hat tipped back, and smiled. "Hey there, Parker. I'm doin' fine – how 'bout you?"

"Hanging in there."

Bill sat on the log beside Parker, a toothpick protruding from the side of his mouth. "Heard ya had some trouble with that storm the other day."

Parker tugged at the line and reeled it in a little, his eyebrows arching briefly. "Yep – lost part of the roof and the electricity besides. We've set up a generator now, so it's not too bad. At least there's hot water for showers again. Felt like I was back in boot camp for a while there." He chuckled and tugged the line again.

"Sorry to hear that. Hopefully you can get it fixed before much longer."

Parker frowned. "I hope so too, though the insurance company's giving us grief, saying they won't pay. And Dalton's got all those hospital expenses ..."

Bill slapped his thigh with a curse. "Now that just ain't right." He went quiet, and both men watched the surface of the lake, lost in their own thoughts. A dragonfly buzzed close by, dancing through the air between them and the lake before settling on a blade of grass. "What'll you boys do?" he finally asked.

Parker shook his head. "Not sure yet. I guess we'll think of something, but it'll have to be soon. I don't like the idea of living without a roof through winter, and it can't be good for Hazel's health."

Bill's eyes flashed. "Lemme see if I can sort somethin' out. We're neighbors, Parker, and neighbors take care of each other."

CHAPTER 11

*J*en shut the lid of her suitcase and jumped in place to get it to close. She zipped it up and set it on the ground beside the bed with a huff. It was time for her to move out of the ranch house. Parker was sleeping on the couch, the roof was still in disrepair, and they didn't need extra people making things more difficult than they needed to be. Thankfully, Emily had invited her to come and stay with her and Eamon at their apartment in Tifton, so that's what she'd do.

She hadn't run the idea by Parker yet, since she knew from their previous conversations that he'd likely object. But it was time, and she didn't intend to let herself be dissuaded on the subject again.

She tugged the suitcase and her purse down the narrow hallway just as Parker came in the front door, a fishing pole in one hand and a bucket in the other. "Where are you off to?" he asked with a frown.

Her cheeks warmed. "I'm going to stay with Eamon and Emily for a while. They invited me, and with the roof the way it is and the house so full ... well, I just thought it was the best option. Besides, now you can sleep in my room – I washed and changed the sheets for you, so it's all ready. You won't have to sleep on the couch anymore."

Parker sighed and ran a hand over his face. "Thanks Jen. You're right, it's probably best for now."

She frowned. That wasn't the reaction she was expecting. "Okay, well ... I guess I'll see you soon. I'll still be coming over to check on Hazel. Then I may head to Alabama to see my folks once Hazel's feeling better."

He nodded, and she thought he looked uneasy. What was going on with him? "That sounds good," he said as he walked into the kitchen.

Jen headed for the front door, her throat tightening. He hadn't seemed at all concerned she was leaving, didn't try to talk her out of it – not that she'd intended to listen to his arguments anyway, but it would've been nice to hear some. He didn't even offer to help her load the car. She pushed open the door and lugged her bags down the stairs, wondering what it was that had Parker so distracted.

JEN SIGHED and reached for her purse. She'd eaten some toast, cleaned up, showered. Time for her to head off to work.

Eamon and Emily's apartment was quiet and peaceful. With only two bedrooms, the guest bed shared a room with a desk covered in papers, a laptop and a multi-function printer. But while it was nice, it wasn't the Cotton Tree. She missed the buzz of activity, the hum of conversation, the country air and the beautiful vistas.

Most of all, she missed the company. Eamon and Emily had welcomed her in, then left for work themselves a few minutes later, telling her to help herself to whatever she needed. So when Hazel insisted she return to the ranch that night for supper, she'd agreed, looking forward to seeing them all again even though she'd only been gone an hour. There was something very homey and inviting about the ranch house and the Williams family, something she didn't want to miss out on.

Most of all, she missed Parker. She'd grown accustomed to their camaraderie and easy banter, and her heart ached at the thought that she might never get the chance to spend as much time with him again. Soon she'd likely be back in Alabama – and if her parents had anything to say about it, she'd stay there. The Cotton Tree Ranch would be just a memory and perhaps a place to visit on vacation. She sighed, and picked up her purse to head out the door, pulling it shut behind her,

* * *

HAZEL FROWNED and laid her head back on the arm of the couch. "You know, Jen, you really don't have to rub my feet. I feel as though I'm taking advantage of you." She laughed and her eyes drifted shut.

Jen chuckled and kept massaging Hazel's foot. "You might as well take advantage now. I don't know how much longer I'll be around."

Hazel's eyes flew open. "What do you mean?"

"You know I can't stay here forever."

She frowned. "Yes, but you said you thought you might stick around – you have a job here now and I thought you were enjoying it."

Jen shrugged. "That's true, I did say that. It's just that ..."

Hazel sat up straight and set her feet on the ground. "What?"

"I don't know ... I don't really belong here, I guess. You've got Dalton and you're part of the family, but I'm not. I guess I forgot that for a while, but now I'm feeling a bit out of place."

Hazel smirked. "Does this have something to do with a certain handsome ex-Ranger?"

Jen's cheeks burned. Of course it did. "No, of course not."

Hazel scooted closer to Jen on the couch. "I don't want to pressure you to stay. I want you to do what feels right for you. If going home to Birmingham will make you happy, do it. If staying here is what you want, I'm right here with you, supporting your decision. I'll miss you if you leave, but I don't want you to stay if you don't feel like this is the place for you. I live here because my heart and home are here. But you can go wherever you want."

"Thanks, Hazel – you're a good friend. And I'll miss you too. But I promise I'll come and visit whenever I get a chance."

Hazel leaned back again with a smile. "But if it did have anything to do with Parker, I'd completely understand. He's such a great guy – I've really grown fond of him since I've been here. And Dalton says he's doing so much better than he was."

Jen frowned and crossed her legs on the couch. "What do you mean 'better'?"

"Well, you know he's had a hard time of it since he was discharged. Apparently he wasn't doing too well at first, but he's been seeing a psychologist and he's adjusting to life stateside."

Jen's curiosity kicked into overdrive. "Did Dalton say how he could tell Parker wasn't coping before?"

Hazel's brow furrowed. "Um ... I think he was just kind of blue all the time, and he wouldn't talk to anyone about it. None of us know what went on with him over in Syria, because he doesn't like to talk about it. But maybe he's opening up to his psychologist. Either way, he seems better now. And Dalton's really happy with how he's doing."

Jen frowned. "Well ..."

Hazel's eyes widened. "What is it?"

Jen shook her head. "It might be nothing. It's just that I've mostly known Parker as a fun, happy guy. Yeah, he's a bit dark and mysterious, not chatty or exuberant – he didn't say much at your wedding. But in the time I've been here, he's been friendly and open ... until the last couple of days. Something is bothering him."

Hazel chewed her lower lip. "Hmmm ... I'll pay more attention next time I see him. I wonder what it could be."

Jen hated talking about Parker behind his back. And really, it wasn't any of her business. Perhaps she shouldn't have said anything, but she couldn't help it – she cared about him and wanted to make sure he was okay. And if he wouldn't open up to her, maybe he'd be willing to tell Hazel or Dalton what was really going on with him.

"So what's going on with your car?" asked Hazel.

Jen grimaced. "The insurance company wants to

write it off. Can you believe that? There's nothing wrong with it, apart from pockmarks all over it. It just looks like it has acne."

Hazel laughed. "Well, I guess you'll be able to get a new one, then."

Jen nodded. "I guess, but I hate to give up on it, you know? I love my car. I think I'll keep driving it and bank the money from the insurance company to use when I'm ready to buy another vehicle." She pouted, thinking about her little hatchback, now covered in tiny hail-shaped craters. It really was such a shame.

Parker burst through the front door in his stocking feet and froze at the sight of the two women. "Uh, hi." His voice was low and his eyes immediately focused on the floor as he headed down the hallway to the guest room, now his bedroom.

Hazel met Jen's gaze with arched eyebrows. "I see what you mean."

Jen nodded slowly. "Right?"

Hazel folded her hands in her lap. "You should go talk to him."

"Me? He isn't likely to talk to *me*."

"Uh, didn't you hear the toast he made at Thanksgiving? You're exactly the person he'll talk to – you're the one 'showing him the light' or something like that." Hazel chuckled and nudged Jen in the ribs with her elbow.

Jen shied away. "Ouch! Okay, fine, I'll go and talk to him. But I know he won't open up. It's just a sixth sense I have – I can tell right away when I have a connection with someone, and Parker and I have definitely lost any connection we had. You'll see."

Hazel smirked. "Uh-huh."

Jen frowned and stood, still rubbing her ribs where

Hazel's bony elbow had connected. She wandered down the hallway, looking back to see Hazel still watching her progress. Hazel shooed her forward with a wave of her hand, and Jen's eyebrows lowered. She shook her head, waved Hazel off, went down the hall to Parker's door and knocked, hoping her friend's eyes weren't still boring into her back.

She heard shuffling inside, and the door creaked open. Parker stared out at her, a half-smile creeping across his face. "Hey, Jen. What's up?"

She could feel her cheeks burning. "Um … can I come in?"

He nodded and opened the door further, waving her in. "Sorry it's a bit of a mess. Still not unpacked."

She nodded. "It's fine, really."

He cleared a pile of clothes from the end of the bed and patted the spot. She sat there and took a deep breath. This was harder than she expected – she didn't know where to start and didn't want to say anything that might offend him or hurt his feelings. Anything that came out of her mouth right now could be construed as nosy, insensitive and a lot of other unhelpful things.

He sat across from her on a chair he'd just cleared of T-shirts. "Are you all right?"

She nodded, forcing a smile. "Yeah, I'm fine, thanks for asking. But I came here to ask about you. If you're okay."

He crossed his arms and frowned. "I'm fine, I guess. Why do you ask?"

"You don't seem yourself. Something's on your mind – bothering you, or worrying you, or …" Her cheeks flamed further.

He shrugged. "Yeah, there's something bothering

me. I didn't realize it showed quite so much, but I should've known you'd figure it out – you can read me like a book." He grinned and leaned forward, setting his elbows on top of his knees.

She sighed with relief. "So what is it? Unless you don't want to talk about it ..."

He shook his head. "It's fine. I don't mind talking about it. I need to work at that, anyway – talking. Having a shrink forcing me to is probably loosening up my tongue a bit ..." He chuckled, then sighed deeply. "It's the ranch and Dalton and Hazel and everything. The insurance company's refusing to pay for the roof and the storm damage. Hazel's medical bills are piling up. We might lose the ranch and everything we've worked so hard for so long to build ..." The words tumbled out until he was done. Then he rubbed his eyes and groaned.

She frowned. No wonder he was anxious - apparently there was a lot going on at the Cotton Tree that she wasn't aware of. She didn't think Hazel knew about it either, though she could understand if Dalton felt she didn't need the stress right after major surgery and while possibly still fighting for her life. They were still waiting to hear the results of her tests. "I'm sorry, Parker. That really stinks."

"Yeah." He ran his hands over his face again. "It does. And we don't know what to do about it. Dalton, Eamon and I will get together and figure it out soon. Which is hard, considering we haven't seen much of Dalton the last few weeks. Getting time to talk has become harder than finding hen's teeth."

She chuckled, then covered her mouth. "Sorry, it's not funny. Really." But she couldn't stop laughing at the mental picture. Before long, Parker joined her and they howled together, tears streaming down their cheeks.

Finally they were both spent, and Parker leaned on Jen's shoulder and took a long breath. "I … don't even remember … what we were laughing about. Why is it that whenever I'm with you, Jennifer Barsby, I forget all my troubles and we can just laugh together?"

She caught his gaze and held it, feeling a warmth rising from her gut up to her head. Her scalp tickled with goosebumps and she smiled. "I don't know. But it sure is fun."

Still smiling, he raised a hand to her cheek and traced a line down it. "Yeah."

"Have you seen your psychologist lately?" she asked.

His hand fell abruptly into his lap and his brow furrowed. "No."

She faltered. "Well … um, perhaps you should. I mean, this is the type of thing they're good for – helping you navigate life's ups and downs, you know."

He crossed his arms again and leaned back in his chair. "I guess so."

She pointed a finger at him. "Don't snarl at me, Parker Williams. You know I'm right."

He chuckled and the lines in his forehead smoothed away. "You are, as usual. I should go and see the doc. I've been using my strategies, though, you'll be pleased to know."

"And has it helped?"

"I think so. I'm talking to you about it, aren't I?"

She laughed and nodded. "Yes, you are. You know, I used to see a psychologist when I was younger."

"You did? What for?"

"Oh, you know, the things rich kids are always

seeing shrinks for. My parents thought they'd screwed me up, so they sent me to talk to someone else for three hundred dollars an hour so *they* didn't have to deal with it."

His eyebrows arched high. "Oh."

She chuckled. "I'm not being fair to my parents. They love me and they showed it when I was a kid – they still do. But they were also very preoccupied, and I was so shy that I couldn't talk to adults, so they thought there was something wrong with me. There wasn't, but I got to add shrink visits to my weekly routine, between soccer practice and piano lessons."

He shook his head with a chuckle. "I keep forgetting you come from money. But you don't seem …"

"Snooty? Stuck-up? Spoiled?" She laughed.

So did he. "No. You seem very down to earth. Normal, you know."

"Yes, but in part that's because I didn't want that life. I know, that sounds crazy, but my parents were always working when I was a kid. I hardly saw them – if I wanted to spend time with them, I had to go to work with them. They were and are very successful, so of course it paid off. But they only had one child, me. It got mighty lonely at times with no one to play with but the nanny."

He frowned. "I'm sorry."

"Well, as soon as I was old enough to leave and go to college, I did. I set up a life for myself – a different kind of life, where I got to spend time with animals and people and enjoy myself. I don't want work and making money to be my only priority. They didn't take too kindly to that. They wanted me to get an MBA., come back to Birmingham and join the family business. But instead I became a vet and stayed in Atlanta."

He shook his head. "Wow. You're such a rebel."

"They try to hook me back into their life all the time, offering to buy me fancy cars and condos and all sorts of things. But I know there are always strings attached. So since college, I've supported myself. It's the one thing I insist on. I love my parents and I appreciate all they've done for me. I enjoy visiting them when I can. But I'll never let them control my life. And they tend to try to – if I give them an inch, they'll take a mile."

He grimaced. "That sounds dangerous."

She chuckled. "You have no idea. But what about you? I can't imagine it was your family's dream to have you join the Army right out of school."

He shook his head. "Definitely not. Mom cried for a week when I told her. She wanted me to be a doctor or lawyer or … anything else, really."

"Do you regret it?" asked Jen, setting her hand on his knee.

He looked at her hand, then covered it with his, sending a thrill up her arm. "Nope. But it's taken me a while to realize that."

"Well, we both have a chance now to set up the kind of life we want."

He nodded. "You make it sound like anything's possible."

She smiled. "It is."

*D*alton slammed his fist on the table, making the glasses shiver. "I just can't believe they won't pay!"

Eamon smoothed his hair back and stared at the spreadsheet on the laptop in front of them. "Sorry, it just doesn't add up. We can't afford to replace the roof and fix the two bedrooms and bathroom. Not with the ranch bank accounts the way they are. And Dalton's got nothing left after he pays Hazel's medical bills."

"I put all my savings into the ranch and my truck," added Parker with a grimace. "I shouldn't have bought the truck. I knew it was too big an expense."

"Don't blame yourself," replied Eamon. "You needed a vehicle and there's nothing you can do about it now. I've got a little bit saved, but I've been eating away at it ever since I left Chattanooga. I keep thinking things will pick up at the Cotton Tree and we'll be able to draw a decent wage, but it hasn't happened yet."

"Do you think it ever will?" asked Dalton.

Eamon nodded. "I do. We're so close. We've finally reached several of our big goals with the herd and breeding stock. The barn has been renovated. We've got all the equipment we need. There were a lot of capital expenses in the first year or so, but that should've slowed down by now. Except that the roof got blown off."

"Shoulda, coulda, woulda," Dalton grumbled, rubbing his hands over his face.

"There's no point in us turning on each other," said Eamon, his eyes narrowing.

"I'm sorry – I just don't know what to do. I feel like I've led you both into an impossible situation. And it's all on my shoulders …"

"No, it's not," replied Parker. "It's all on *our* shoulders. This is *our* ranch. We decided to go in on it with you – that was *our* choice. We didn't have to do it, we wanted to. And now that it's in trouble, that's on all of us."

The three of them fell silent, resting their chins in their hands.

The phone rang and Parker stood to retrieve it from its cradle on the kitchen wall. "Hello, Cotton Tree Ranch."

"Is that Dalton?" a man said.

Parker shook his head. "No, sir, this is Parker."

"Oh, hey, Parker – this is Alton Conway over at the Conway Farm down the road. How're you doin', son?"

Parker smiled. "I'm well, thanks, Mr. Conway. And you?"

"Well, I just heard from Bill Pullen about your roof situation over there at the ranch house. Blown clean off, huh?"

Parker rubbed his eyes. "Yes, sir, that's right. Not the whole thing, but near enough."

"Well, I'd like to come over sometime this week and help you repair that ol' thing. I've got some sheets of Colorbond roofin' you're welcome to – we just re-roofed our farmhouse last month and we got leftovers."

Parker's eyes widened. "We'd sure appreciate that, sir! Any help we can get is more than we have now."

"You got it, Parker. Just give me a call and let me know when, and I'll be there." The phone line went dead and he set it back in place.

"Who was that?" asked Dalton.

Just then, the phone rang again. Parker frowned and picked it up. "Cotton Tree Ranch, this is Parker."

"Hello there, Parker me boy. It's Will Hart. How're things?"

"Hello, Will. What's up?"

"Well, I was just talking to Bill Pullen at the feed store, and he told me about the storm damage you got. A few of us were there and we decided we'd offer our services to help you fix it up. Shouldn't take more than a few days with enough men. And Andy Harmon – you know, the plumber? He said he'd take a look at your piping. My son-in-law Jackson's a tiler and he's more than happy to re-tile your bathroom, said he's got a good bit of leftover tiles you can choose from if you like. Free of charge."

Parker rubbed his chin. "Wow, Will, that would be amazing. Thanks!"

When he hung up, he didn't even get a chance to raise an eyebrow in his brothers' direction before phone rang again. By the end of the evening, much to the Williams brothers' surprise, they had an entire team of volunteers and tradesmen lined up to do the repairs on their house the following Monday. And Parker sat with hunched shoulders at the kitchen table, exhausted by all the conversations he'd had with neighbors from all over the county to organize the work.

"Do you think it'll be enough?" asked Eamon, nursing a cup of coffee in his hands.

Dalton shook his head in wonder. "I don't know. But it's sure a good start."

* * *

JEN STIRRED the pot of beans one last time. Using oven mitts, she picked up the pot, emptied it into a long glass baking pan, laid strips of bacon across the top and slid it into the oven. She stood with her hands on her hips and surveyed the kitchen, full to the brim with women from the surrounding farms. The Cotton Tree was the only ranch in the county. Everyone else grew cotton, peaches or one of a dozen other crops that thrived in the red dirt of south Georgia.

"How's that sweet tea comin'?" asked Esther Pullen, a tea towel draped over her shoulder.

Jen turned to check the saucepan, with tea bags bubbling. "I think it's about done. I've added the sugar and I think it's dissolved."

"Good. Here you go." Esther set a large jug full of ice on the counter by the stove.

Jen picked up the saucepan, poured it into the jug, filled it to the brim with cold water from the tap and carried it out to the front porch. A row of tables set up along the porch held jugs of ice water, sweet tea and Coke, along with trays of crackers, cheese and buttered biscuits. She set the jug on one of the tables and hurried back inside, wiping her hands on the apron around her waist.

She glanced down the hall as she passed. She couldn't see the work being done – one of the men had hung a sheet to prevent dust sifting into the rest of the house – but she could hear it. They'd begun just after breakfast, the families arriving in trucks and SUVs, finding anywhere they could in the front yard to park, most laden with building supplies or some kind of food.

Back in the kitchen, the din of conversation drowned out the banging and clanging of work going on overhead. The women chatted and laughed as they bustled around, putting together a lunch that looked as though it would feed Parker's old Army unit, though there were only about thirty people there from Jen's count. Still, she supposed they'd be mighty hungry after a full morning of work.

There were trays of fried chicken to go with the pans of beans and the biscuits, a truckload of macaroni and cheese, hot dogs, hamburgers, fries and onion rings and collard greens. And for dessert there were banana cream pies, apple pies and peach and black-berry cobblers. She licked her lips and her stomach growled. Just the sight and smell of so much good food made her hungry.

She picked up a tray of chicken and carried it out to the porch, past Hazel seated in the den with a book in her hands, watching with a frown as everyone buzzed by. Jen hadn't seen her actually *look* at the book – no doubt she was wishing she could join in the fun. She deposited the chicken outside, then returned to sit beside Hazel on the couch. "How're you doing?"

Hazel grimaced. "I feel ridiculous, just sitting here while everyone else is working so hard."

Jen laughed and patted her arm.

"Susan banned me. She *banned* me!" Hazel huffed. "Said my only job today was to keep getting well and let everyone else take care of the rest."

Jen nodded. "Susan is very wise."

Hazel snarled as another woman hurried by with an armful of food. "Yes, I suppose she's just trying to do what's best for me. But seriously, I'm feeling good. I could help out with … something."

Jen stood. "Can I get you a drink?"

Hazel nodded, her face falling. "Yes, thank you."

Jen nodded and made her way back to the kitchen. A group of children pushed past her through the kitchen door, chattering and laughing, and she grinned. It felt good to have so much life filling the house. She piled a plate with food, filled a plastic cup with sweet tea and carried it back to set on the coffee table beside Hazel. "You could come outside and eat with everyone else," she suggested.

Hazel made a face and nodded. "I'll do that. Thanks."

"What's on your mind?"

She sighed. "Besides being bored out of my mind? The test results. They should be done – they said I'd hear back by now, but I haven't heard a thing."

Jen half-smiled. "I'm sure we'll hear soon."

"But what if it's bad? What if they missed some of the cancer and I have to go through chemo? And what if the chemo doesn't work …" She took a quick breath and put her hand on her throat. "I'm in my last year of teacher's college. I was hoping I'd get a job next year, then maybe we'd get pregnant. I mean, you never know for sure if you can get pregnant until you try, but I want to have a family. If I have to do chemo, we may have to wait five years to start a family, if we can have one at all. And if the chemo doesn't work …"

Jen took her hand and squeezed it. "Whoa, calm down there, sweetie. You can't go down that road – it'll only lead to a panic attack. Let's just wait to see what the results are. Maybe they'll be clear. And if they're not, we have to believe the chemo will work. Don't fret – it's not going to make anything better."

Hazel squeezed her eyes shut and nodded as tears rolled down her cheeks. "You're right. I shouldn't think about it. At least not until it's real."

Jen embraced her friend. "I know it's going to be okay. You've come through the surgery so well, and Emily was confident she got it all. Try to enjoy today and not worry about it anymore. We'll get the results soon enough." She glanced over Hazel's shoulder as her friend sobbed into her hair and saw Parker through the hanging sheet. He caught a glimpse of them and smiled, his cheeks dimpling.

Jen's heart quivered. Would Hazel be okay? For that matter, what about Parker? She wished there was more she could do to take care of her friends. But all she could do was be there for them, pray for them and hope that everything would turn out okay in the end.

* * *

JEN ADMIRED the brand-new bathroom and the roof overhead. She was in awe of how much could be achieved when a community pulled together the way theirs had over the past two weeks. The tiling had finally been completed that day, and that was that. She smiled and hurried back to the den where they were playing Monopoly. Susan had gone out shopping earlier that afternoon and hadn't returned yet, so it was just the two couples, Parker and Jen.

She slid onto the couch beside Parker and grinned at him. He seemed better as well. As promised, he'd been visiting his psychologist since they last discussed it, and his smile had returned after their neighbors and friends came together to repair the storm damage. He and Dalton had even gotten a few days' work here and there as laborers, and Eamon had picked up some accounting clients from surrounding farms. Every bit helped to keep the lights on at the ranch, as Dalton liked to remind them. And the lights were back on — once the roof had been repaired, the power company restored electricity to the ranch house within days. They were celebrating the milestone with a pot roast and board games.

"You ready to lose?" he asked, his eyes twinkling.

She laughed. "Please. I already have six hotels on my properties. You're gonna be paying rent every day of the week, buddy."

Hazel stood and maneuvered past them, heading toward the kitchen. "I'm going to make some popcorn," she called back over her shoulder.

"I'll help." Dalton followed quickly behind.

Eamon moved his game piece around the board, passed *Go* and collected two hundred dollars from Emily, who served as the bank. He leaned across to wrest the money from her.

"No, you're cheating!" she cried with a giggle.

"I'm not cheating. You're not very good at this whole bank thing." He dug his fingers into her ribs, eliciting a cackle of laughter. "You're supposed to be impartial and just hand over the money."

In between bursts of laughter, she cried, "But you were in jail!"

"I rolled a double!"

"On the floor – that doesn't count!"

Jen rolled her eyes. "Come on, you two."

Parker smirked and slapped his brother playfully on the thigh. "Em, give him the money this time. But no more cheating, Eamon."

Emily handed over the cash with a pout, then glanced at the kitchen door. Hazel and Dalton were still in the kitchen, but all they heard was the hum of the microwave. She and Eamon exchanged a look and she cleared her throat.

Jen frowned. "What's going on, you two? You look like the cat that ate the canary."

Emily frowned. "We have a secret to tell. But if we tell you, you can't say anything to Hazel or Dalton."

Jen's brow furrowed. "Okay …"

Emily grinned, then whispered, "I'm pregnant."

Jen clapped her hand over her mouth to stop from squealing, then whispered back, "Congratulations. That's so exciting. Wow, that was …" She stopped, her cheeks reddening.

"Fast? Yeah, we know." Emily chuckled as Eamon laced his fingers through hers.

Eamon gazed into Emily's eyes. "It's really early still, but we just wanted to tell you. We only found out yesterday."

Jen felt all warm inside. "Well, that's great news. And we won't say anything, but I have to ask – why tell us but not Hazel and Dalton? I mean, I understand if it's too soon to go public, but they're your best friends."

Eamon took a slow breath. "Well, you know Hazel hasn't gotten her results yet, so we're waiting to see how that goes … anyway, they have other things on their minds."

"And this certainly wasn't planned," added Emily. "I mean, I had a whole heap of other plans, but a baby wasn't one of them. Still, we couldn't be happier." She turned to Eamon and he kissed the tip of her nose.

"Absolutely. We'll still do all those things we'd planned, only it'll be three of us doing them rather than two." He wrapped his arms around her and pulled her close to kiss her on the lips. "Having a baby won't change anything."

Jen smiled and leaned back on the couch. "Well, I'm really happy for you two. And I know Hazel and Dalton will be as well."

Parker slouched forward and whispered, "I think the game's over." His smile made her heart beat faster and her stomach did a flip. His arm pressed against hers and his fingers tickled the side of her leg.

Jen bit her lower lip and was about to slip her hand into his when Hazel and Dalton burst through the kitchen door, both holding bowls. "Popcorn's ready!" called Dalton.

Jen sat up straight and smiled as she took the bowl from Hazel and set it on the coffee table. "Mmmm … delicious."

CHAPTER 13

"We miss you, hon," Jen's mom drawled over the phone line. "You think you'll be home for Christmas? You didn't make it for Thanksgiving and it sure was quiet around this place. I thought you'd be here, given you're our only daughter, but ..."

Jen lay back on her bed with a sigh. "Yeah, I'm sorry about that, Mom. I'll drive out there on Christmas Day I'd like to spend the morning here at the Cotton Tree, but after that I'm all yours."

"So you're back at the ranch, then?"

"Yeah, I moved back in yesterday. I missed it, and now that the power's back on and the bathroom's functioning it made sense."

"Well, I'm glad things are working out for you, hon."

"How are you doing, Mom?"

"Oh, just fine. You know us, we're working ourselves to the bone."

Jen frowned. "You should take some time off over

Christmas, Mom. Have a vacation. You deserve a break." It was always the same thing: excuses upon excuses as to why they couldn't take time away from the family business. She knew the truth – they loved it. It made them feel needed and they didn't want a break, even as it exhausted them. But she'd had this argument with them a thousand times and she knew it wasn't one she could win.

"Oh, maybe we will. You know your father, though – he doesn't think anyone else can take care of things the way he does. I guess he's right about that."

"When I get home, we'll do some fun things together, Mom. Maybe shop the after-Christmas sales, get some coffee, have our nails done – how does that sound?"

"Sounds just perfect, baby girl. I can't wait to see you."

When she hung up, Jen felt a hard ball of homesickness in her gut. She enjoyed being out on her own, making her own way, but she missed home at the same time. Her relationship with Birmingham and with her folks was complicated – she adored both the city and her parents, but at the same time needed space from both so she could be her own person.

She walked to the bathroom, tugging a clean towel from the linen closet on her way. She was looking forward to her first shower in the newly-renovated bathroom. It seemed larger than before, with a much bigger shower, modern tub and dual vanity. She locked the door behind her, undressed and climbed into the running shower. Hot water cascaded over her head and down her back and she ran her fingers through her hair.

When she climbed out, she noted with dismay that

she'd forgotten to turn the exhaust fan on. It was one of Hazel's pet peeves, something she knew well after years as Hazel's roommate. She flicked it on with a grimace.

A scream echoed through the house, followed by shouts and yelling.

Jen threw the towel around herself, tucked it in tight, unlocked the door and ran the length of the hall, dripping water as she went. "What's wrong? What happened?" she yelled when she discovered her friends in the den.

Then she noticed they were jumping around and hugging each other. "Hazel's results are all clear," explained Dalton as Susan threw her arms around him.

Jen raced over and embraced Hazel with tears in her eyes. "I knew it! I knew it would be fine. That's such great news!"

Tears streamed down Hazel's cheeks. She couldn't speak, just buried her face in Jen's shoulder. Dalton grabbed Hazel from behind and pulled her into another embrace, leaving Jen standing with her arms wrapped around herself, watching with a watery smile.

She felt Parker's arms sneak around her waist before she saw him. She spun around and embraced him, his eyes glistening. "Isn't it great?"

He nodded, his hands linked behind her back. "So great." Then he raised an eyebrow and chuckled. "Nice dress. I think you're leaving a watermark."

She gasped as she remembered the towel. "Oh yeah, this old thing – I just wear it around the house, you know …" Her heart jitterbugged in her chest, and her cheeks burned.

Parker laughed. "Well, it suits you." He leaned forward and kissed her, catching her completely off guard. His lips were soft and warm and they lit a flame deep inside, as her eyes drifted closed.

Through a haze, she heard laughter and whistling, and suddenly felt very underdressed. She pushed away from Parker, glanced around and saw everyone watching them. "Uh … sorry. I was taking a shower …" She spun on her heel and ran to her bedroom, shutting the door behind her, then leaning against it with a groan. She knew one thing – they would never let her live that down.

Needless to say, Jen took longer to get ready for work than usual. She spent extra time on her outfit, and decided to make an effort and put on some makeup – anything to postpone seeing her friends so soon after that embarrassment. It mostly worked – by the time she made her way to the kitchen for breakfast, Hazel had gone to college, Dalton and Eamon were out in the barn and Parker was running errands in town.

All this was according to Susan, who was the only other person left. She was bustling around the kitchen cleaning up the breakfast mess left behind by everyone else.

"What would you like to eat?" she asked Jen over her shoulder as she scrubbed a pan caked with scrambled egg remnants.

"Just a piece of toast, I think. I'm running late for work."

"Well, you look lovely today," replied Susan with a wink.

Jen's cheeks burned. "Thank you."

Susan put a slice of bread into the toaster. "Do you have a lot of work to do today?"

"Just a few house calls, then I should be home late afternoon."

"Well, I packed some lunch for you." Susan handed her brown paper bag. "Here you go. I hope you like tuna salad."

Jen's brow furrowed. She couldn't remember the last time someone had packed lunch for her. "Thanks so much. That's very thoughtful of you."

Susan waved a hand dismissively. "Oh, I love it. I miss having my boys at home, and it makes me happy to take care of people. Can I let you in on a little secret?"

Jen nodded, wondering just how many secrets she'd have to keep for this family and how on Earth she'd manage it. "Sure."

Susan leaned close, her gloved hands dripping and blue eyes sparkling. "I'm moving to Tifton."

Jen's eyes widened. "Really?"

Susan returned to the sink and continued scrubbing the pan. "Yeah. I can't bear being up there in Chattanooga all by my lonesome while my boys set up their lives down here. It's time for me to sell out and move south." She glanced at Jen. "What do you think? Bad idea?"

Jen smiled. "No, not at all. I think it's wonderful."

* * *

"Thanks for staying, Mom," said Parker, wrapping his arms around her.

"It was good to see you, hon, you and your brothers."

"Yeah, sorry they couldn't be here to see you off, but they had to collect a mare from Louisiana and it's quite a drive."

"I understand." His mom stood on tiptoe to kiss his cheek, then whispered in his ear, "That Jen's a lovely girl. Don't let her get away – she makes you happy. And it warms my heart to see you smiling again, my darling boy."

Parker raised an eyebrow as his mother hurried down the porch steps and got into the driver's seat of her VW. His mother had never encouraged him to pursue a woman before, and his cheeks warmed at her concern. She was a good judge of character – and if she liked Jen, it was a good sign. He stood on the porch and waved as Mom pulled away. She rolled her window down and waved back, then was gone.

He rested a foot on the porch rail and sighed. It was good to have her stay, but it'd be nice for things to get back to normal after the craziness of the past few weeks. Hazel had been officially classified as "in remission," so she could move on with her life. The roof, bedrooms and bathroom were fully renovated and repaired, and the power was back on. Mom was heading home to Chattanooga. And he, Dalton and Eamon could get on with to what they loved doing most – running the ranch.

The only thing still nagging at his mind was Jen. She'd said she was leaving Christmas morning for Birmingham, but whether she'd be visiting or leaving for good was unclear. It wasn't too far away, but he knew they wouldn't see each other much. He'd learned firsthand that friendships generally dwindled over such a distance. Of course, he wanted more than friendship and he'd made that pretty clear to her.

Or had he? From her response so far, he wasn't sure how she felt about him, but he hadn't been able to stop thinking about their kiss the other night – she in nothing but a towel, water falling from her hair like raindrops and leaving a puddle around their feet …

Parker sighed. Mom was right – he shouldn't let her get away. But how could he stop her from leaving?

* * *

PARKER POURED some ice-cold Coke into a Solo cup and headed out the back door, balancing a tray of pork ribs in his other hand. He set the tray down by the grill and opened up the lid to light it. Once it was heating up, he took his cell phone from his back pocket, hit shuffle on a country music playlist on Spotify and set it on a stump nearby. He smiled and took a sip of Coke. This is what he loved about life on the ranch – a quiet night, time with family and friends and the scent of barbecue in the air.

The kitchen door swung open and Jen appeared, a tray in her hands. She approached the grill and smiled. "Bratwursts."

"Set them here, please," he said, making room beside the ribs.

"It's nice out," she responded. But then shivered despite her coat and hugged herself tight.

He glanced up at the black sky filled with glowing stars. "I love it out here in the winter. You can feel the chill in the air, but it ain't bad. And the sky's so clear."

"There aren't this many stars in the Atlanta sky, that's for sure." She sighed and studied the expanse.

He watched her with a sly grin. He hadn't been able to get Jen off his mind all day. Mom's words had

453

finally cemented his resolve – she was the woman for him. He'd known it for a while, but hadn't admitted it fully to himself with everything else going on. He'd always known she'd be moving on, but now something inside him had changed. If she felt about him the way he did about her, maybe she didn't have to leave after all.

But there was no way he'd find out unless he said something, and talking to women had never been his strong suit – especially about things like feelings. He shuffled his feet and cleared his throat, still studying her profile. "Um … Jen?"

"Yes?" She turned to him, the stars still gleaming in her eyes. Tendrils of blonde hair drifted around her face, and her cheeks were flushed with pink. She looked stunning and it took his breath away.

"You've been a good friend these last weeks."

She nodded and half-smiled. "Thanks. You too."

"But you've probably noticed my feelings for you have changed. Grown." Her eyes widened as he stepped toward her. He set the grilling tongs down beside the platter of ribs, took her hands in his and looked her in the eye. "I know you're the one for me."

She gasped, her eyes widening.

"I've known it for a while, but with everything that's been happening, I haven't said anything. But that kiss …" He grinned and lifted her hand to his lips, kissing her fingertips. "And all our talks. You've brought me back to life and gave me a reason to laugh again. I don't want you to leave – I want us to be together. I don't know how you feel about me, but I hope you'll give us a chance." He stopped and waited for her response.

Her chest heaved and her hands trembled. Would

she pull away? Had he said too much? The silence between them grew and his heart beat a staccato rhythm against his ribcage as her eyes searched his.

Harley pushed between them, the dog's tail thumping against the base of the grill. Parker glanced down at the dog and tried to nudge him out from between them with his boot. The adorable mutt really had the worst possible timing.

Jen leaned forward, tripped over Harley's back and landed against Parker's chest with a huff, her lips ramming into his.

"Ouch!" he mumbled, his eyebrows arched in surprise.

"Sorry!" She giggled into his mouth, and he chuckled in reply. Then they kissed for real, and he lifted her over Harley and set her down to stand on top of his boots. He pulled her closer, feeling the warmth of her body on his. She trembled in his arms, as he felt a glow of love fill him up from the tips of his toes to his crown.

CHAPTER 14

*J*en reached up to hang an ornament on the tree, one with a gold outline of the White House on a dark blue background. It glowed in the soft light of the fireplace in the den. "Where'd you get this one?"

Hazel glanced at the ornament. "My aunt gave it to me. It's beautiful, isn't it? The White House has an official ornament each year – this one was from a few years back. I keep thinking I should get them every year, since they really are stunning, but I never remember to do it."

Jen picked another ornament from the box at her feet as Hazel took a sip of eggnog, then set her glass back on the coffee table. She scooted closer to the tree and crossed her legs as she searched through the box for the next ornament to add to the tree. The strains of Harry Connick Jr.'s Christmas album filled the air, along with the scent of apple and cinnamon from the wassail brewing on the stove top in the kitchen. "So you're headed back to Alabama tomorrow?" asked Hazel.

Jen had a swallow of eggnog before replying. "Yeah, I'm going to Birmingham tomorrow. But I'll be back before long."

Hazel's eyebrows flew skyward. "You will?"

Jen's cheeks blazed. "Yes. I've decided to stay here. Well, in town – I'm getting an apartment in Eamon and Emily's complex. A unit just opened up and I already signed a lease."

Hazel leaped to her feet and threw her arms around Jen's shoulders. "That's fantastic –you're not leaving after all! I was trying to be brave for your sake, but I really didn't want you to go. It's been so wonderful having you here, but I felt like it would be selfish to ask you to stay. So what made your mind up?" She released Jen and watched for her reaction with a sparkle in her eyes.

Jen still hadn't spoken to her friend about what'd happened with Parker. She'd felt like keeping their relationship to herself for a while so she could ponder what she wanted to do without everyone else having a say in it. It was a big decision to make – was Parker the one? Should she change her life for him? Her parents were so excited about her visiting Birmingham, hoping she'd remain there. If she stayed in Georgia, it'd have to be for the right reason. She knew Hazel would be delighted, but she needed to think without any pressure from her or anyone else.

The past few days had given her the clarity she needed. Parker was everything she'd always hoped for. Already her relationship with him was more fulfilling and exciting than any she'd ever had. She couldn't imagine living without him – and that meant staying where she was, since he couldn't very well move to Birmingham and leave the ranch behind. She only hoped her parents would understand. "Well, actually Parker and I ..."

Hazel interrupted her with another hug and a shout. "I hoped that was the reason! He's such a great man and I knew from the first moment I met him that you two would make a perfect match."

Jen frowned. "Why didn't you say so?"

Hazel chuckled. "You know you don't listen to a word I say."

Jen set her hands on her hips. "That's not true."

"Oh, yes it is. I didn't like Chris, but you just went on ahead and dated him."

"Well ..."

"So with Parker, I thought I'd wait and let you figure it out for yourself. And I'm so glad you did." Hazel embraced her friend again.

Jen's brow furrowed. "Just as well I did ..."

Hazel sighed. "Oh, come on – you know you can't hold a grudge against me, so you might as well let it go now."

Jen's face relaxed. "You're right, I can't. And I'm glad you approve."

The front door opened and Emily blew in with the frigid breeze. "Phew! It's getting cold out there." She stamped her feet and unwound her scarf from around her neck.

"Yeah, it's supposed to drop into the thirties tonight," said Hazel, hurrying to greet her.

"Welcome to the tree-decorating party," added Jen as she hung another ornament on the tree. "We're almost done, but you can help with the final touches."

"I can't believe it's Christmas Eve," said Emily,

settling down beside the box of ornaments with a smile.

"*I* can't believe I'm only getting the tree up on Christmas Eve," added Hazel with a grimace. "But better late than never, I suppose."

"Would you like some eggnog?" asked Jen.

Emily nodded. "That would be amazing. I've been on my feet all day in surgery and I'm exhausted and starving."

"Are you done for the year?" asked Hazel.

"Nope. I've got five days off, but then it's back to the grind." She grinned. "I love it."

Jen went into the kitchen, poured Emily a large glass of eggnog, set some chocolate-covered almonds on a plate, grabbed a bowl of pretzels, carried it all back into the den and set it on the coffee table.

Emily's eyes shone. "Oh, perfect!"

"Dinner will be ready in about an hour," Hazel informed her. "We're expecting the men home from Pensacola any moment – the auction finished yesterday, but they needed this morning to load up. Dalton called a few minutes ago to say they weren't far off."

Emily nodded as she munched on pretzels. "Sounds good. I can't wait to see Eamon – it's the first time we've been apart overnight since the wedding." Her cheeks flushed.

Hazel and Jen both chuckled, and Jen rolled her eyes. "You two are sickening."

Emily laughed. "I remember saying that about Hazel and Dalton. And now it's my turn. How strange – I would never have thought …" She went silent, and the three women went back to decorating as the fire snapped and sparked in the hearth.

"You missed the big announcement," Hazel finally

murmured as she fixed a Nutcracker ornament to a low branch.

"What's that?" asked Emily, adjusting a glass angel that faced the wrong direction where it hung.

"Jen just told me she and Parker are officially an item. And she's moving to Tifton."

Emily's eyes and smile widened. "Wow, that's great. I'm so happy for you, Jen."

Jen nodded, feeling suddenly shy. "I'm going to live in your apartment complex. Already signed a lease – I'll be moving in after the Christmas break."

Emily chuckled. "Oh, so that's why you were asking so many questions about the place. I wondered what the sudden interest in rental rates, rental contracts and carpet cleaning signified."

Jen shrugged. "Uh-huh. Thanks for your help. And Will's happy I'm staying – he's got more work than he can handle on his own, and apparently some of his oldest clients are asking for me now."

"What about your folks?" asked Hazel cautiously.

"I haven't told them yet." Jen chewed the inside of one cheek. "I figured I'd do it after Christmas – let them have a little bit of joy before I destroy all their hopes and dreams." Her heart sank at the thought. She loved her parents, hated to disappoint them, but she'd never really wanted to move back to Birmingham and had no intention of taking over the family business the way they wanted her to. She'd seen how Barsby Enterprises had eaten her parents alive. They'd never done anything they'd dreamed of doing because work consumed their every waking moment, and likely invaded their sleep as well.

She forced a smile. "But I refuse to be unhappy. My best friend is well. My other best friend helped her get better. You're both happy and healthy, you have wonderful men in your lives who love you. And now I have Parker." She paused to grin wider. "Life is good." She squatted beside Hazel, who was seated on the floor, and leaned over to hug her. "I'm glad you're here and you're well."

Hazel's eyes glistened. "I am too. And thank you for being here for me and helping me through it. You and Emily are the best friends a girl could ask for – I don't know what I would've done without you both." She waved Emily over and welcomed her into their embrace.

Emily joined them, and the three women swayed as one, then overbalanced and crashed, with Emily on the bottom. But she just giggled. "My goodness, what is in that eggnog? You're crushing me." They all laughed as they tried to find their feet and extricate themselves from the tangle of arms and legs on the floor.

Emily got free first, then all of a sudden made a mad dash for the bathroom. Hazel and Jen watched her go, Hazel in confusion. She covered her mouth and grimaced when she heard Emily throwing up. "Oh no."

Jen frowned – she knew what was wrong with Emily, and that Hazel didn't. "I hope she's okay –"

Hazel jumped to her feet, ran to the bathroom and started hurling herself.

Jen stood slowly and waited until both women emerged, their faces pale. "What's going on?" she asked with a grimace. "Either you've both gotten food poisoning or you're both pregnant …" Then she realized what she'd said, and hoped Hazel hadn't been paying too much attention, or else she'd just given Emily's secret away.

Emily's cheeks flushed. Hazel looked between her two friends. Finally, Hazel grinned. "I *am* pregnant."

Emily broke into a joyous smile. "So am I!" They embraced, then reached for Jen, and all three laughed as they held each other and danced in a circle in the middle of the den. "I can't believe it!" cried Emily. "When …?"

"Well, it happened faster than we thought it would," replied Hazel shyly. "Pretty much as soon as I found out my results were clear. It's still very early and I've only started feeling unwell, but when you threw up it triggered me." She laughed. "And how about you? How far along?"

"Um … I think I'm at about eight weeks now. Though, it's hard to keep track, as busy as we've been."

"Well how about that? Talk about a honeymoon baby!" exclaimed Hazel.

Jen burst out laughing all over again and Emily soon joined her.

A cool breeze at her back made her turn around, and she almost collided with Parker, who'd just come in the front door. He grabbed her with both hands and drew her close to kiss her. "I was ready for you that time," he whispered in her ear.

"You're here!" cried Hazel, running past them to embrace Dalton. Eamon swept Emily up into his arms as well and all three couples enjoyed a romantic reunion.

Just then the buzzer sounded in the kitchen. "Oh, that's the yams!" cried Hazel, hurrying to pull them from the oven. "Dinner's ready!" she called over her shoulder.

The others followed her into the kitchen, talking excitedly about all they'd done since they last saw each other. Parker threaded his fingers through Jen's and gazed lovingly at her while she recounted a story about work from that day. They all sat at the table, now laden with ham, yams, potato salad, ambrosia, green bean casserole, squash casserole, maple-glazed carrots, golden biscuits and corn muffins.

"I'd like to get us started by saying a blessing," Dalton declared. He bowed his head and Jen watched the rest of the table follow his example. Then she did too.

"Thank you, Lord, for this food. Thank you for the hands that prepared it and for all of your protection and blessings this year. We are so grateful, God, for Hazel's health, for good friends and neighbors who helped us repair the ranch house and who've been here for us and with us as we went through the most difficult time of our lives. Thank you for this day and for your son who was born so many years ago to save us. In his holy name, amen."

"Amen," came the chorus from around the table.

Jen's throat burned as everyone began handing food around. Her chest tightened and her eyes filled with tears. She wasn't used to this kind of family, where they shared life together, talked about everything, and helped each other through the hard times. Her parents weren't on speaking terms with most of their extended family, and their lives were so consumed by work that they'd barely had time for holidays and celebrations.

But this – this was the kind of family she'd always longed for. Maybe one day it would be hers as well. The thought made a single tear overflow and wind down her cheek. She wiped it away and stared down at her plate.

"Yams?" asked Parker beside her, a baking dish in one hand.

"Yes, please." She smiled and took the dish from him.

"Are you okay?" he asked.

She nodded, unable to speak.

"We have an announcement to make!" called Eamon, breaking through the buzz of conversation. He glanced at Emily and smiled. "Em and I are expecting a baby!"

Emily laughed. "Yes, it's true. Though I'm sorry, honey – I already told Hazel and Jen."

He pouted. "What? I thought we were going to wait and tell everyone together?"

"Well, I didn't have much choice once I vomited in front of them."

Everyone laughed and Eamon grimaced. "Okay, that makes sense. I guess it's all out in the open ... wait, let me rephrase that!" he clarified as the men laughed even harder.

"Literally all," interrupted Hazel. "Since I threw up as well."

Eamon and Parker stopped dead and stared at her.

Dalton smirked proudly, laying an arm around Hazel's shoulders and kissing the top of her head. "Yep. We're expecting too."

The men cheered. Jen couldn't help grinning widely at it all.

Then Parker cleared his throat and slid his arm around Jen. "And that's not all ...," he began.

"What?!" shouted Dalton, his brow furrowing.

Parker laughed and waved him off. "I'm just kidding, big brother, relax. We're not expecting."

"Darn right we're not," Jen said with a laugh.

"But," Parker continued, "we are dating now." He turned to look Jen in the eye. "And I'm in love with her."

Dalton and Eamon hooted and hollered as Jen's cheeks burned crimson. When they calmed down, she said, "And I'm in love with you too."

He bent toward her and kissed her full on the mouth as the rest of the room erupted in approval. He tasted like salt and cinnamon, and as his arms wrapped around her she knew there was nowhere else in the world she'd ever feel as safe, loved or happy as she did there.

CHAPTER 15

*J*en leaned on the top rail of the fence and watched the fillies frolicking in the pasture beyond the yard. They were almost six months old now and had lost their gangly awkwardness. They moved with grace and ease, strong legs and arched necks.

She smiled. The first hint of sunshine glimmered on the horizon, lighting up the sky in a golden glow. She didn't usually rise this early, but it was Christmas morning – ever since she was young she'd always watched the sun rise on Christmas day. It was one of the few traditions she'd shared with her father, and even when she moved out of home she'd carried it on.

The phone in her pocket buzzed, and she pulled it out and held it to her ear. "Merry Christmas, Dad," she croaked hoarsely, as it was the first word she'd spoken since crawling out of bed. She shivered and tugged her coat tighter around her.

"Morning, princess, and Merry Christmas to you as well." His deep voice was soothing.

"What are you looking at?" she asked. It was what they always did whenever they didn't share a Christmas sunrise in person.

"I'm staring out across the lake. I can see the sun rising over the water and lighting up the boat house."

She closed her eyes and pictured the image. She loved the lake house where her folks went on the rare occasions they took time off from work. Some of her fondest childhood memories had been formed there. "Sounds divine, Dad. I'll be there later today, okay?"

He murmured approval. "What about you – what do you see?"

Her eyes flicked open and she glanced around. "There's a barn still in shadow. Across the pasture in front of me the sun is rising and I can see a herd of horses basking in the golden light, grazing silently. Some of the foals are dashing around the place, chasing each other, kicking their heels up and flicking their tails."

He chuckled. "That sounds pretty good too, Princess. Drive safe when you head this way. There'll be a ton of traffic."

She nodded. "I will, Dad. Actually, I hope you don't mind, but I'm bringing someone with me."

There was a long pause on the other end of the line. "Someone?" he finally asked.

"Yeah, his name's Parker Williams."

"Oh, *that* kind of someone."

She chuckled. "Yes, Dad. I would've asked earlier if it was okay, but it was kind of a last-minute decision."

"He's welcome to join us. If he's important to you, he's important to us."

She sighed and blinked rapidly. "He *is* important to me."

"Well, then I'm happy you're bringing him. I guess this means you won't be staying too long, though. Am I right?"

Jen's lips pursed. "Sorry, Dad. I know you and Mom want me to move back to Birmingham. But Parker lives here, and he co-owns a ranch with his brothers, so he can't leave. I've got a job here and I've really grown to love the place."

He sighed. "I understand, Princess. We're just looking forward to having you home again."

"I promise to come see you whenever I can."

"We'll hold you to that."

When the call was done, Jen shoved the phone back in her pocket and continued to look out over the ranch. It was growing lighter by the minute and soon every vestige of the night would be gone, chased away by the light.

She sighed again and headed back toward the house. There was no telling how long it would be until the rest of the group woke. Likely they wanted to sleep in, but she hadn't been able to – she was too excited. Perhaps she should go for a run ... or better yet, make everyone a big breakfast. That would surprise them all. She hurried into the kitchen, flicked on the overhead light, tied on an apron and opened the refrigerator door to assess its contents. Hmmm, what could she make?

She pulled eggs, bacon and butter from the fridge, then stood staring at them. Bacon and eggs were always a hit, but not very exciting. What else could she do with them? She pulled out her phone again, searched recipes and found a Paula Dean breakfast casserole that sounded perfect. She foraged for everything else she needed to make the casserole, and found it all except for horseradish. Come to think of it, she wasn't sure she'd ever used horseradish in anything. What was it, some kind of vegetable?

Well, maybe carrot would do in its place. The recipe only called for a teaspoon, so it wouldn't make much difference. Only, it didn't make sense to waste part of a carrot. She might as well throw the whole carrot into the mixture. It couldn't hurt. She grated the carrot and tossed it in with the eggs, milk, buttered bread and diced bacon, mixed in some mustard and surveyed the results. It looked good to her, if a little strange with the orange flakes in it. She grated cheese over the top then pushed the baking dish into the oven. She put her hands on her hips and smiled, proud of herself. And still no one else was awake.

She spun around, ready to clean up, and gasped. She couldn't believe how much of a mess she'd made just preparing one breakfast casserole! Flour coated the countertop and drifted down to the floor below. There were egg shells scattered around and egg mixture and carrot peelings had landed everywhere. She pushed a strand of hair behind her ear and rubbed her face. Oh well – best start on the clean up now while the casserole was cooking. She picked up a handful of egg shells, then dropped them when the kitchen door opened.

Parker walked in, and his eyes widened and eyebrows arched when he saw her. "Merry Christmas," he said, scanning the room and obviously trying not to smile. "What's going on in here?"

"Um, making breakfast." She grinned.

"Oh? Well, if the mess is anything to go by, it's bound to be delicious." He grabbed her and wrapped her in his arms, pulling her into his chest.

She gazed up into his deep brown eyes which crinkled around the edges as he smiled. "Hi," she whispered.

"Hi," he replied, then kissed the tip of her nose. "You've got flour everywhere."

She nodded and glanced at the soiled floor. "I know. I'm just cleaning up now."

"No, I mean *everywhere*." He turned her until she could see her own reflection in the window of the microwave. Flour coated her nose and cheek and ran through one side of her hair making it look as though she had a thick gray streak.

She set her hands on her hips. "Wow. I look dazzling!"

He spun her back toward him and kissed her. "You sure do."

She chuckled and nestled into his chest, enjoying the warmth that enveloped her. That space was reserved just for her, or at least it felt that way. It made her heart race and her knees tremble.

"So did you tell your folks you're not moving back to Birmingham?" he asked.

She nodded. "I did. Dad wasn't very happy about it, but I think he'll understand once he meets you." She stepped back and searched his face. "Are you still okay coming home with me for Christmas? I know it's a bit early to meet the parents, so I'll completely understand if you want to back out."

He laughed. "You'd understand? Hmmm … maybe I should rethink this whole thing."

She slapped his chest playfully. "Don't you dare! I already told them you're coming."

He squeezed her tight and kissed the top of her head. "I wouldn't miss it."

* * *

Jen tucked her feet beneath her on the floor and leaned back against Parker's legs. He sat behind her on the couch, his hand on her shoulder, teasing her hair occasionally. A fire crackled in the hearth, and lights lit up the Christmas tree against the wall. A small stack of gifts lay beneath it, and everyone was seated around the tree, sipping coffee and listening to soft Christmas carols.

She smiled as Harley trotted to her side, turned in a circle, then laid down against her leg. He sported a set of reindeer antlers on his head and his doleful eyes begged her to remove them. "Sorry, bud – Hazel wants you to wear them, and I haven't got a say in it," she whispered into his floppy ear. His tail thumped the floor in response, then he picked up a new dried pigs ear between his paws and gnawed on it.

Susan, having arrived late on Christmas Eve after a long drive south, hurried out of the kitchen with a plate of breakfast casserole in her hands and sat on the love seat. "Wow, Jen, this looks delicious. What are the orange flecks?"

"Carrot," replied Jen.

Susan's smile grew. "Oh, yum." She took a bite and chewed, her eyes widening. "It's different, that's for sure. But I like it."

Jen grinned. "Thanks."

Dalton and Hazel were squeezed into the armchair across from Jen and Parker. Dalton handed Hazel a gift and she unwrapped it carefully, setting the paper aside. Jen knew she liked to use the paper for gift cards the following year. It was just like Hazel to do something so thoughtful. She wished she was more organized, but at the same time she knew wishing was futile. She was herself, and she'd learned in the past couple of years that she'd better accept herself the way she was or she'd never be content.

Hazel cried out at her gift – a necklace with a pendant that had been carved to resemble a mother holding a child – and threw her arms around Dalton. "Thank you, it's beautiful." She held it in the air to admire it, then let Dalton clasp it around her neck.

Just then, there was a loud knock on the front door. Susan hurried to open it, then stepped back, revealing Hazel's parents in the dull morning light. Hazel gasped and stood. "Mom? Dad? What are you doing here?" She ran over and threw her arms around each of them.

Her mother dabbed her eyes with a handkerchief. "I'm so sorry we weren't here sooner, darling. It's just that … well, I don't cope very well with things like… well, you know."

"Things like what?" asked Hazel.

"Like that my daughter might not … might …" Her mother's voice faded and she clamped a hand over her mouth to stifle a sob.

Hazel embraced her again, and Jen could hear the emotion in her voice. "It's okay, Mom. I'm just glad you're here now. Come on in, both of you, take a seat. We just started opening gifts."

They both stepped tentatively inside and followed Hazel. Dalton and Hazel gave up their place on the armchair, and Eamon vacated his as well to sit on the floor in front of the loveseat, at Emily's feet. Jen hurried to the kitchen to fix them each a plate of casserole and a cup of coffee. She carried them back to the den on a tray, setting it on the coffee table in front of them. "It's good to see you again, Mr. and Mrs.

Hildebrand," she said, giving Hazel's father a hug and her mother a kiss on the cheek. "I made some breakfast – I hope you're hungry."

They both looked stunned, and Mrs. Hildebrand managed a wobbly smile. "Thank you, Jen."

Jen returned to her place on the floor in front of Parker and rested her hand on Harley's back, petting his soft shiny fur. It was a Christmas miracle – Hazel's parents were finally here. She knew how much it meant to her friend and it filled her heart with warmth.

She pulled a small box from beneath the tree and handed it to Parker. It was wrapped haphazardly in Santa-print red paper, and she'd run out of tape at the last moment, so it was folded oddly. She felt her cheeks warm as he turned it over in his hands. She hoped he'd like it, but she'd never been any good at selecting gifts.

He ripped off the paper and opened the box to find a pair of limited-edition Army Ranger cufflinks. "Wow, thanks!"

"I wasn't sure what to get and I saw these. Well, I thought you might … do you like them?"

He nodded and leaned forward to kiss her. "I love them."

She grinned and laid her head against his knee.

"I got you something as well," he said. He pulled a gift from beneath the tree and handed it to her.

She nodded. "Thank you." It was a small box as well – maybe he'd gotten her cufflinks also. She chuckled to herself as she opened it.

"What's so funny?" he asked.

She winked at him. "Oh, nothing." But when she pulled off the wrapping, he took it from her and she frowned. "Hey, that's mine. You can't take it back once it's been given."

He laughed, but there was an intensity in his gaze that wasn't usually there. He got up, kneeled in front of her. Then, he opened the box and held it up to her. "Jennifer Barsby, first you were a friend, one who opened my eyes to see that there was still life ahead for me and that I could respect the past without living in it. And now, I love you and can't imagine my life without you. Will you marry me and make me the most grateful man alive?"

The rest of the room stilled as everyone watched the exchange.

Jen covered her open mouth and nodded as her eyes filled with tears. "Yes, I'll marry you," she whispered, her throat choked with emotion.

"What was that?" he quipped, setting a hand behind one ear.

She laughed. "I'll marry you!" she cried and threw her arms around his neck, knocking him off balance. They landed in a tangle on the floor as Dalton hooted and Eamon laughed.

But Jen didn't care. She kissed Parker beneath the Christmas tree as hot tears poured down her cheeks, kissed him fully and completely, holding nothing back. The kiss was full of promise and hope for a future not yet written. And as his lips returned it, she wished it would last forever.

THE END

EXCERPT: MAKE-BELIEVE FIANCÉ

MAKE-BELIEVE SERIES

Take one billionaire cowboy in need of a fiancée, add one divorced teacher with trust issues and mix in a fake engagement. What could possibly go wrong?

Gwen Alder is starting over — divorced and broke, she's come to Billings, Montana for a new beginning. But waitressing in a roadside diner for the summer isn't paying the bills, and she finds herself in over her head with no hope of catching up.

Heath Montgomery has it all — fame, fortune and a

mega-watt smile, but one thing he doesn't have is a date for his cousin's wedding.

When they cross paths, Heath has an idea — what if he paid her to be his date? No strings, no complications, just a simple business transaction — a way to finally win his father's trust, and get his parents off his back about settling down once and for all.

She's poor and plain. He's wealthy and arrogant.

They didn't want anything more than a simple arrangement. They never planned to fall in love. But sometimes cupid has a mind of his own.

CHAPTER ONE

Some things, Heath Montgomery understood. He knew about horses, and about ranching, and how to run a business. And he understood poker. Women? Nope. But poker he got.

He leaned forward in his chair and peered over the cards in his hand to survey the three faces staring back at him. The air stank of stale peanuts and sweat. His mouth turned up at one corner. He chuckled silently and drew in a long slow breath as his friends frowned and squinted at their own hands. Finally, he fanned his cards out on the table. "This is it, then."

Adam Gilston, his co-worker and best friend, lay down his hand and rolled his eyes. "You're cruel." He pushed the pile of chips in the middle of the table toward Heath. "Remind me why I ever thought it'd be a good idea to play poker with you?"

Heath laughed and ran his fingers through his hair. "Sorry, dude, I can't help it. I was born to win."

Adam punched him in the shoulder.

"Hey!" complained Heath with a chuckle. "Sore loser."

"Someone's got to bring you back to earth."

"Anyone need another drink?" asked Tim, holding up a pitcher of Coke with ice, his dark eyes gleaming in the dim light.

Heath shook his head. "No thanks, I've had enough. It's just about time to head home. How many hours have we been at this?"

Heath's kid brother Dan groaned and covered a yawn with his fist. "Too many."

"We're getting too old for this," added Adam, blinking reddened eyes as he scooped the cards into a pile.

"But it's tradition," Tim insisted, stacking his chips neatly, his biceps bulging beneath the sleeves of his plain white T-shirt. Every time Tim was around, Heath made a mental note to go to the gym more often. He had a home gymnasium, but preferred the outdoors – riding a horse or roping cattle always seemed preferable to pumping iron.

"Maybe we could come up with a new tradition," Dan offered. He'd always played the peacemaker, even when they were young.

"One that doesn't involve staying awake for an entire weekend to play poker," added Heath, rubbing his tired eyes. He pushed his chips into a drawstring bag and handed it to one of the casino staff standing against the wall. The man, dressed in a black uniform with red trim and a badge that said "RAMON – I'm here to help," took the bag, nodded and headed for the cashier's cage.

"You're all soft," Tim huffed.

Heath laughed. "Old and soft. That sounds about right."

Adam stood and stretched. "Thirty is hardly old."

"It feels a lot older than twenty," said Heath. "We used to be able to stay up all night and keep rolling all day without so much as a single yawn." He missed those days, but at the same time he was glad they were behind him. He liked a quieter life these days – his ranch suited him just fine. He reached for his Stetson and put it on with another yawn. "Let's get some breakfast on the way back. I'm starved." He walked to the door and pushed it open, letting the bright lights of the casino filter into the small dark room.

Ramon returned with the bag, now full of cash. He almost ran into Heath, then took a step back and pulled out a pile of hundred-dollar bills. "Here you go, sir."

"Thank you." Heath stuffed the bills into his jeans pocket as Ramon nodded and hurried off. It was surreal the way the casino always looked the same – day or night, who could tell. Patrons wandered between the tables, drinks in hand, ready to gamble their savings away.

He frowned. There wasn't much about the place that he liked, but he'd put up with the stale air, bright lights and piped-in music for the three men who followed him. He, Tim and Adam had become fast friends at the private high school he'd attended in San Francisco all those years ago, and they met up at least once a year ever since to play poker. His brother Dan joined the group several years ago, tagging along with Heath as he often did.

"Hello, Heath."

The voice to his right made him squeeze his eyes

shut for a moment. Then he turned to face the speaker, pasting a smile onto his face. "Chantelle. Fancy seeing you here."

She flicked her long blonde hair over one shoulder and grinned. "I get around."

He resisted the temptation to agree. The last thing he wanted in that moment was to have it out with his ex-girlfriend in the middle of a crowded casino on zero sleep. Instead he nodded and set his hands on his hips. "We're just heading out. Good to see you." He stifled a yawn and managed a farewell smile.

But she stepped in front of him, resting a perfectly manicured hand on his shoulder. "You don't have to go just yet, do you?"

"It's 7 a.m. and we've been up all night," explained Tim, coming up behind him. "We're going to grab some breakfast and hit the hay. And you are?"

"I'm Chantelle. Pleased to meet you." She gave Tim her most dazzling smile.

Heath willed his eyes not to roll. She really knew how to turn on the charm, but after dating her for six months he'd seen that charm was her only asset. Ever since they broke up, he'd done his best to steer clear of her, but she kept showing up like an unlucky penny everywhere he went. It was like she'd pinned a tracking device to him.

Tim smiled knowingly at Heath as he shook Chantelle's hand. "The famous Chantelle. What a pleasure."

Her eyes glinted. "I'm famous now, am I?"

"In our little circle you are," said Adam, kissing her on the cheek. "How are you doing?"

By the time she'd greeted Dan, Heath was itching to get out of there. "Well, good to see you, Chantelle." He spun on his heel and headed for the exit, hoping his entourage came with him.

When he glanced over his shoulder, he saw they were following. But he also saw them smirking and grinning. Great. He knew what they were thinking – why'd he let go of Chantelle Ryan? She was beautiful, charming, accomplished – everything his parents were hoping for in a daughter-in-law.

Which is where she'd set her sights. Never mind that he wasn't in love with her. She didn't care about that – she even told him so. She was happy to get married and wait for the love to come later, she'd said. Just so long as they could be together. That's when he'd known it was over. How could he love someone so shallow, so manipulative, someone who only wanted to be Mrs. Montgomery.

And then she'd laughed at his return to church. She not only refused to join him in his weekly attendance, but her mockery had been like a knife in the gut. How could anyone settle for someone who treated his beliefs like that? He'd rather stay single the rest of his life than marry a woman he wasn't head-over-heels in love with, a woman who'd scorn his faith. And he hadn't found anyone else yet – much to his family's dismay.

The automatic doors slid open and he walked out into the glaring sunlight. His pupils constricted and he held up a hand to shield his eyes, trying to locate the valet parking stand. He saw it to his left and headed toward it, feeling around his pocket for the ticket stub.

Tim bumped his elbow and grinned. "So that's Chantelle, huh? How come you never mentioned she was so hot?"

"Eh, I guess she is." Heath wasn't in the mood to talk about his ex.

"You guess?" exclaimed Tim, with a whistle. "I can't imagine how high your standards must be if you think she's mediocre."

Heath shrugged and rubbed his eyes as they waited for the parking attendant to retrieve their vehicles. "I know she's pretty. But when you get to know her ..."

"Oh, I'd love to," said Tim with a chuckle and a backward glance.

Heath's eyebrows arched.

"Don't worry, bro, I know the code – I won't date your ex. No matter how hot she might be." He sighed and held a hand to his heart as though it were broken.

Heath laughed. "In this case, I'd say you're welcome to her. But I don't think you'd be happy."

Tim frowned. "Oh?"

"She's only interested in a thick wallet, if you get my drift." Heath shook his head. It had taken him longer than it should've to figure that out. But once he had – and once she'd aired her views on his beliefs he'd parted ways with her and hadn't looked back.

Tim nodded, his short brown hair shining in the bright morning sunlight and his blue eyes twinkling. "Ah, I get it. Only *in it to win it*, then. Shame ..."

"It's not like you don't have your pick of women throwing themselves at you, *Fireman Tim*." Heath grinned.

Tim laughed. "It's not like that – trust me. Anyway, none have really caught my eye yet."

"Yeah, me neither."

"So what type of woman are you looking for?" asked Tim.

"Someone real and genuine, fun, down to earth ... I

don't know. Just someone who isn't impressed by my name, but who really *sees* me. You know?"

Tim, Adam and Dan looked at him as though he'd lost his mind. "And where do you think you'll find someone like that?" asked Adam, one eyebrow raised high.

"That's the question," said Heath. "Probably not in a place like this." He nodded toward the casino.

"You might be right about that," replied Tim with a chuckle.

A beat-up blue truck rumbled into the space in front of them. The attendant jumped out, jogged around the front of the truck and up to Heath. "Here you go, Mr. Montgomery," he said with a smile.

Heath handed him a tip. "Thanks."

"Why do you keep this old thing?" asked Tim as he climbed in the passenger side.

Heath sat in the driver's seat and shut the door behind him. He sighed and relaxed against the upholstery, glad to be back behind the wheel. It felt like home. "Because I like it. It's comfortable."

"You could afford to buy every truck on the lot," replied Tim with a chuckle.

"So what? Shiny things don't impress me. I want something that feels right, that I know I can depend on." Heath pressed on the accelerator and glanced into his rearview mirror to see Adam's car following them with Dan in the passenger seat. He pulled out onto the main road, his mind wandering over everything they'd discussed.

His own words rang in his ears – is that what was missing? He'd dated plenty of women through his twenties, but none had ever felt quite right. Since Chantelle, he'd sworn off dating – he was sick of the awkwardness, the games, and how it never resulted in anything but heartache. He was older now, and knew what he wanted. Someone genuine, a woman he could depend on, who was loyal and loving and real.

Heath sighed as he remembered Adam's words. Where would he find a woman like that?

* * *

Heath turned the truck into the *Lucky Diner* lot and shut off the engine. "Does this place look okay?" he asked.

Tim nodded and licked his lips. "It looks fine to me. I could eat a horse and chase the rider, I'm so hungry."

Heath chuckled. "Where on Earth did you pick up that saying?"

"In Australia. I was there last year running a collaborative training program for disaster preparedness."

Heath arched an eyebrow. "You really do live a crazy life, you know that?"

Tim shrugged. "I guess. I'm traveling more than I'd like to – staying in hotels, eating in restaurants, meeting different people everywhere …"

"My heart bleeds," replied Heath with a laugh.

Tim chuckled. "Okay, I do love it. But lately it's been a bit lonely."

"I guess I can understand that."

They climbed out of the truck just as Adam's Prius pulled up beside them. The two tall, strapping men climbed out, Dan unfolding his limbs with a groan. "Did you buy the smallest car you could find?" he grumbled. Adam lunged for him, but Dan danced out of the way.

Heath smiled. Those two were always going at it,

trying to one-up each other. They'd been that way even in high school, both so competitive, neither willing to give in. Even though Dan was two years younger, he'd always tried to keep up with the older group of friends.

"It's good for the environment," Adam growled as the foursome marched into the diner. "Anyway, my wife picked it out."

A bell rang over the door. Heath glanced up at it and his eyes narrowed. A sprig of mistletoe hung beside the bell. It was July.

The smell of fried potatoes mingled with apple pie and coffee distracted him from the incongruous greenery. He stopped, wondering if they should seat themselves or wait to be seated. After a few moments, when no one came to assist them, he led the group to an empty booth against a window at the far end of the diner. Adam and Dan were still rough-housing. He glared at them, slid in beside Dan and quietly dug an elbow into his brother's side.

The waitress walked over, tugged a pencil from behind her ear and held up a pad of paper, barely looking up as she asked for their order. Heath studied her with a half-smile. There was something about her that intrigued him. She was beautiful, but not in an obvious way. She wore no makeup, her blonde hair was pulled back into a tight ponytail and dark circles lined her eyes – it made her seem almost plain at first glance.

The other men gave their orders. Finally, it was Heath's turn. She glanced up at him, then back at the pad. He smiled, watching her closely. She looked tired. Not that he knew what she usually looked like, but she seemed a couple of years younger than him and those dark circles couldn't be there for any other reason. He wished he could ask her about it. "What do you recommend?" he asked.

She arched an eyebrow and chewed on the end of her pencil before answering. "Um ... the waffles are good."

He nodded. "Waffles then, please, and two eggs over easy."

"Coffee?"

"Yes, please, with cream."

With a curt nod and brief smile, she turned and headed for the kitchen.

Heath pushed himself out of the booth and jogged after her. "Excuse me?"

She faced him with a startled frown. "Yes?"

"I'm sorry. I noticed you're not wearing a name tag – just wondering what we should call you, since you're our server and all."

One eyebrow arched. "Gwen. You can call me Gwen."

"I'm Heath. Pleased to meet you, Gwen ... is that short for something?"

Her eyes narrowed. "No."

He chuckled. He seemed to be striking out at every turn. She wasn't interested in a conversation or anything else with him, that much was clear.

His phone buzzed in his pocket. He yanked it out to see who was calling at such an early hour. He swiped his finger across the screen, nodding an apology to Gwen. She pasted a smile on her face and walked away. "Dad. How can I help you?"

"Where are you?" Graham Montgomery's voice boomed down the phone line.

"I'm having breakfast."

"It's almost eight o'clock and there's a senior leadership meeting at the office in ten minutes."

Heath slapped his forehead. "Sorry, Dad – it's my annual weekend with the guys from school. Dan's with us too. We're just having breakfast before heading home." Silence on the other end of the line. "Hello? Dad?"

"So what have you been up to all weekend? All kinds of debauchery, no doubt."

Heath frowned and shook his head. "No, Dad, we just played poker at Montana Nugget, and before that we were out at the ranch. I'm heading back to the ranch now and can be in the office within an hour or so. What's the meeting about?"

"Forget it. Finish your breakfast."

"Come on, Dad …"

"No. I'll take care of it this time, son. But let me ask you … when are you going to take yourself seriously?"

"Dad …"

"I mean it. It's time for you to settle down, son. You're not twenty anymore."

"I know that, Dad." Heath took a quick breath. It was always the same thing. "I know I gave you trouble when I was younger, but like you said, I'm not a kid anymore. I work hard every single day, Dad. You know that. I've earned a weekend off."

"You should be married by now. At your age, I had two children and was running my own ranch."

His eyes closed and he frowned. "I know."

"It's time to take responsibility, son. Responsibility for your life, for the company … you can't live this way forever. These weekends with the boys are just another symptom of you trying to hold onto your childhood. But you're not a child any longer – you're a man. It's time you started acting like one."

A hint of sarcasm crept into his voice. "And what does that mean, Dad, to act like a man?"

"It means... well, who are you bringing to your cousin's wedding?"

"What?"

"The wedding this weekend. Who are you bringing? You do have a date, don't you?"

Heath bit his lip. Not only didn't he have a date for the wedding, but he'd forgotten all about the event. "Of course I do – I'll tell you all about her soon. But right now I have to go."

His father grunted into the phone. "Well, that's good to hear. You're not getting any younger, you know? I want to give you the CEO position and take a step back, son, but I'm still not convinced you're ready. If you could show me you're growing up ... well, maybe we could finally take that trip I've been promising your mother."

"I hear you, Dad – I just don't agree I have matured. I've been busting my tail running the company and we're bringing in higher profits than ever before. We've added four ranches to our portfolio in the past twelve months, along with half a dozen feed and produce stores, and we'll be expanding into more stores in other states next year. Business is good and it's getting better. That should be all you need to know to make your decision. And if you can't see that, I don't know what to tell you."

Graham seemed to sense he'd crossed a line. "Now, son..."

But now Heath was boiling. His father had a way of bringing out that side of him and he didn't like it, yet couldn't seem to stop it. "Since you insist on nosing into my private life, I'll be sure to keep you updated on my relationship status from now on. If you like, I can even get Social Security numbers so you can run background checks."

His father sighed. "I know you're doing well, Heath. I keep up with what you're doing at work. I just have some concerns. I want you to be settled, happy. And I'm looking forward to meeting this mystery date of yours."

"She's no mystery, Dad. Look, I have to go – I'm being rude to the guys, and our food is on the table."

His father rang off with a promise to let him know how things went in the meeting. And Heath wandered back to the booth to find Gwen setting plates on the table. He slid into his seat, the aroma of freshly-made waffles with maple syrup and butter drifting up to greet him. His stomach growled and he smiled at Gwen.

She returned his smile half-heartedly as she finished delivering the meals. "I'll be back with your coffee – let me know if you need anything else," she said, wiping her hands on the apron tied neatly about her trim waist.

He watched her leave, then sliced off a piece of waffle. As he put it in his mouth, Tim glanced up at him from his stack of pancakes. "Who was that on the phone?"

"Dad."

"You didn't look real happy about whatever he was saying," Dan added between mouthfuls of egg.

Heath chewed, swallowed and cut another piece. "Yeah. You know the usual – when are you gonna get married, settle down and grow up?" He was tired of hearing about it, from both parents. According to his mother, thirty was far too old to be a respectable bachelor; according to his father, it showed he wasn't sensible enough to run the company. Never mind that he'd basically been managing it for two years already, since his father's heart attack slowed him down.

For some reason, they were both so invested in the idea of him marrying and having a family, they couldn't swallow the idea that perhaps he was the man they wanted him to become already, just single. And they never gave him a break about it, let alone the benefit of the doubt.

Dan chuckled. "I've heard that speech before. So what are you gonna do?"

"Find a date for our cousin's wedding this weekend. Seeing as I already told him I had one, just to get him off my back."

"I get that. Who do you have in mind?"

Heath shook his head. "No one. But I'd better fix that, and fast."

Keep reading...

ALSO BY VIVI HOLT

Visit my website at www.viviholt.com for an updated list of my books

ABOUT THE AUTHOR

Vivi Holt was born in Australia. She grew up in the country, where she spent her youth riding horses at Pony Club, and adventuring through the fields and rivers around the farm. Her father was a builder, turned saddler, and her mother a nurse, who stayed home to raise their four children.

After graduating from a degree in International Relations, Vivi moved to Atlanta, Georgia to work for a year. It was there that she met her husband, and they were married three years later. She spent seven years living in Atlanta and travelled to various parts of the United States during that time, falling in love with the beauty of that immense country and the American people.

Vivi also studied for a Bachelor of Information Technology, and worked in the field ever since until becoming a full-time writer in 2016. She now lives in Brisbane, Australia with her husband and three small children. Married to a Baptist pastor, she is very active in her local church.

Follow Vivi Holt
www.viviholt.com
vivi@viviholt.com

Made in the USA
Monee, IL
26 November 2019